LIO

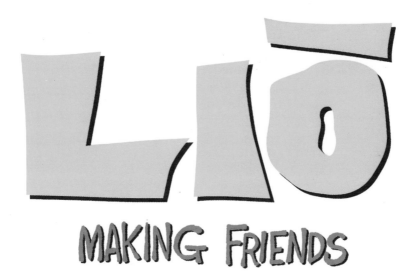

MAKING FRIENDS

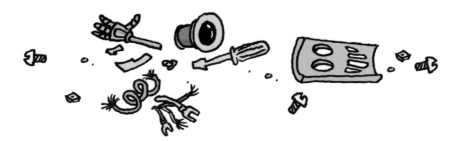

Other *Liō* books by Mark Tatulli

Liō: Happiness Is a Squishy Cephalopod
Silent But Deadly
Liō's Astonishing Tales
There's Corpses Everywhere
Reheated Liō
Zombies Need Love Too
Liō: There's a Monster in My Socks

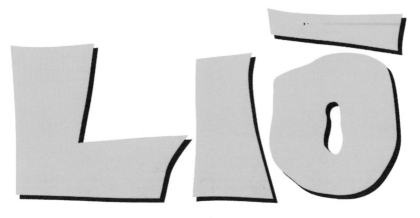

LIO

MAKING FRIENDS

by

MARK TATULLI

Andrews McMeel
Publishing, LLC

Kansas City • Sydney • London

Liō is distributed internationally by Universal Uclick.

Andrews McMeel Publishing, LLC
an Andrews McMeel Universal company
1130 Walnut Street, Kansas City, Missouri 64106

www.andrewsmcmeel.com

13 14 15 16 17 SHO 10 9 8 7 6 5 4 3 2 1

ISBN: 978-1-4494-2558-6

Library of Congress Control Number: 2012952343

ATTENTION: SCHOOLS AND BUSINESSES

Andrews McMeel books are available at quantity discounts with bulk purchase for educational, business, or sales promotional use. For information, please e-mail the Andrews McMeel Publishing Special Sales Department: specialsales@amuniversal.com

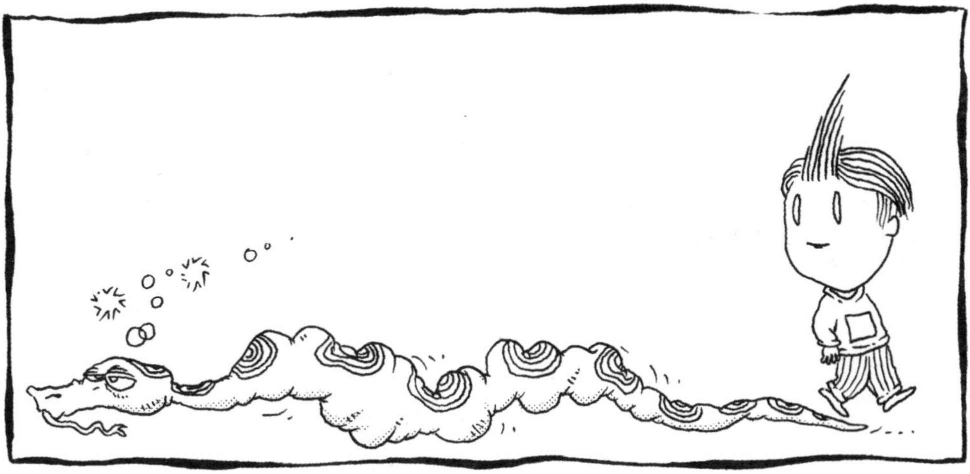

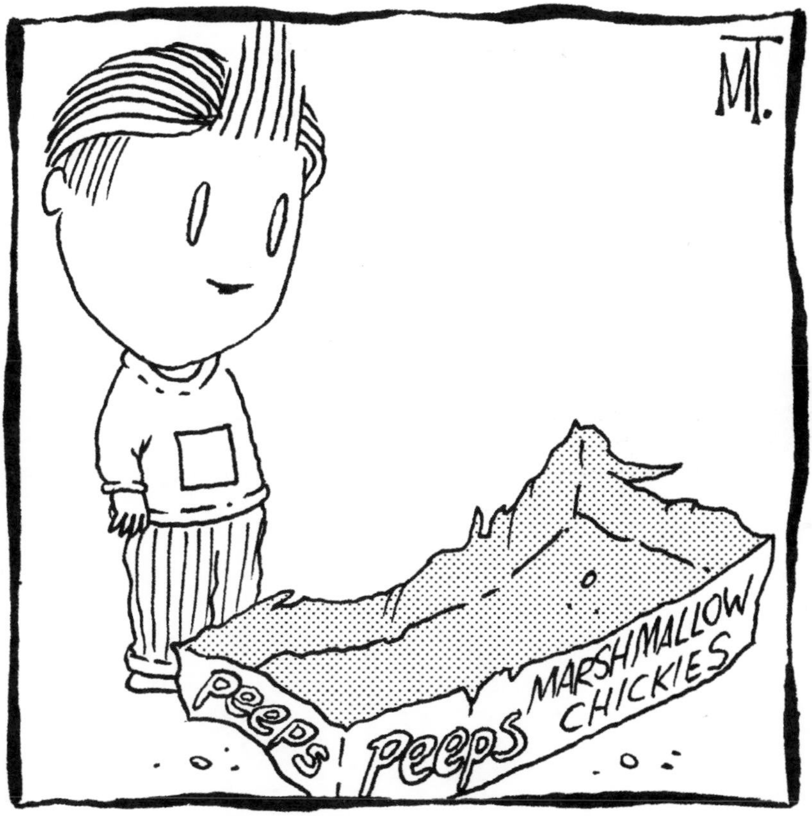
MT.
Peeps
Peeps
MARSHMALLOW
CHICKIES

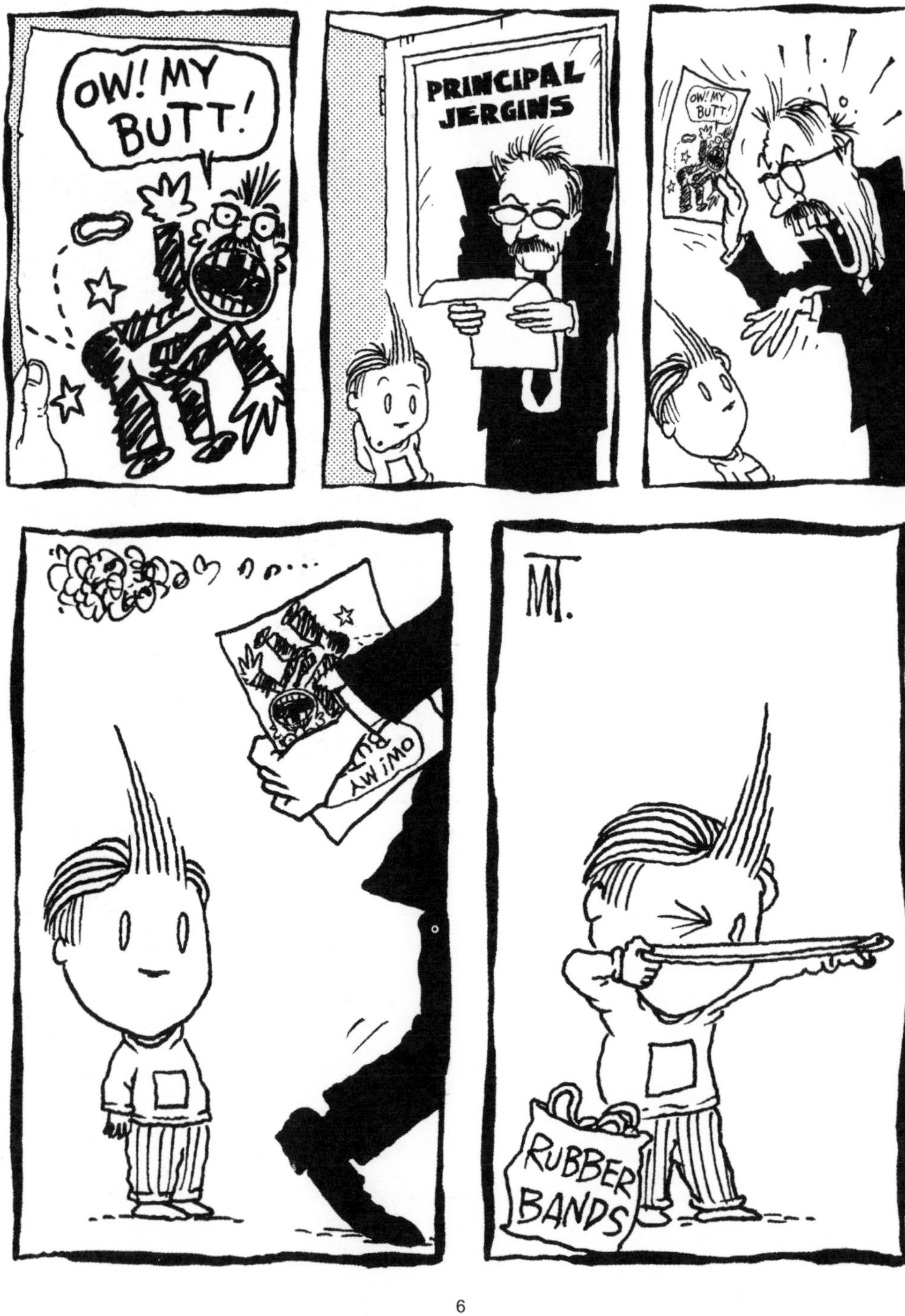
OW! MY BUTT!
PRINCIPAL JERGINS
OW! MY BUTT!
RUBBER BANDS

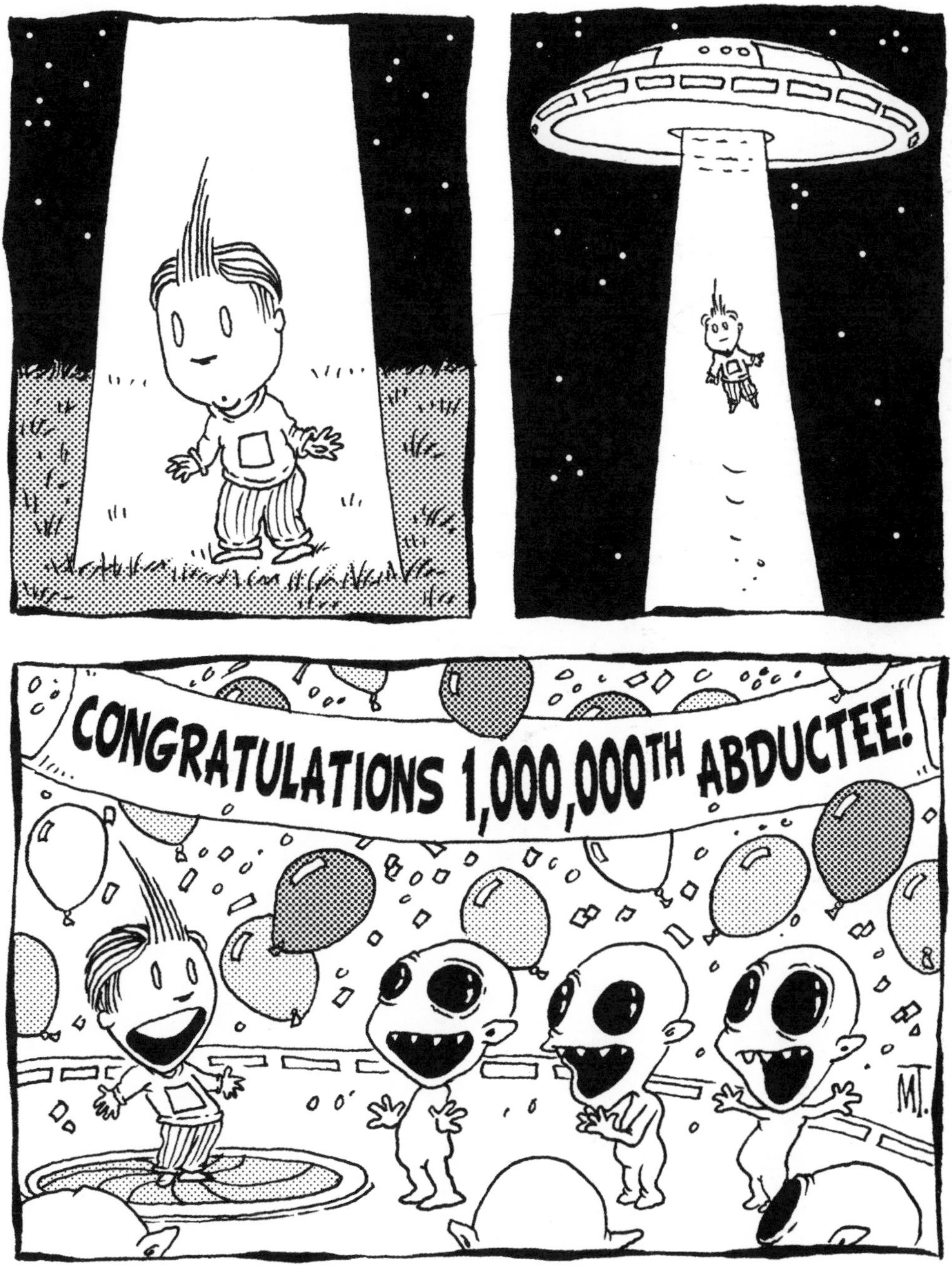
CONGRATULATIONS 1,000,000TH ABDUCTEE!
MT.

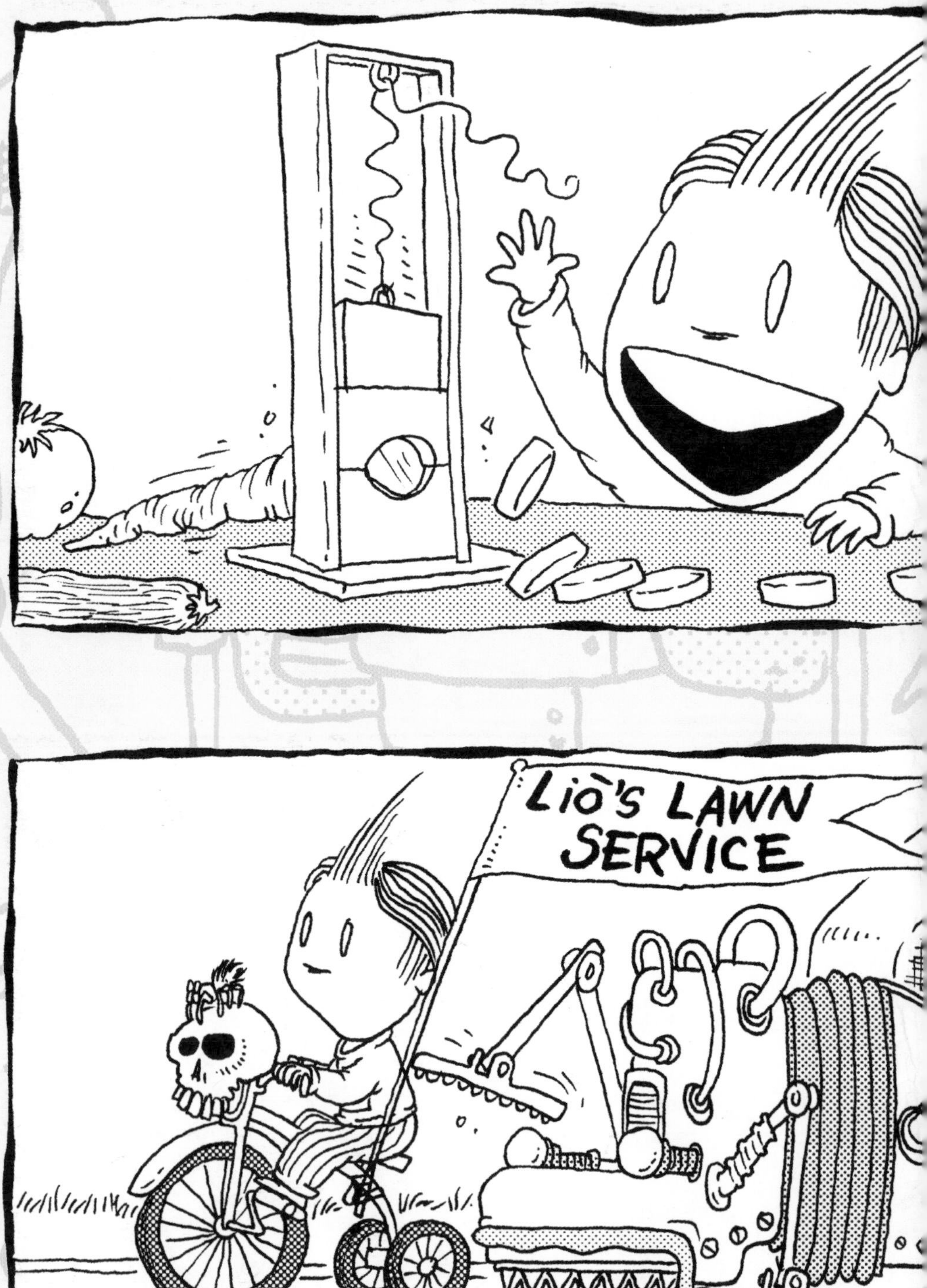
LIO'S LAWN SERVICE

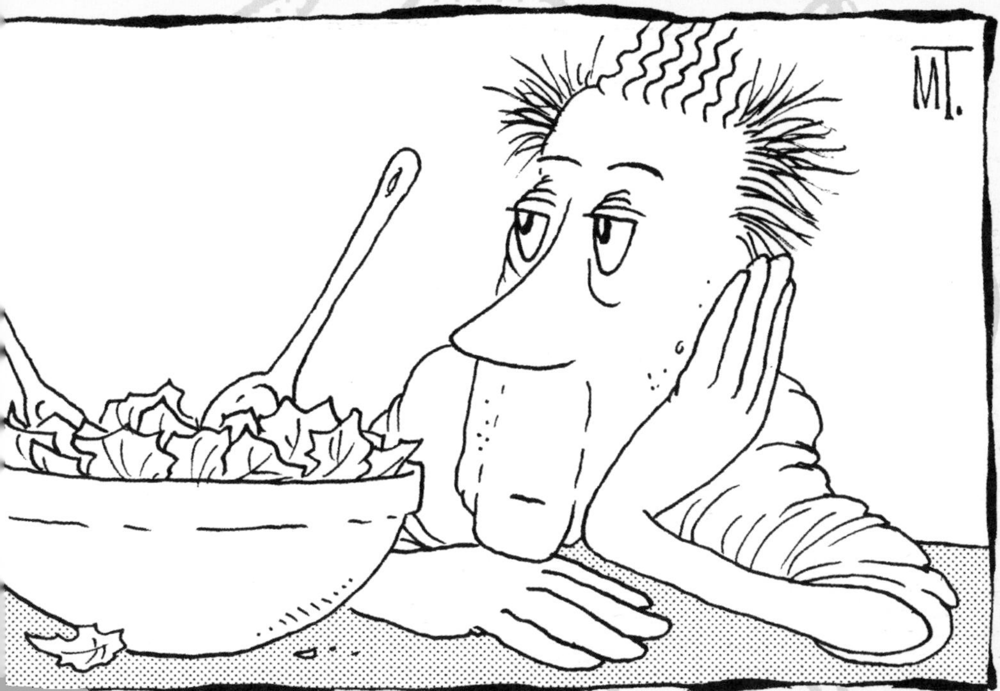

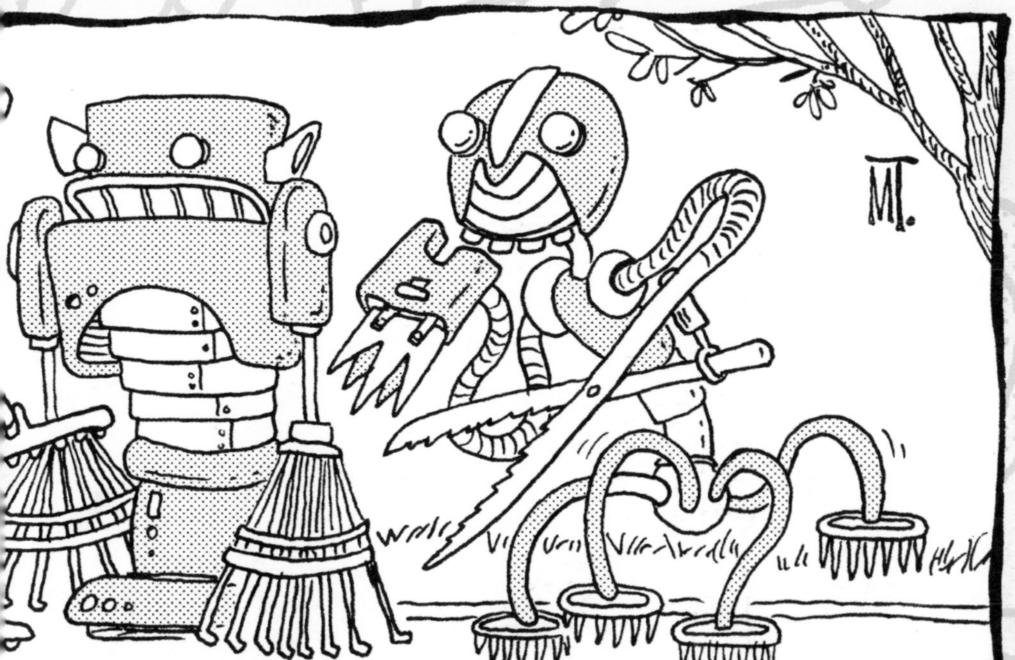

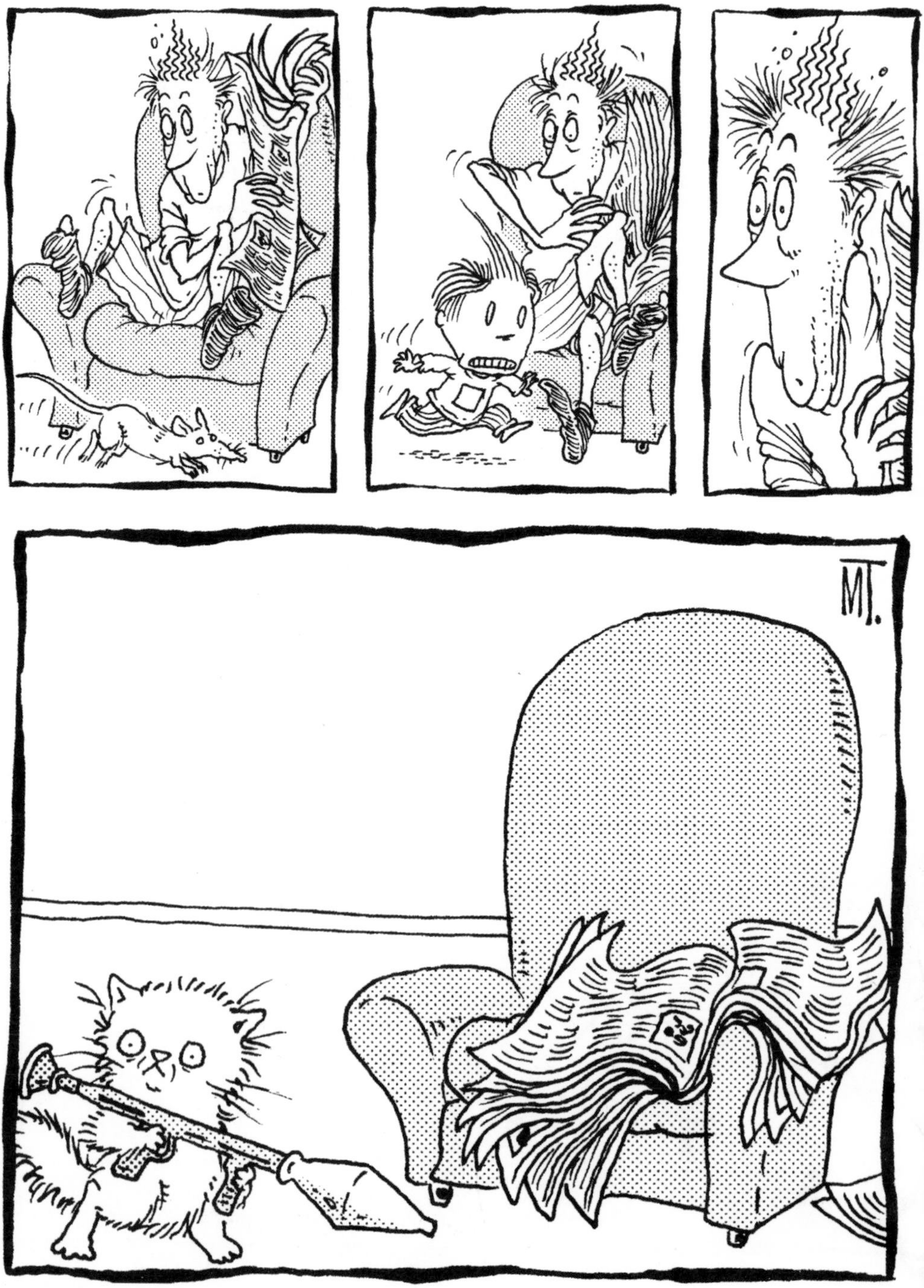

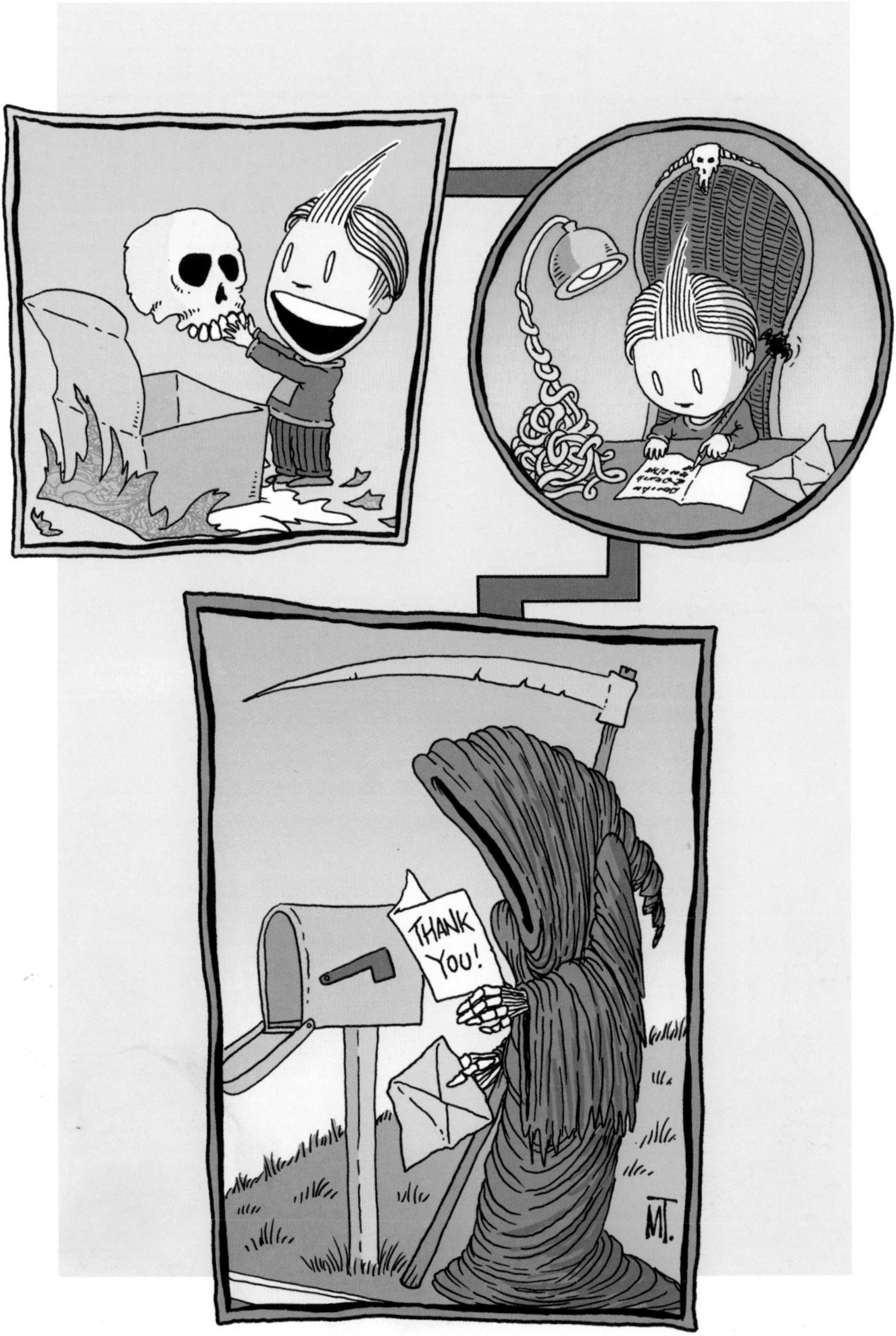
THANK YOU!
MT.

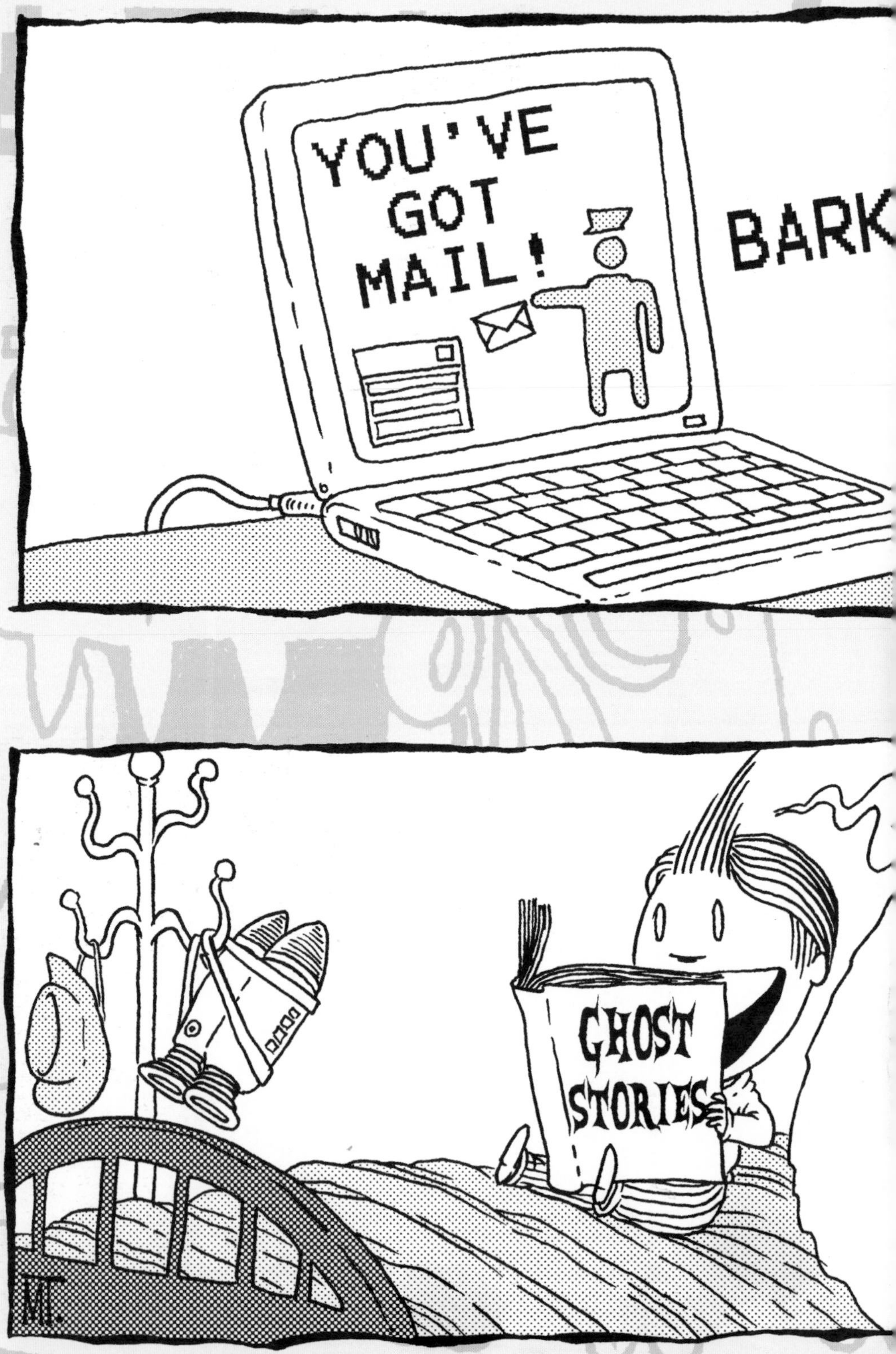
YOU'VE GOT MAIL!
BARK
GHOST STORIES
MT.

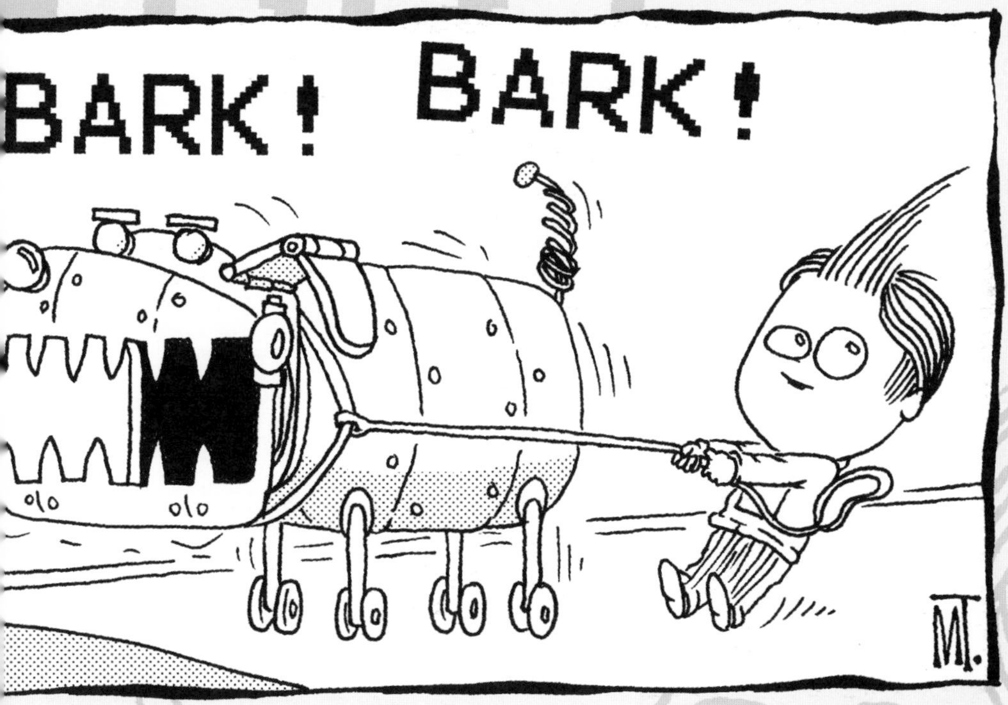
BARK! BARK!
MT.

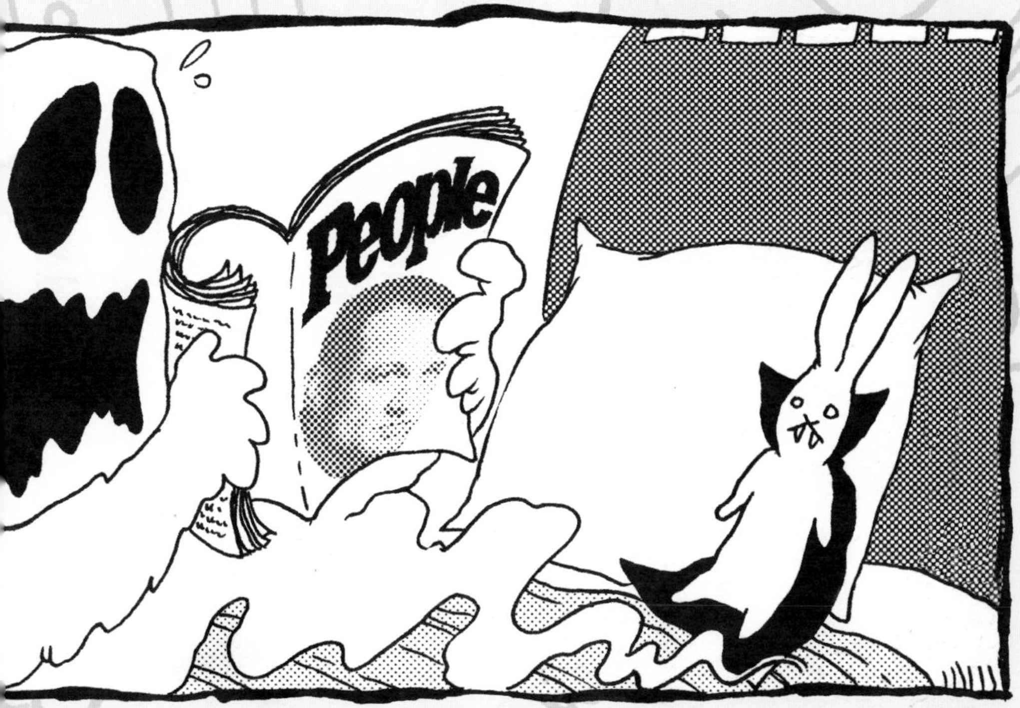
People

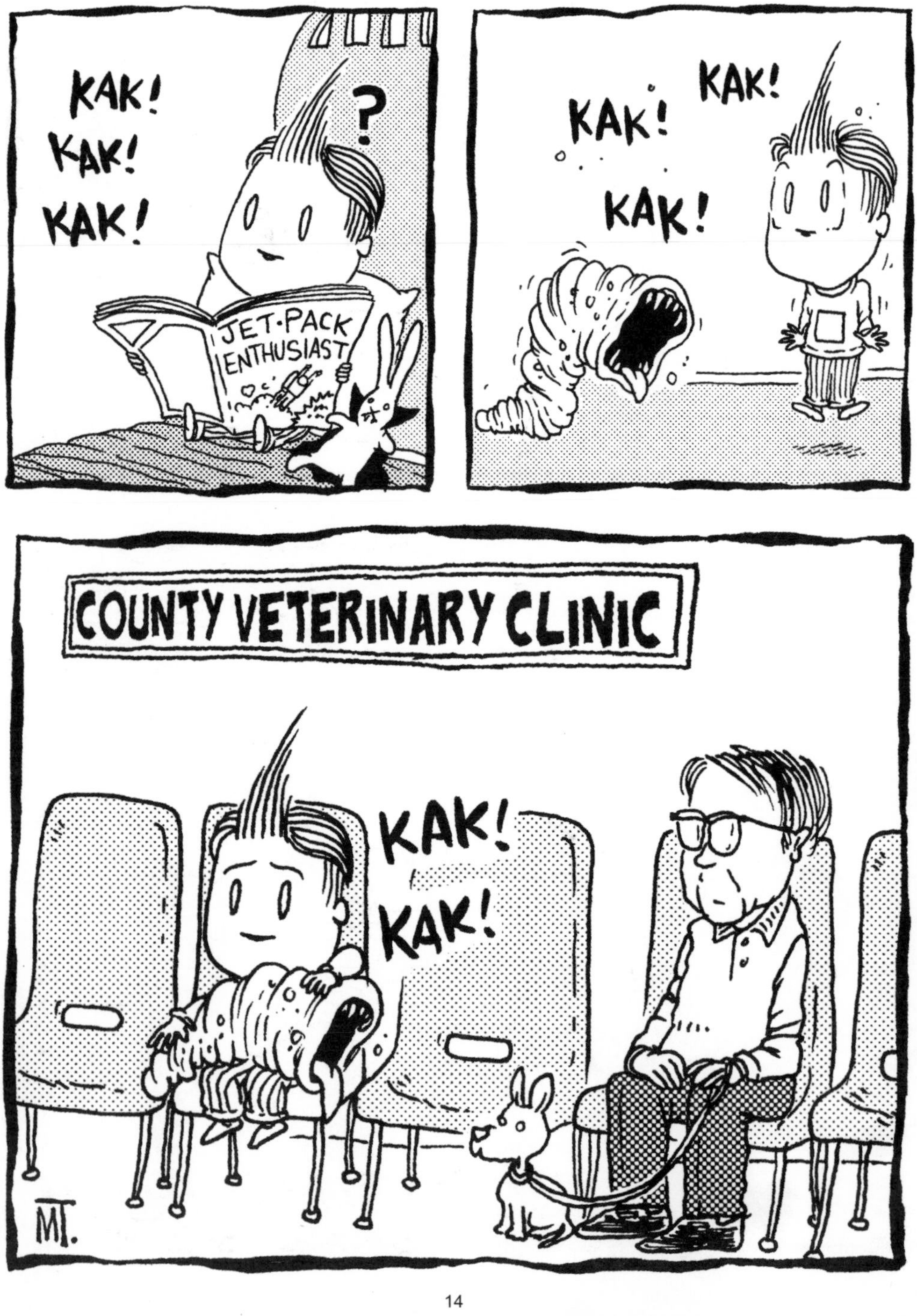
KAK!
KAK!
KAK!
?
JET-PACK ENTHUSIAST
KAK!
KAK!
KAK!
COUNTY VETERINARY CLINIC
KAK!
KAK!
MT.

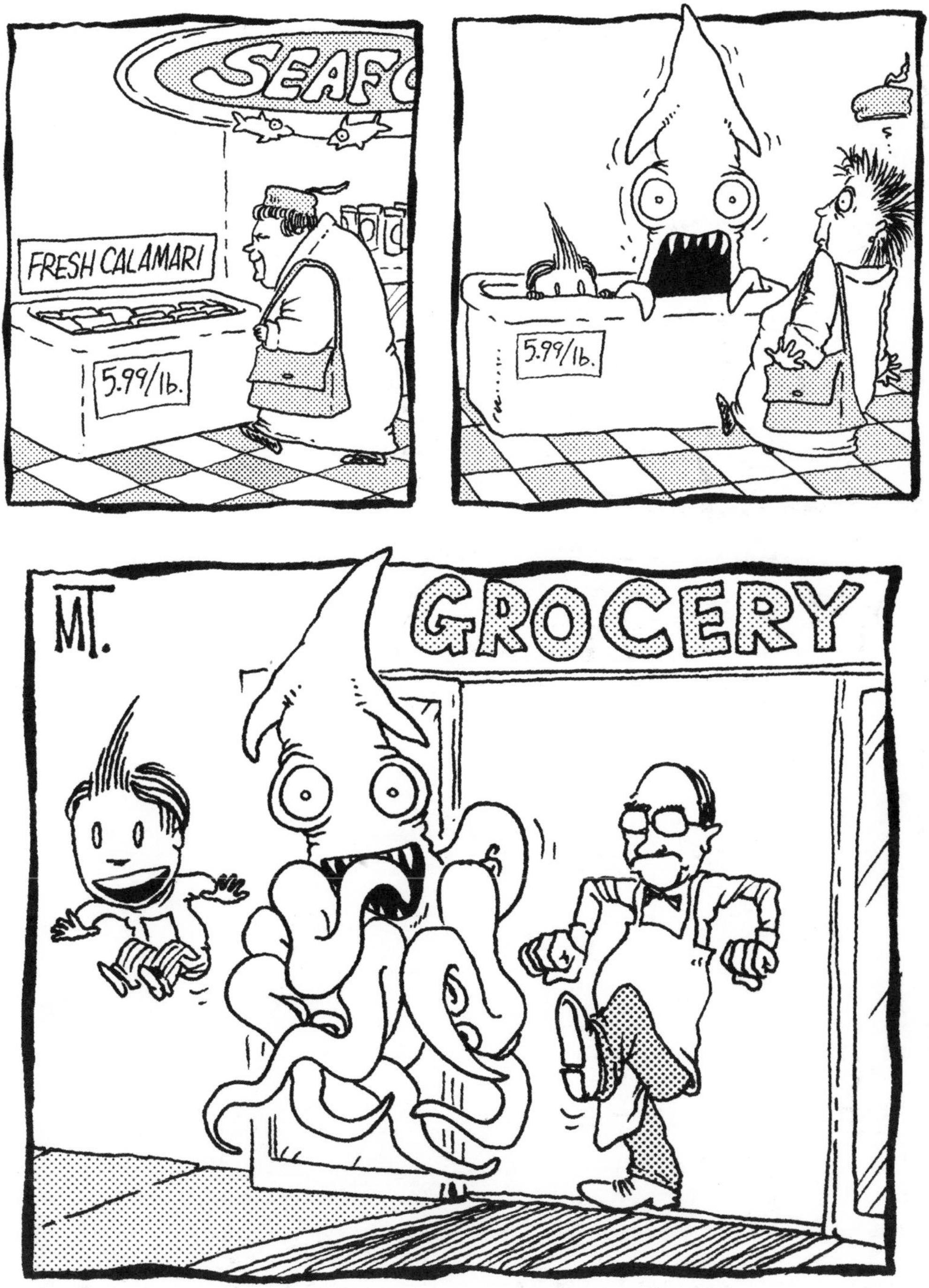
SEAFO
FRESH CALAMARI
5.99/lb.
5.99/lb.
MT.
GROCERY

OFFICE
SUPPLY
MT.

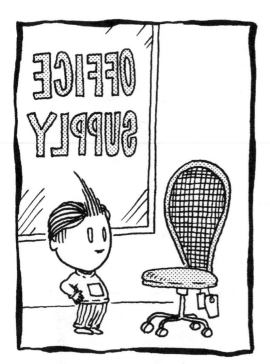

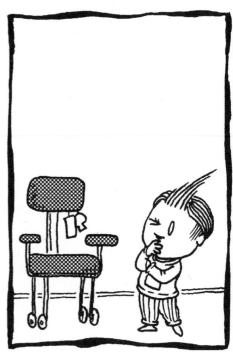

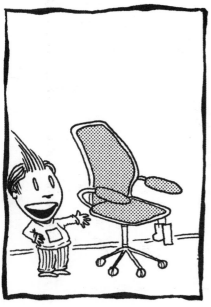

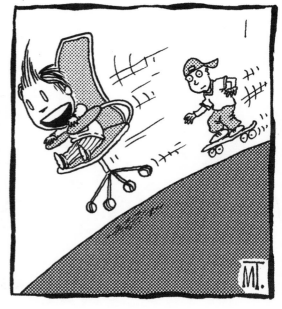

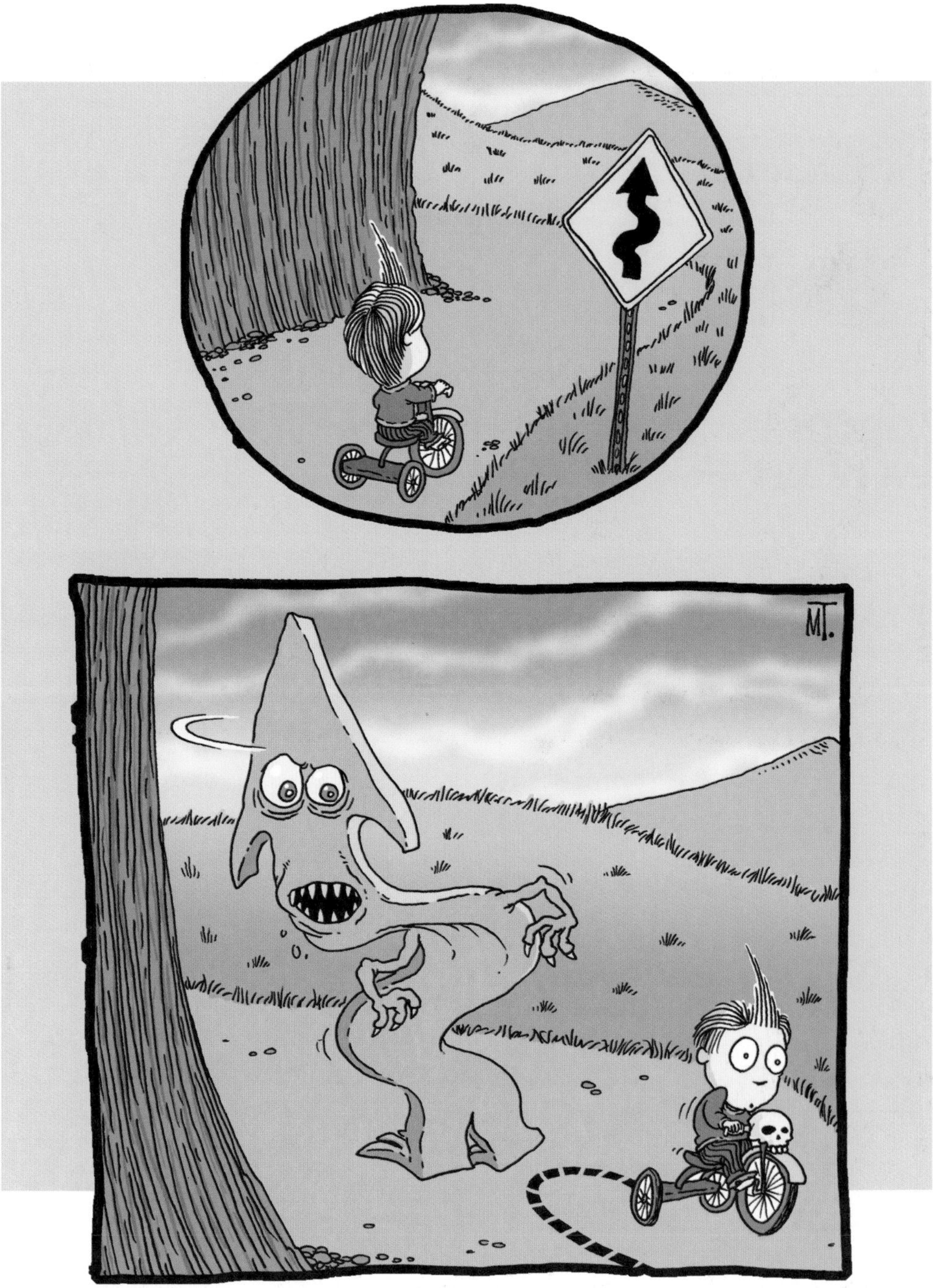

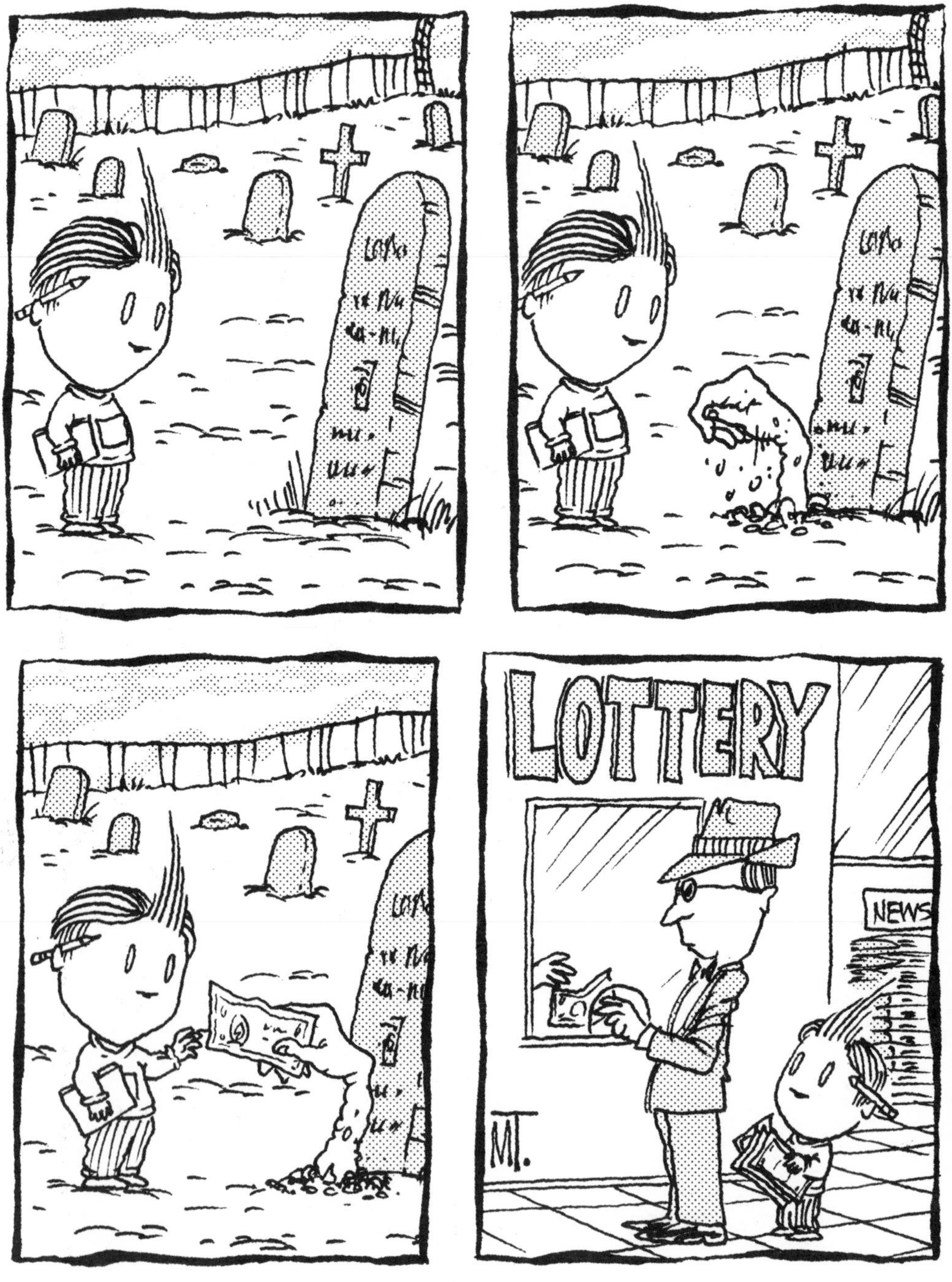
LOTTERY
NEWS
MT.

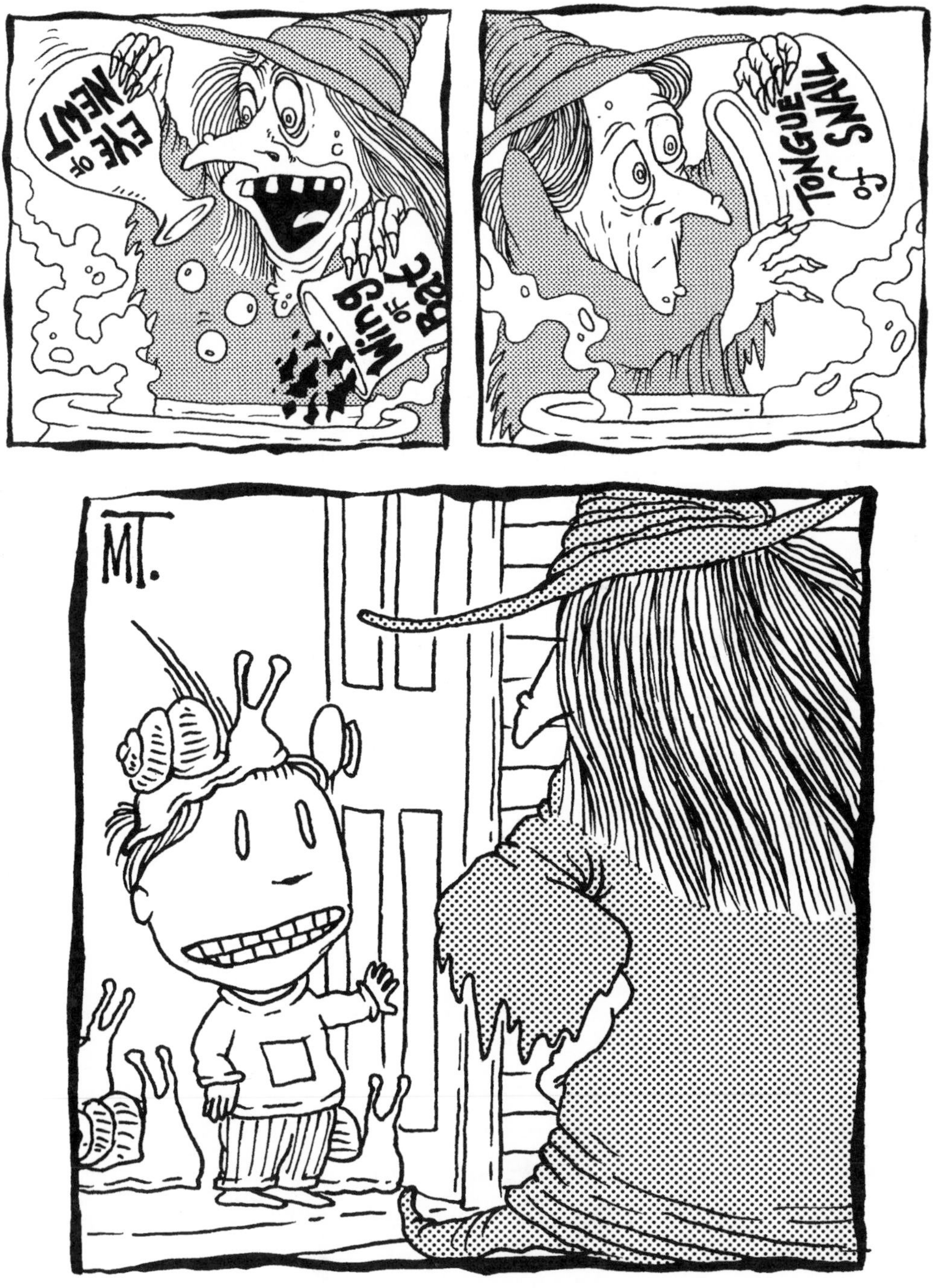
EYE of NEWT
Wing of Bat
TONGUE of SNAIL
MT.

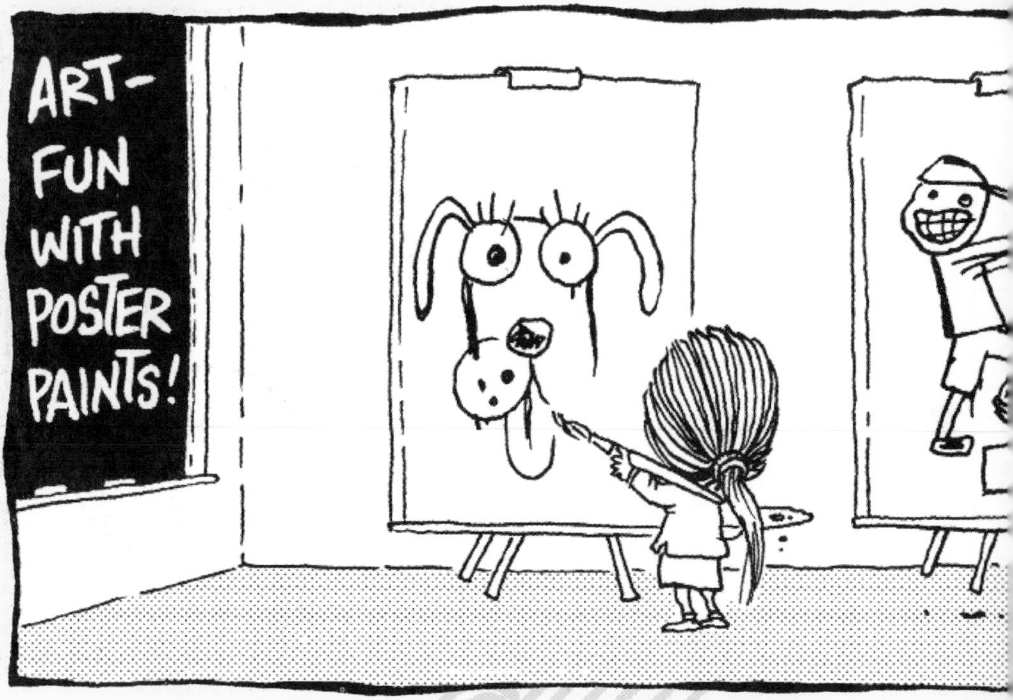
ART-
FUN
WITH
POSTER
PAINTS!

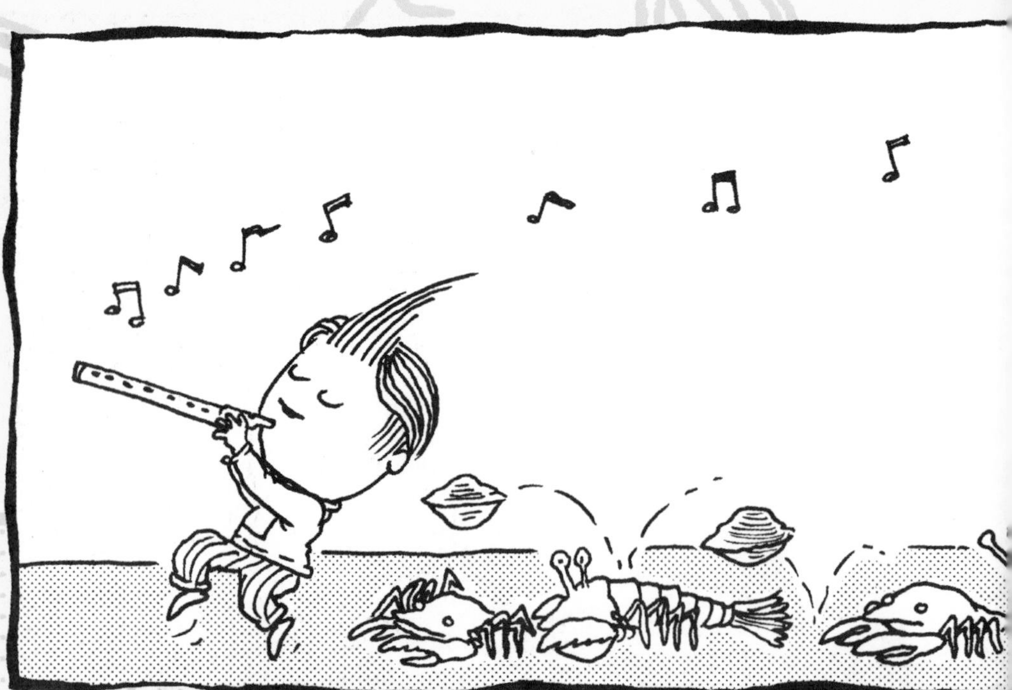

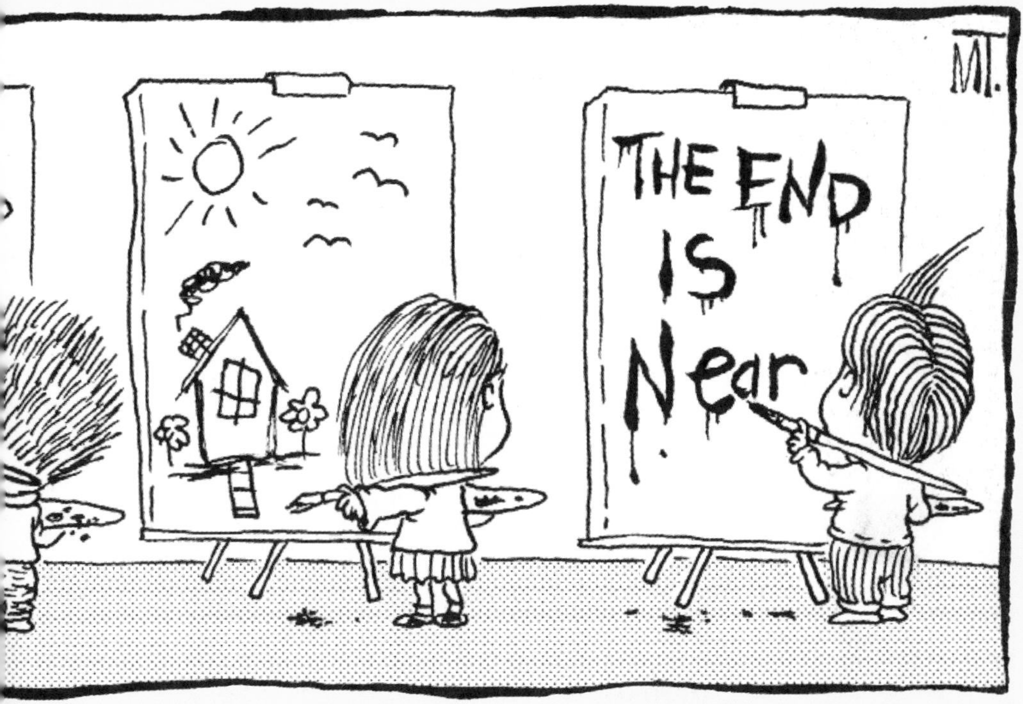
THE END IS Near
MT.

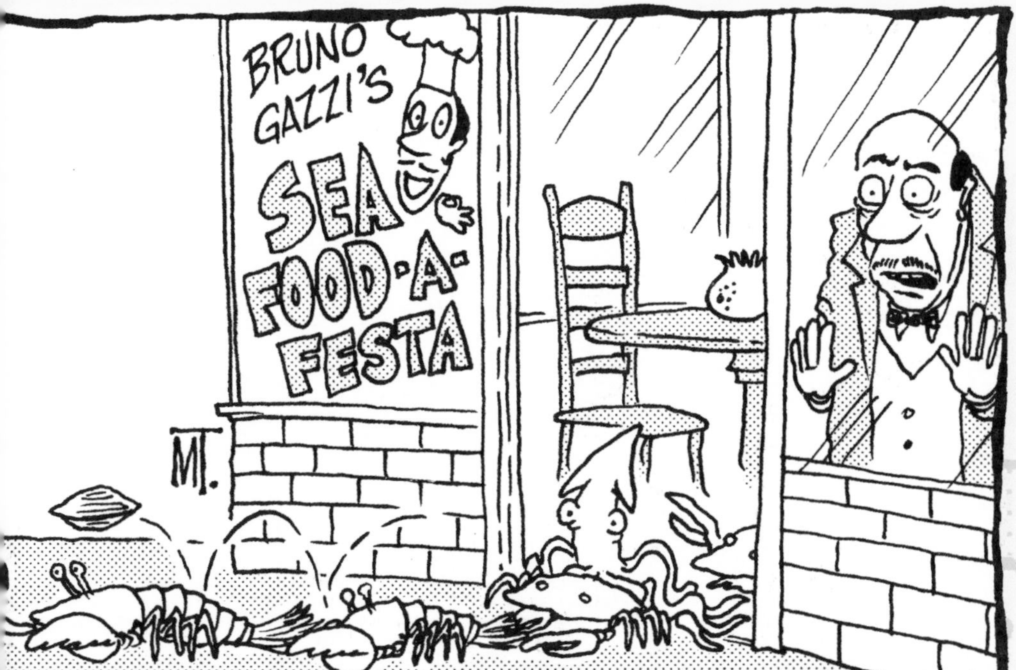
BRUNO GAZZI'S
SEA FOOD-A-FESTA
MT.

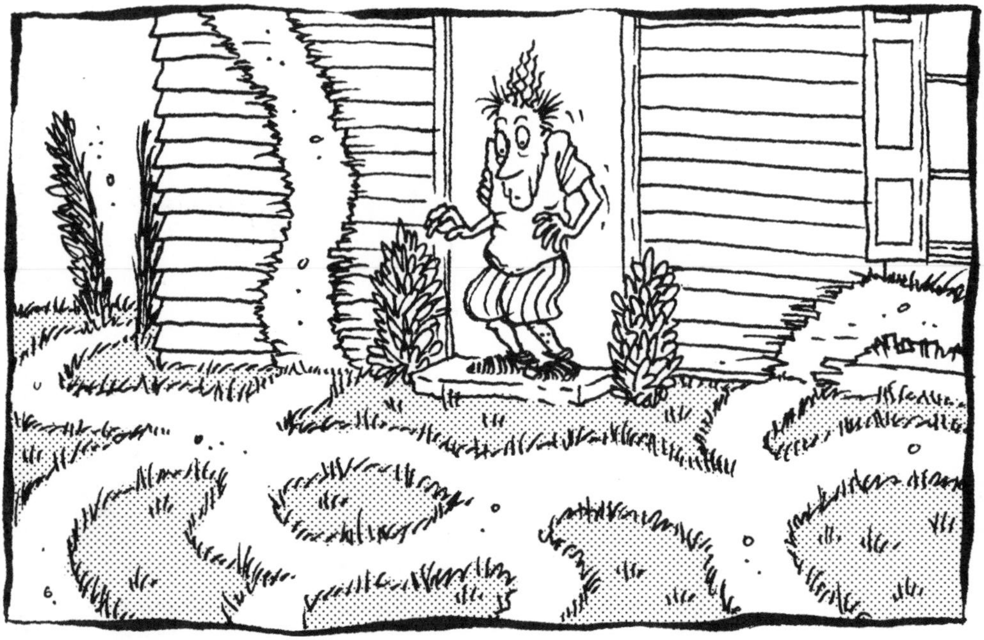

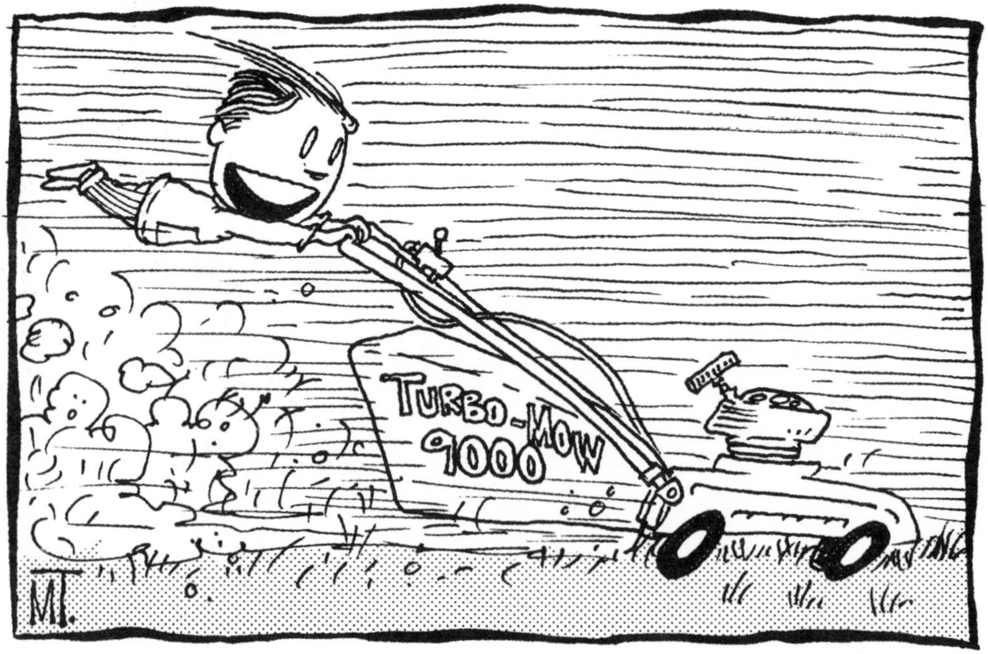
TURBO-MOW 9000
MT.

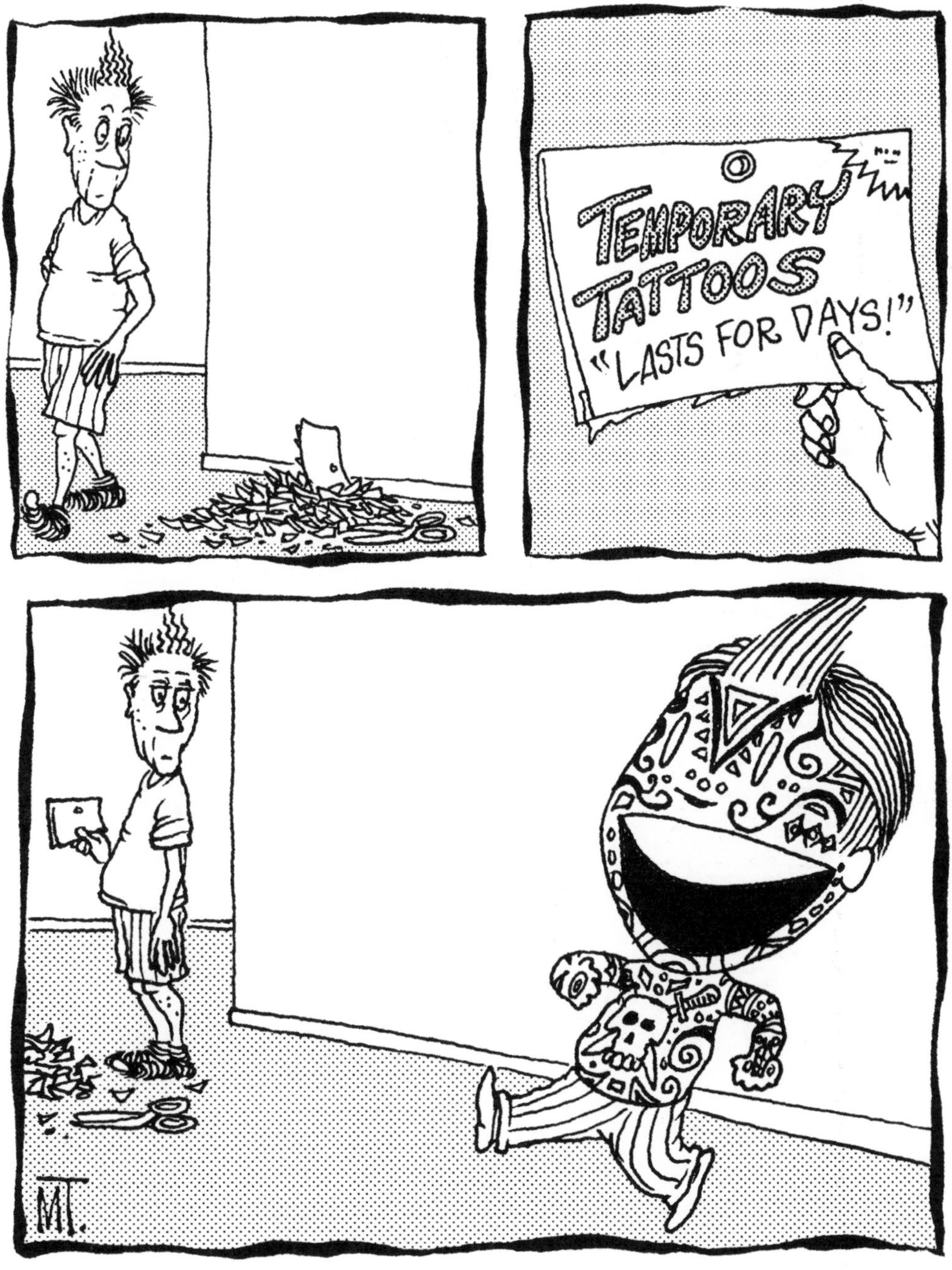
TEMPORARY TATTOOS
"LASTS FOR DAYS!"
MT.

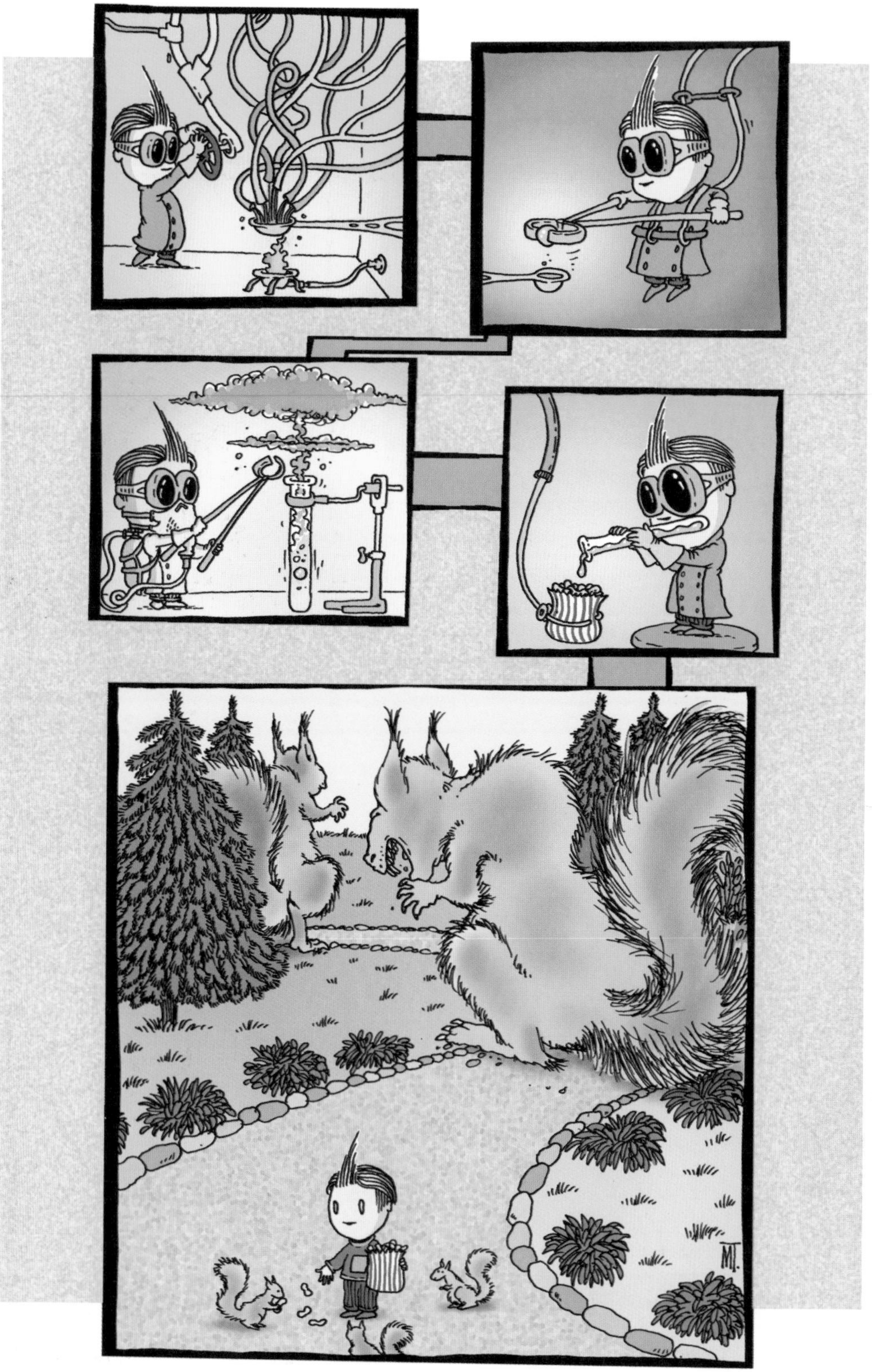

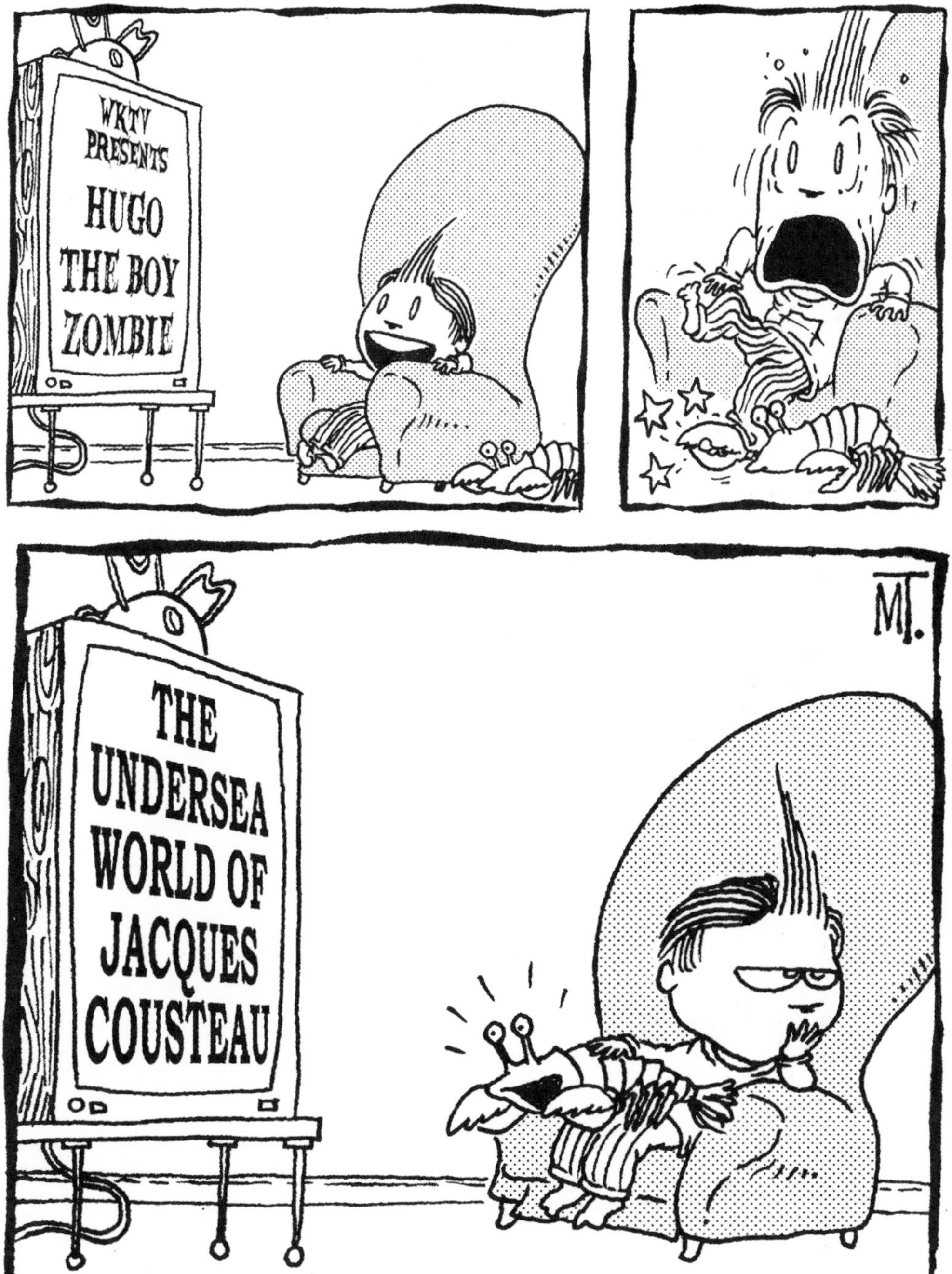
WKTV PRESENTS
HUGO THE BOY ZOMBIE
THE UNDERSEA WORLD OF JACQUES COUSTEAU
MT.

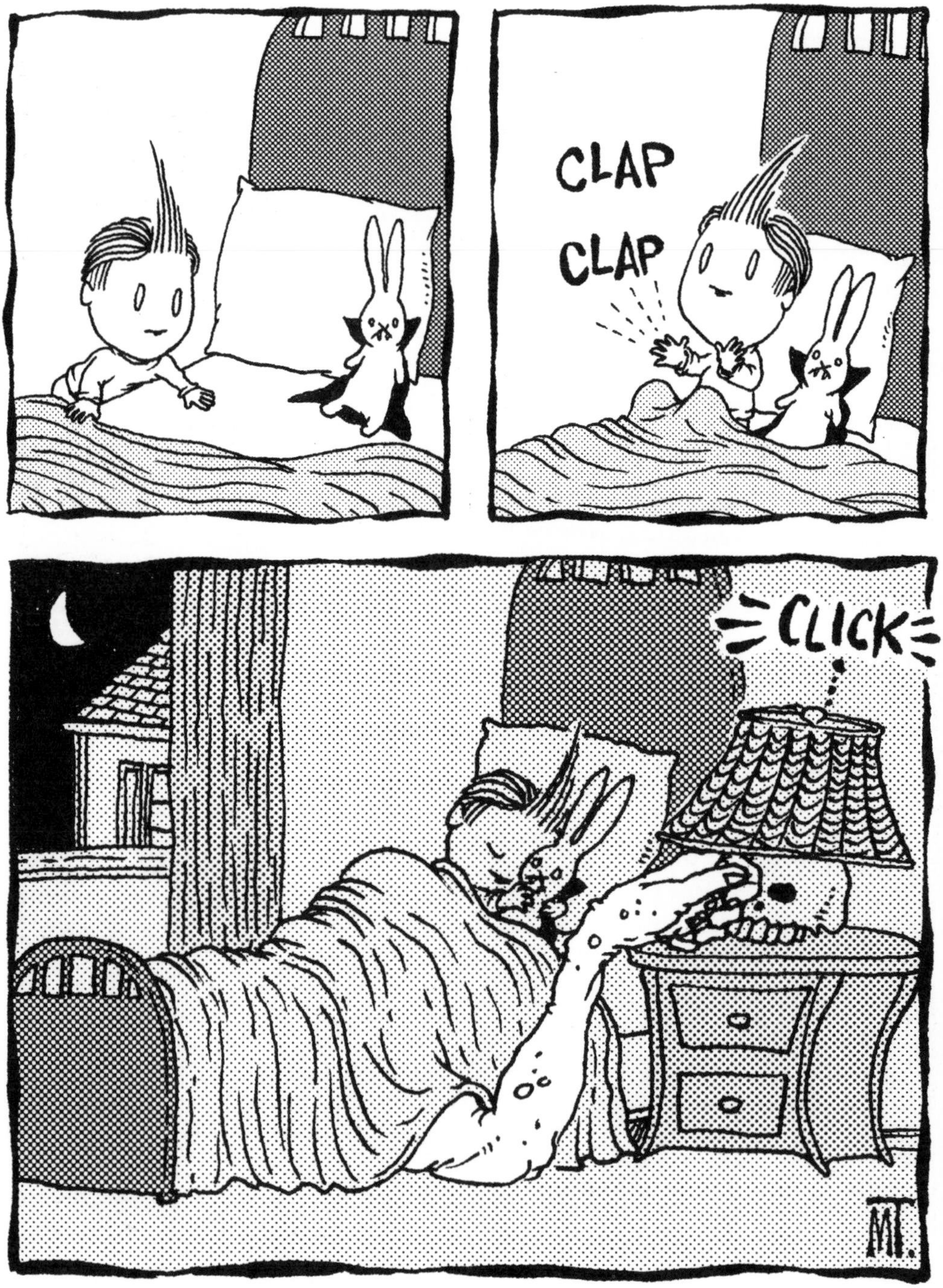
CLAP
CLAP
CLICK
MT.

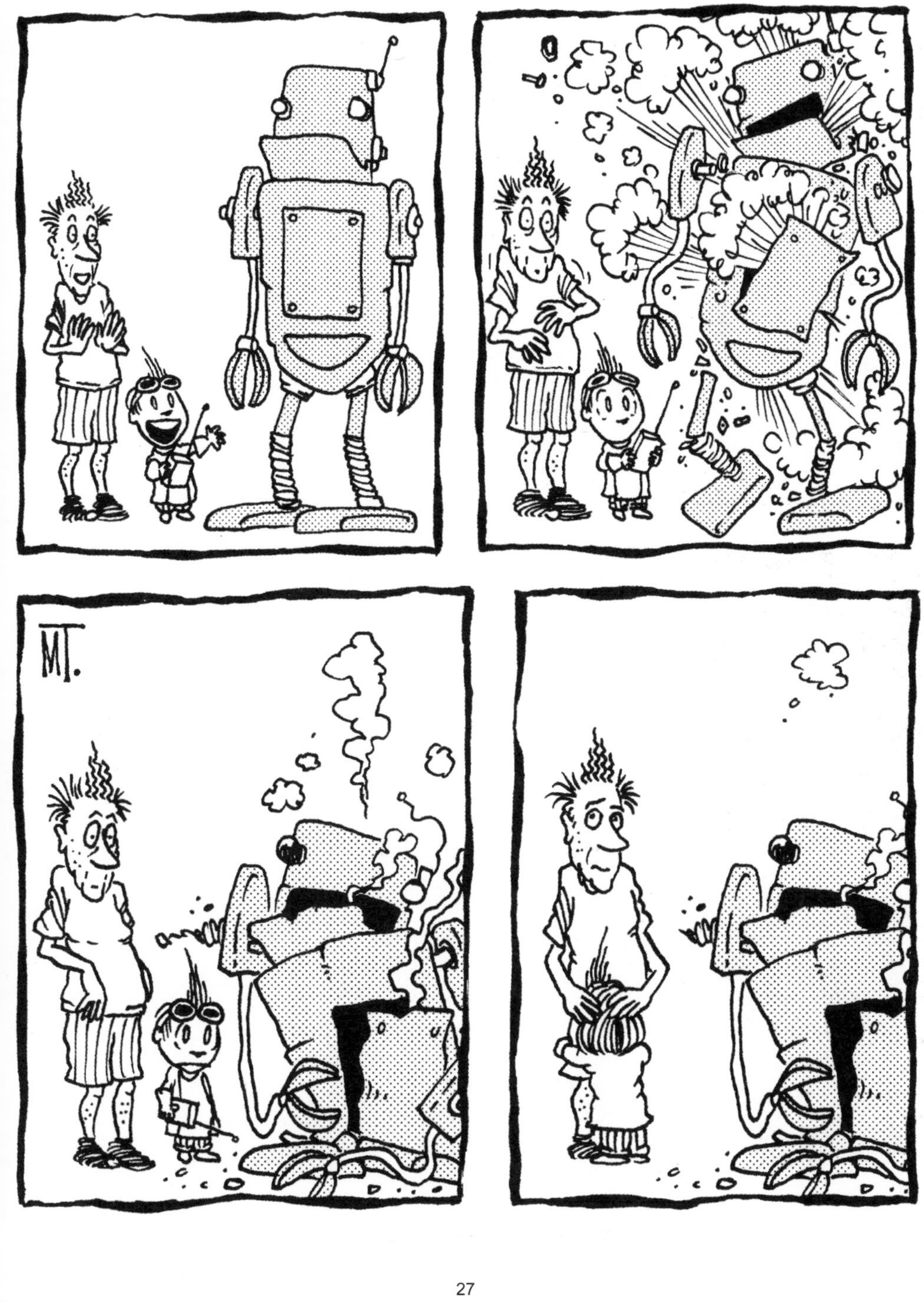

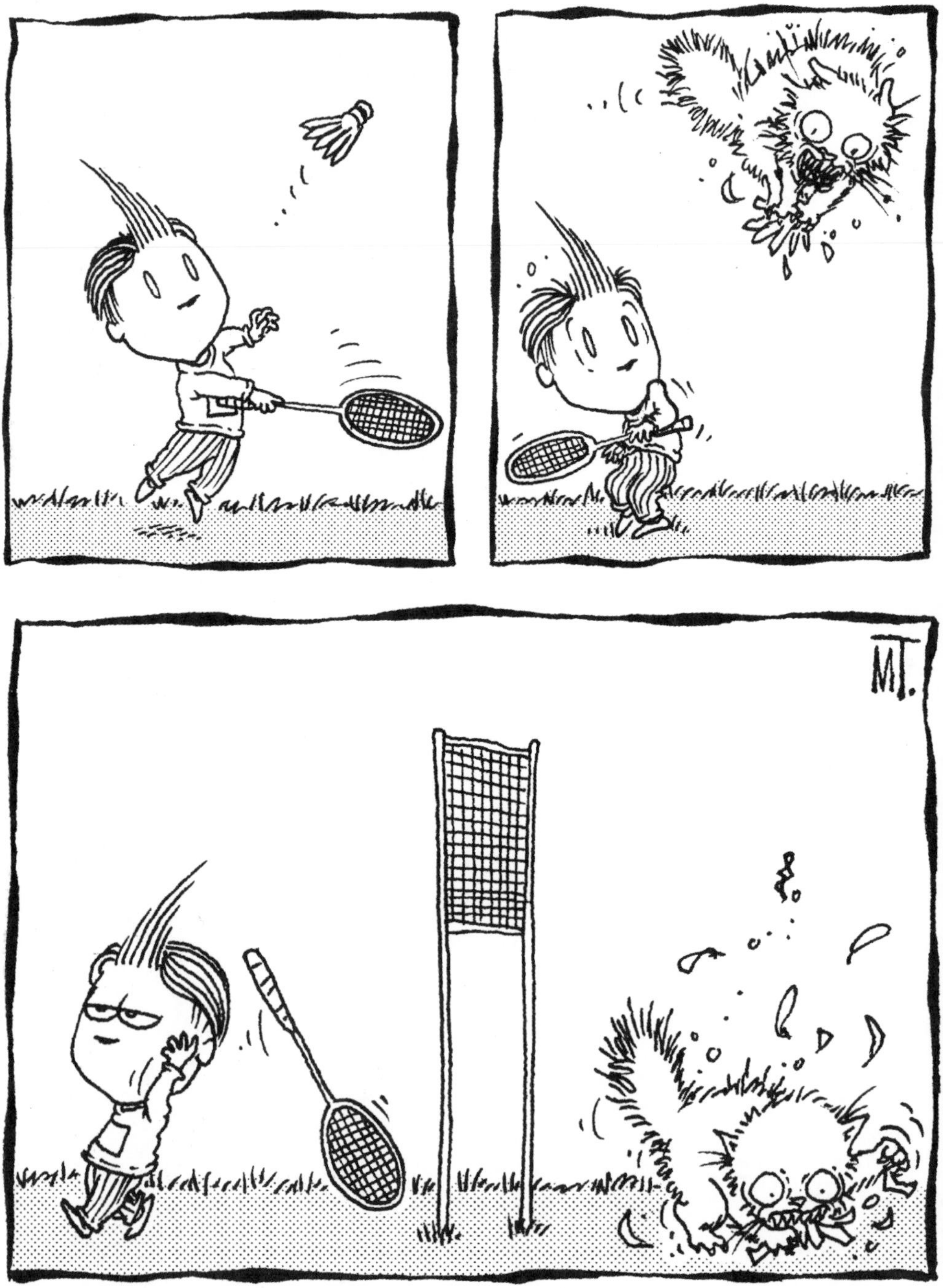
MT.

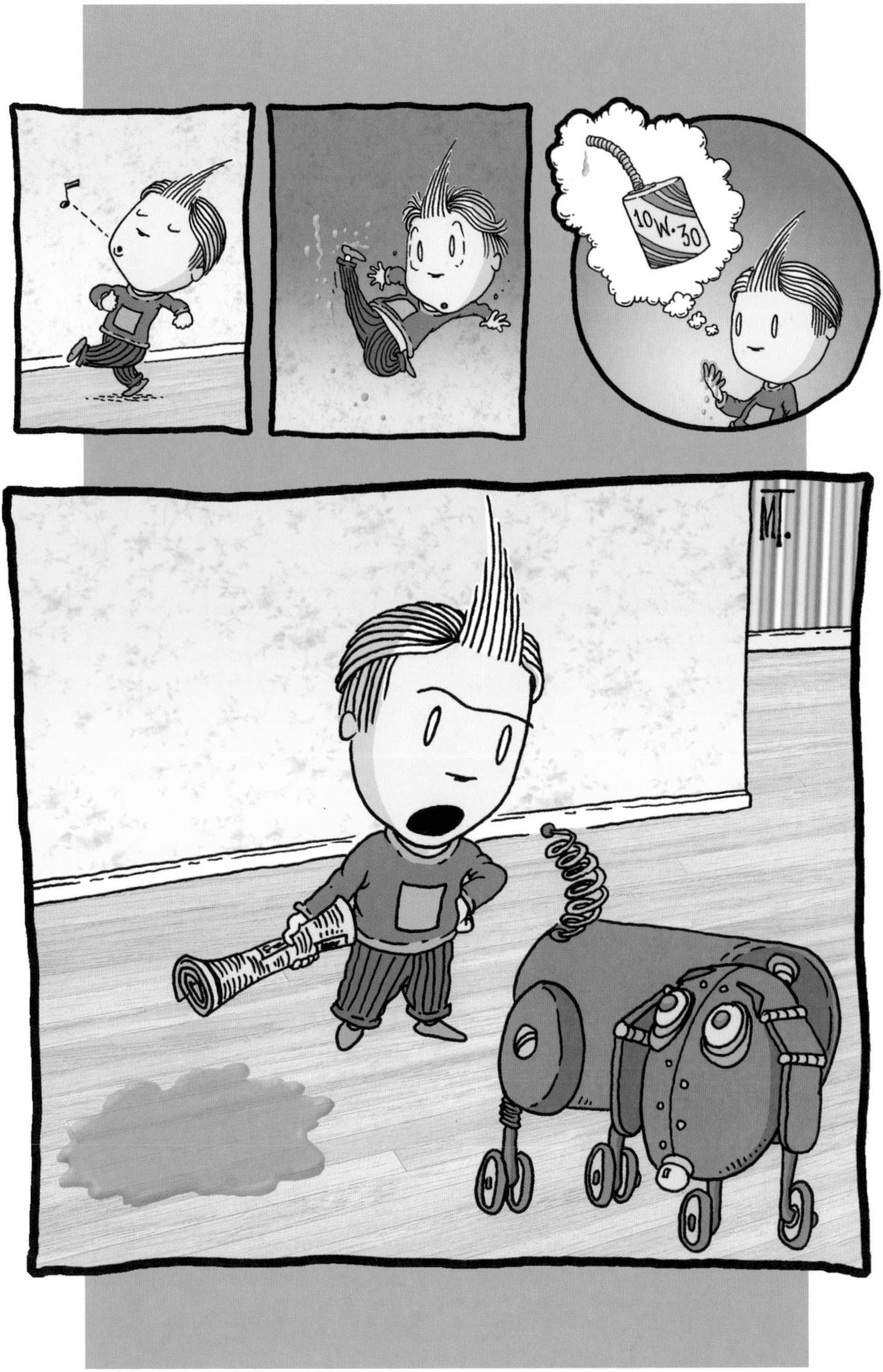
10W·30

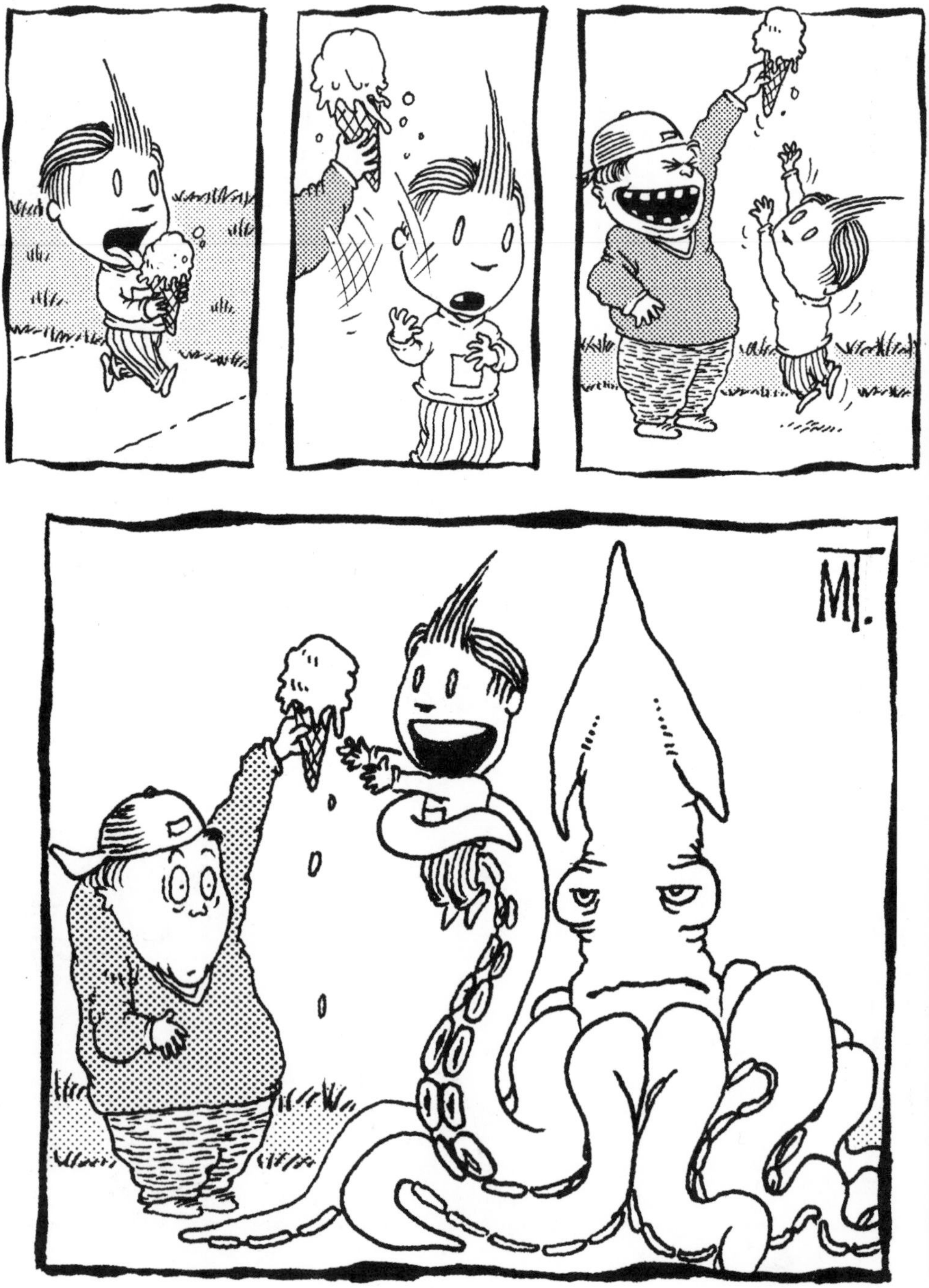
MT.

FRESH
MT.

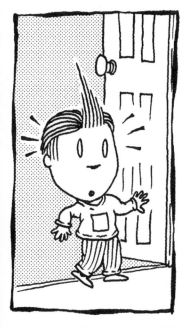

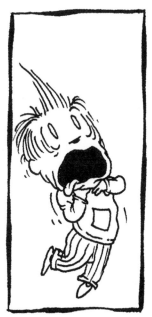

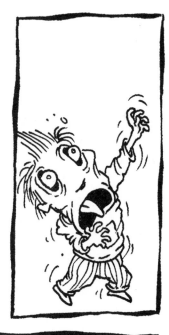

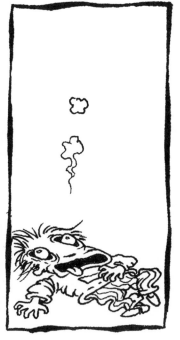

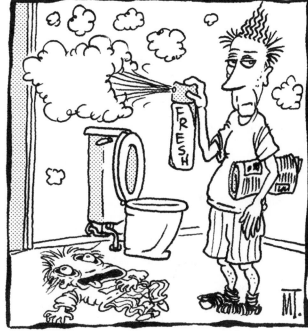

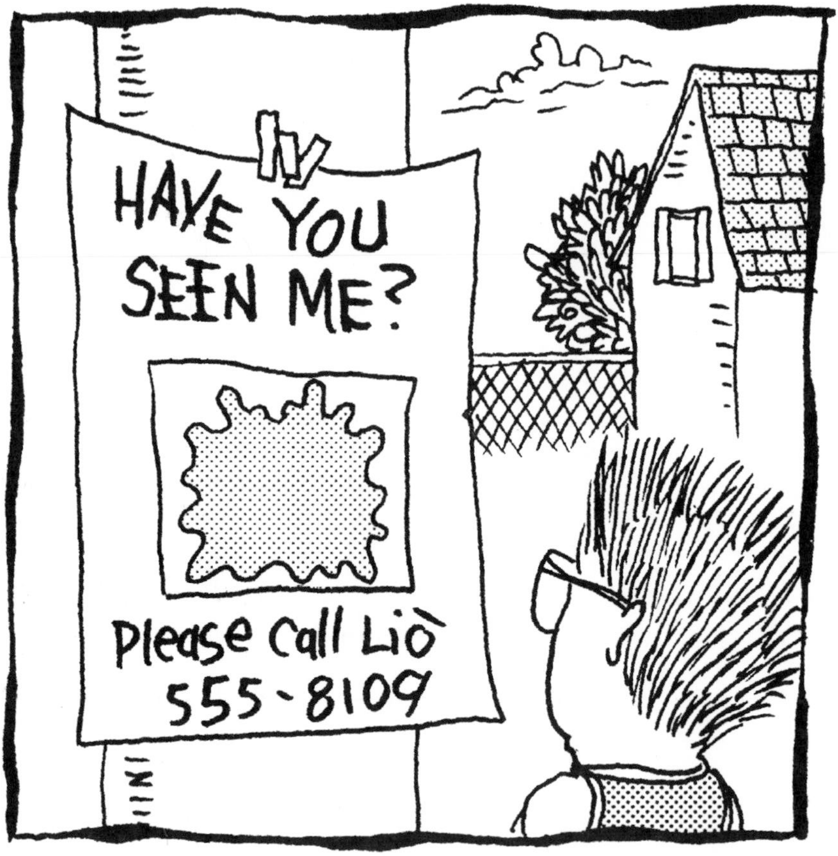
HAVE YOU SEEN ME?
Please Call Liò
555-8109

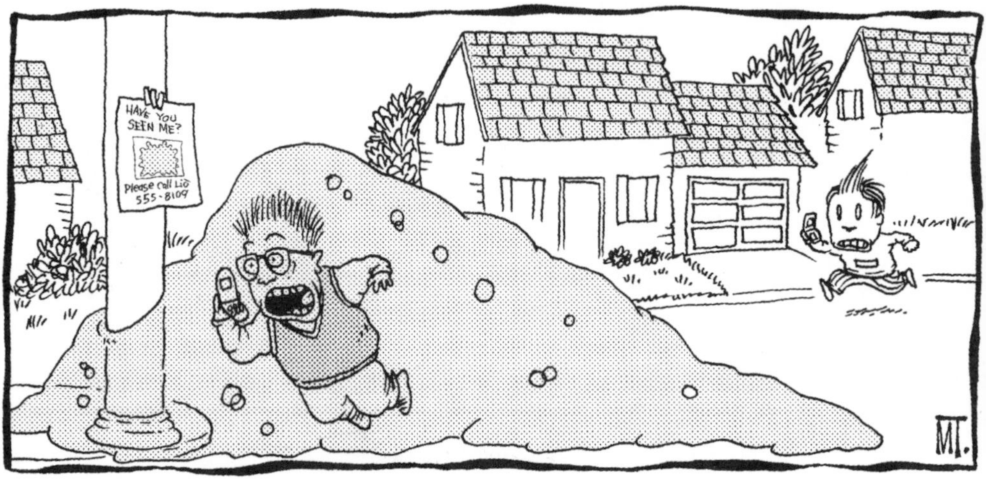
HAVE YOU SEEN ME?
Please Call Liò
555-8109
MT.

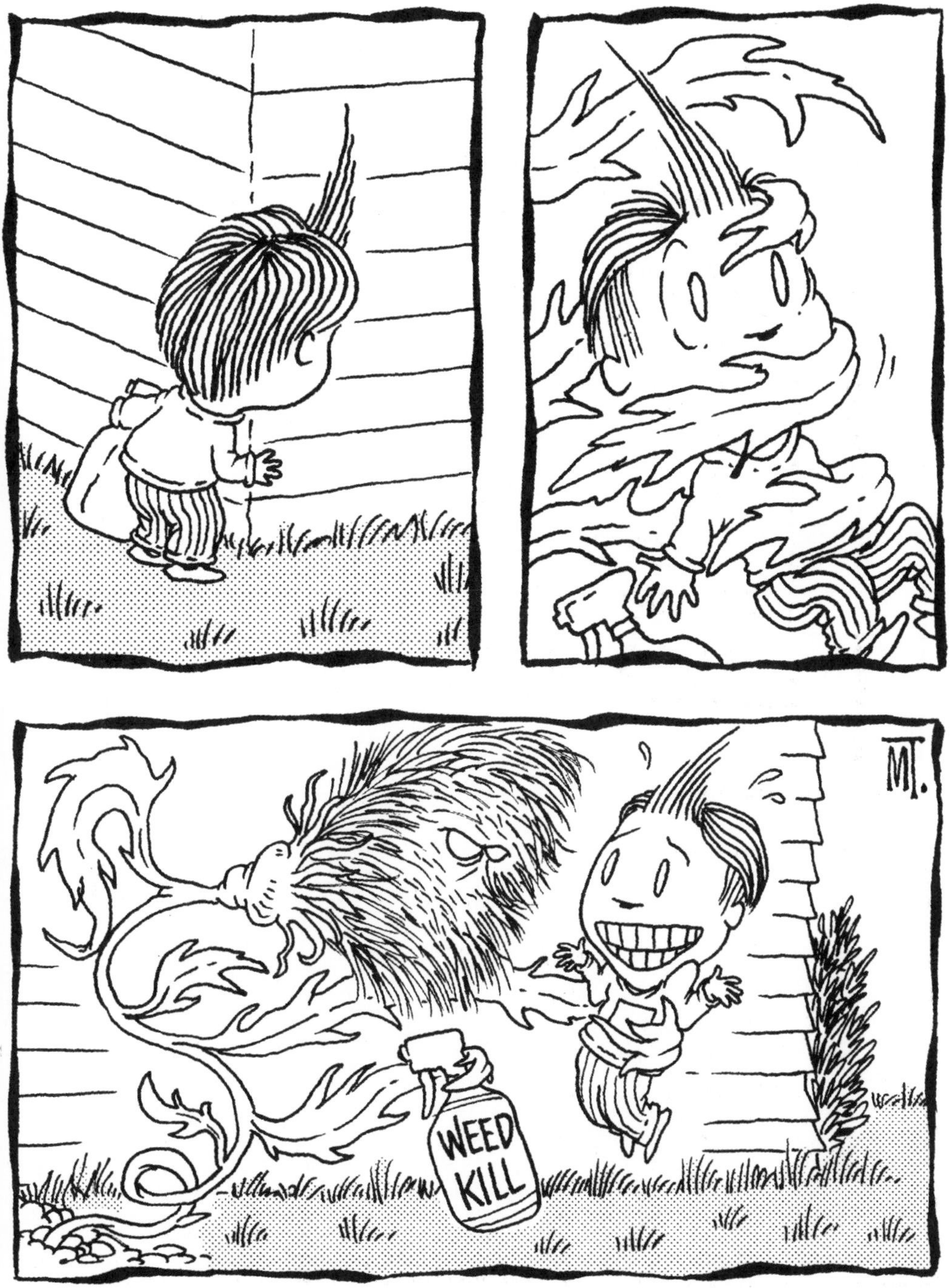
MT.
WEED KILL

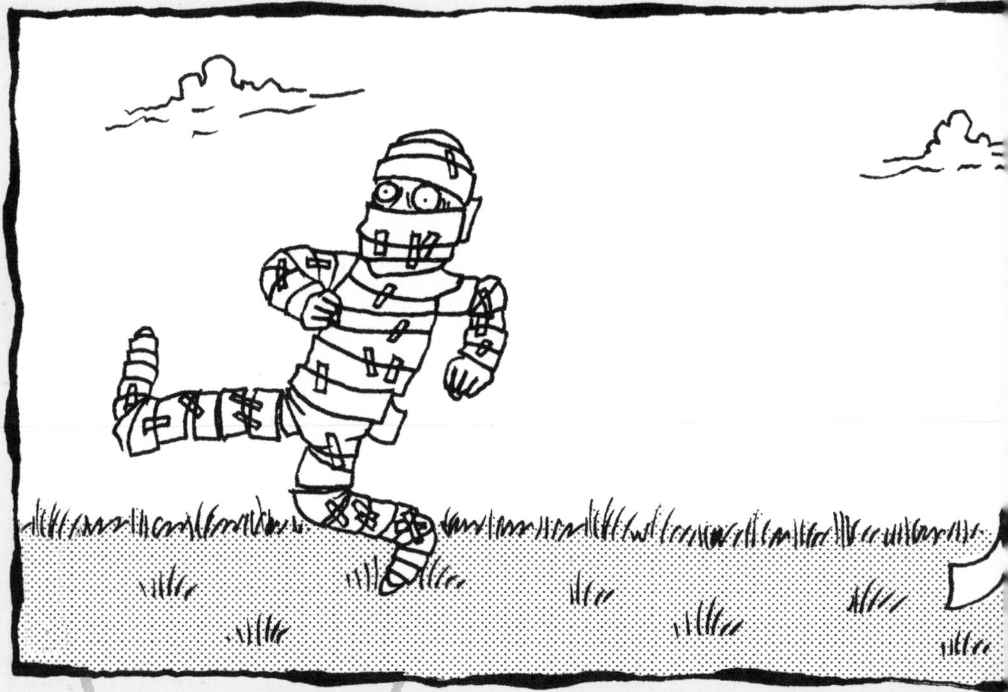

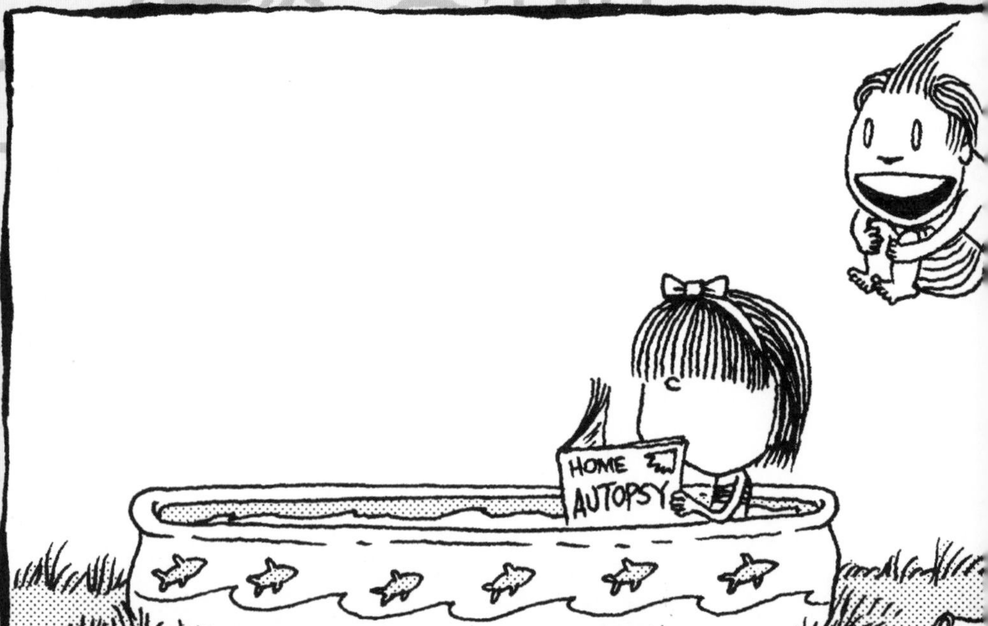
HOME
AUTOPSY

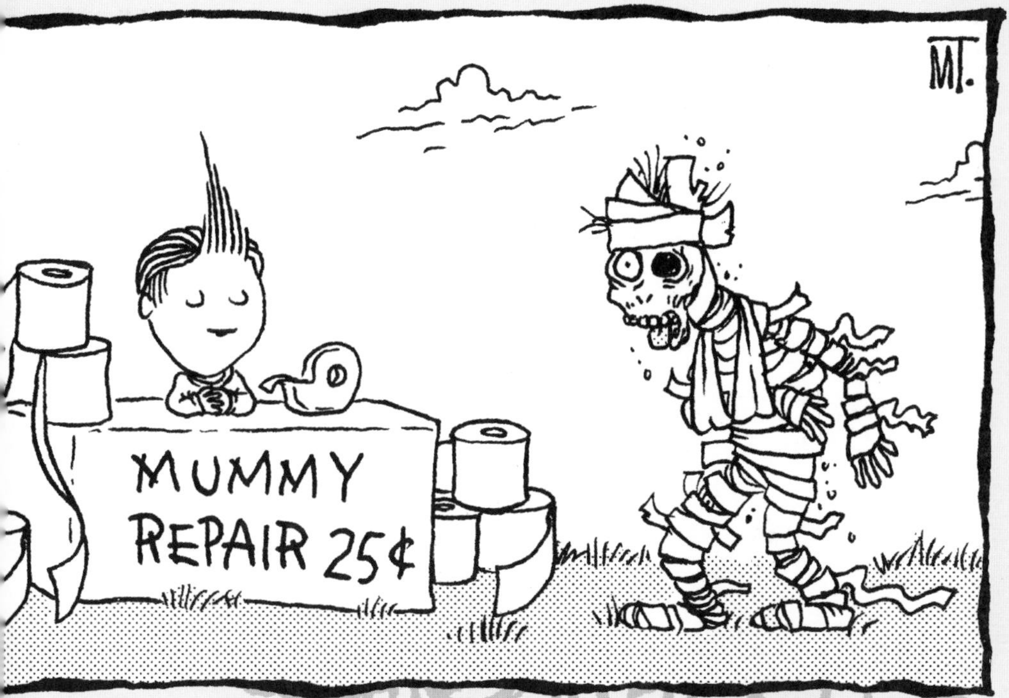
MT.
MUMMY
REPAIR 25¢

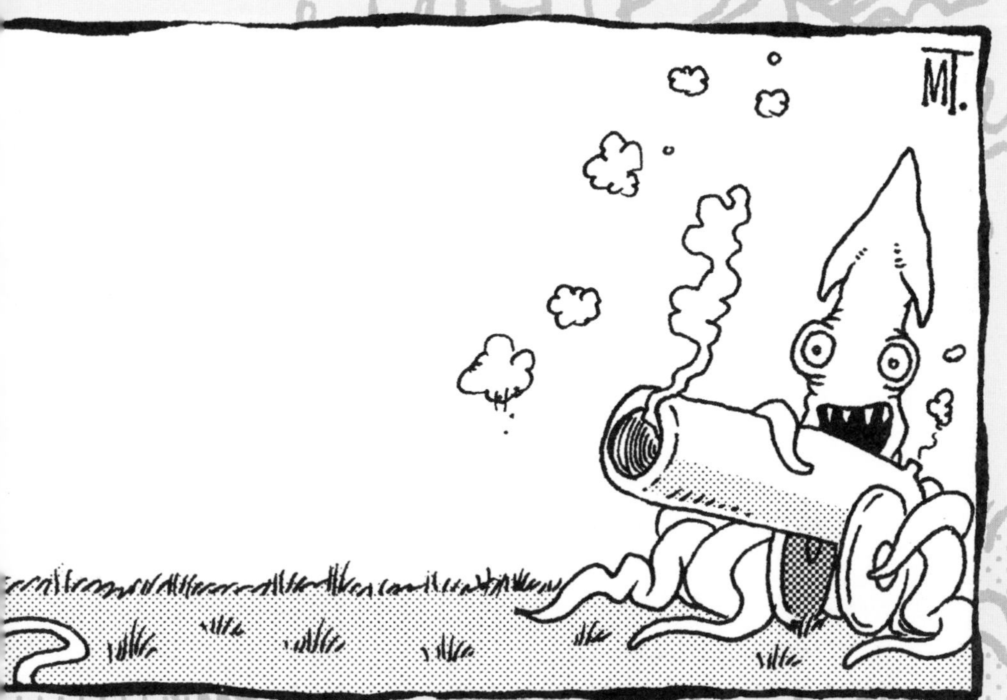
MT.

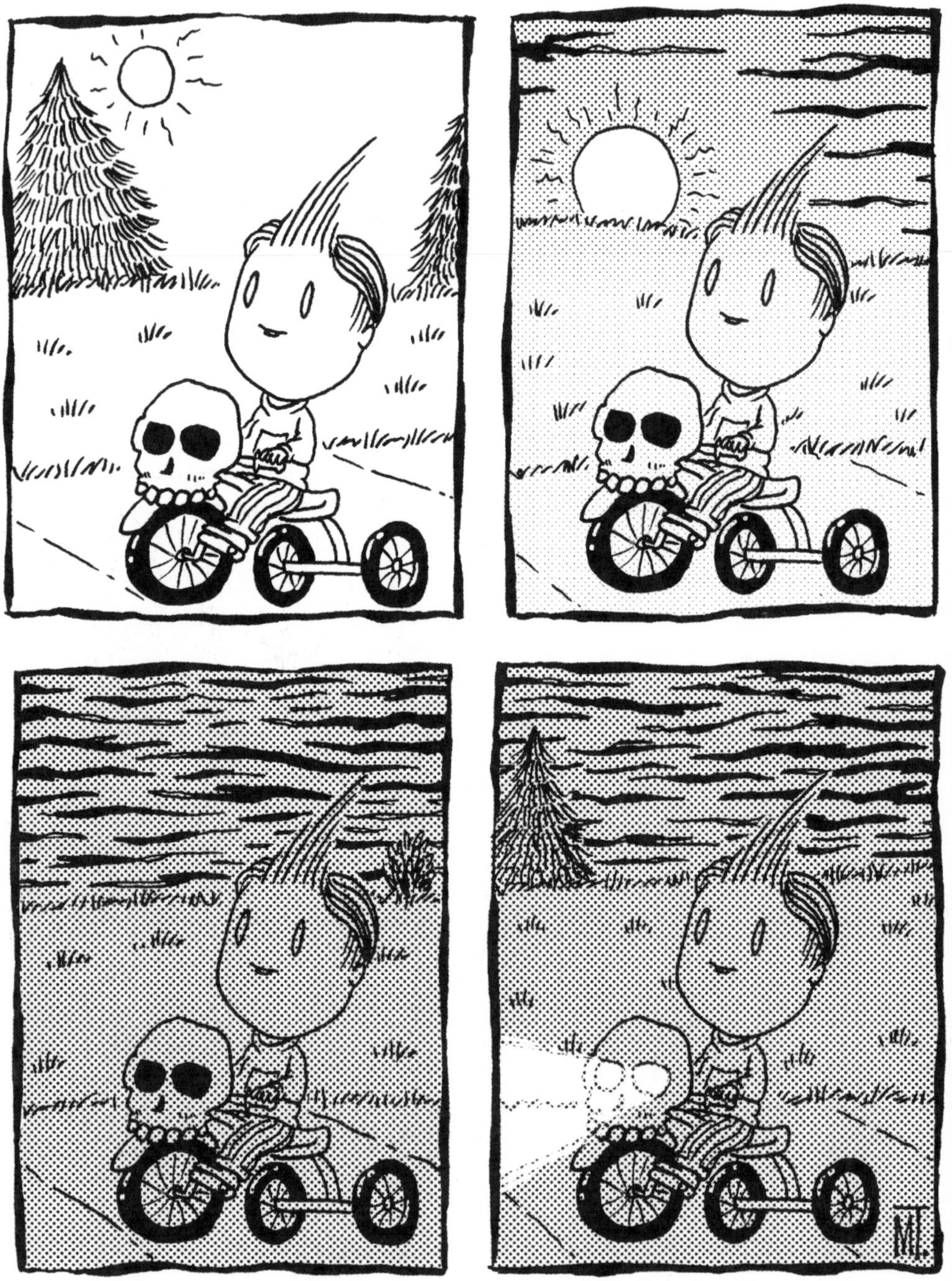

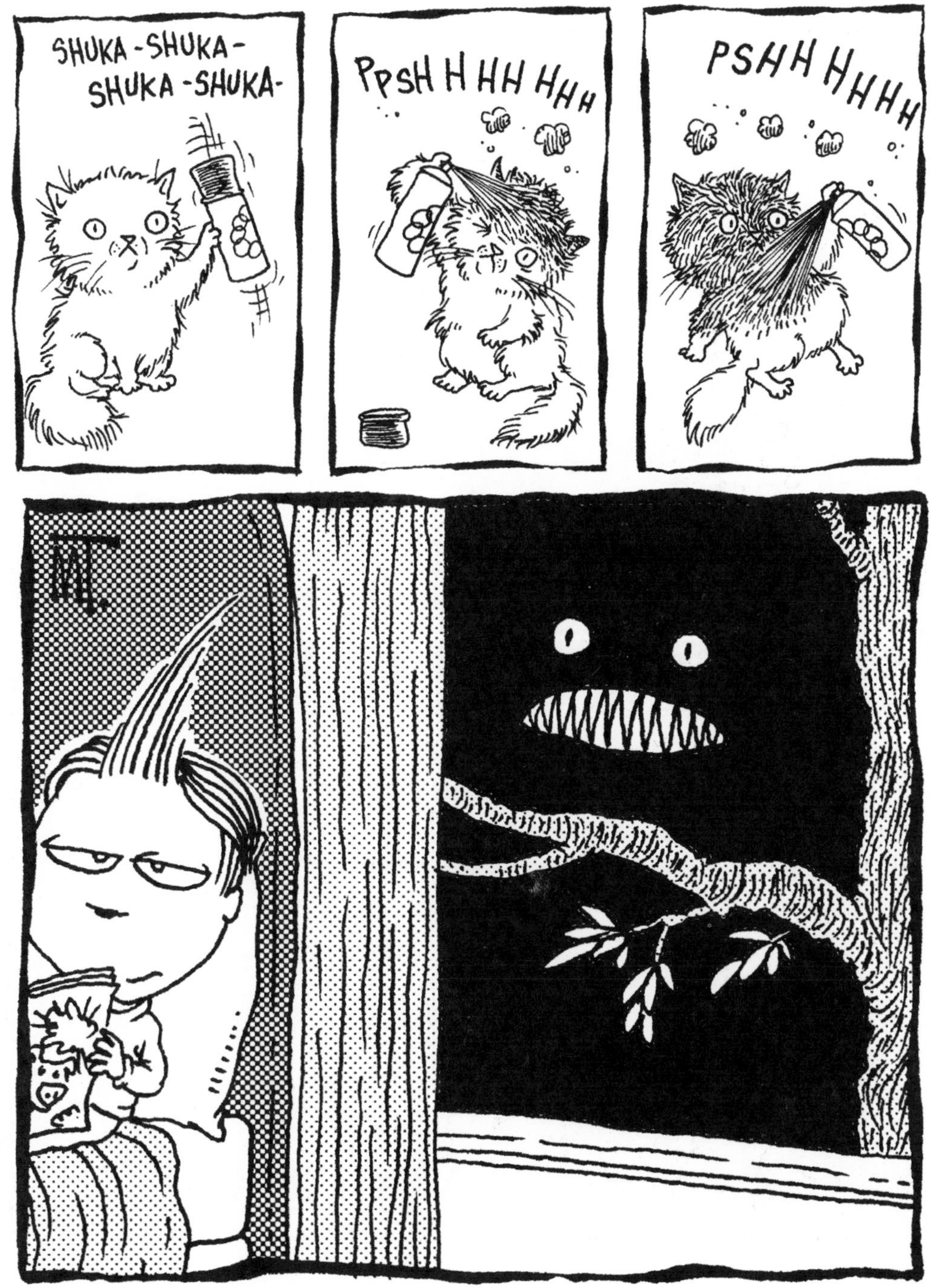
SHUKA-SHUKA-
SHUKA-SHUKA-
PPSH H HH HHH
PSHH HHHHH

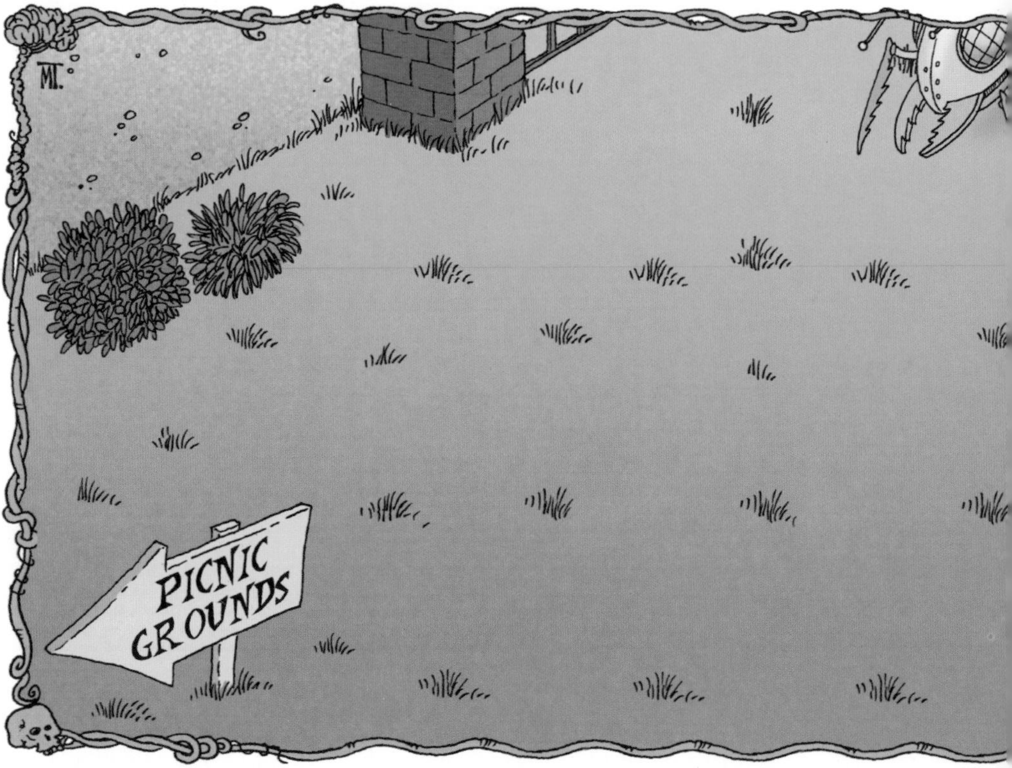
PICNIC GROUNDS

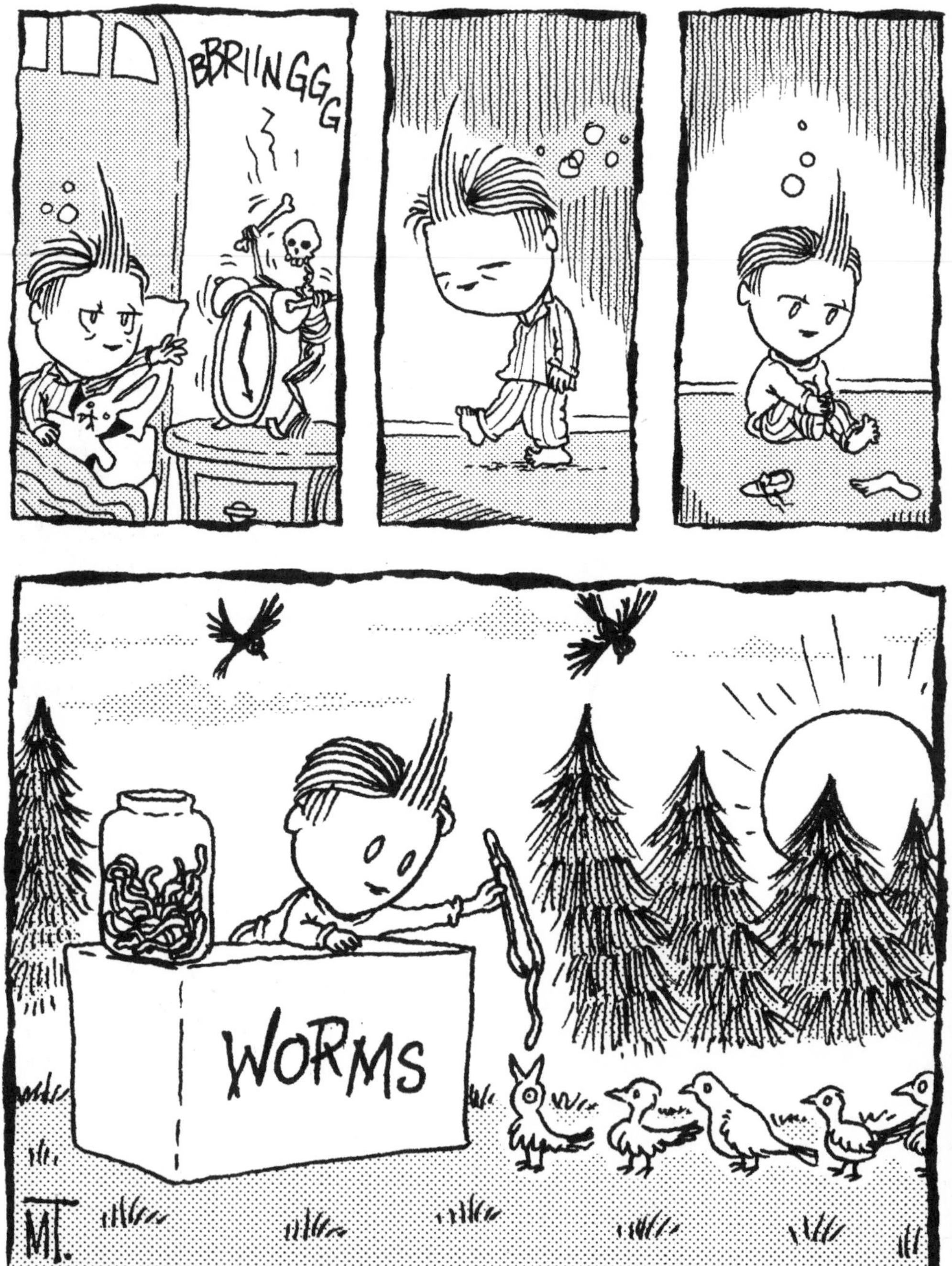
BBRIINGGGG
WORMS
MT.

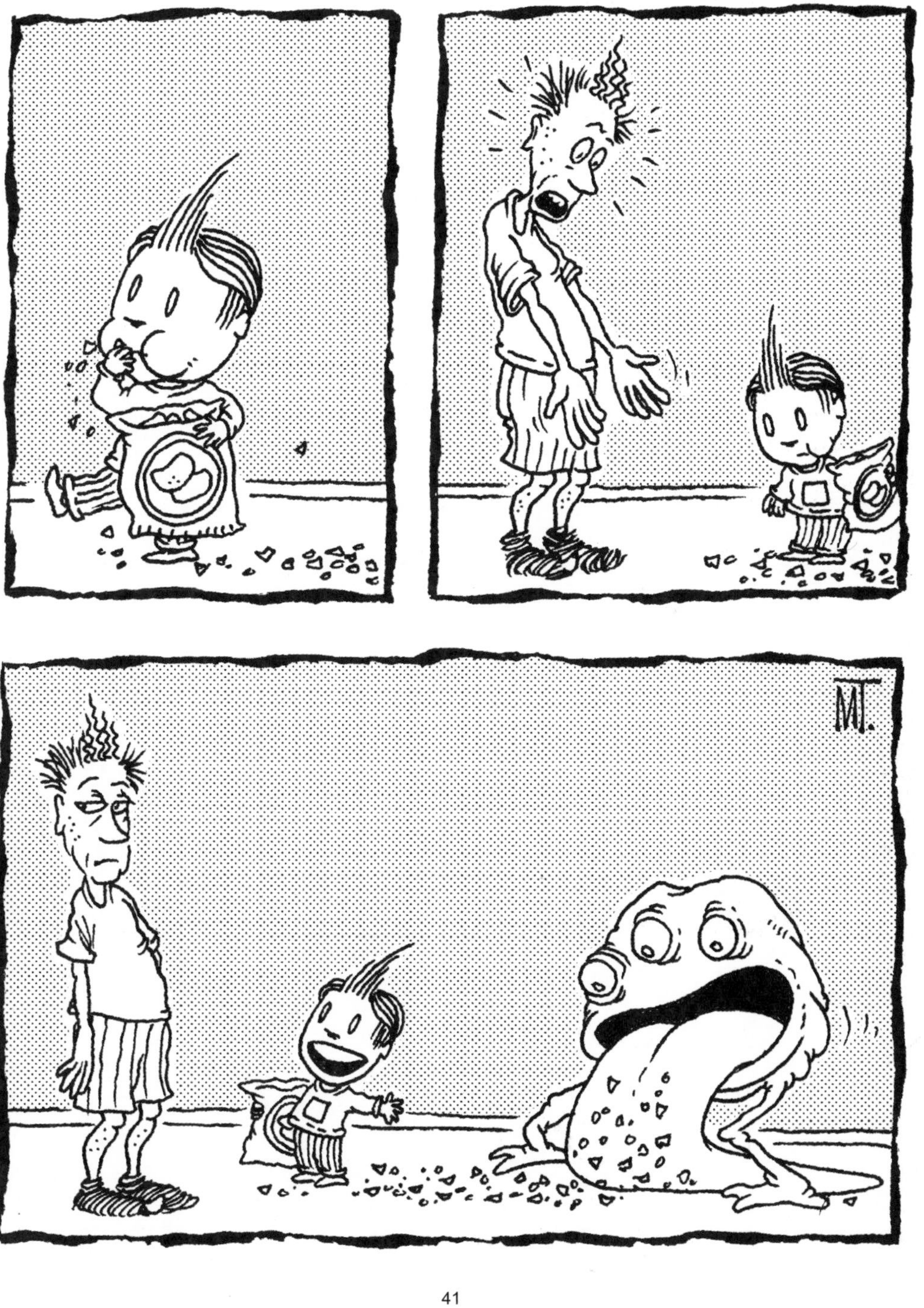

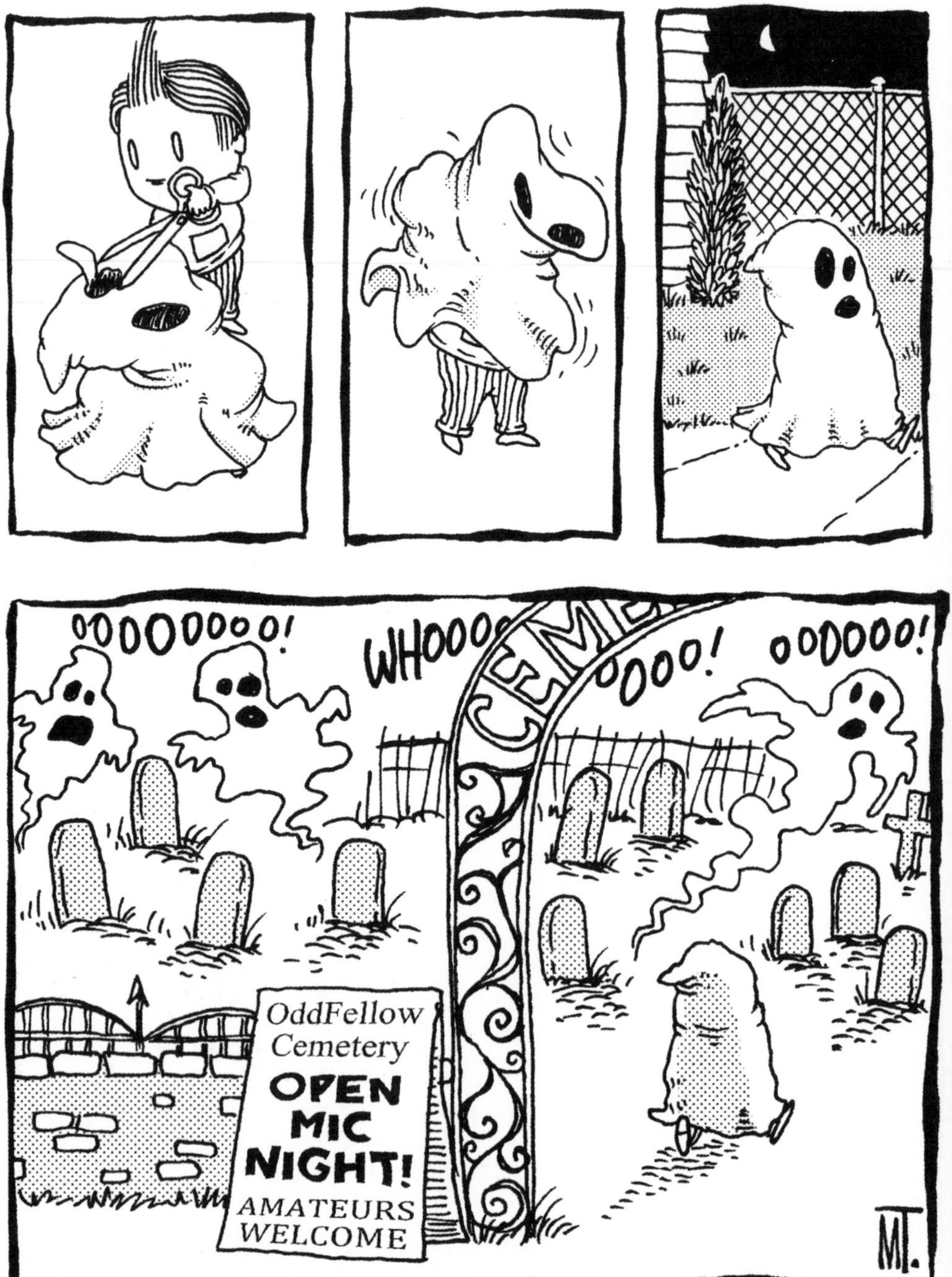
OOOOOOOO!
WHOOO
OOOO!
OOOOOO!
OddFellow Cemetery
OPEN MIC NIGHT!
AMATEURS WELCOME
MT.

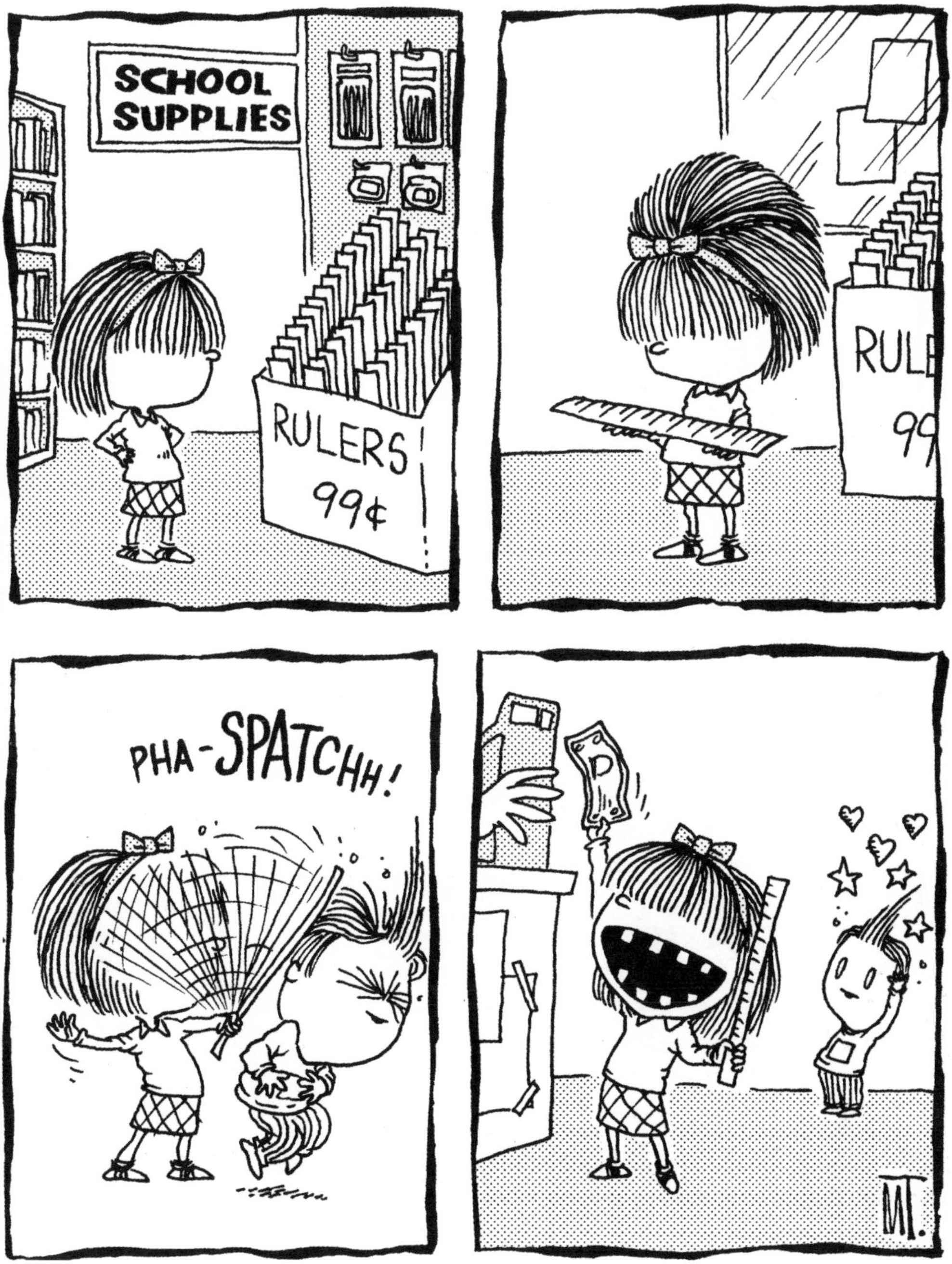
SCHOOL SUPPLIES
RULERS 99¢
RUL
99
PHA-SPATCHH!
MT.

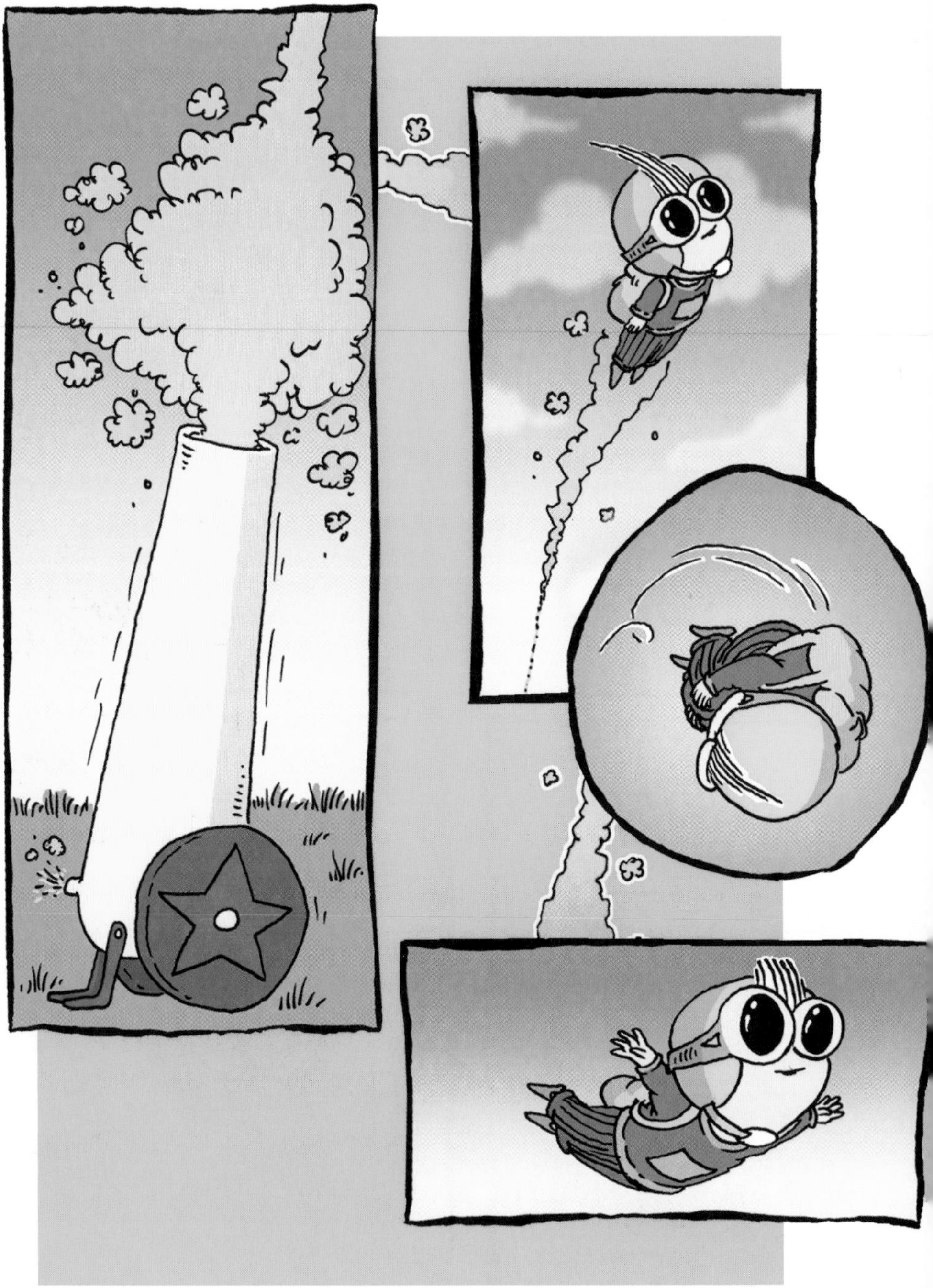

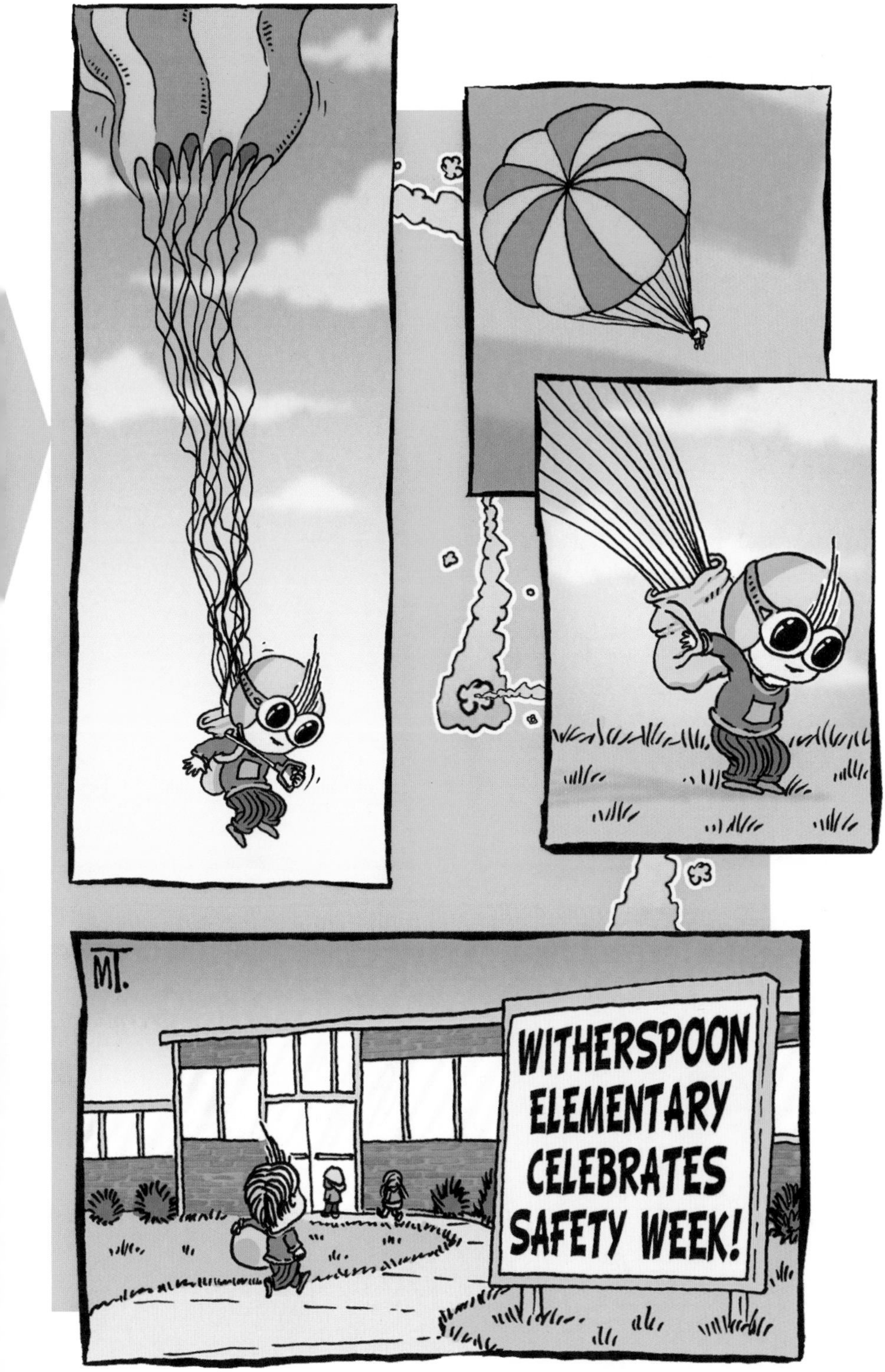
MT.
WITHERSPOON ELEMENTARY CELEBRATES SAFETY WEEK!

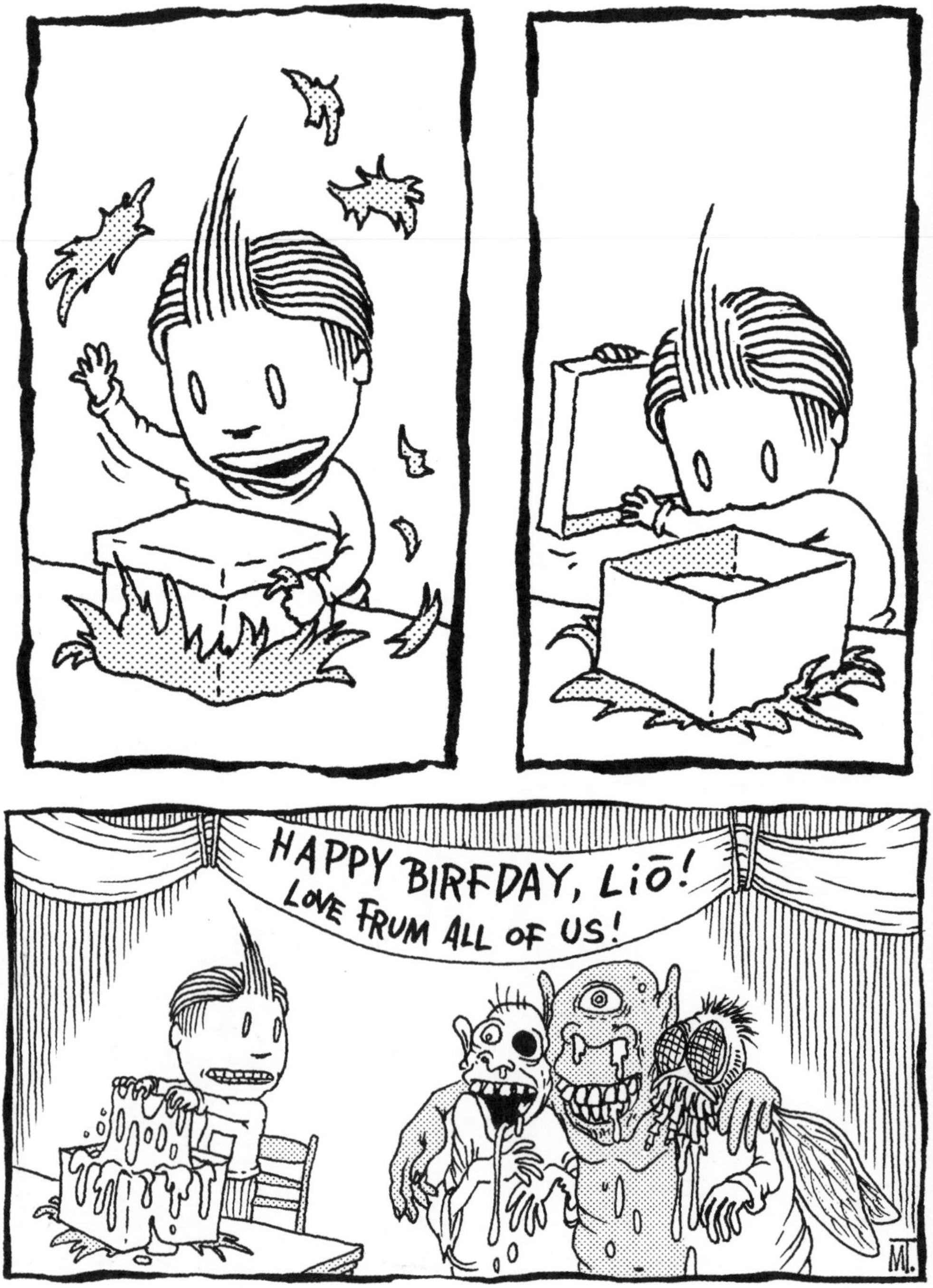
HAPPY BIRFDAY, LIŌ!
LOVE FRUM ALL OF US!
MT.

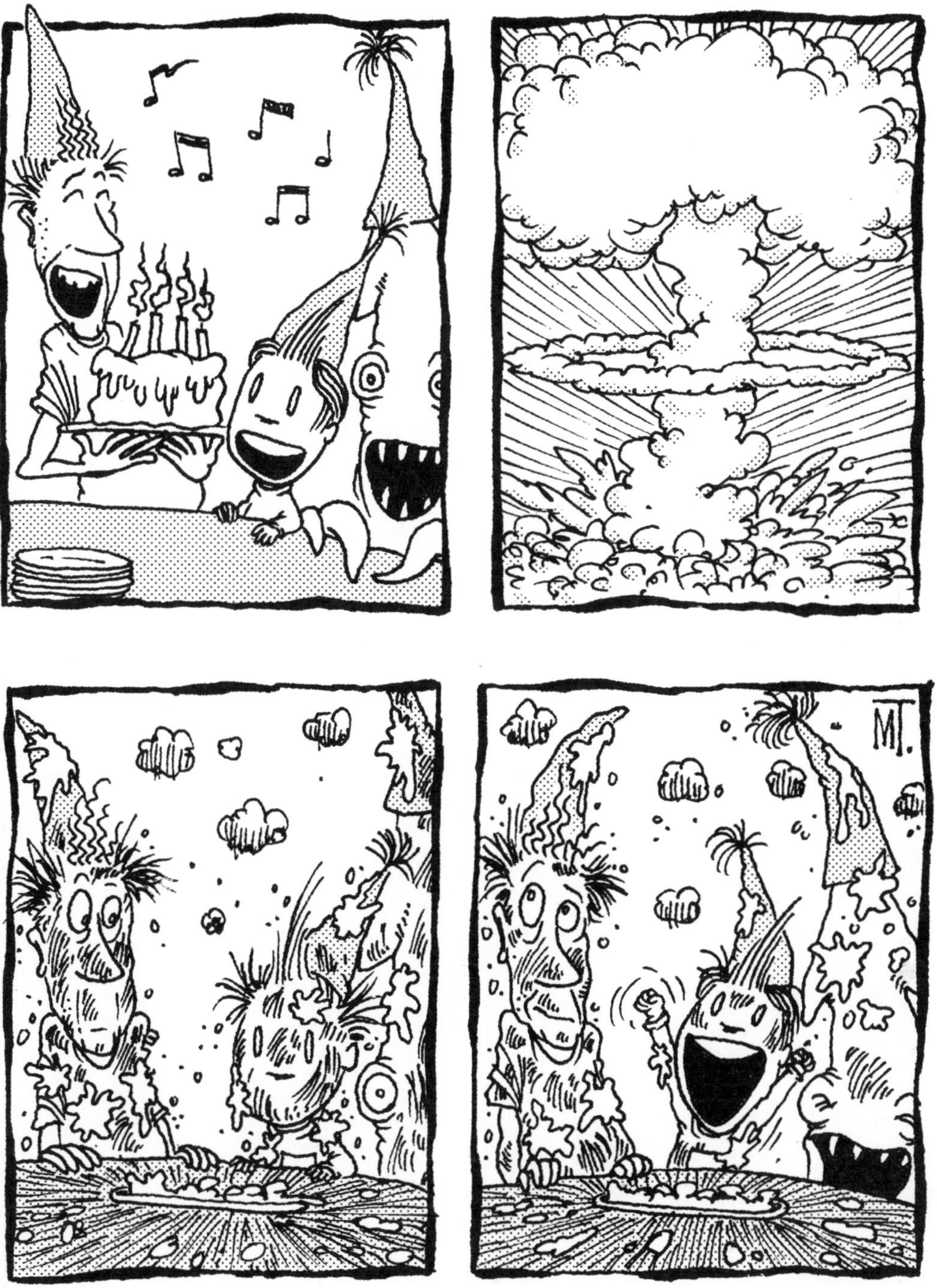
MT.

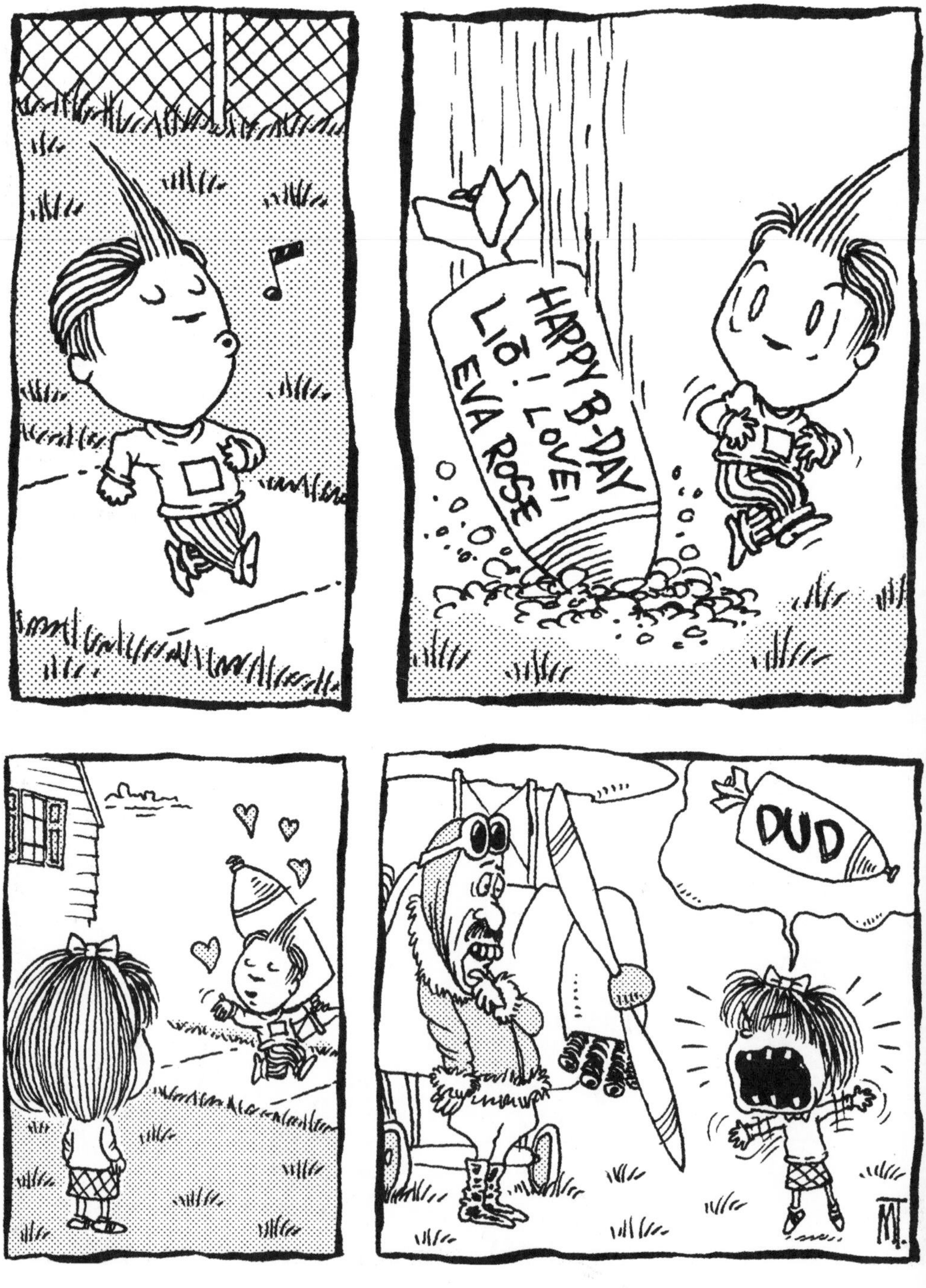
HAPPY B-DAY
LIO! LOVE!
EVA ROSE
DUD
MT.

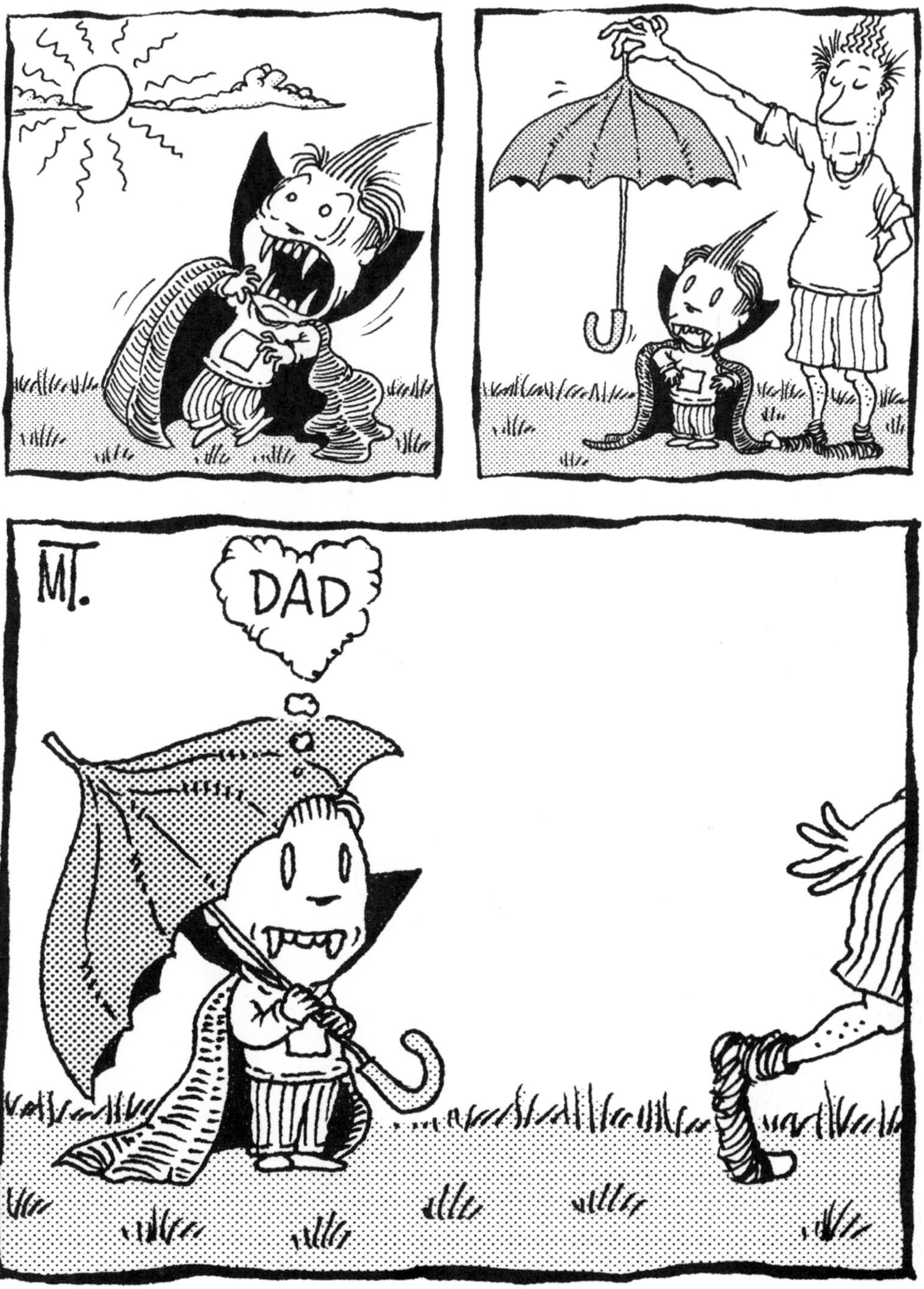

MT.
DAD

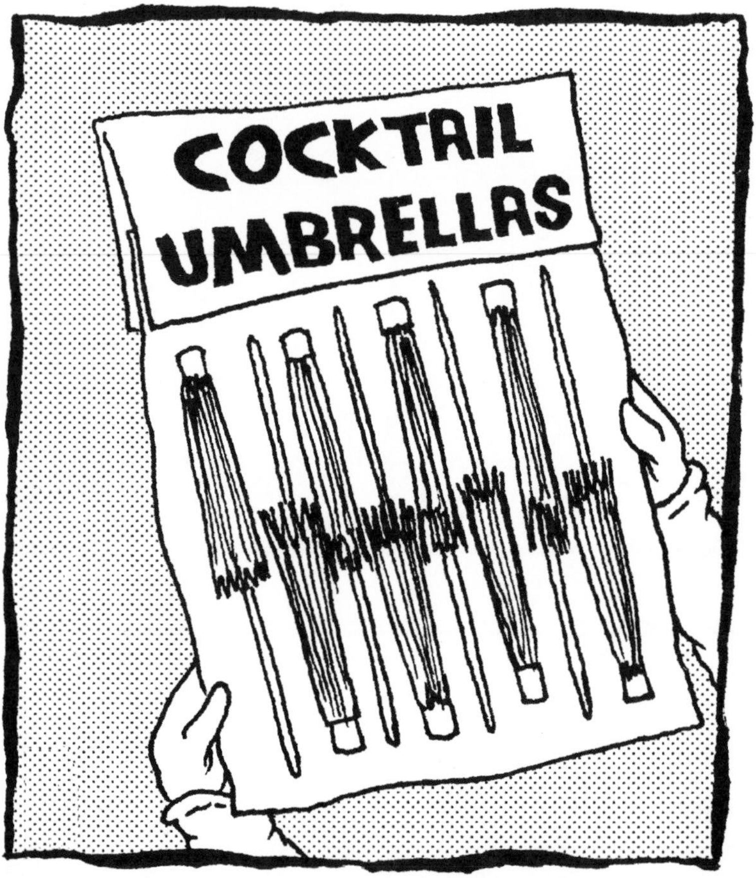
COCKTAIL
UMBRELLAS

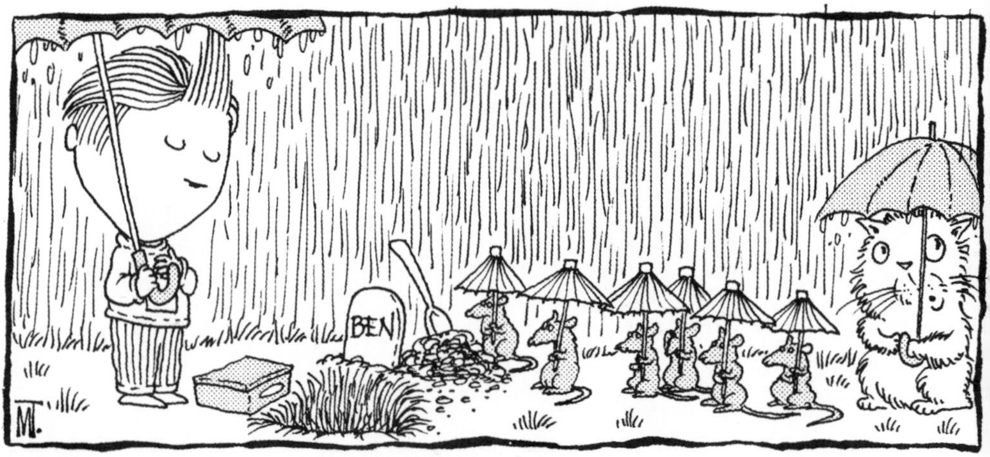
BEN

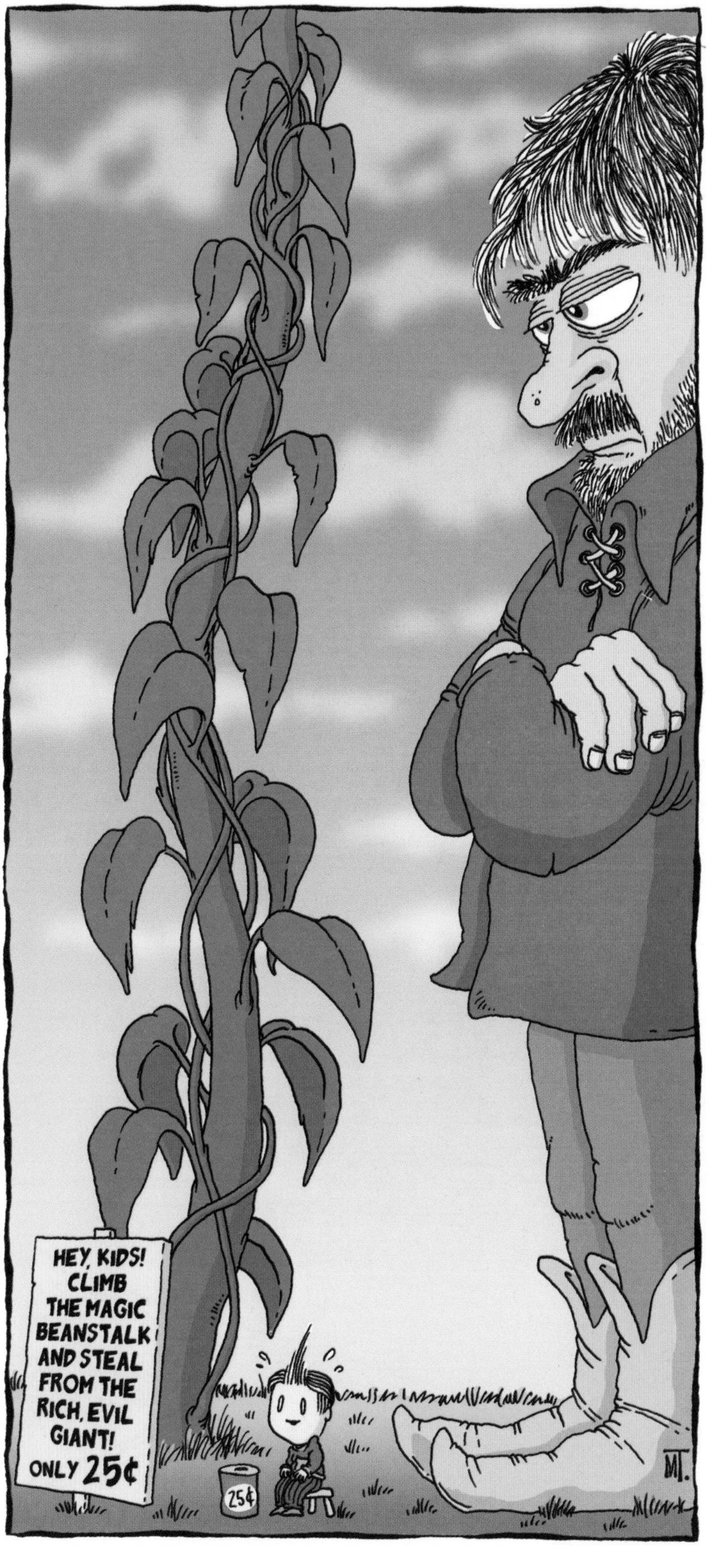
HEY, KIDS! CLIMB THE MAGIC BEANSTALK AND STEAL FROM THE RICH, EVIL GIANT! ONLY 25¢
25¢
MT.

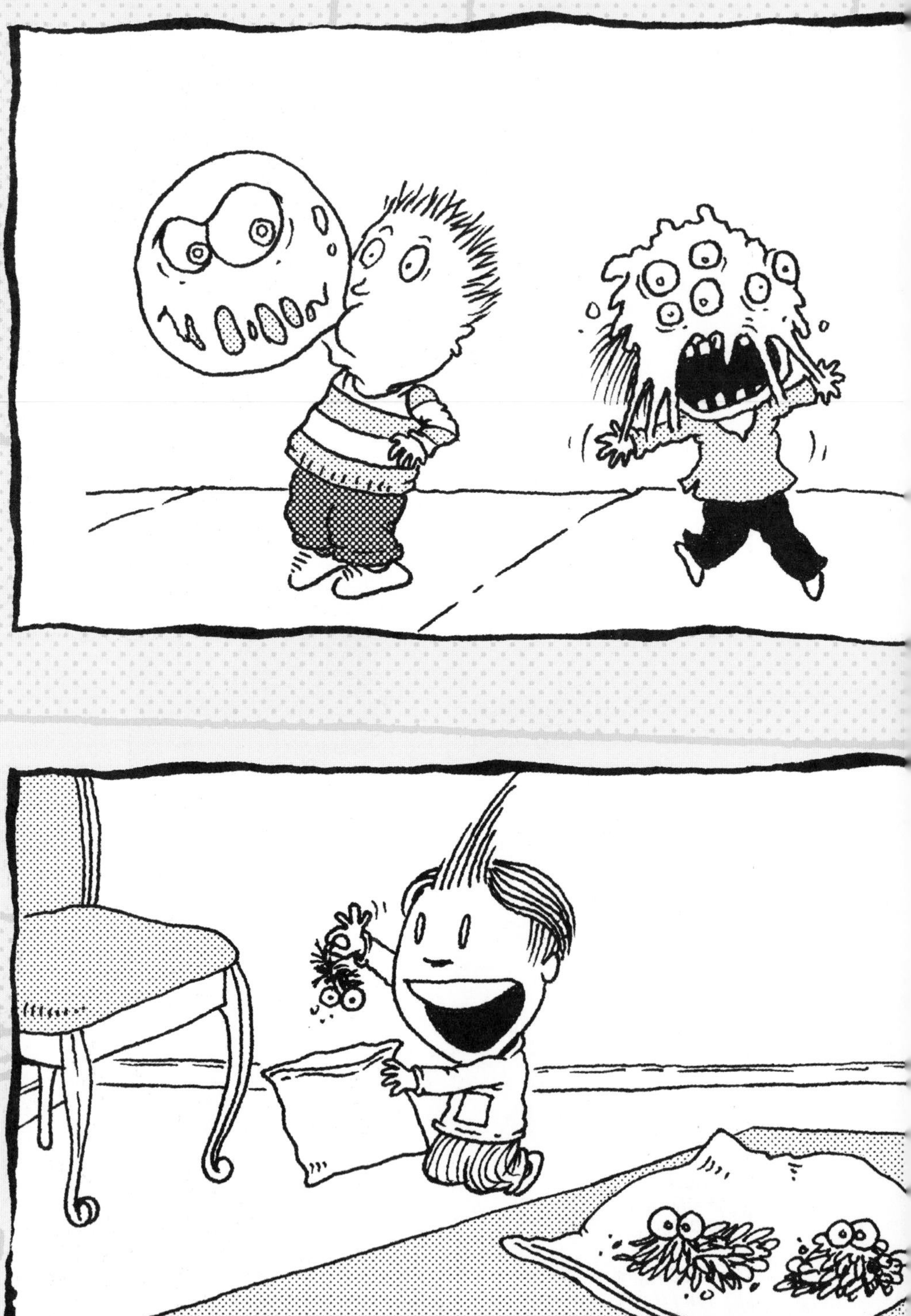

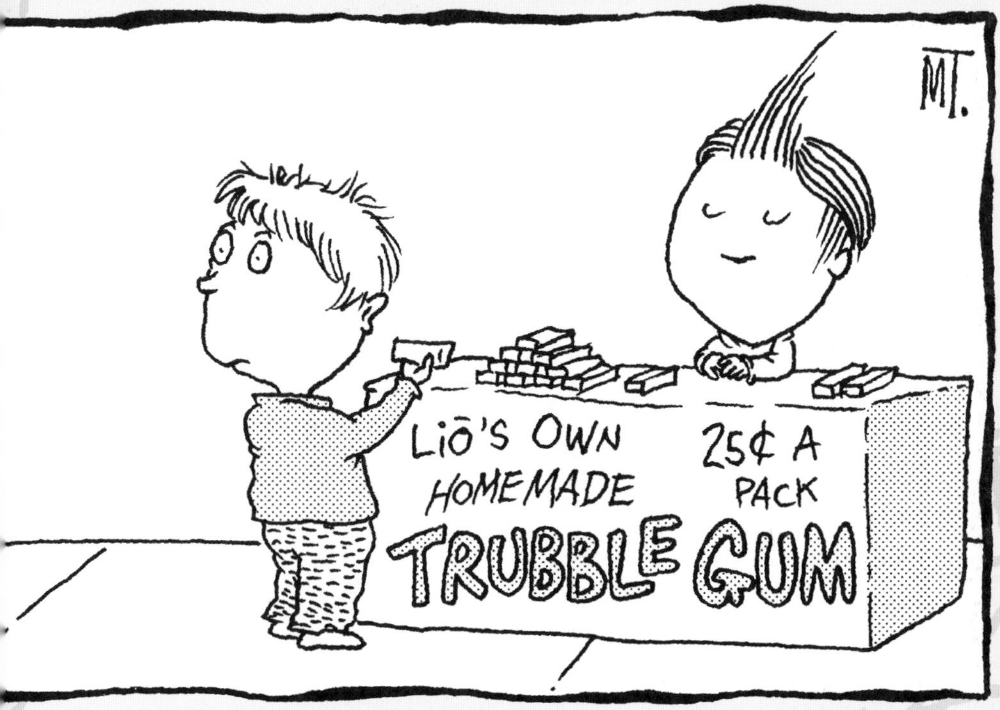
MT.
LIO'S OWN
HOMEMADE
25¢ A
PACK
TRUBBLE GUM

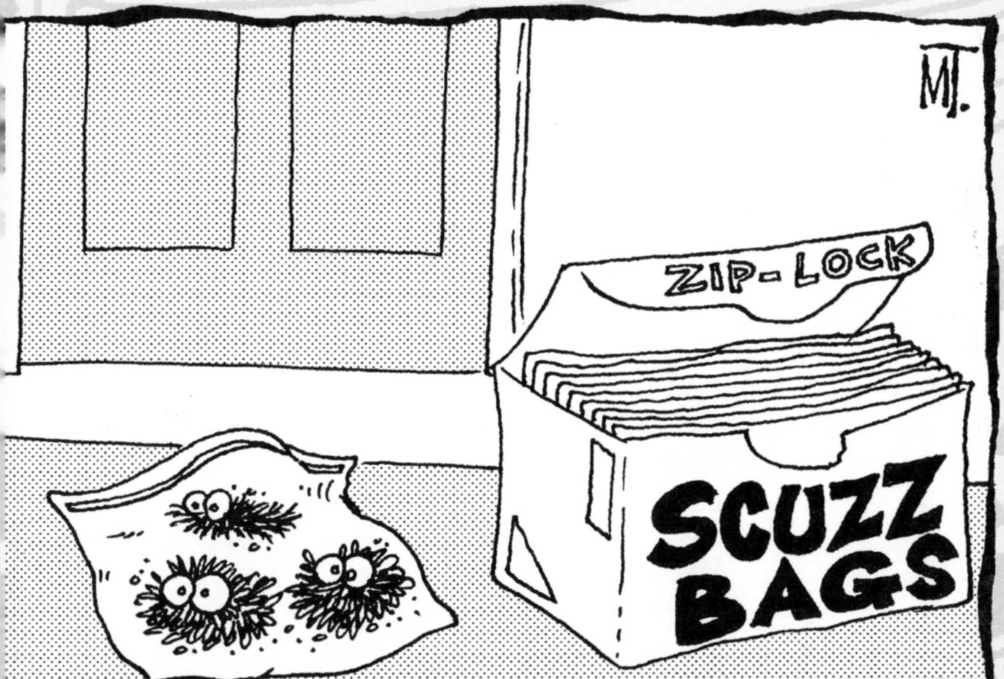
MT.
ZIP-LOCK
SCUZZ
BAGS

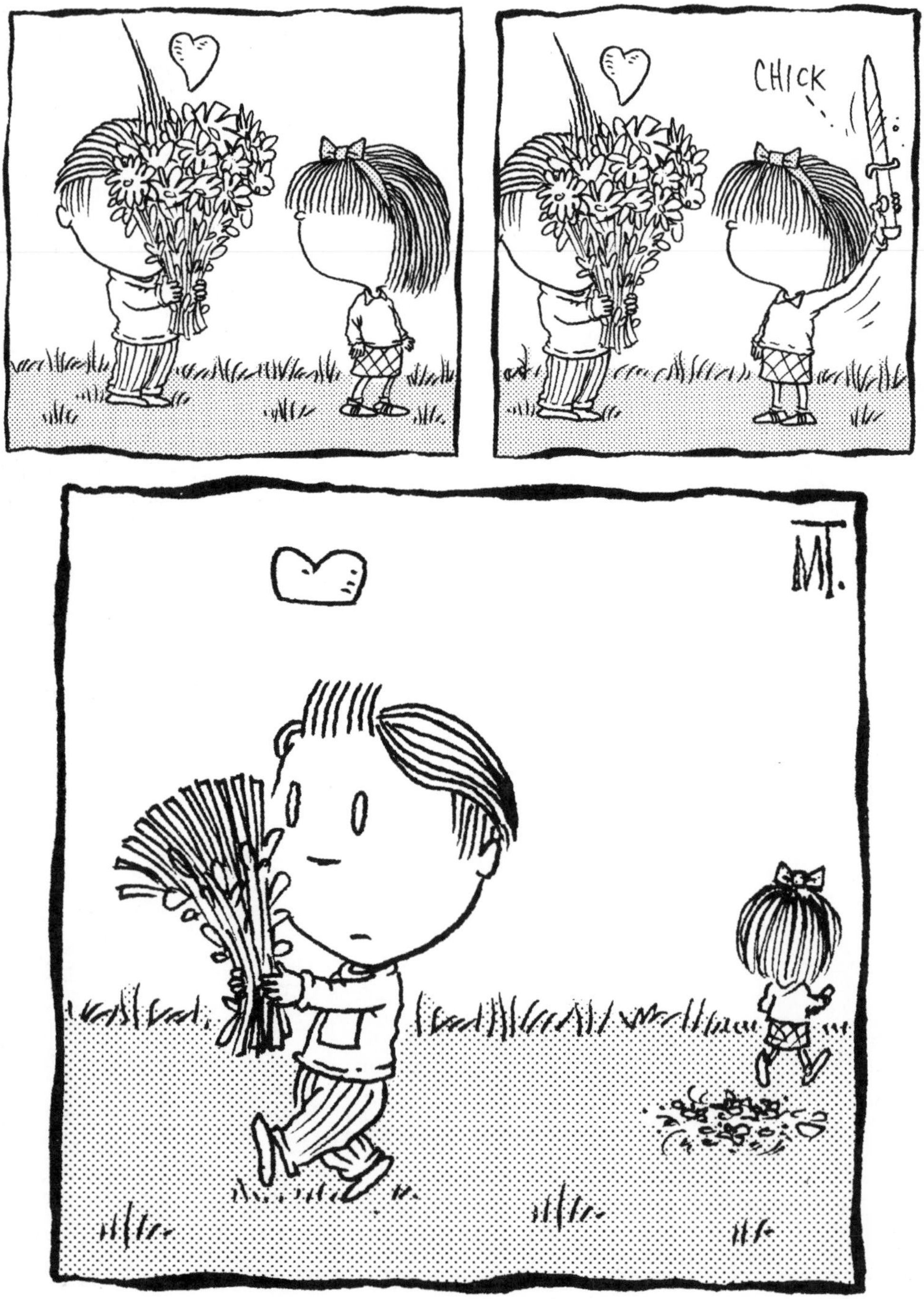
CHICK

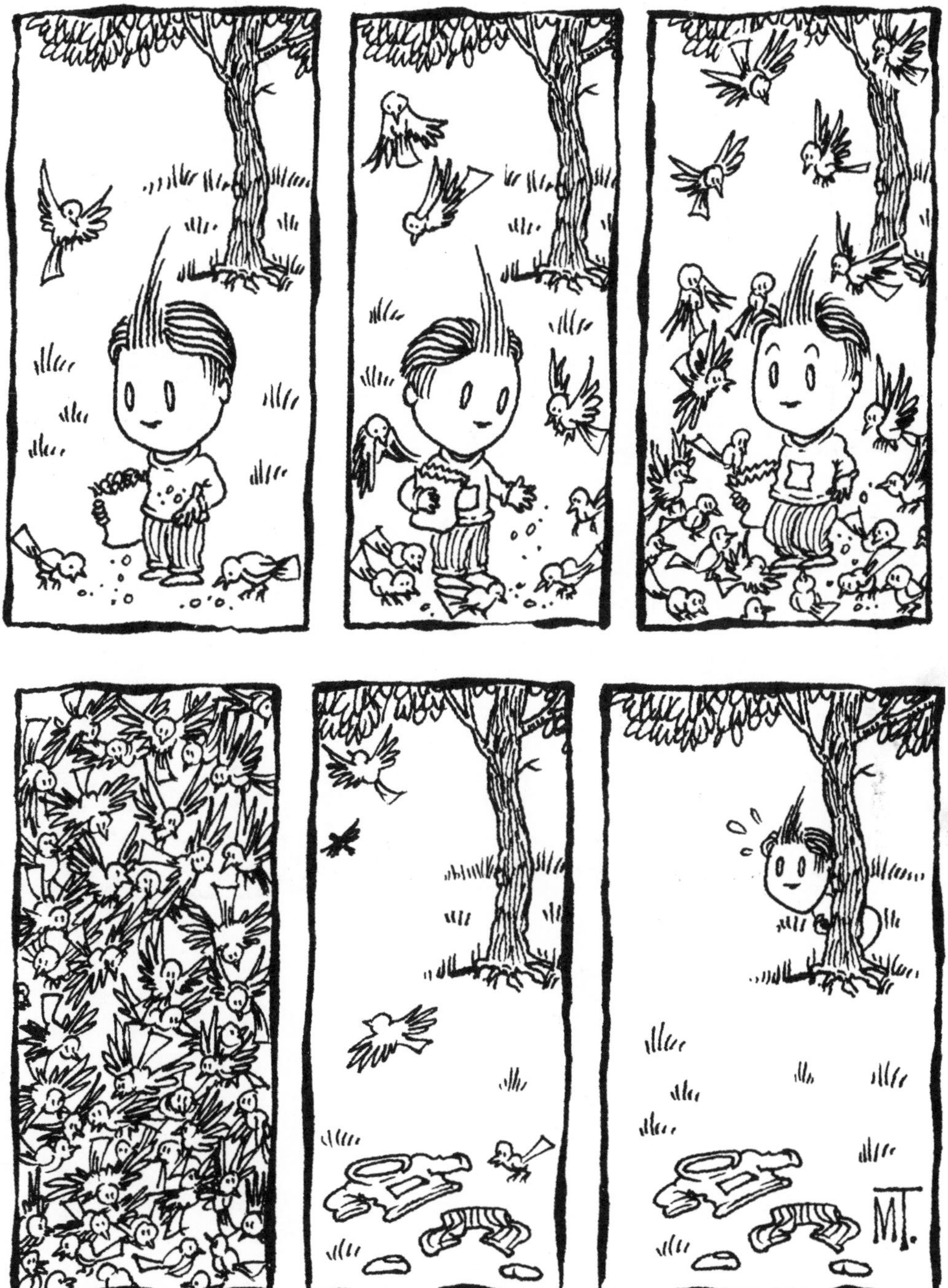

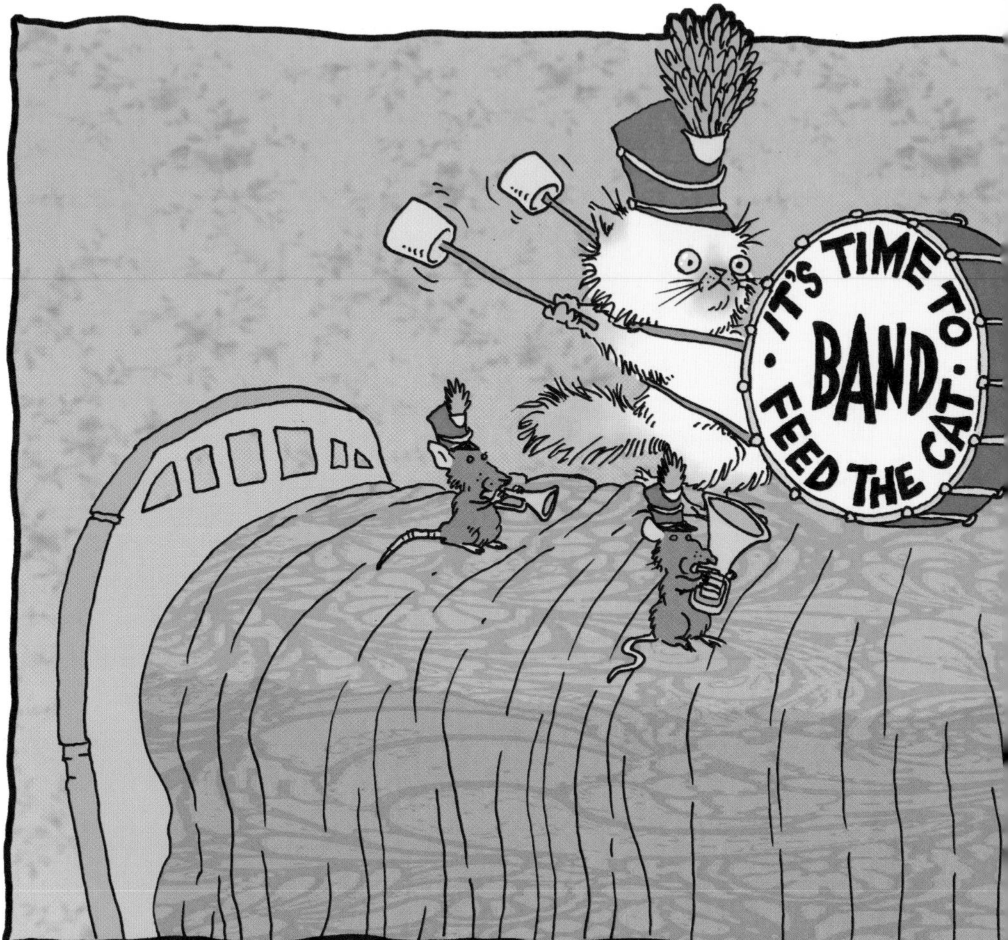
IT'S TIME TO
BAND
FEED THE CAT

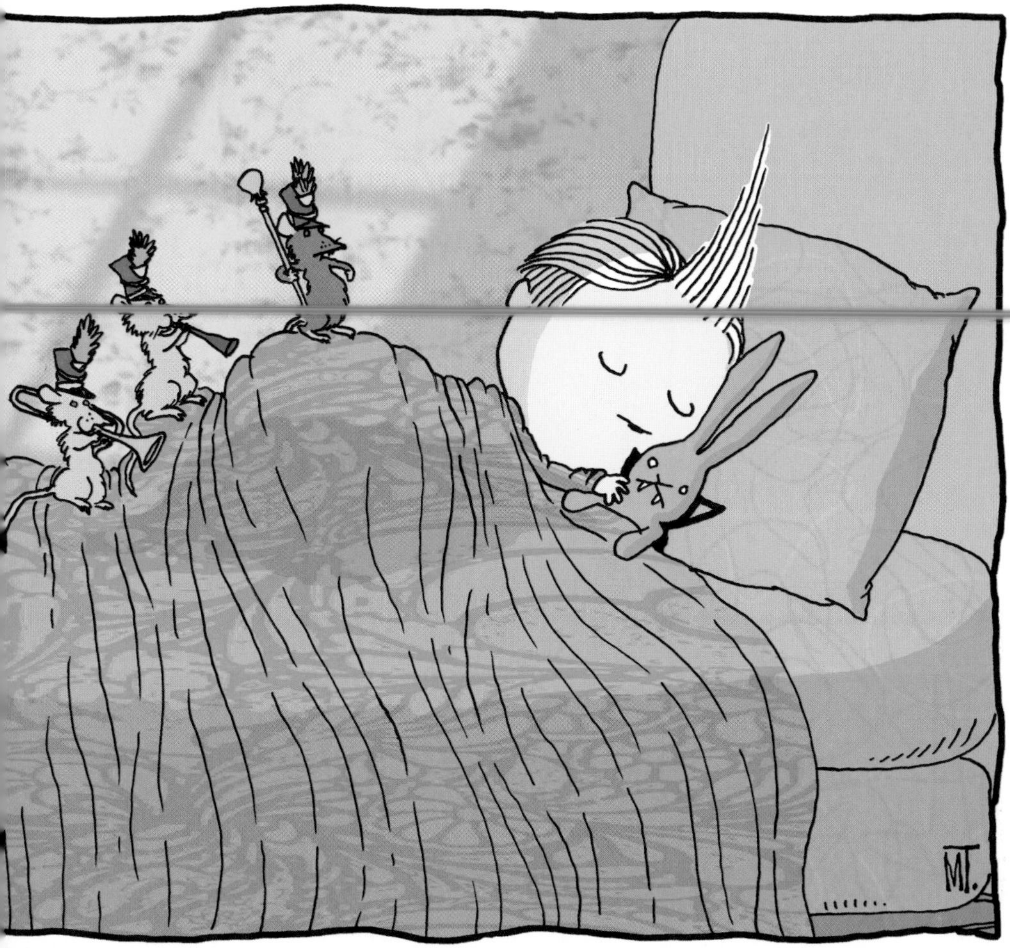
MT.

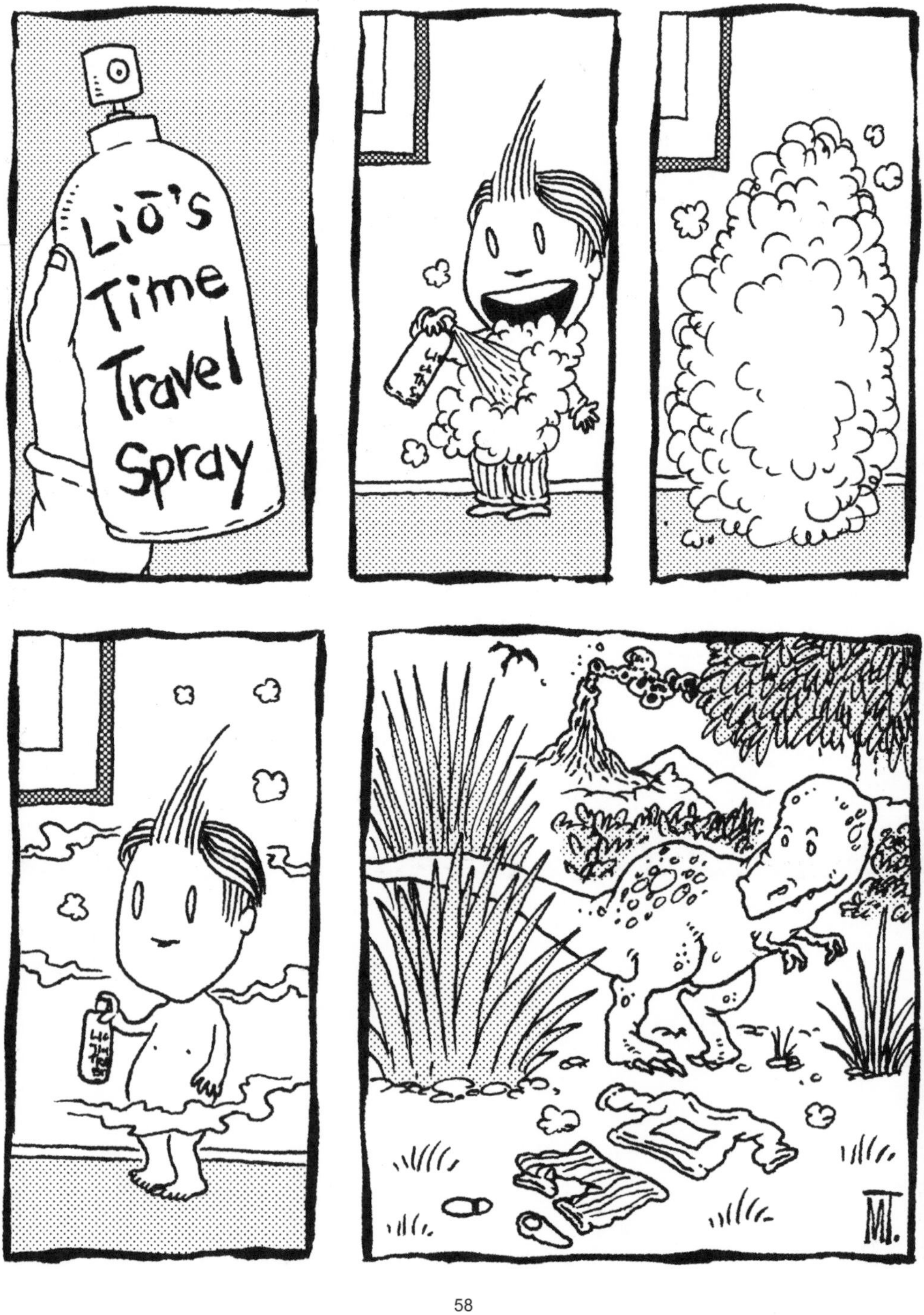
LIŌ'S
Time
Travel
Spray

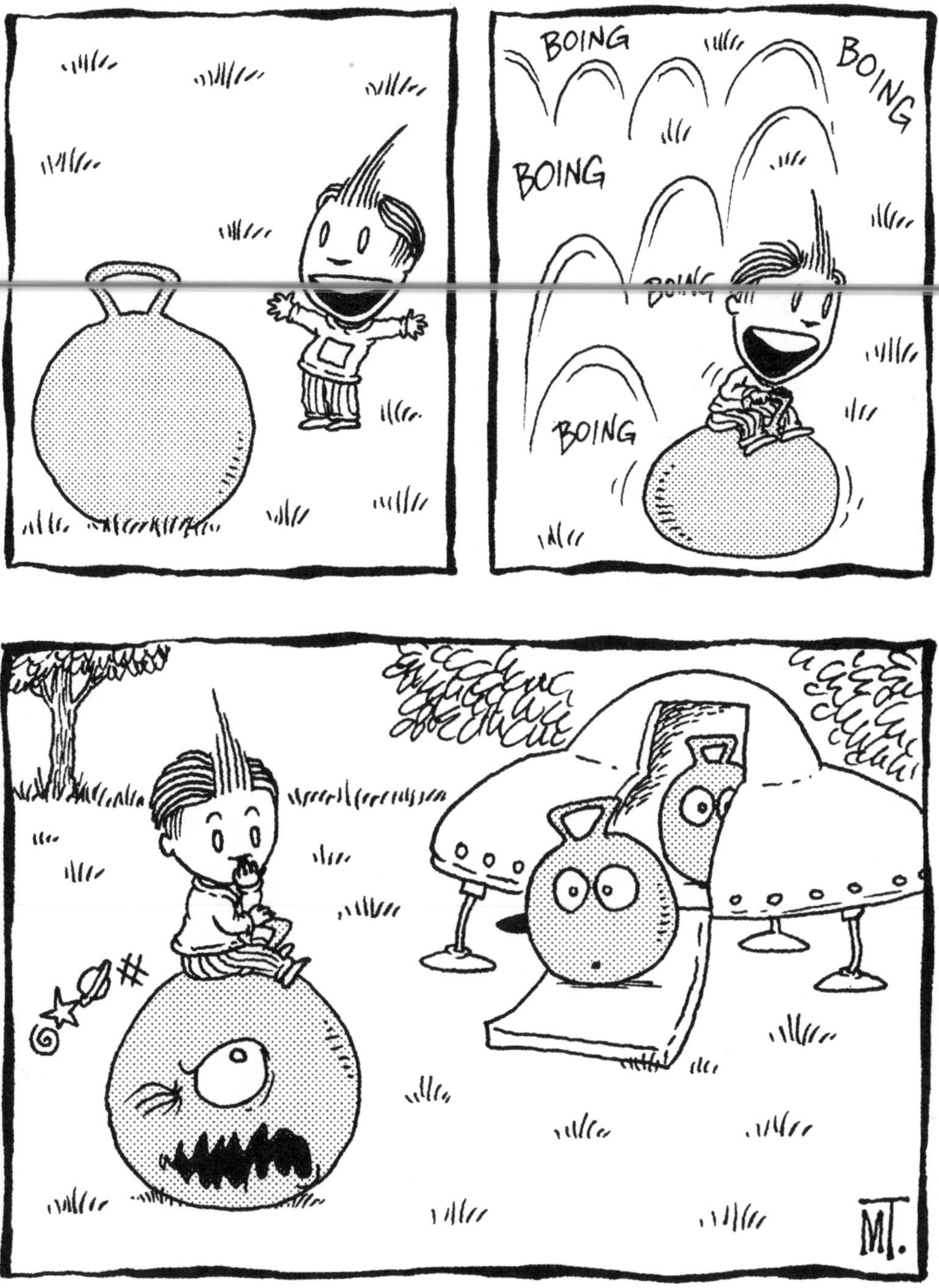
BOING
BOING
BOING
BOING
BOING
MT.

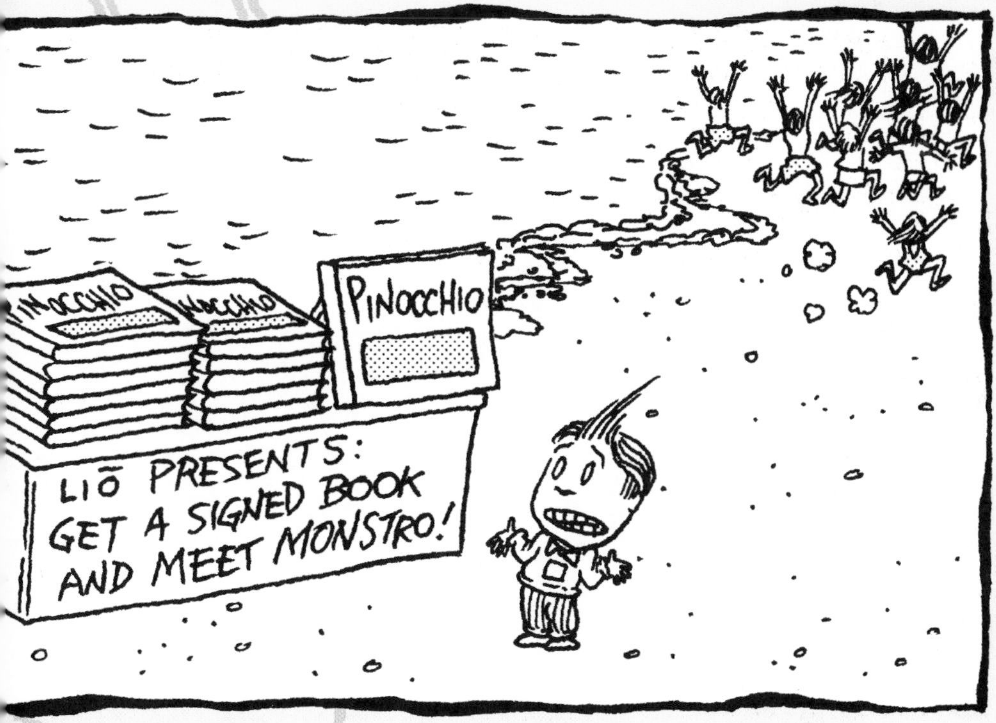
PINOCCHIO
PINOCCHIO
PINOCCHIO
LIO PRESENTS:
GET A SIGNED BOOK
AND MEET MONSTRO!

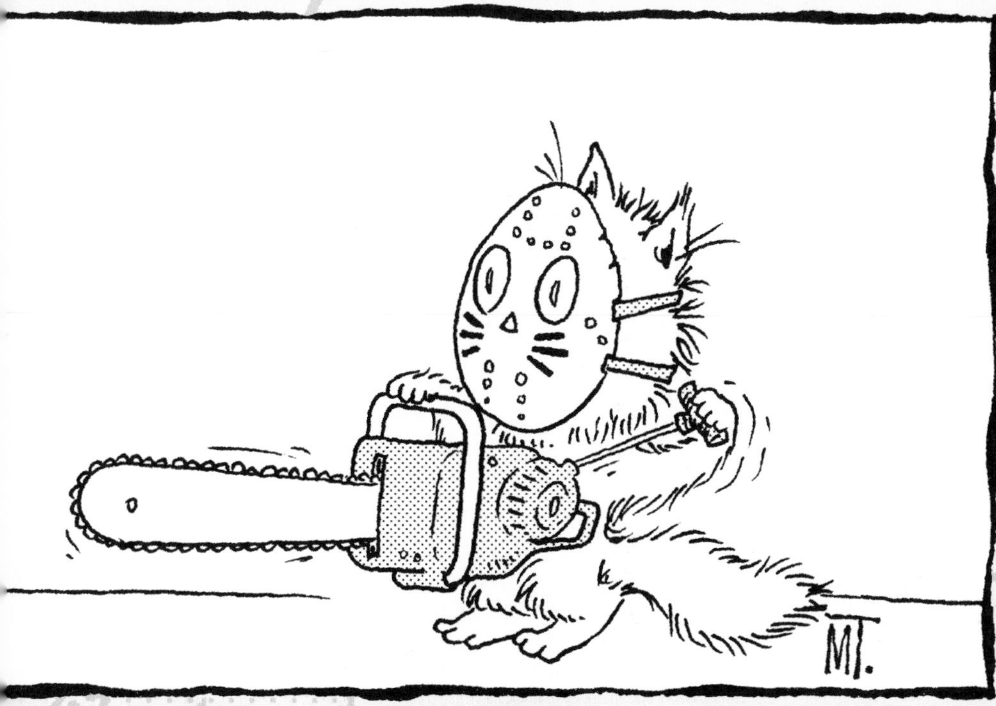
MT.

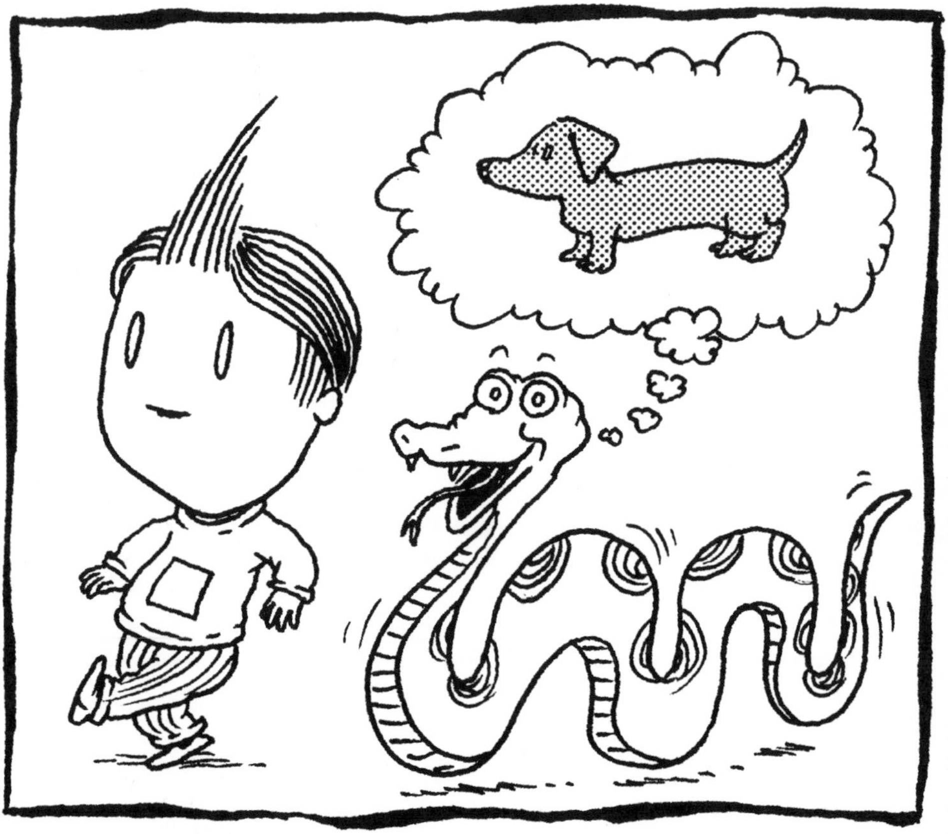

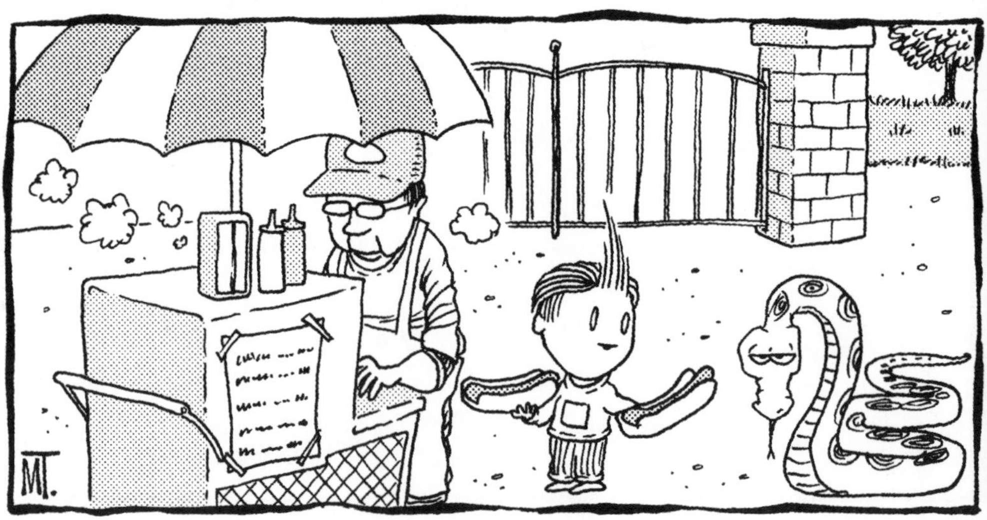

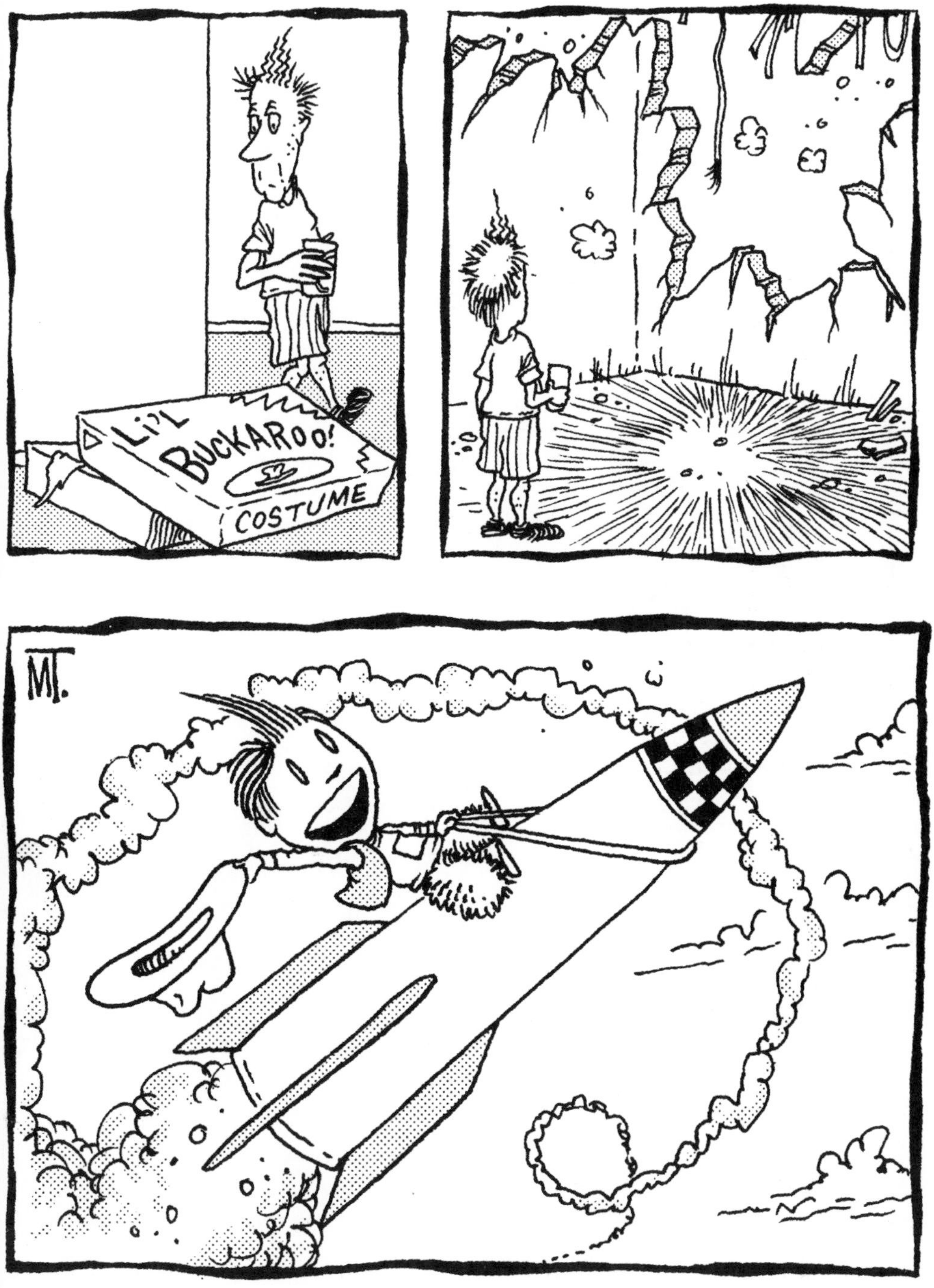

LI'L BUCKAROO!
COSTUME

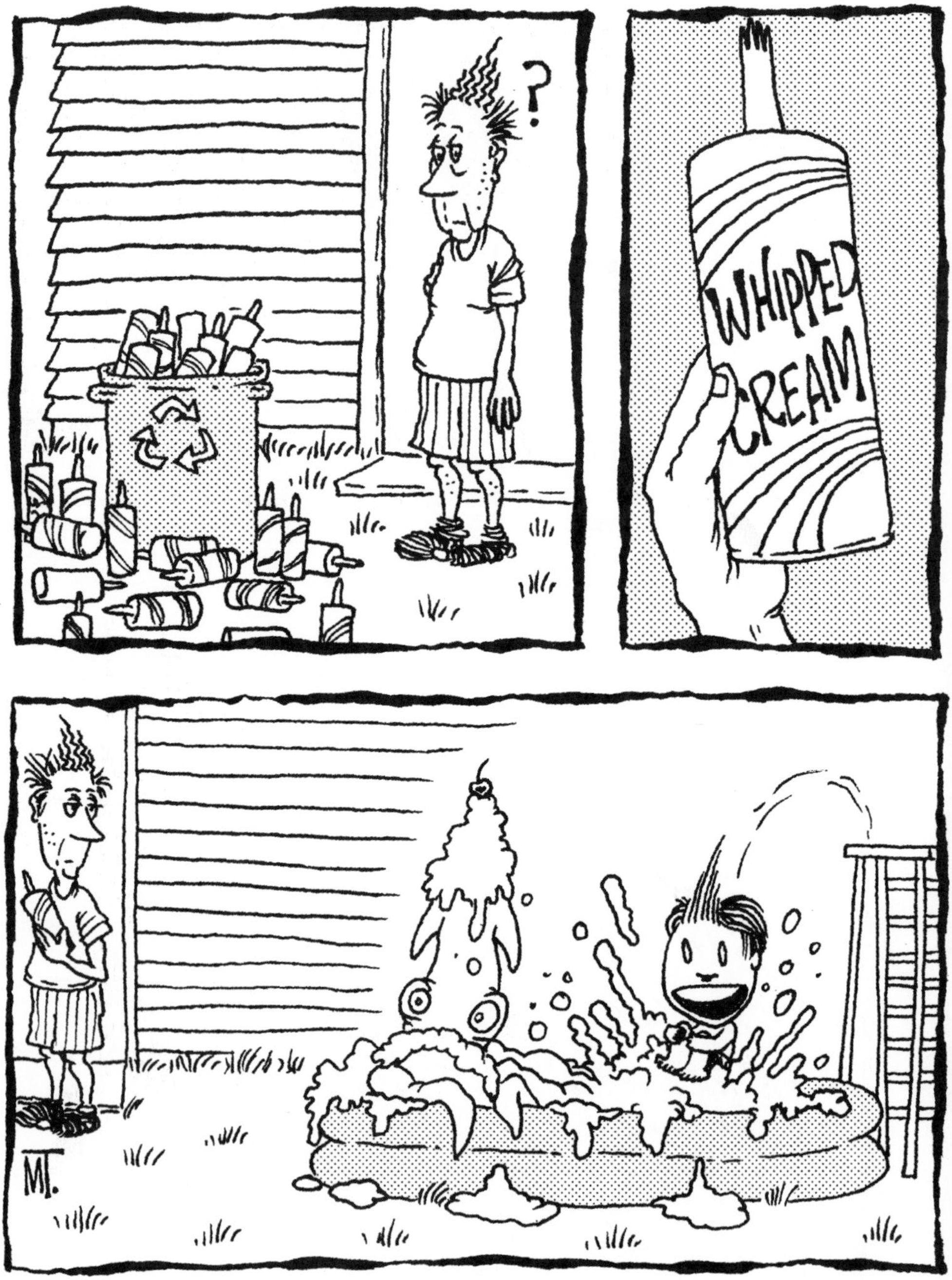
?
WHIPPED CREAM
MT.

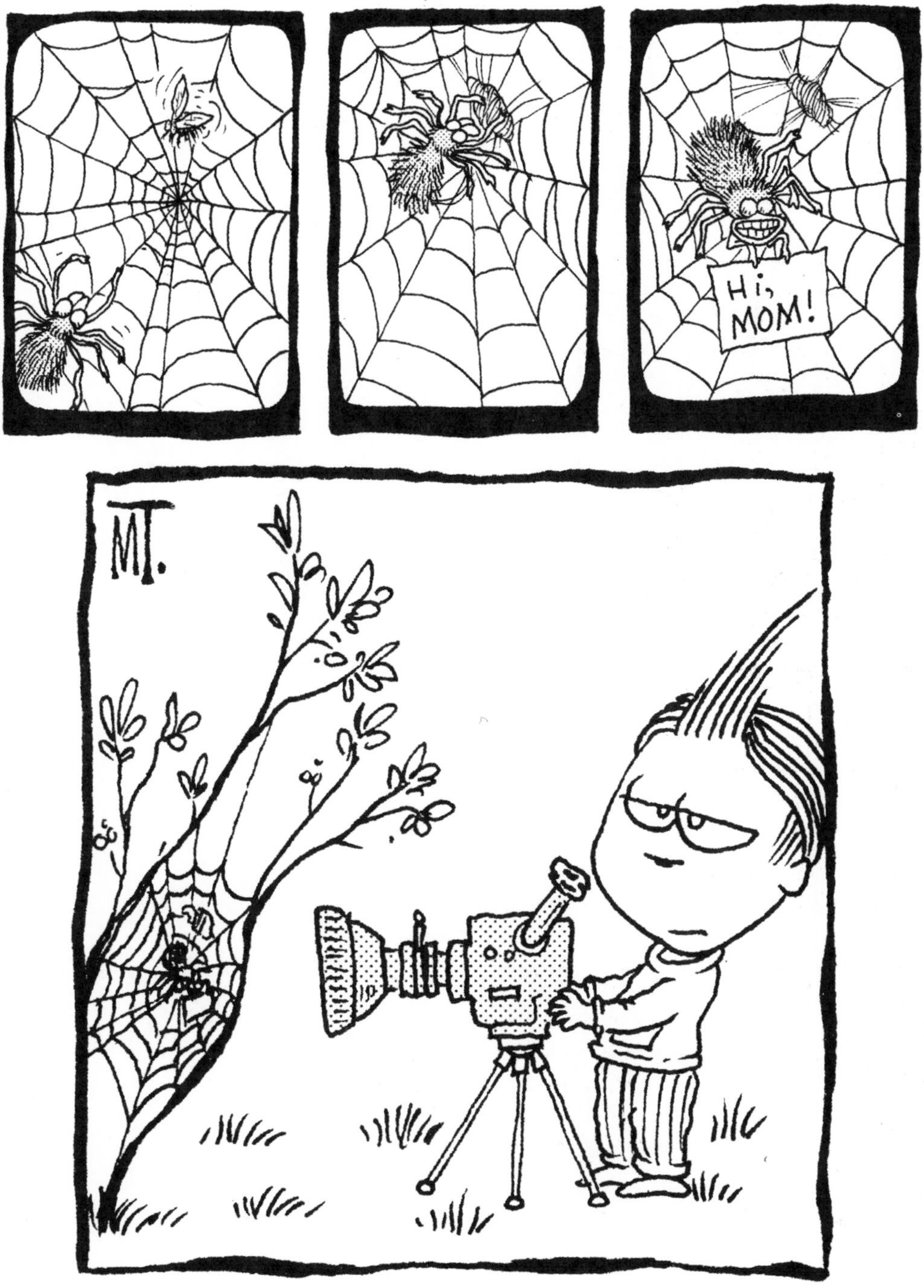
Hi,
MOM!
MT.

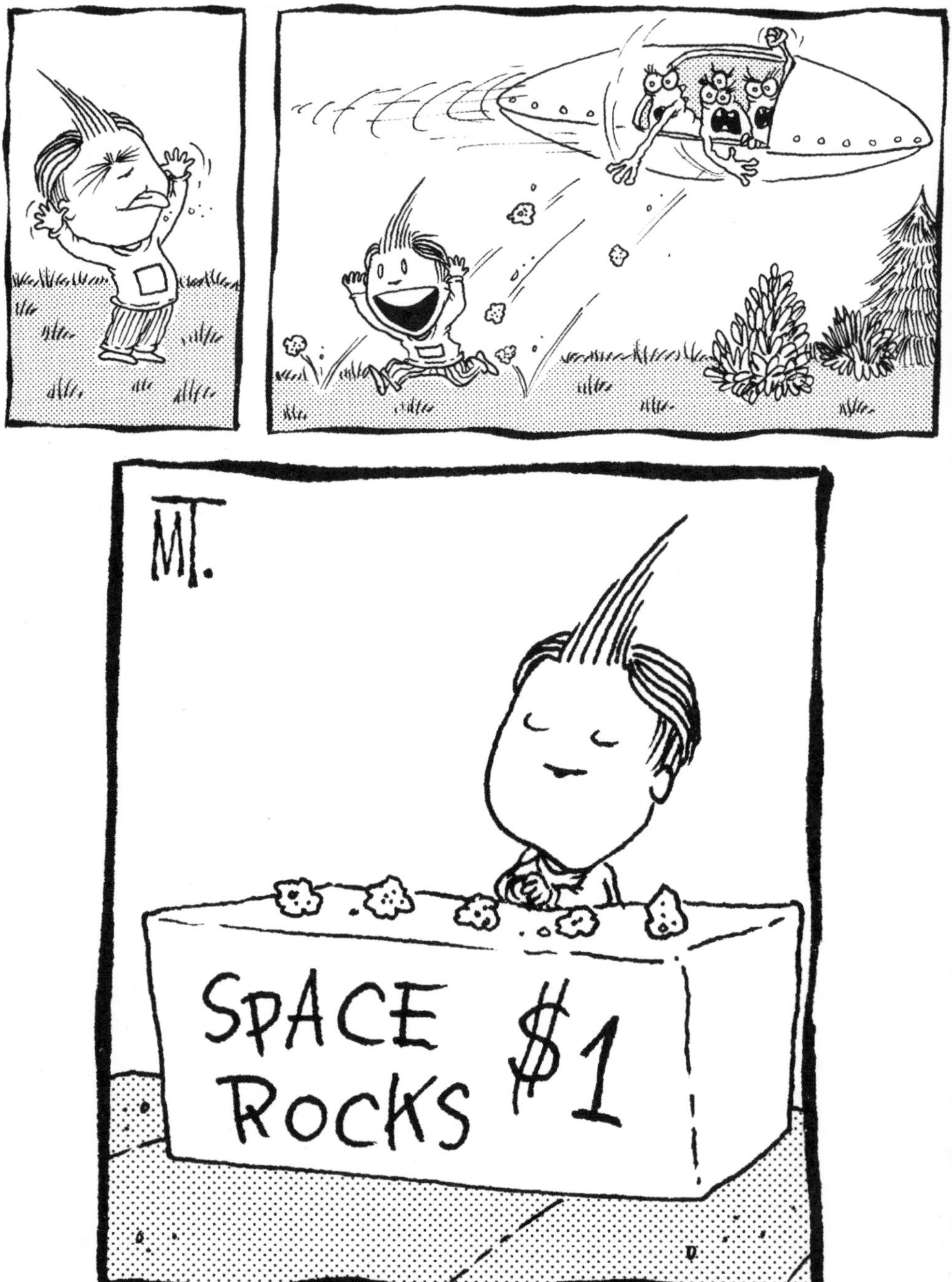
SPACE ROCKS
$1

SOMETHIN'S FISHY
OPEN
TROPICAL &
FRESHWATER
FISH
SUPPLIES
MT.

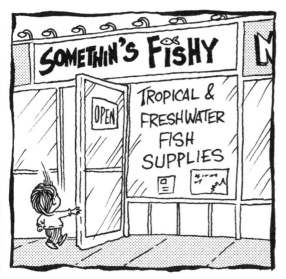

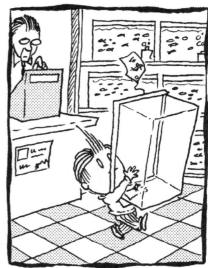

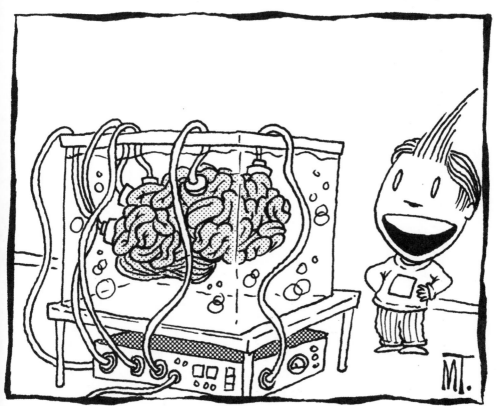

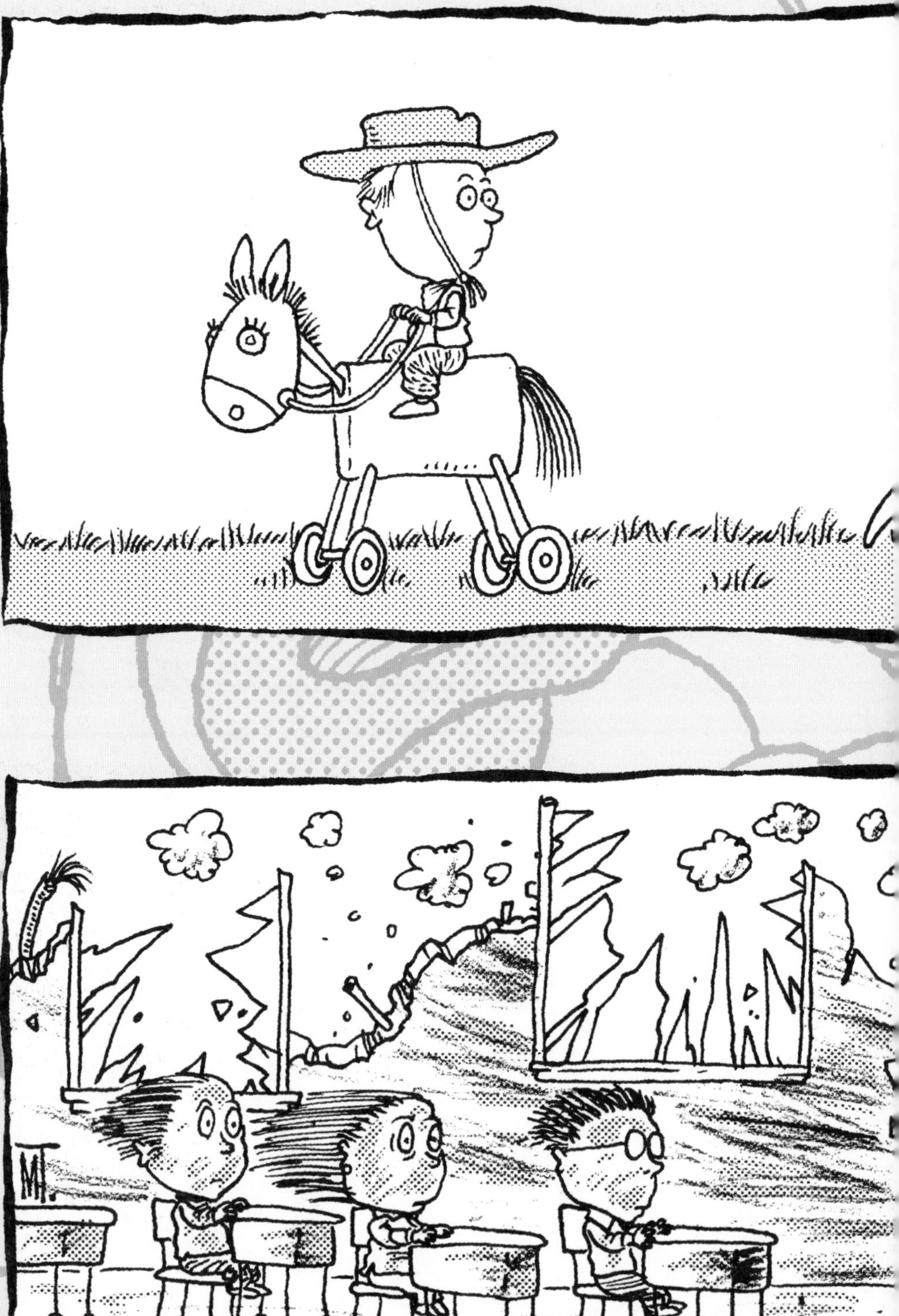

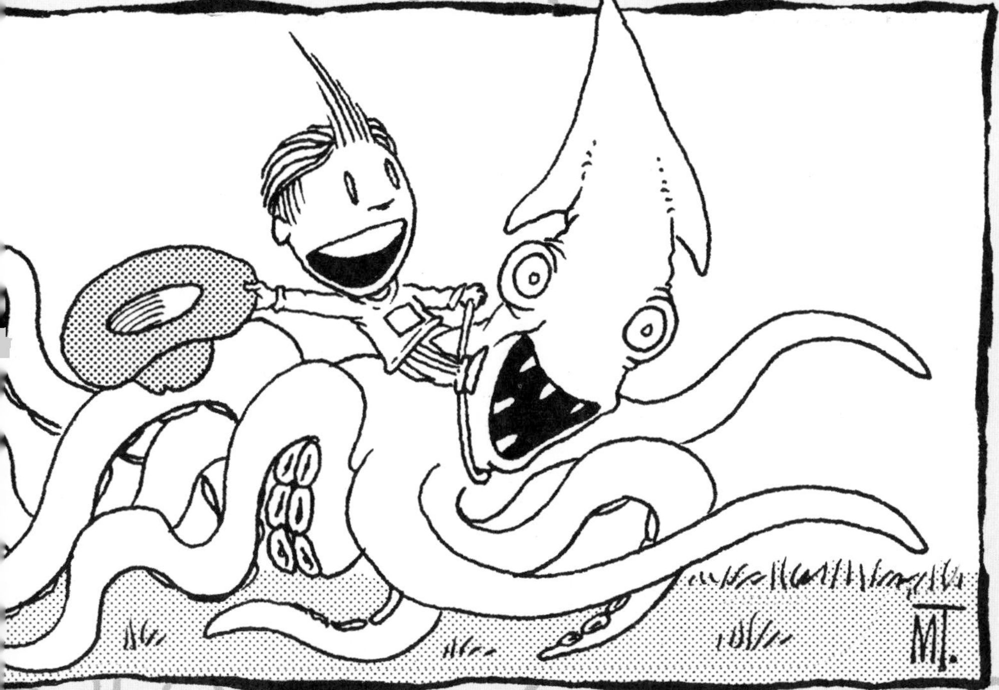
MJ.

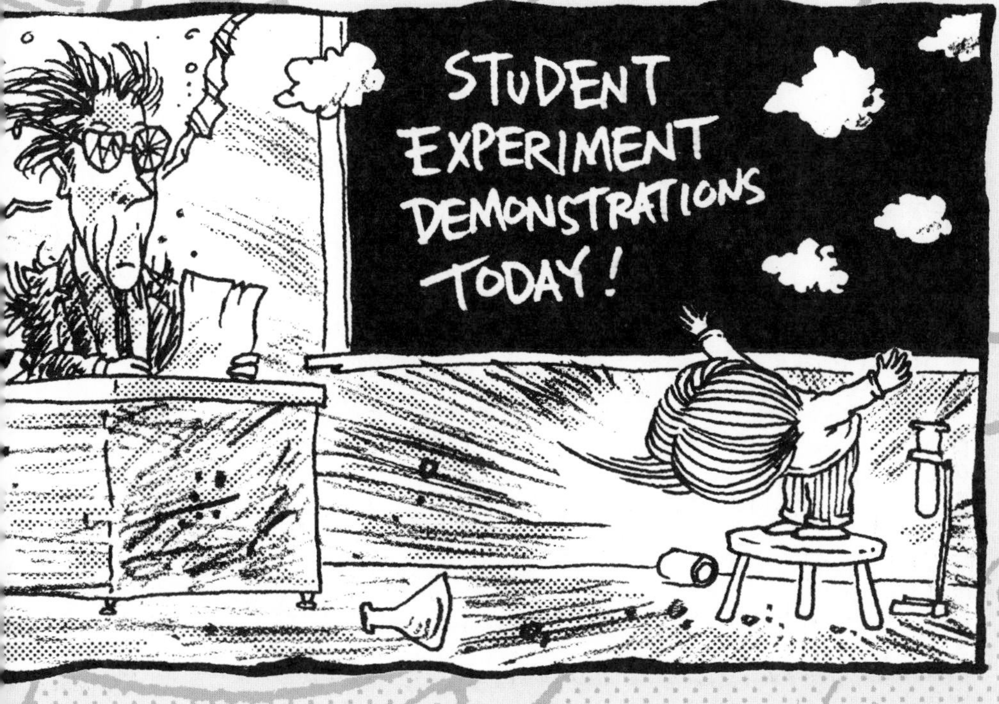
STUDENT
EXPERIMENT
DEMONSTRATIONS
TODAY!

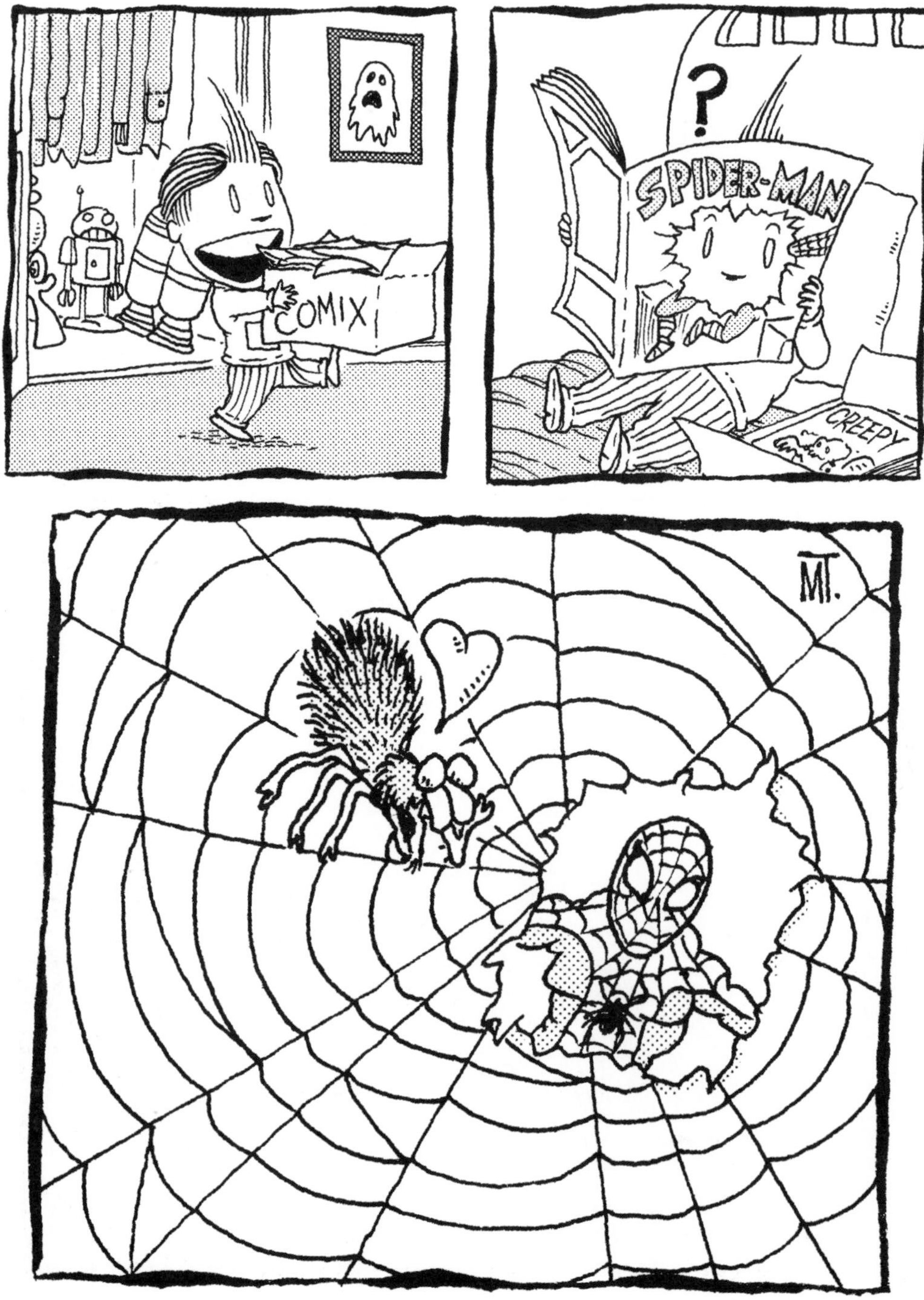
COMIX
?
SPIDER-MAN
CREEPY
MT.

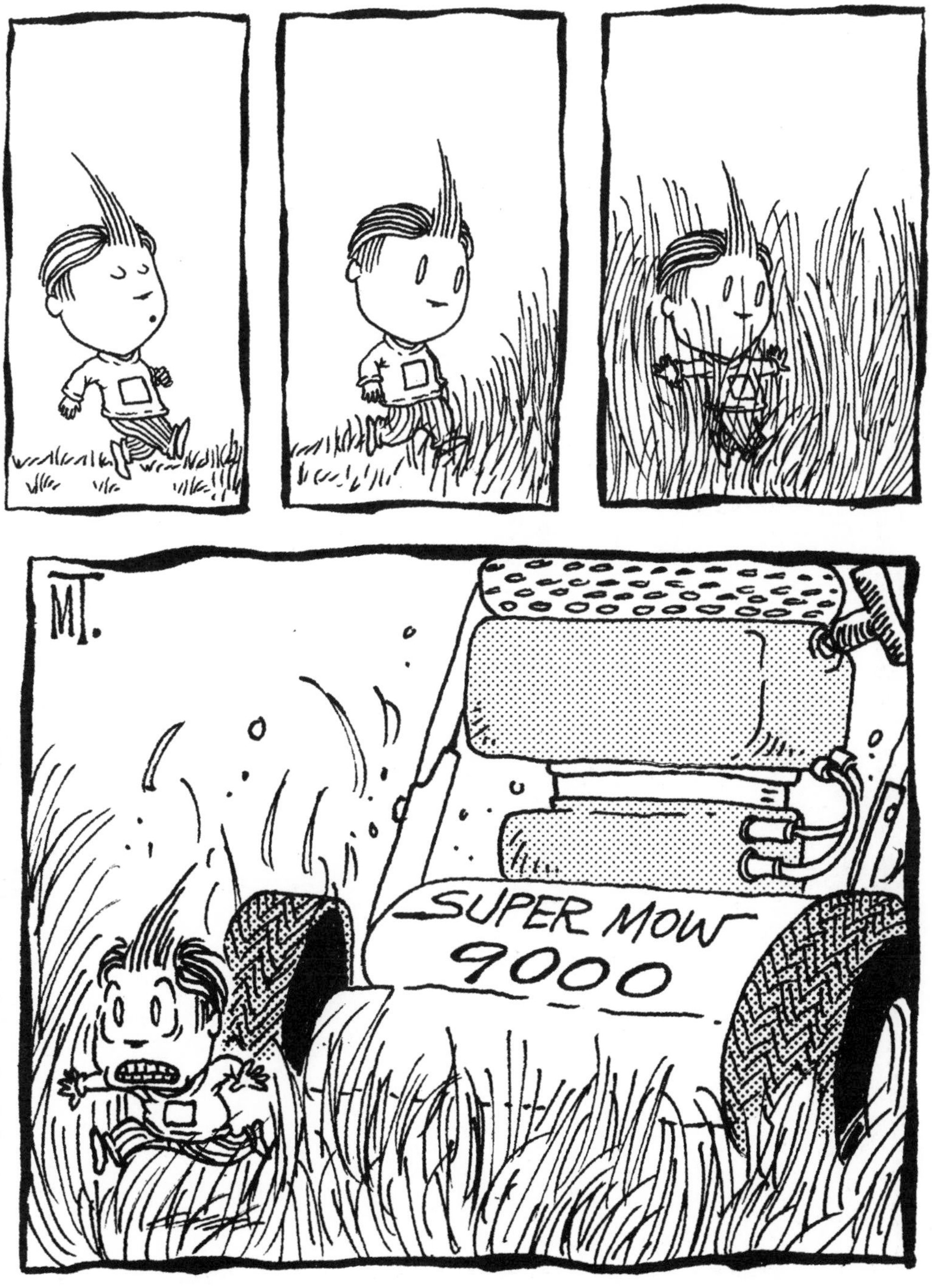
MT.
SUPER MOW
9000

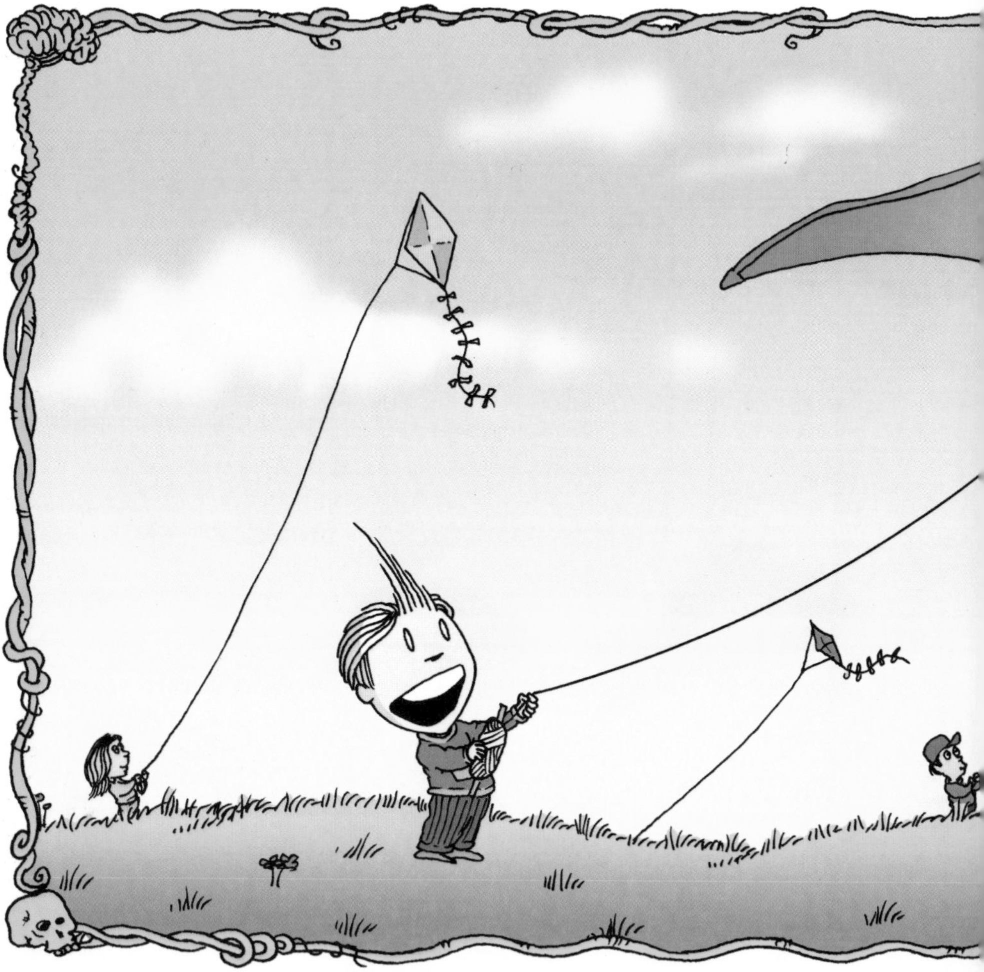

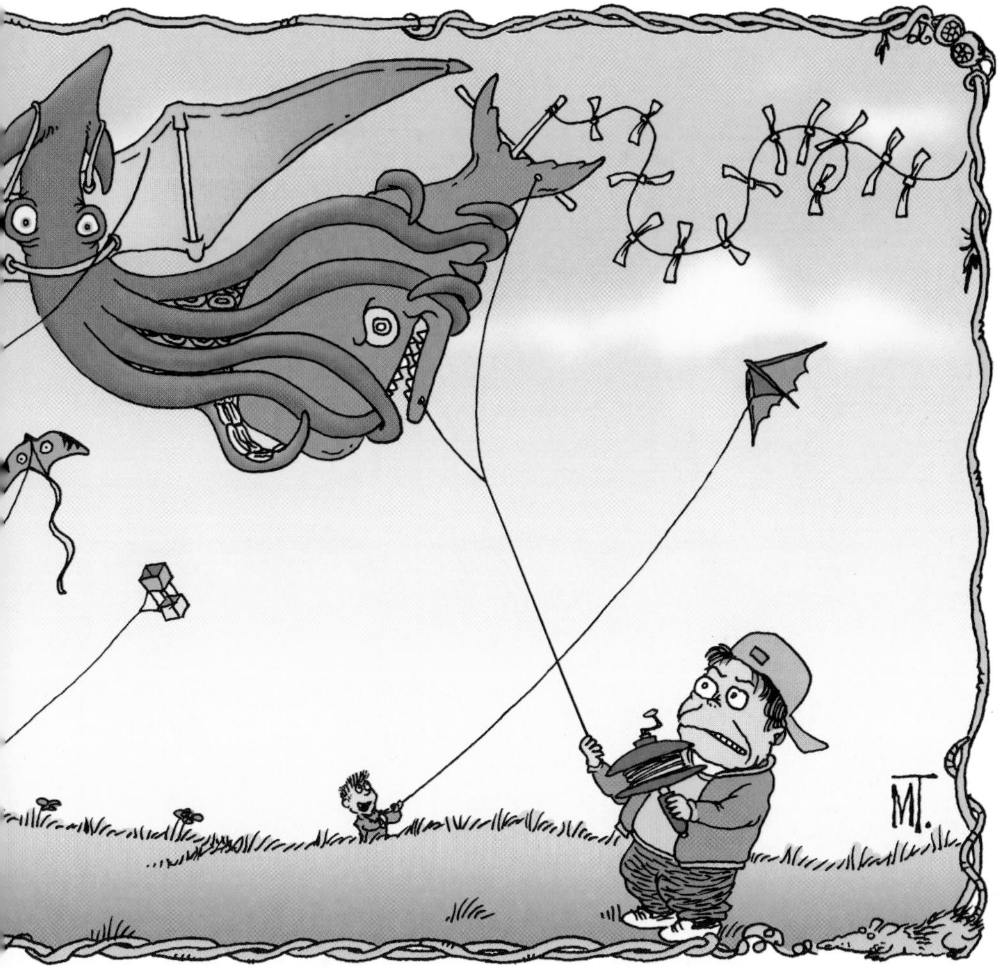

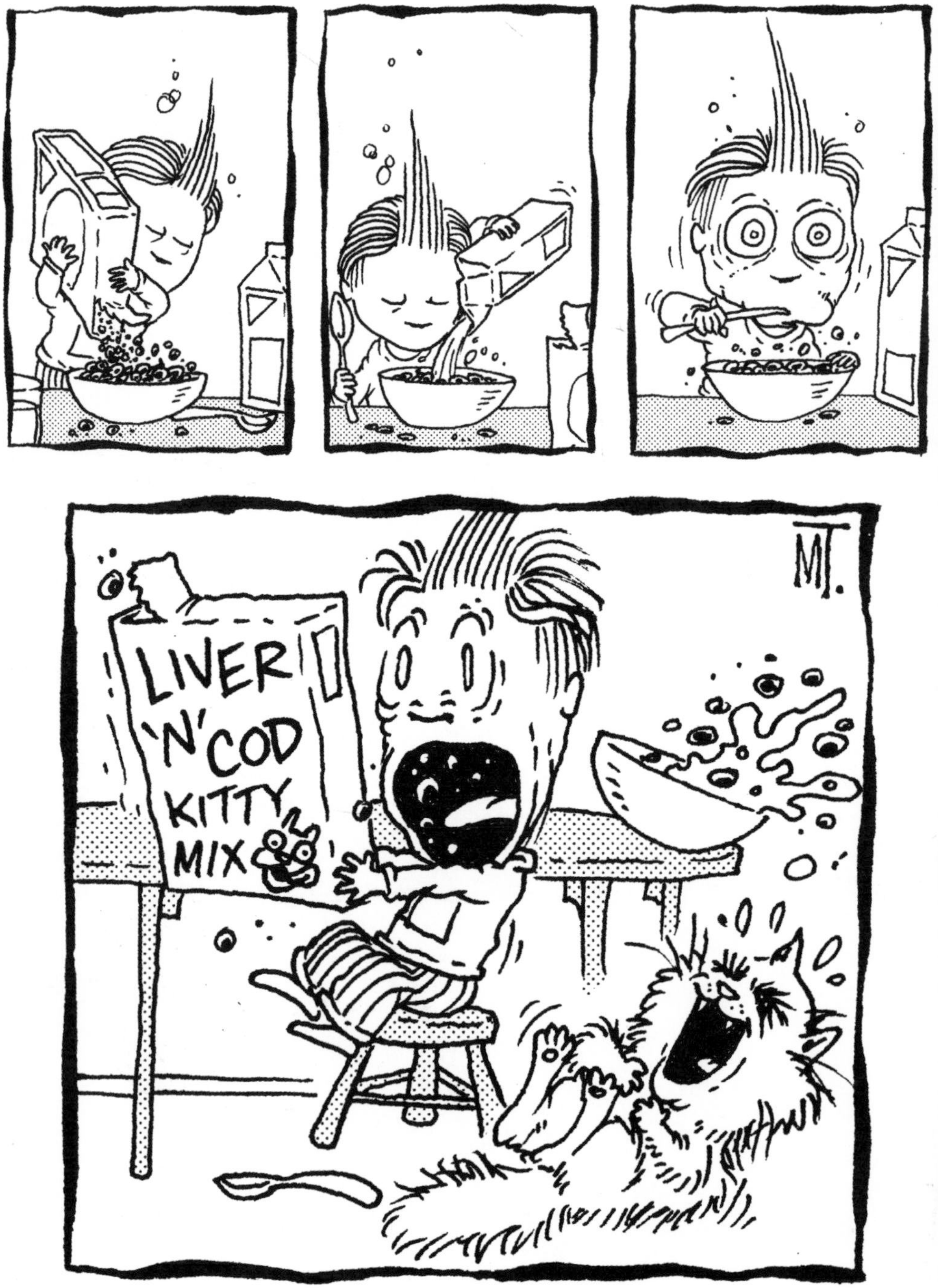
LIVER
'N' COD
KITTY
MIX
MT.

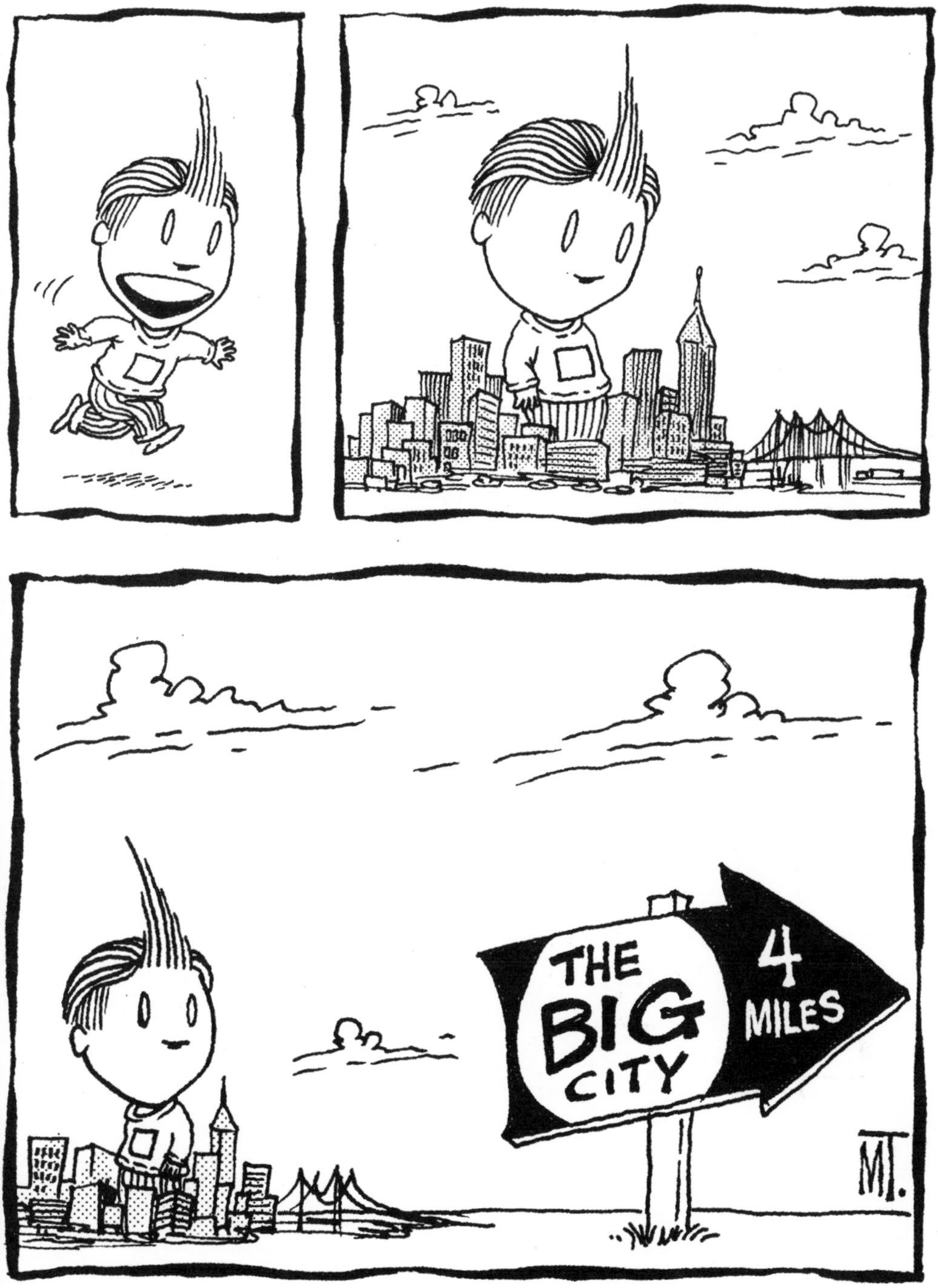
THE
BIG
CITY
4
MILES
MT.

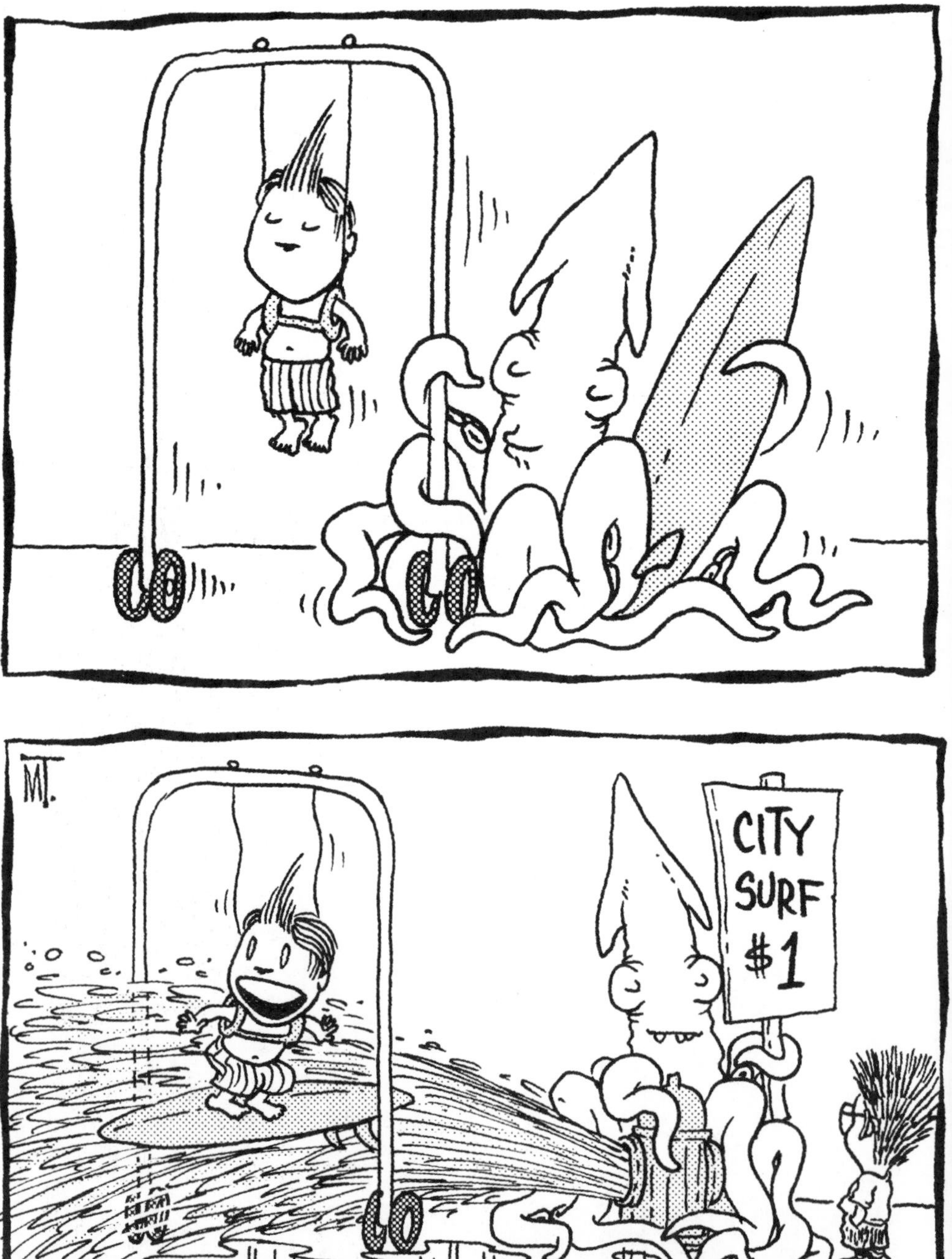
CITY
SURF
$1

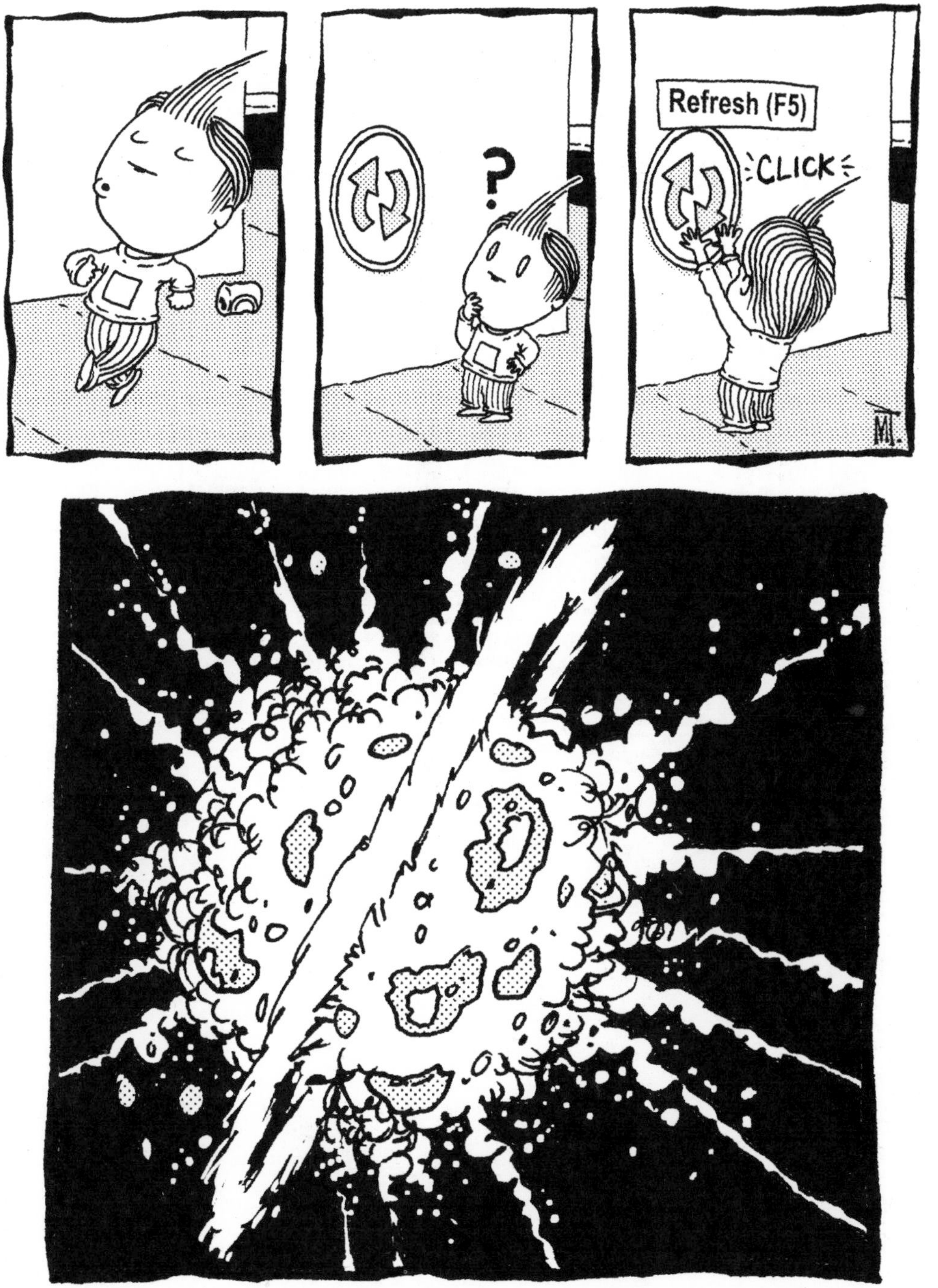
?
Refresh (F5)
CLICK

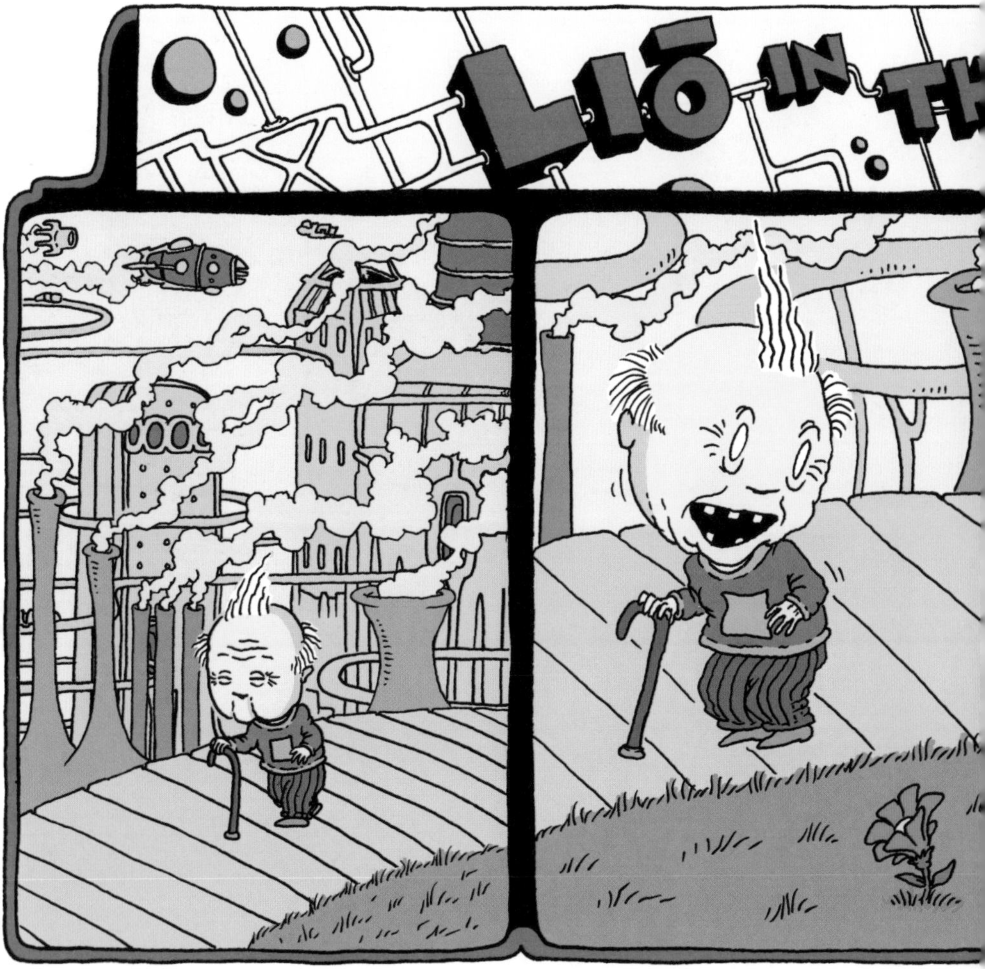
LIO IN

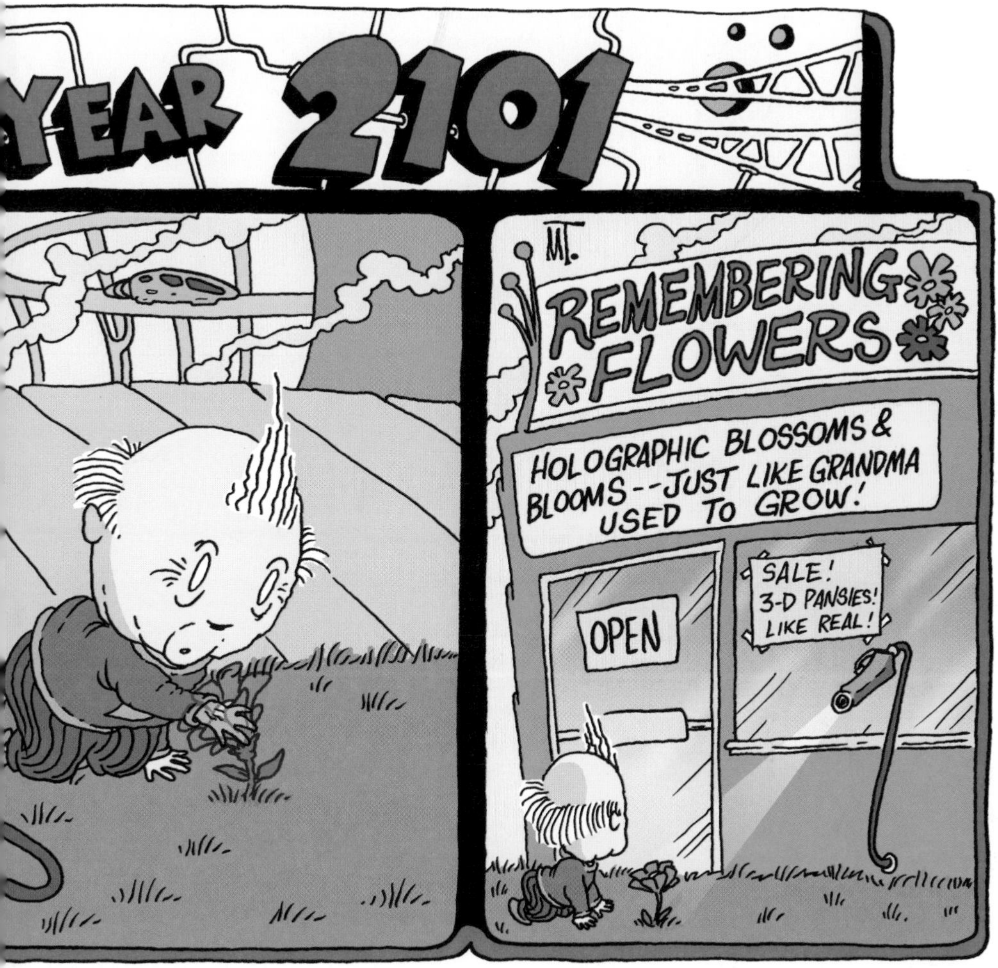
YEAR 2101
M.T.
REMEMBERING FLOWERS
HOLOGRAPHIC BLOSSOMS & BLOOMS--JUST LIKE GRANDMA USED TO GROW!
OPEN
SALE! 3-D PANSIES! LIKE REAL!

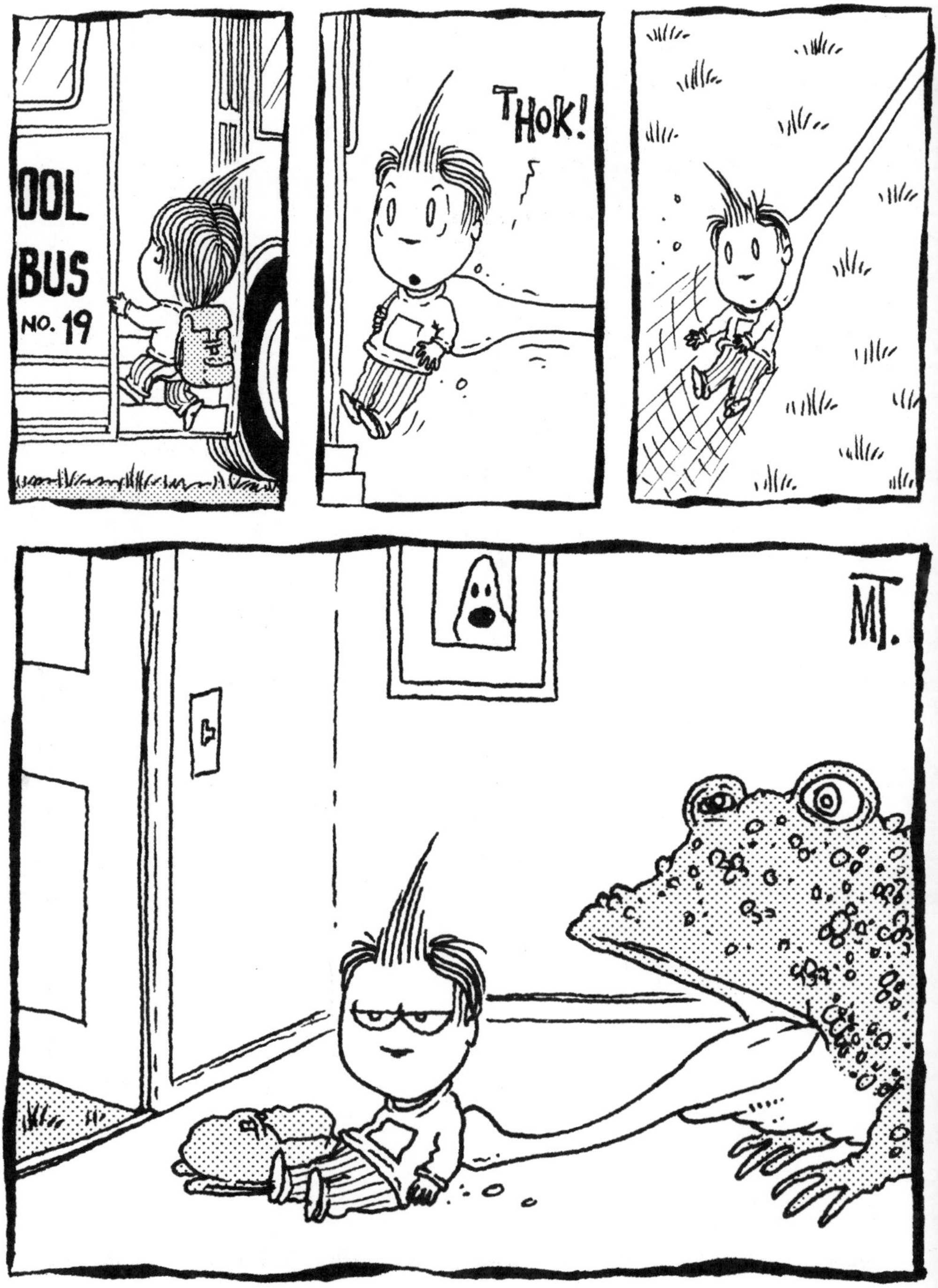
OOL
BUS
NO. 19
THOK!
MT.

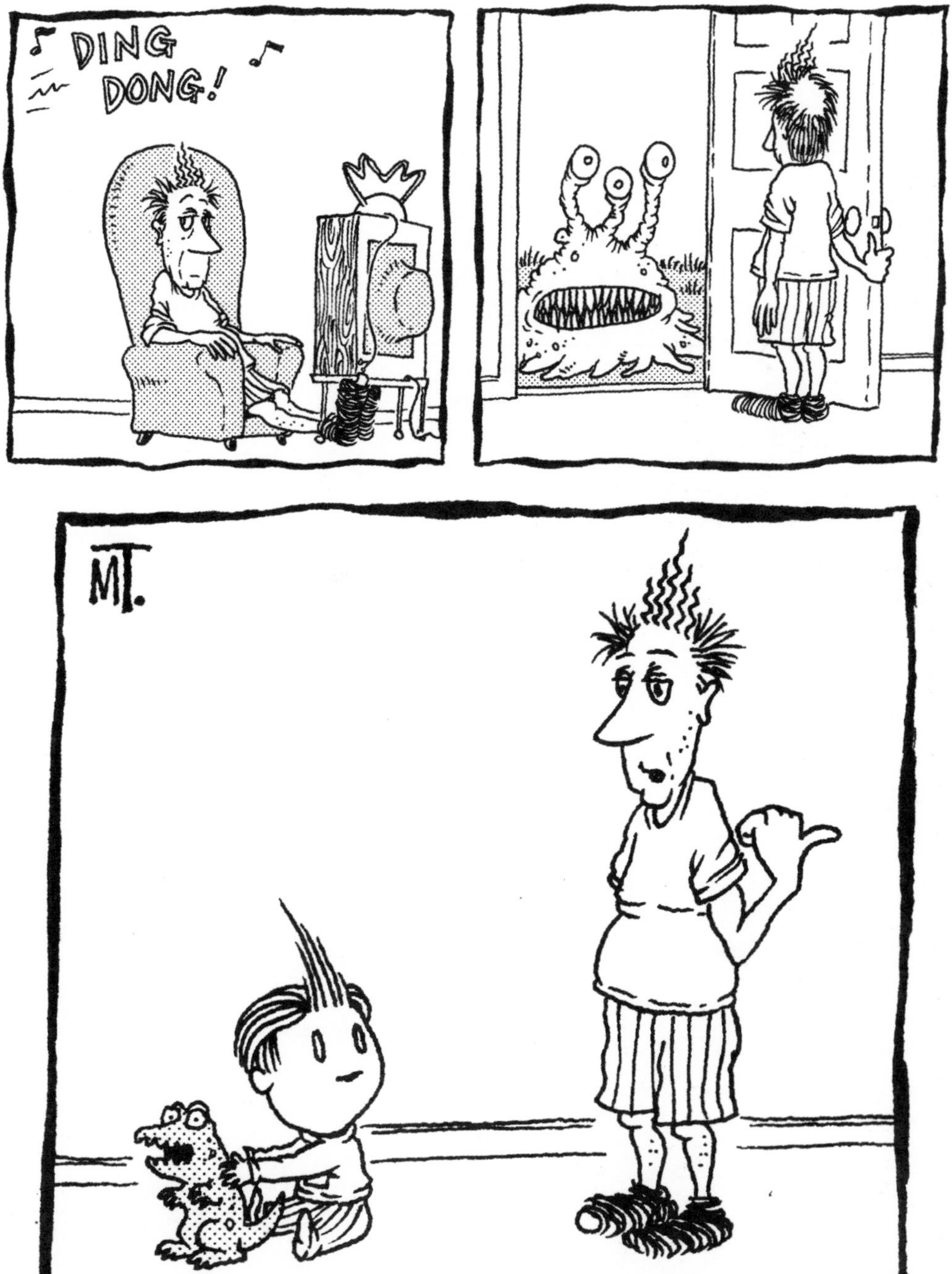
DING DONG!
MT.

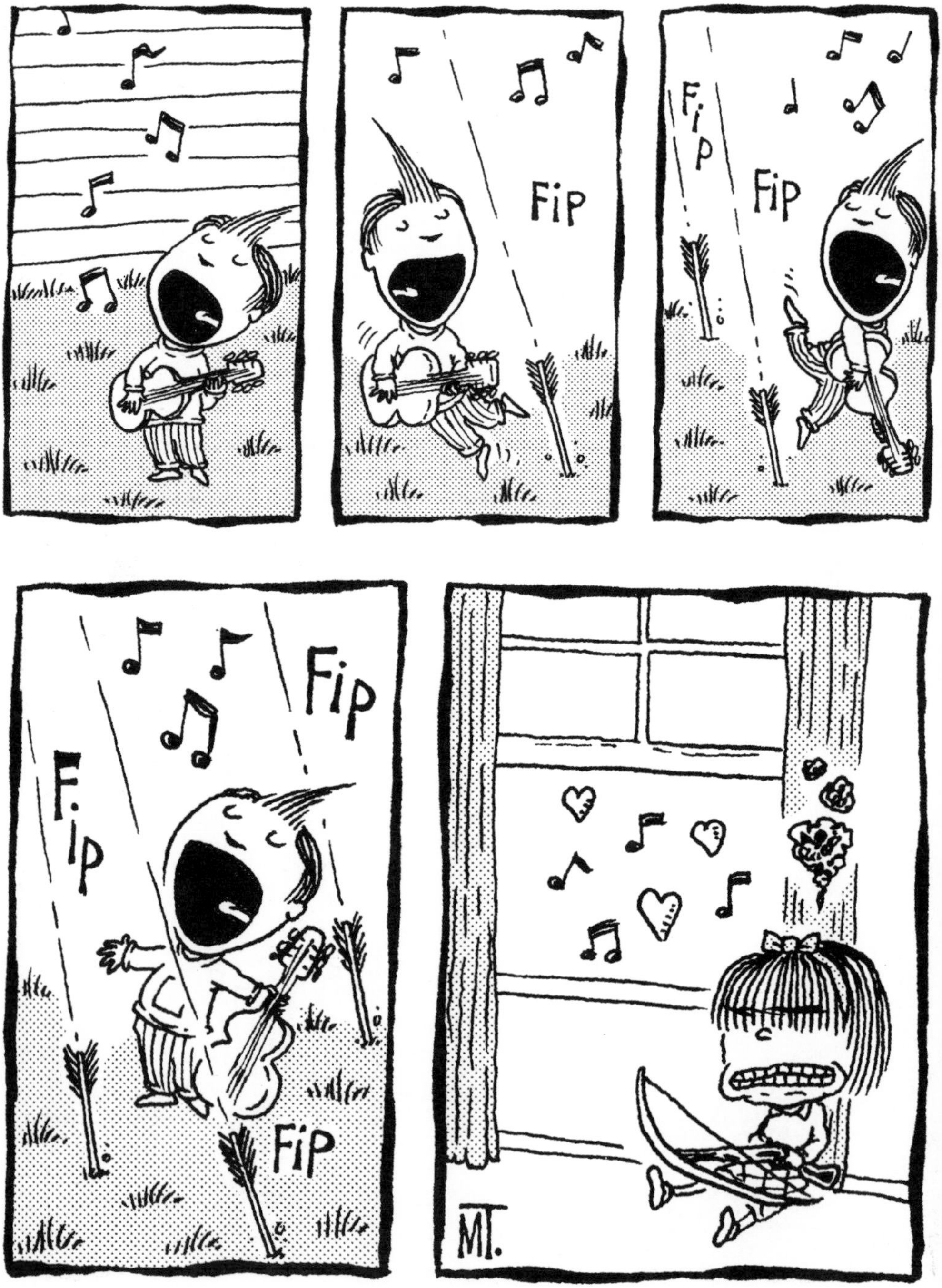
Fip
Fip
Fip
Fip
Fip
Fip
MT.

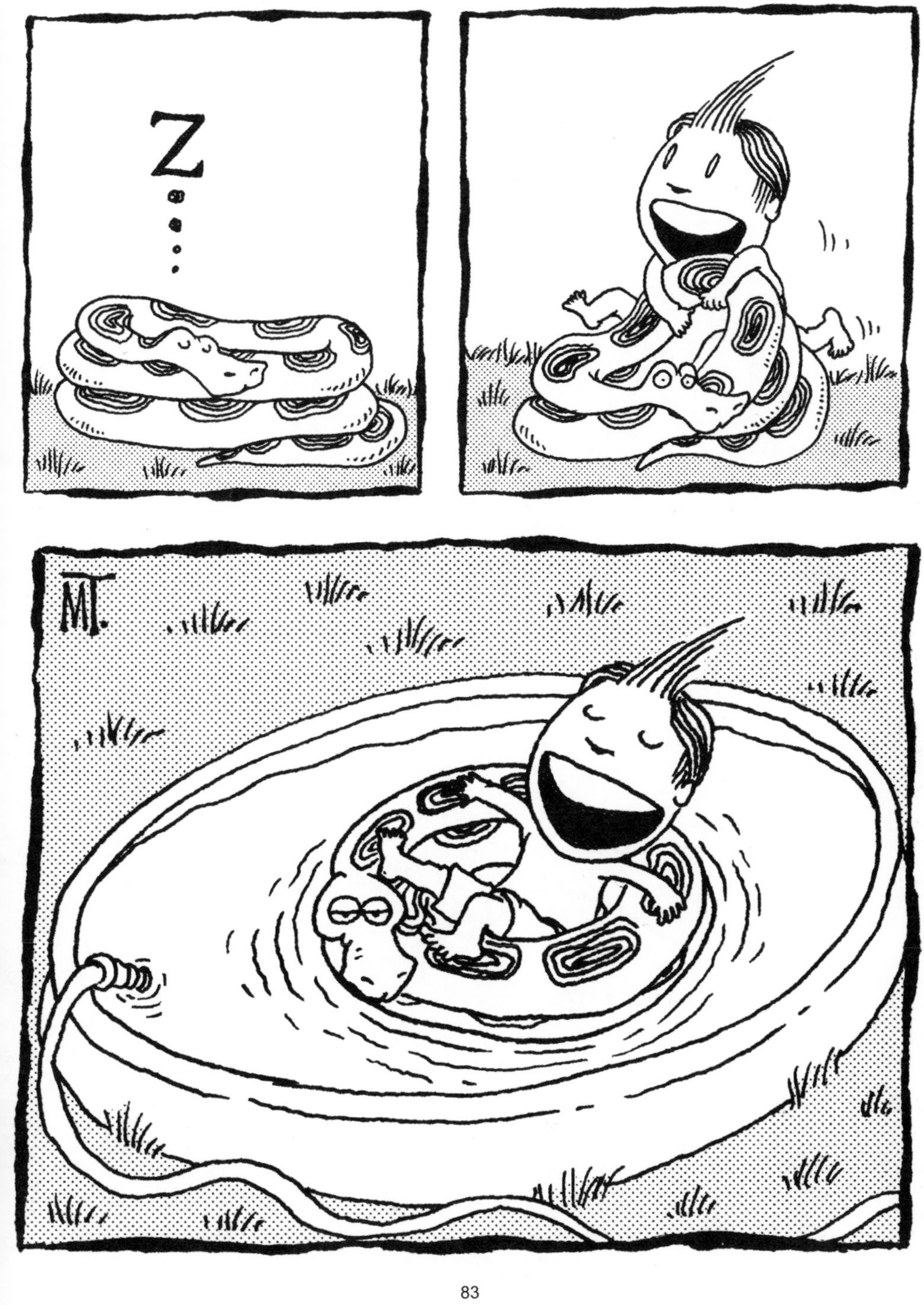
Z

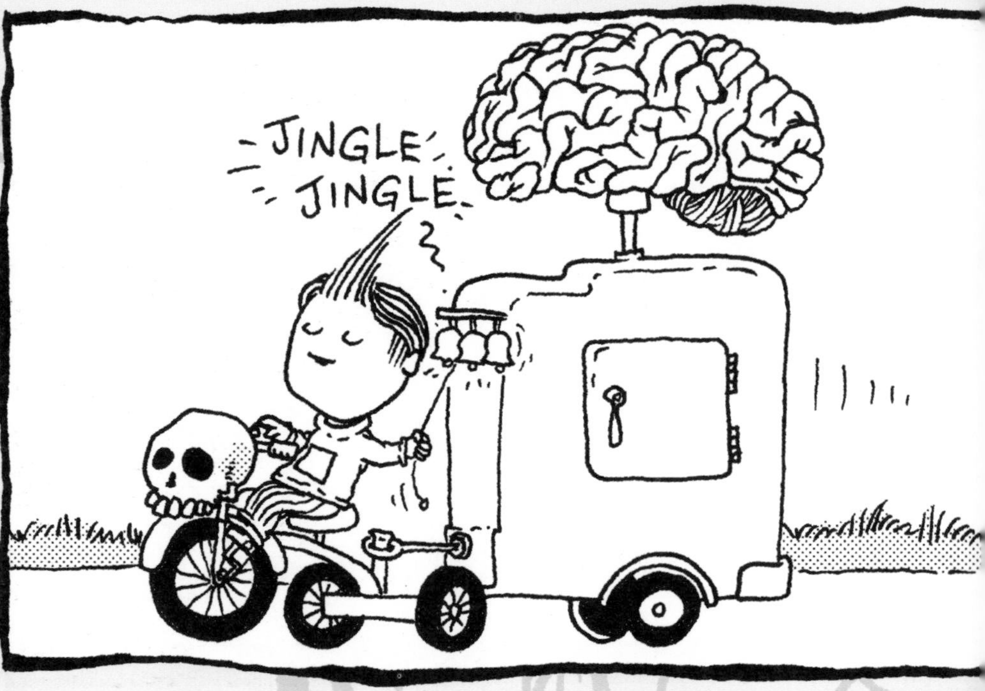
JINGLE
JINGLE

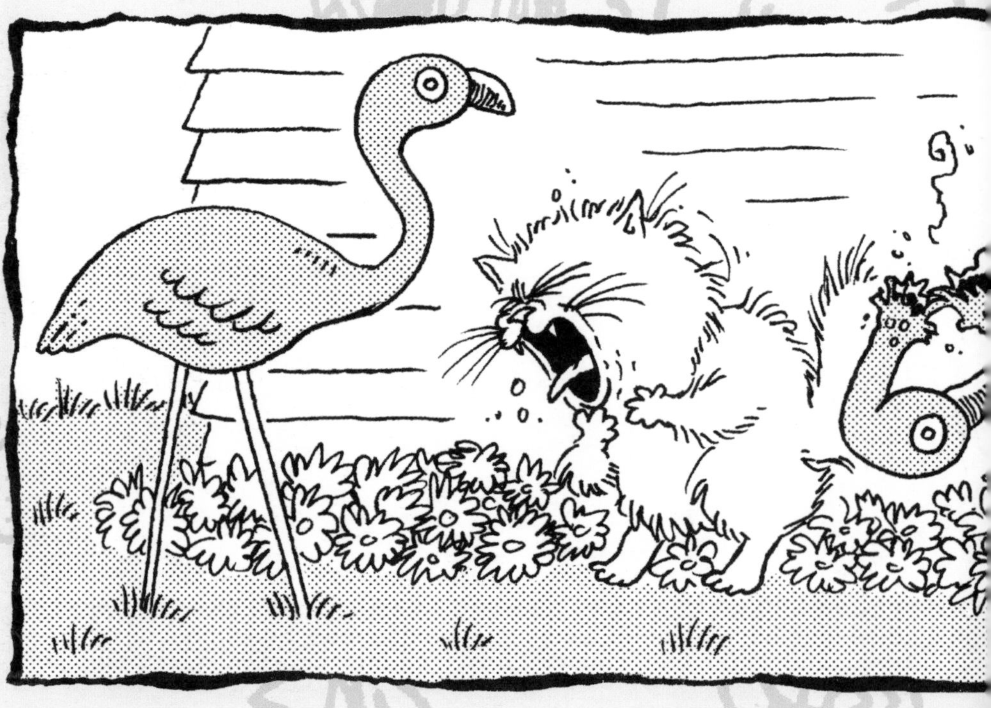

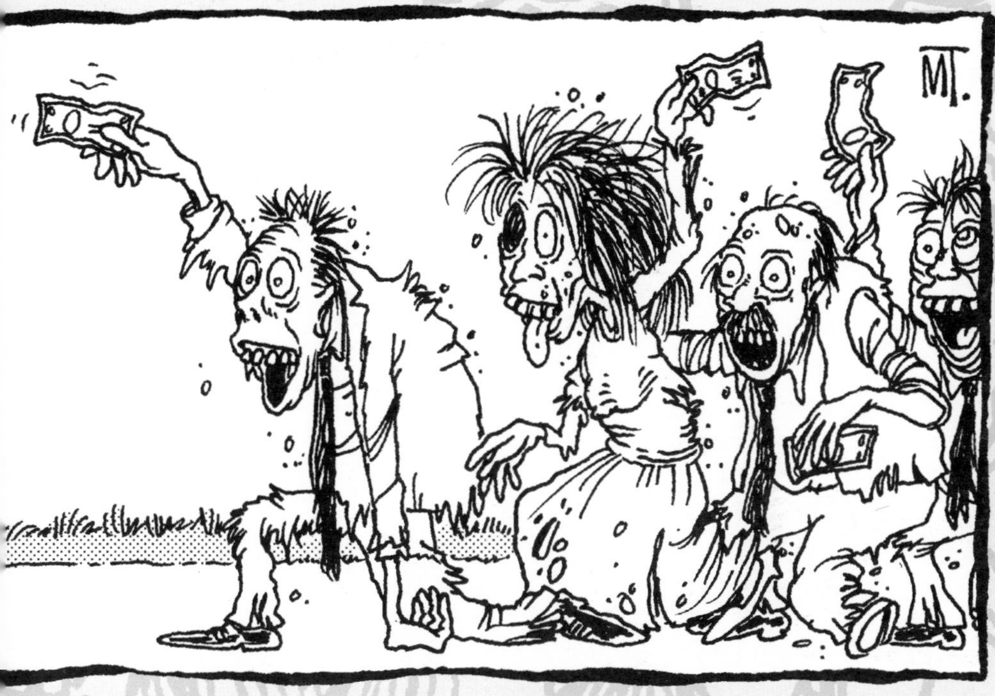

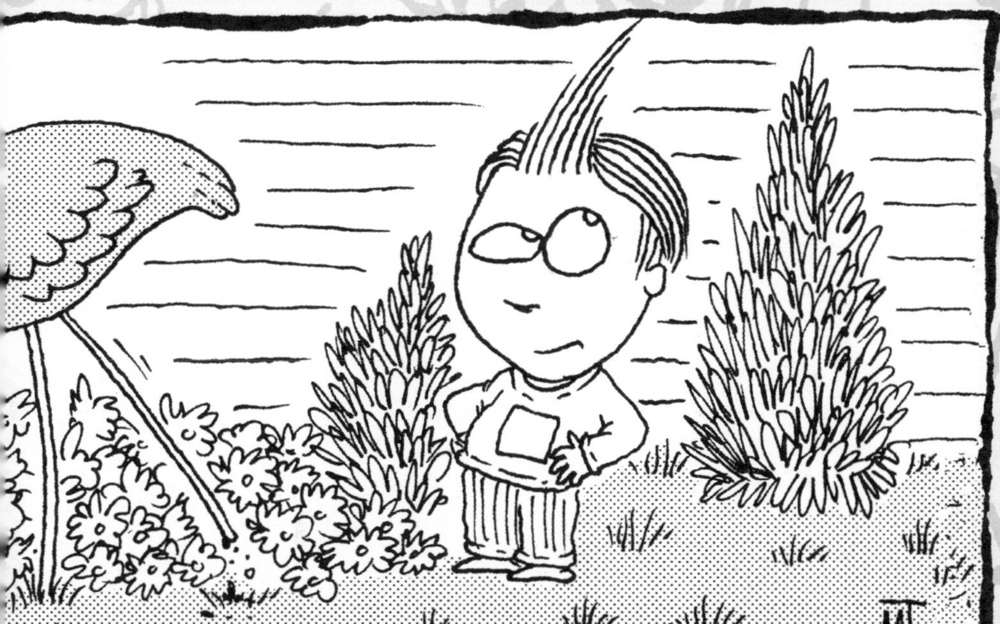

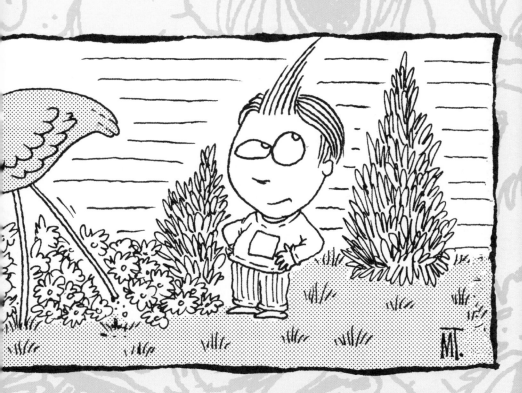

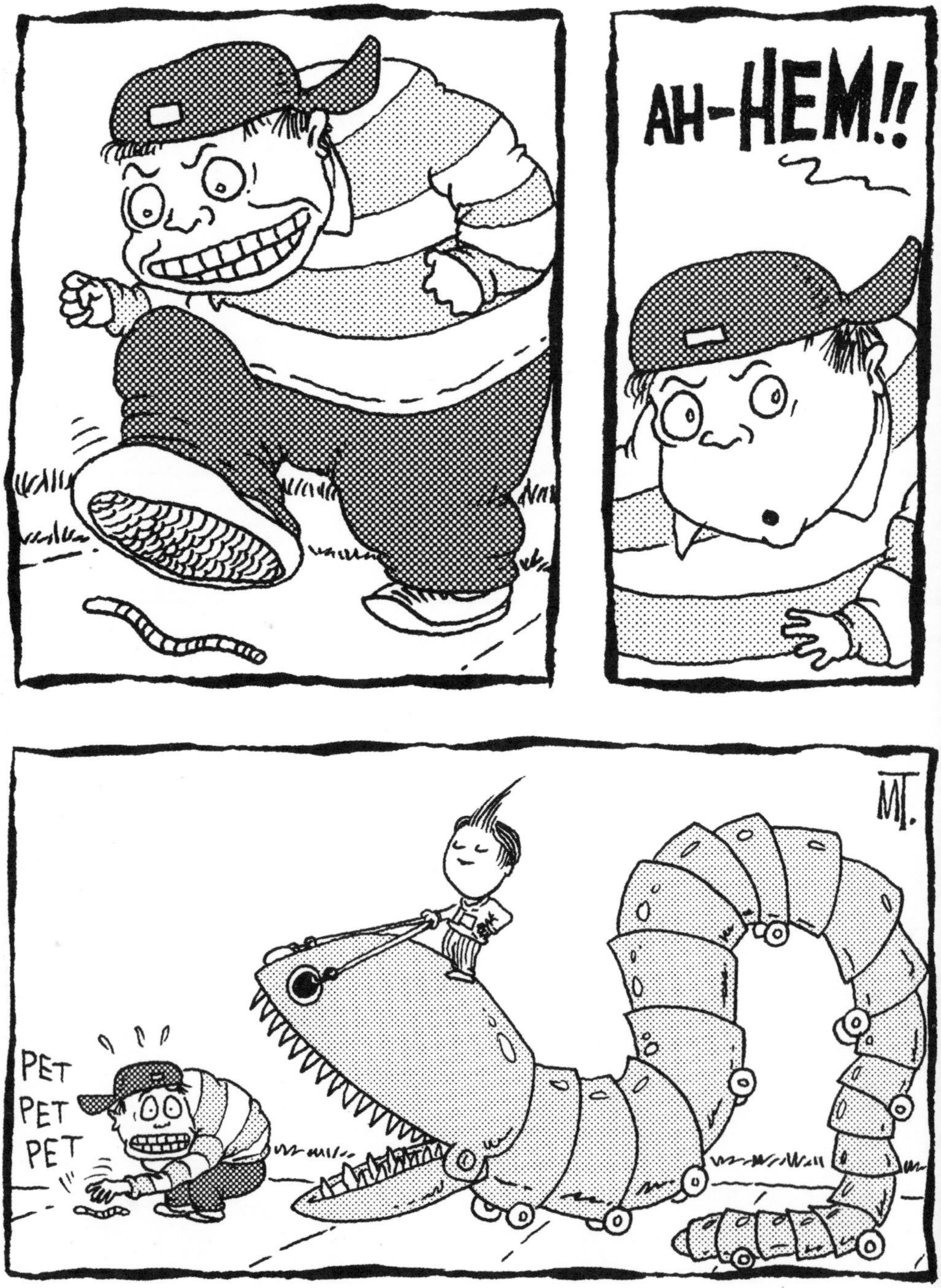
AH-HEM!!
MT.
PET
PET
PET

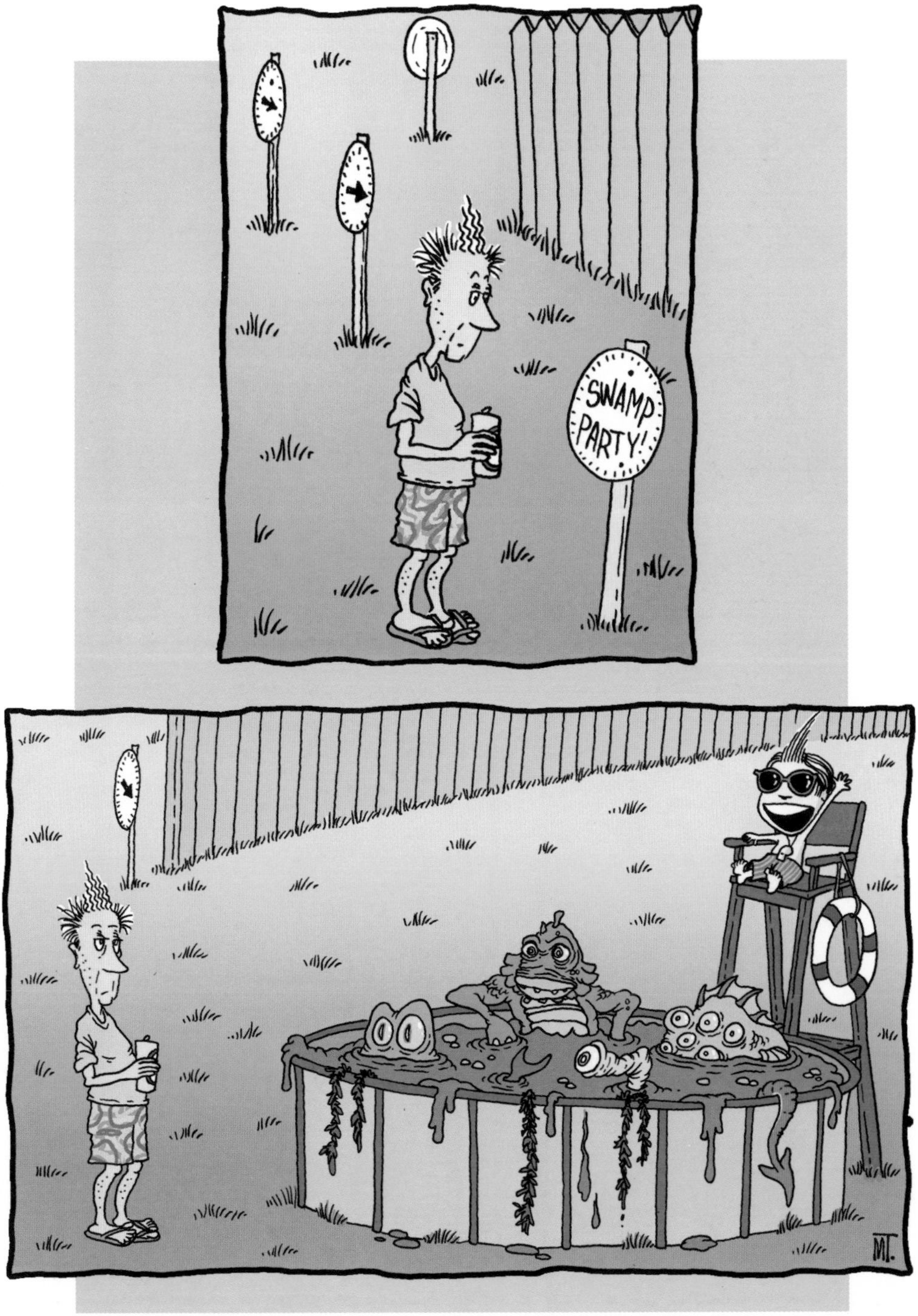
SWAMP PARTY!
MT.

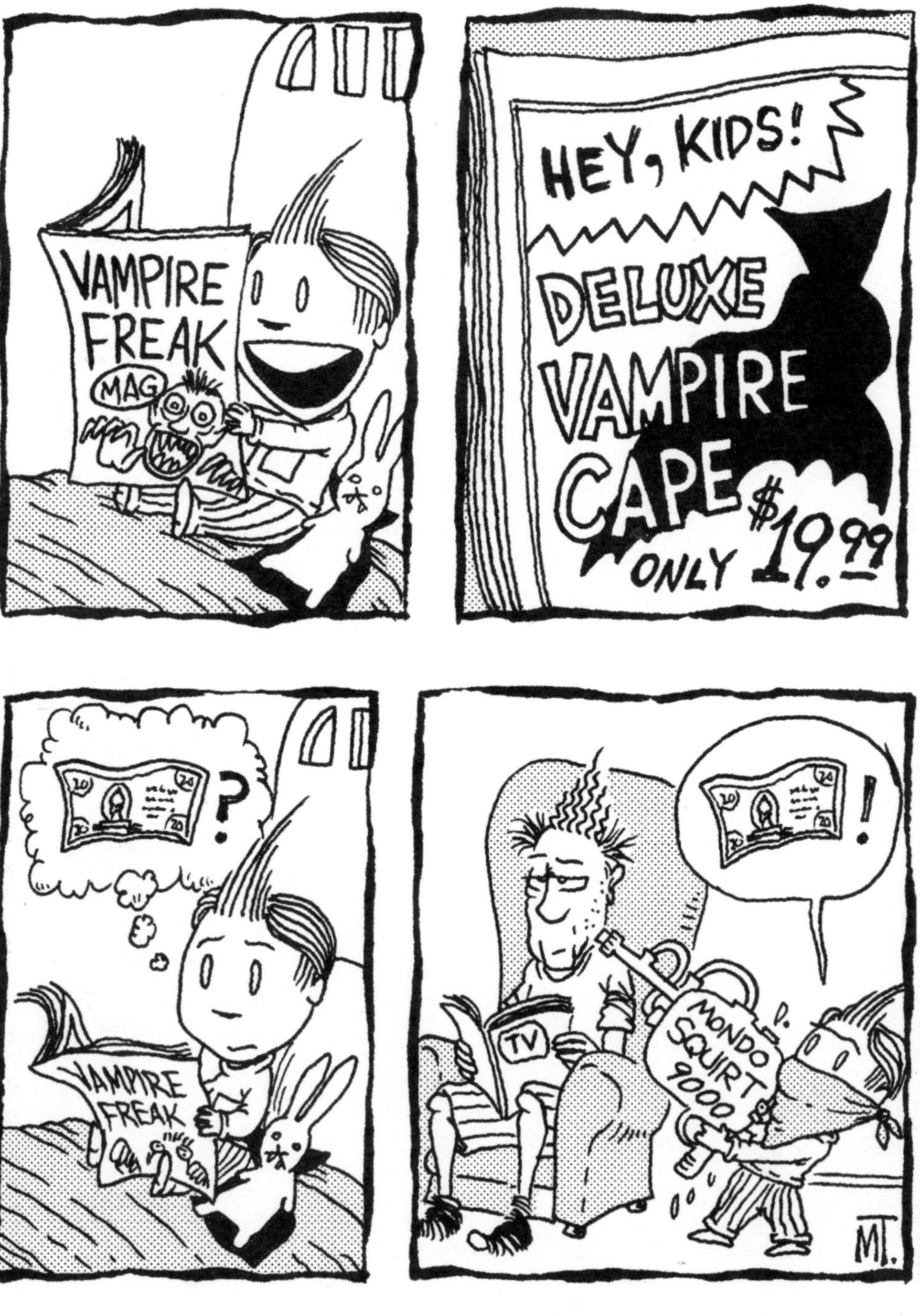
VAMPIRE FREAK
MAG
HEY, KIDS!
DELUXE VAMPIRE CAPE
ONLY $19.99
?
VAMPIRE FREAK
TV
!
MONDO SQUIRT 9000
MT.

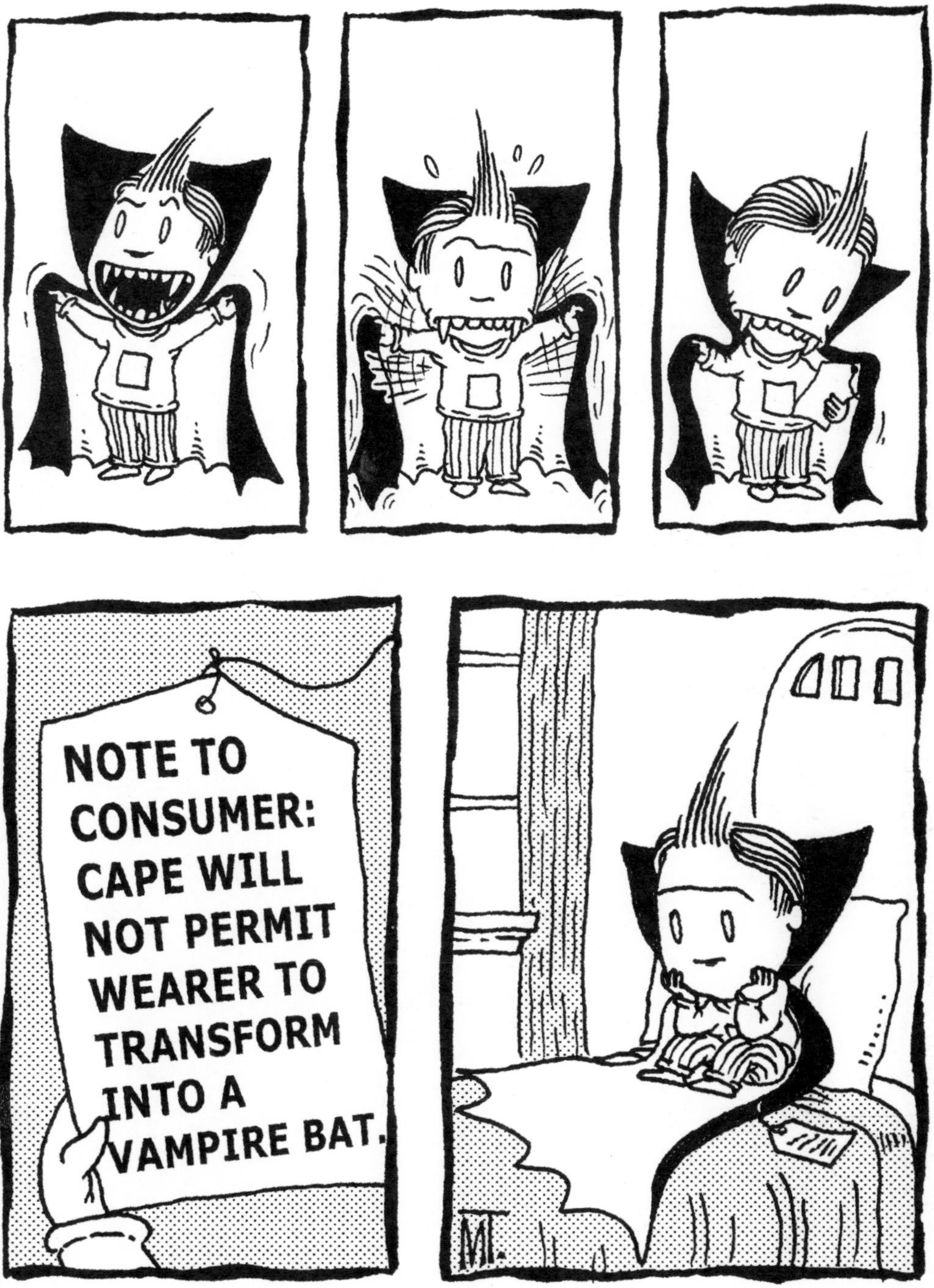
NOTE TO CONSUMER: CAPE WILL NOT PERMIT WEARER TO TRANSFORM INTO A VAMPIRE BAT.
MT.

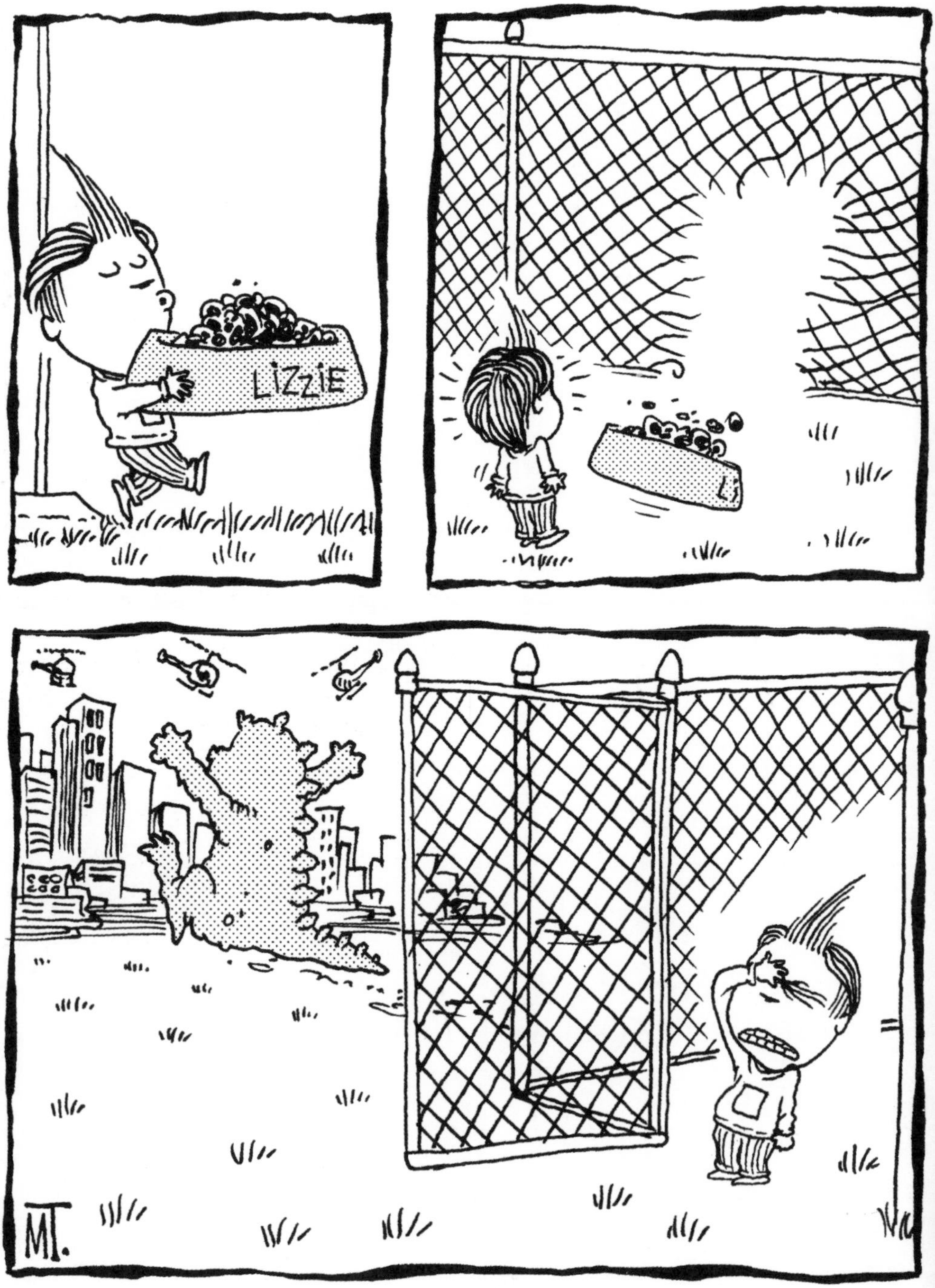
LIZZIE

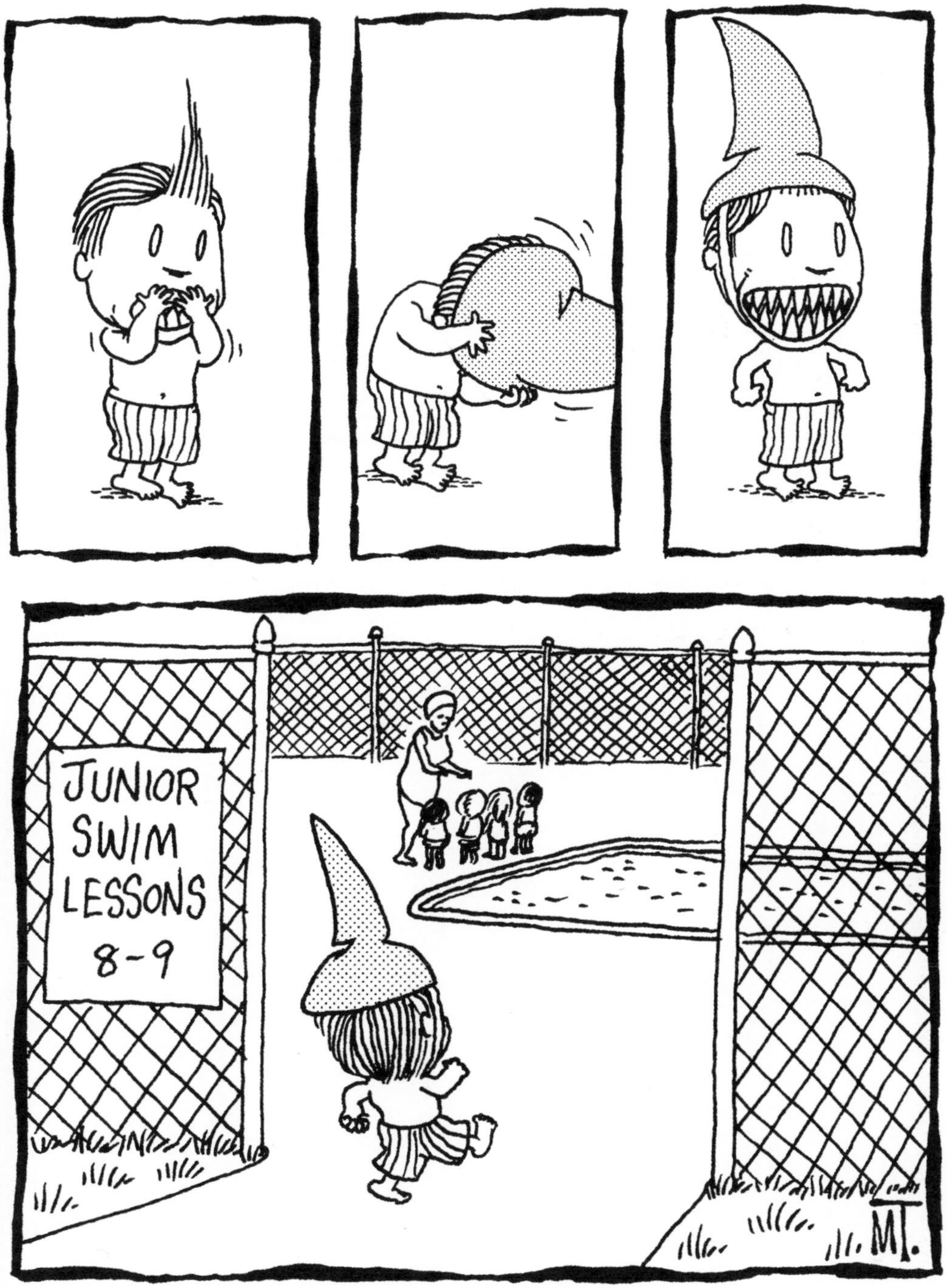
JUNIOR
SWIM
LESSONS
8-9
MT.

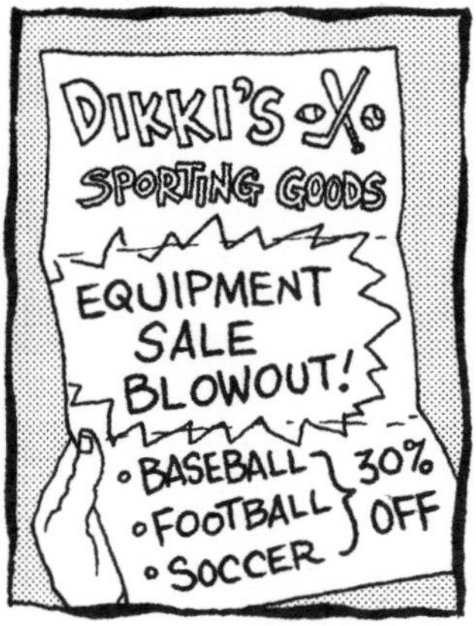
DIKKI'S
SPORTING GOODS
EQUIPMENT SALE BLOWOUT!
BASEBALL
FOOTBALL
SOCCER
30% OFF

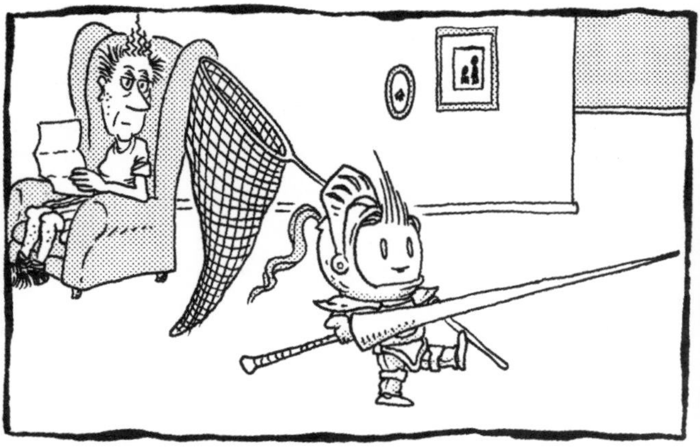

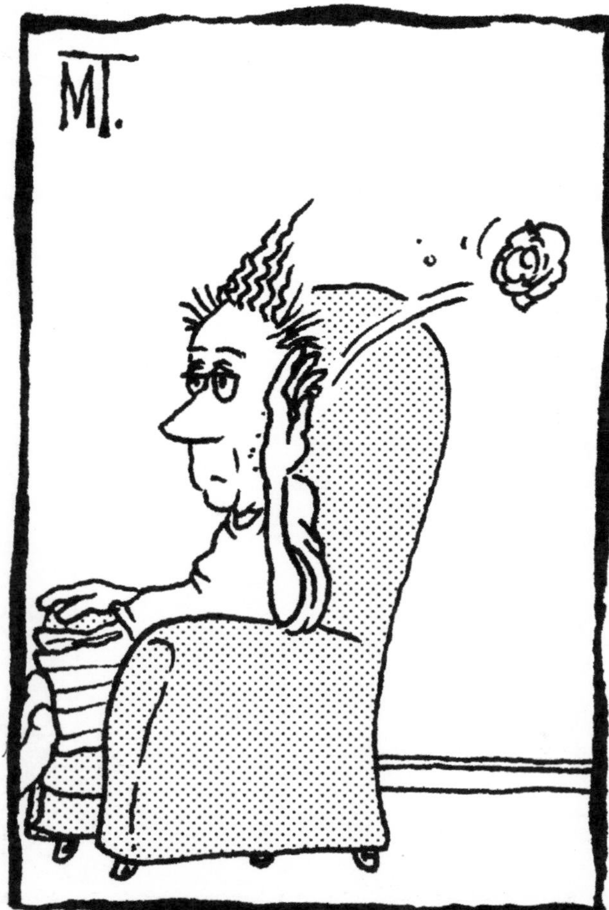
MT.

MT.

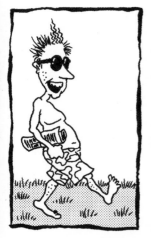

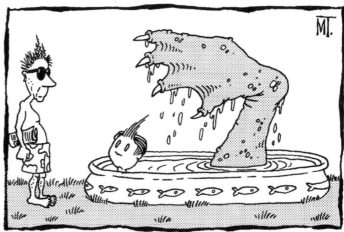

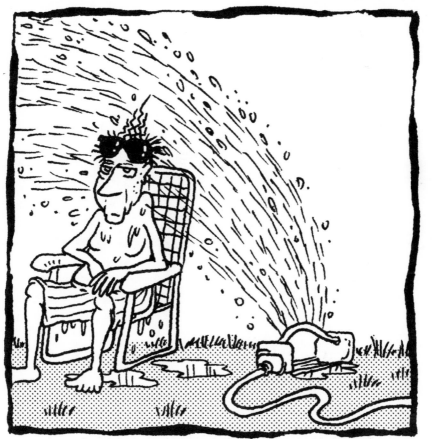

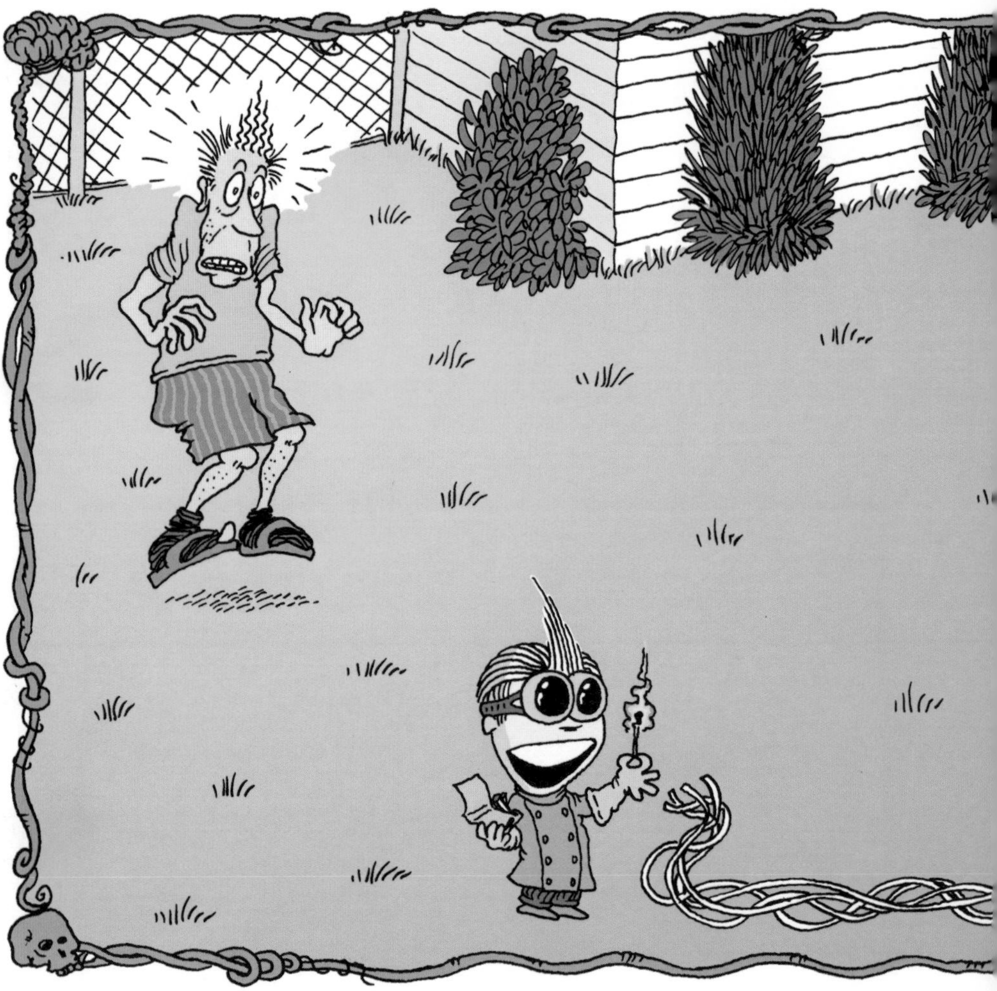

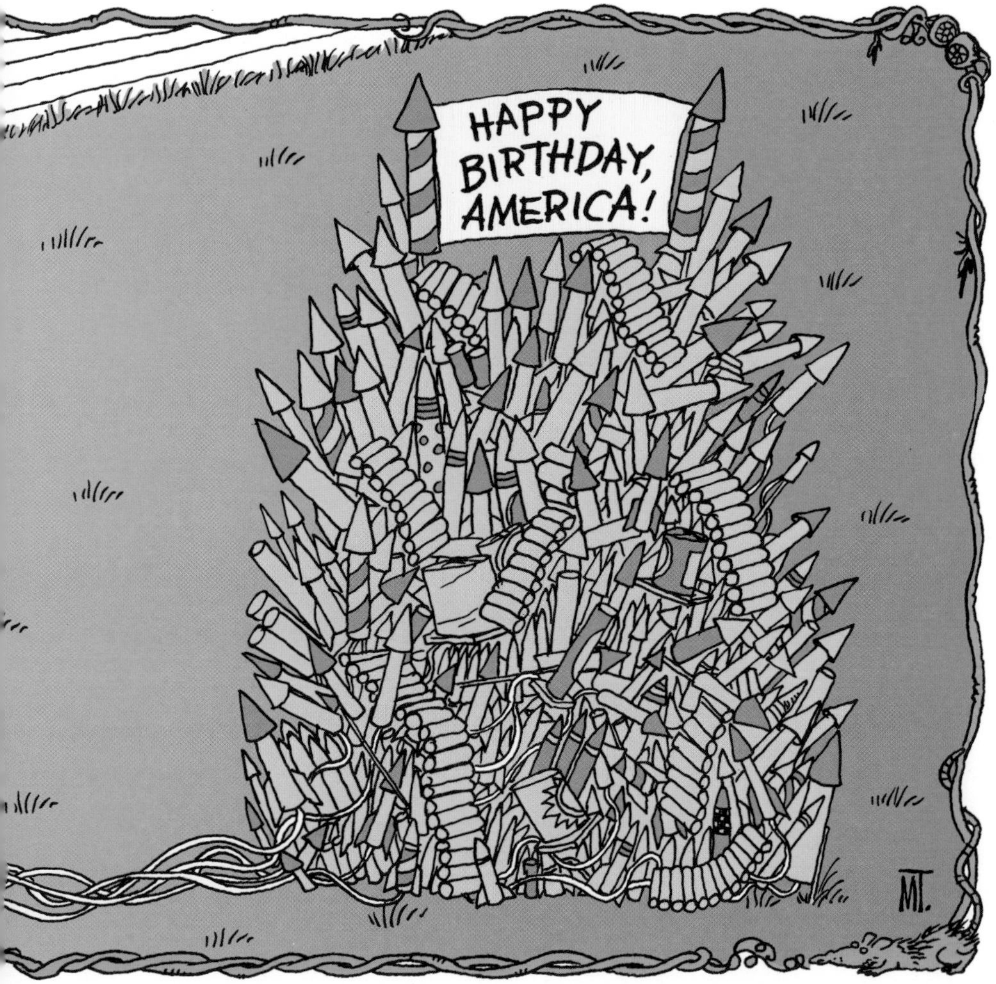
HAPPY BIRTHDAY, AMERICA!
MT.

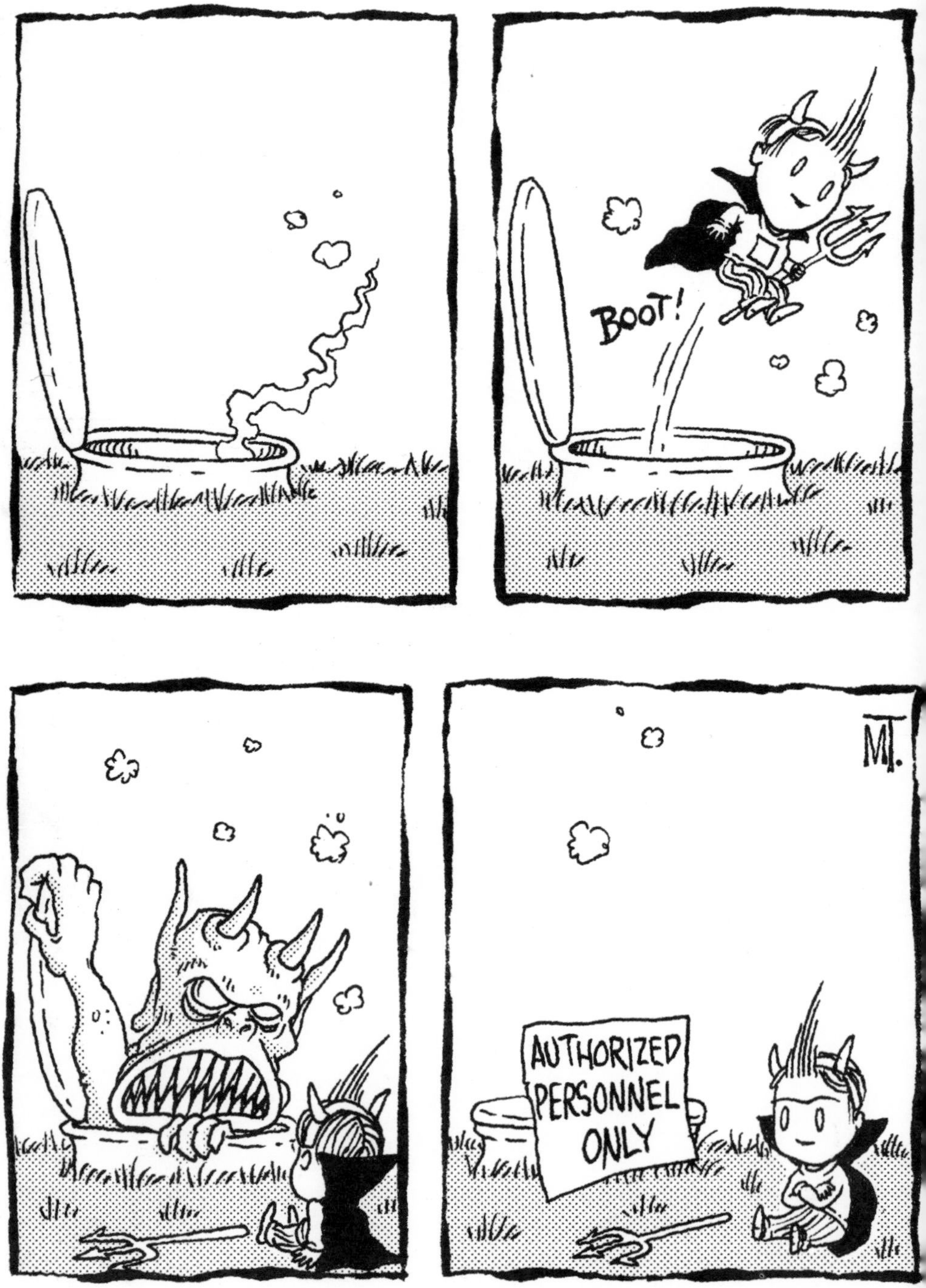
BOOT!
MT.
AUTHORIZED PERSONNEL ONLY

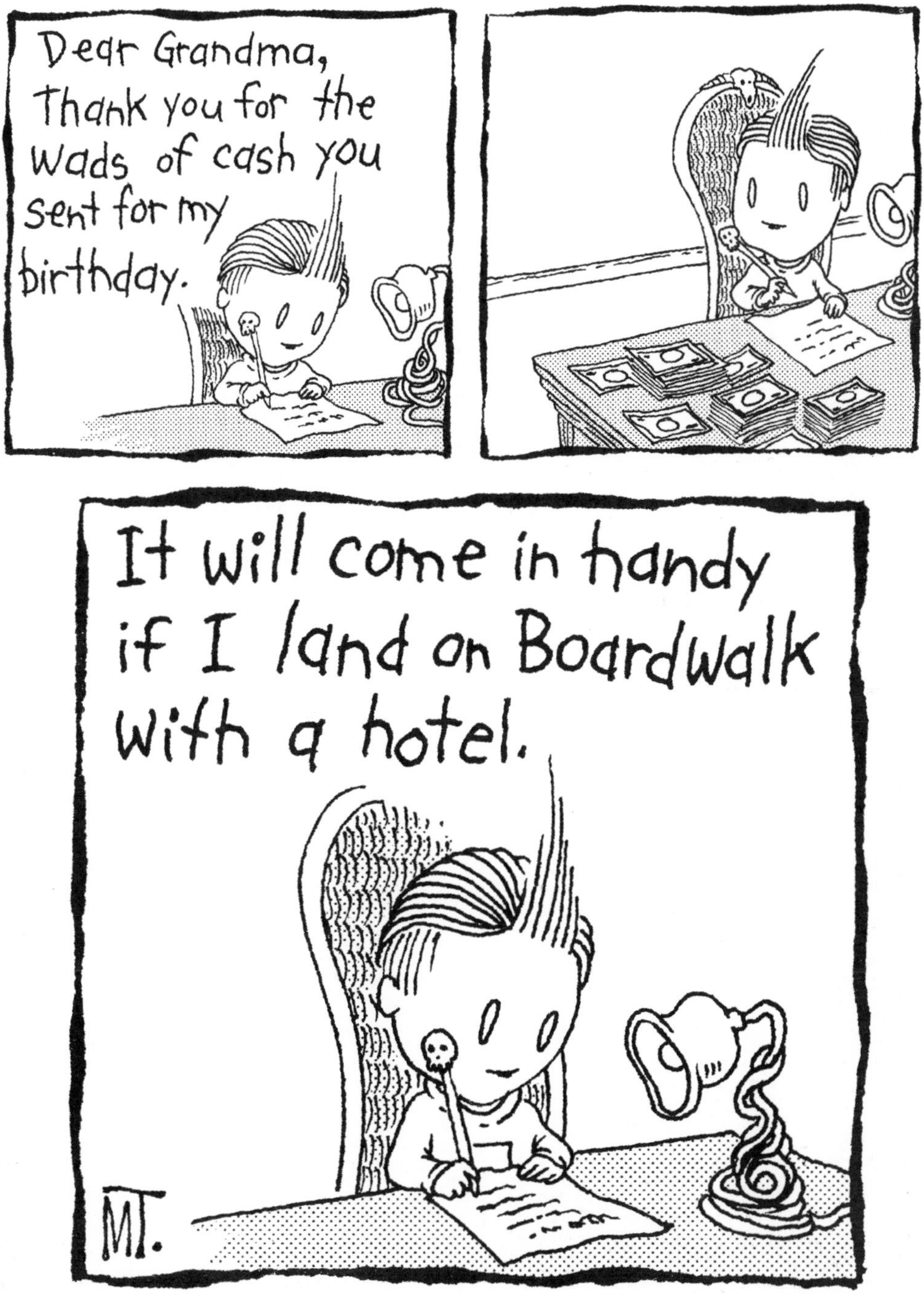
Dear Grandma,
thank you for the wads of cash you sent for my birthday.
It will come in handy if I land on Boardwalk with a hotel.
MT.

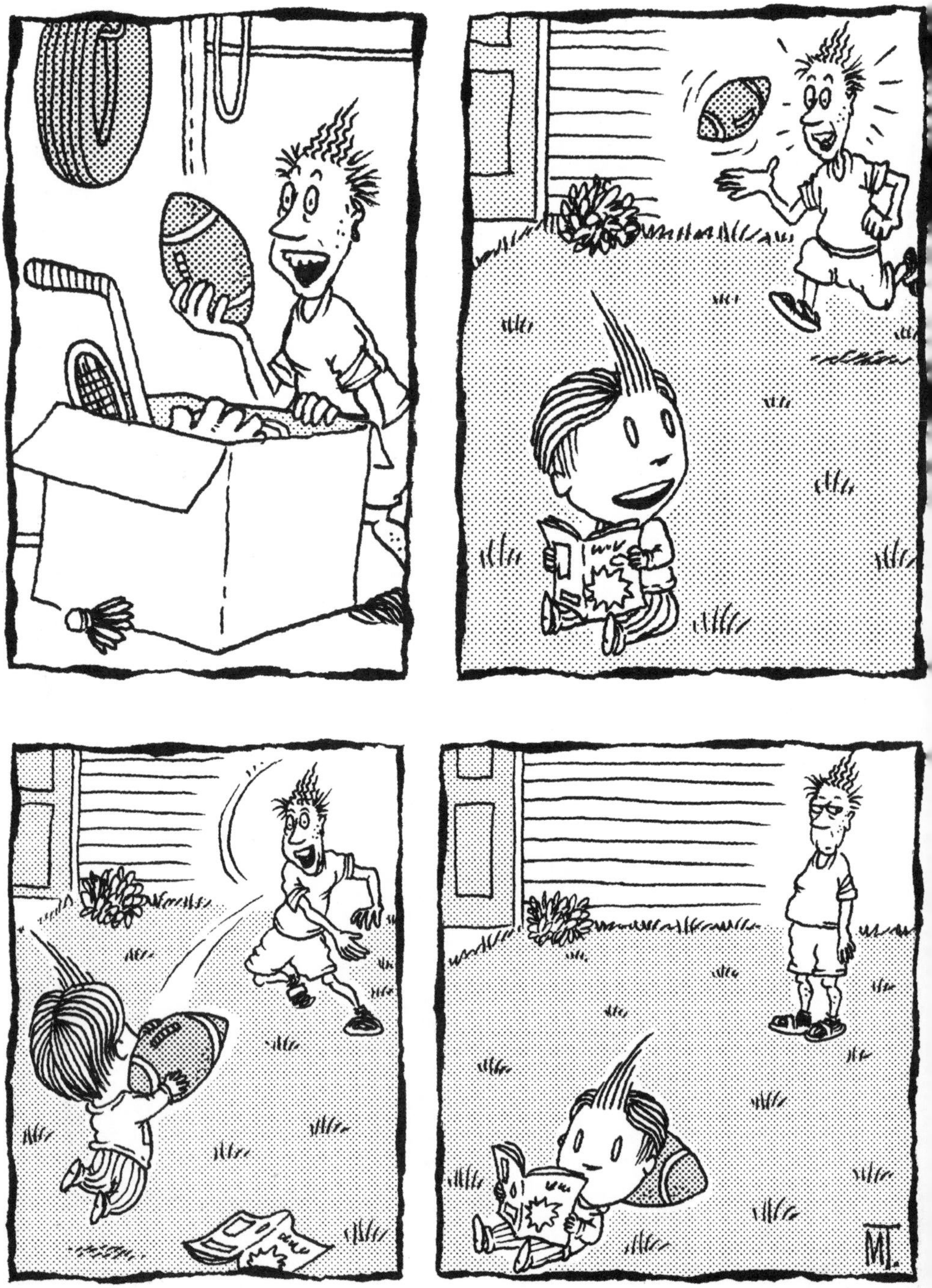

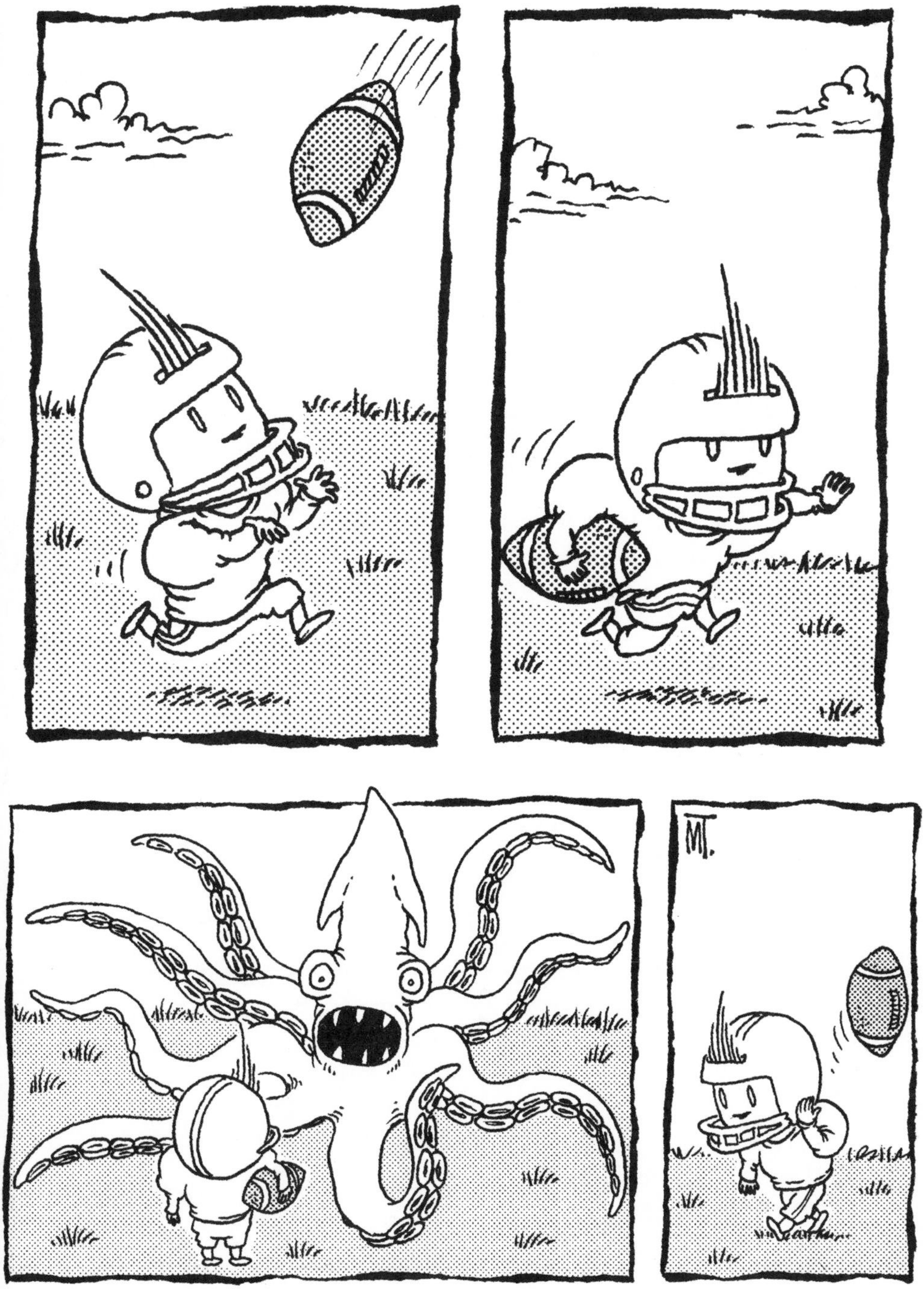

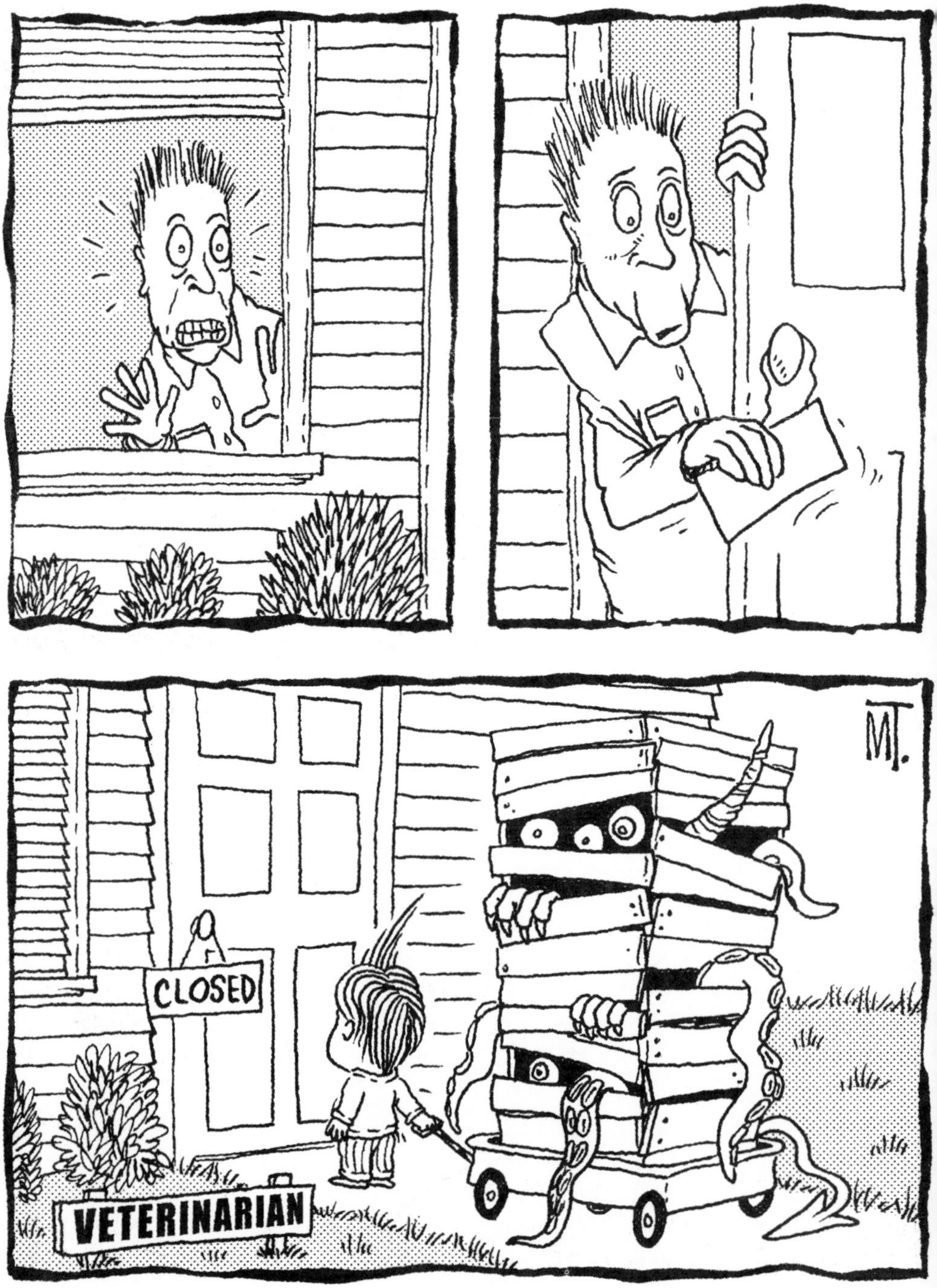
CLOSED
VETERINARIAN
MT.

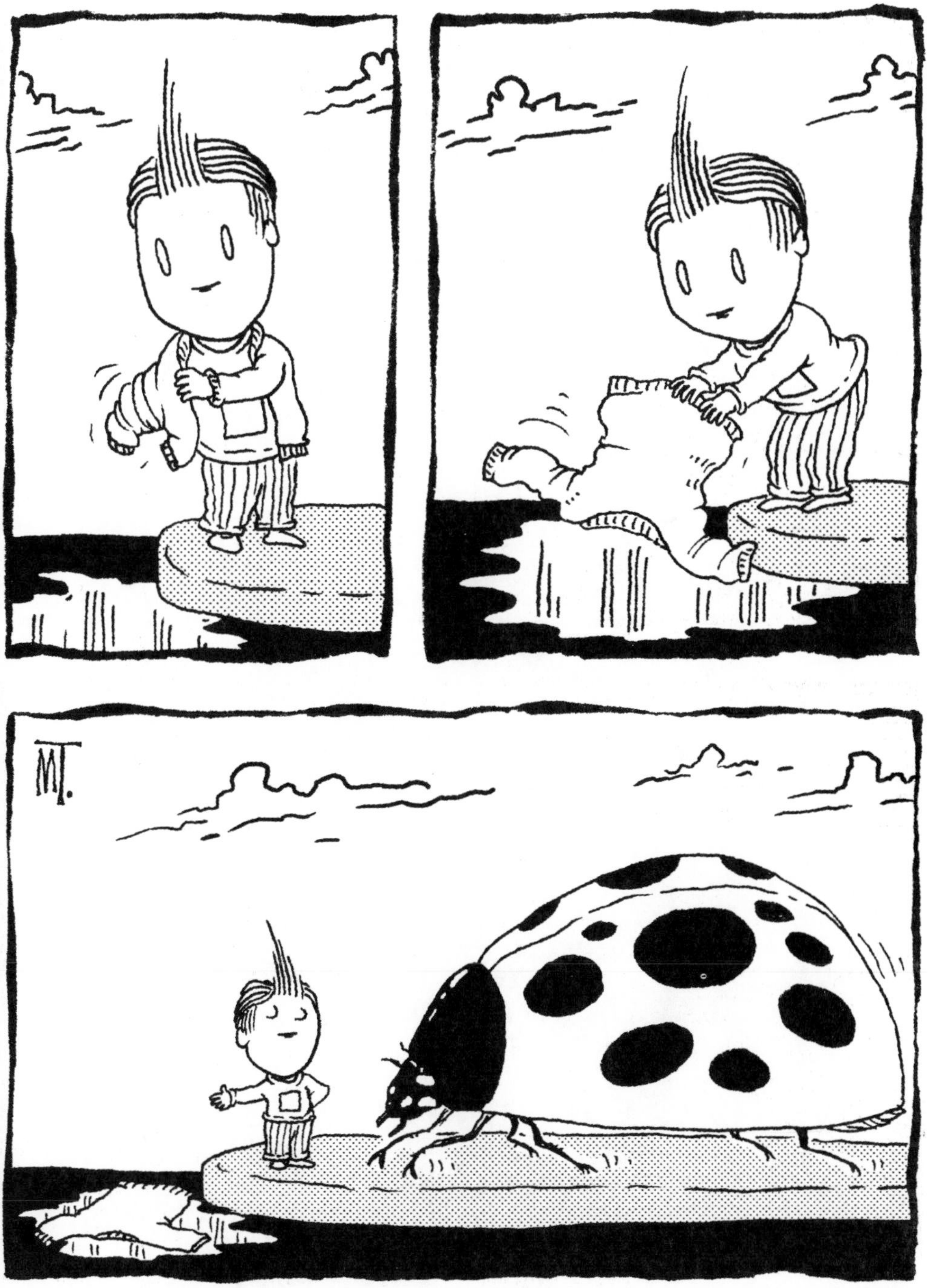

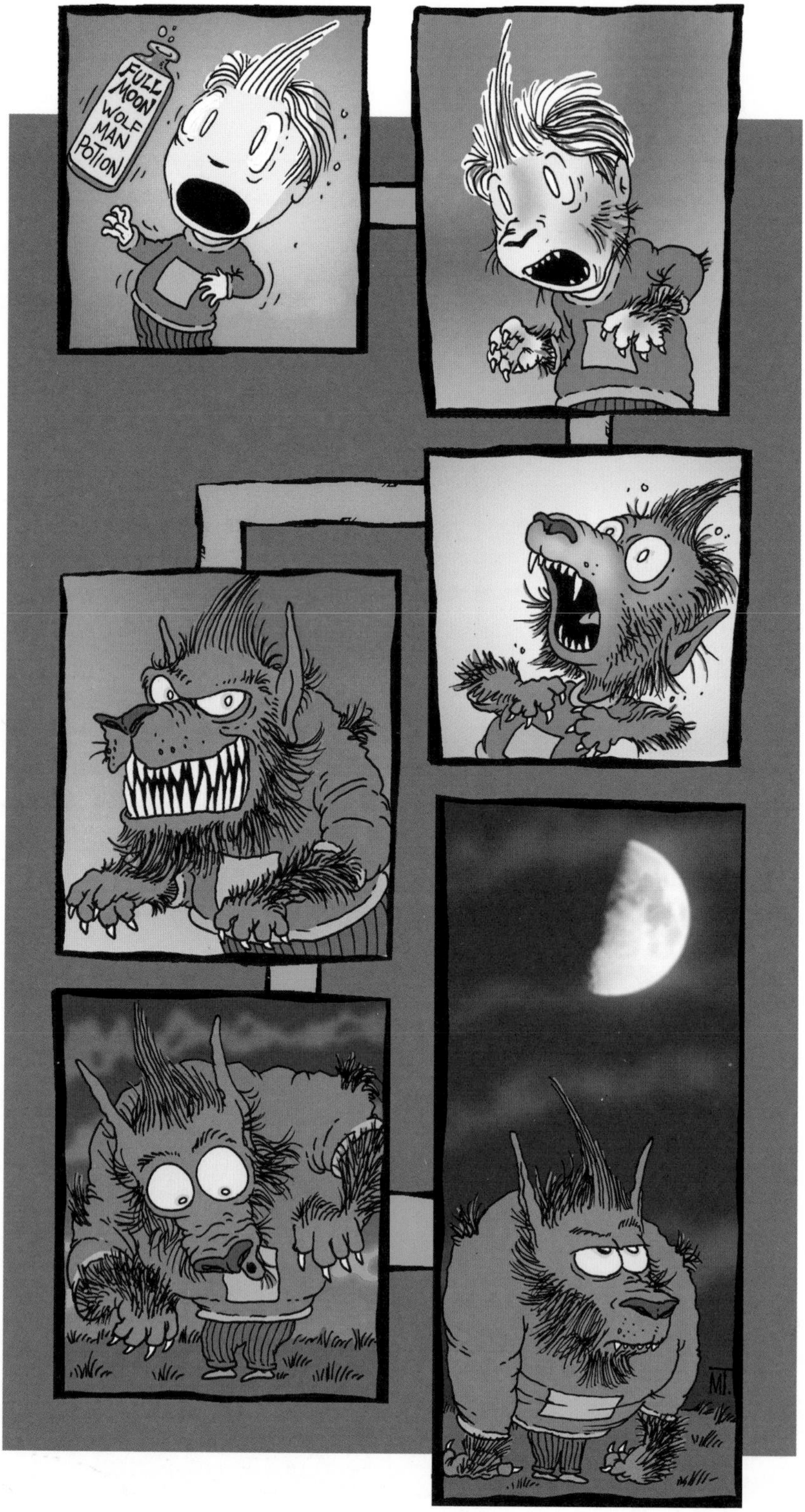
FULL MOON WOLF MAN POTION
MT.

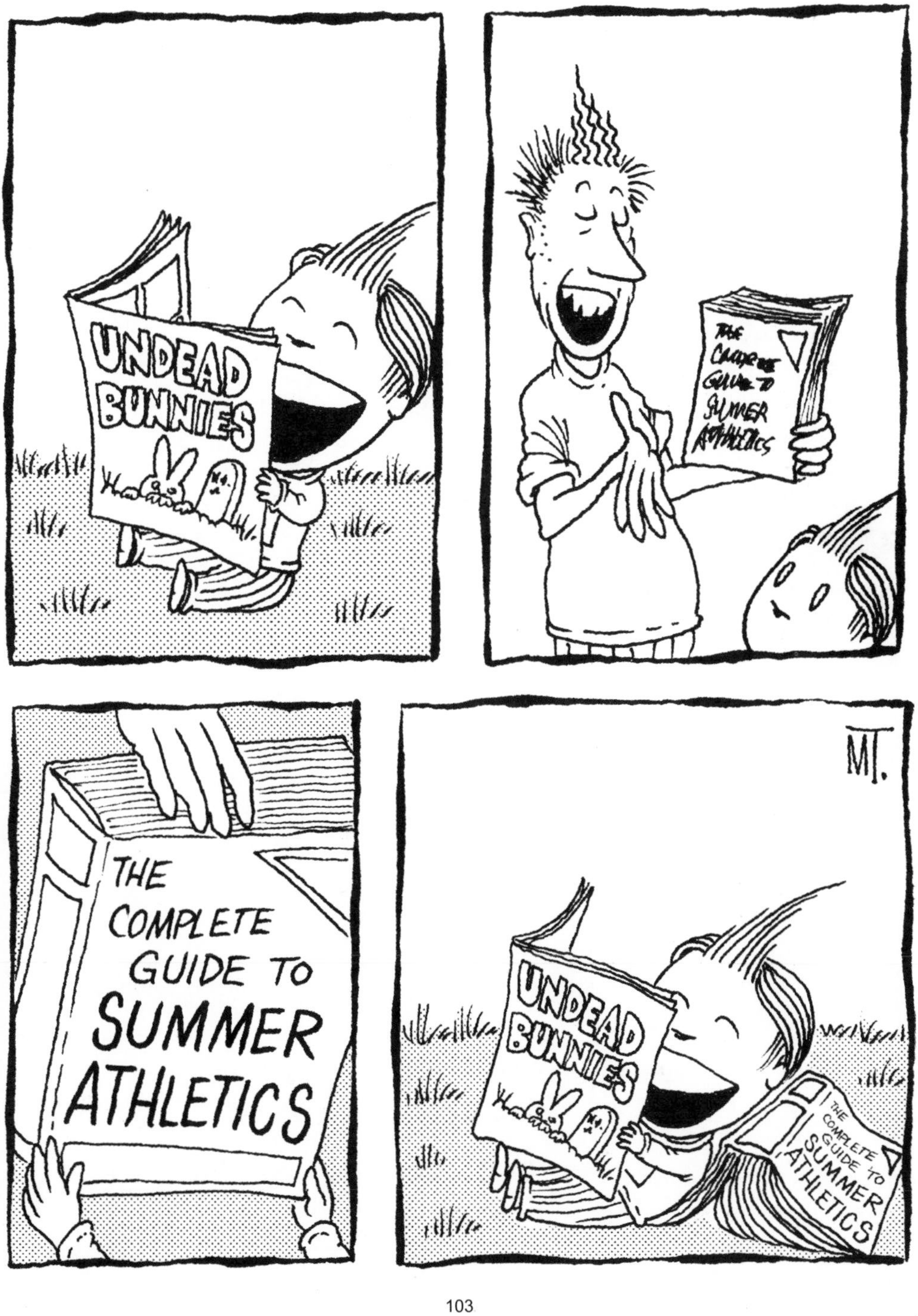
UNDEAD BUNNIES
THE COMPLETE GUIDE TO SUMMER ATHLETICS
MT.
UNDEAD BUNNIES
THE COMPLETE GUIDE TO SUMMER ATHLETICS

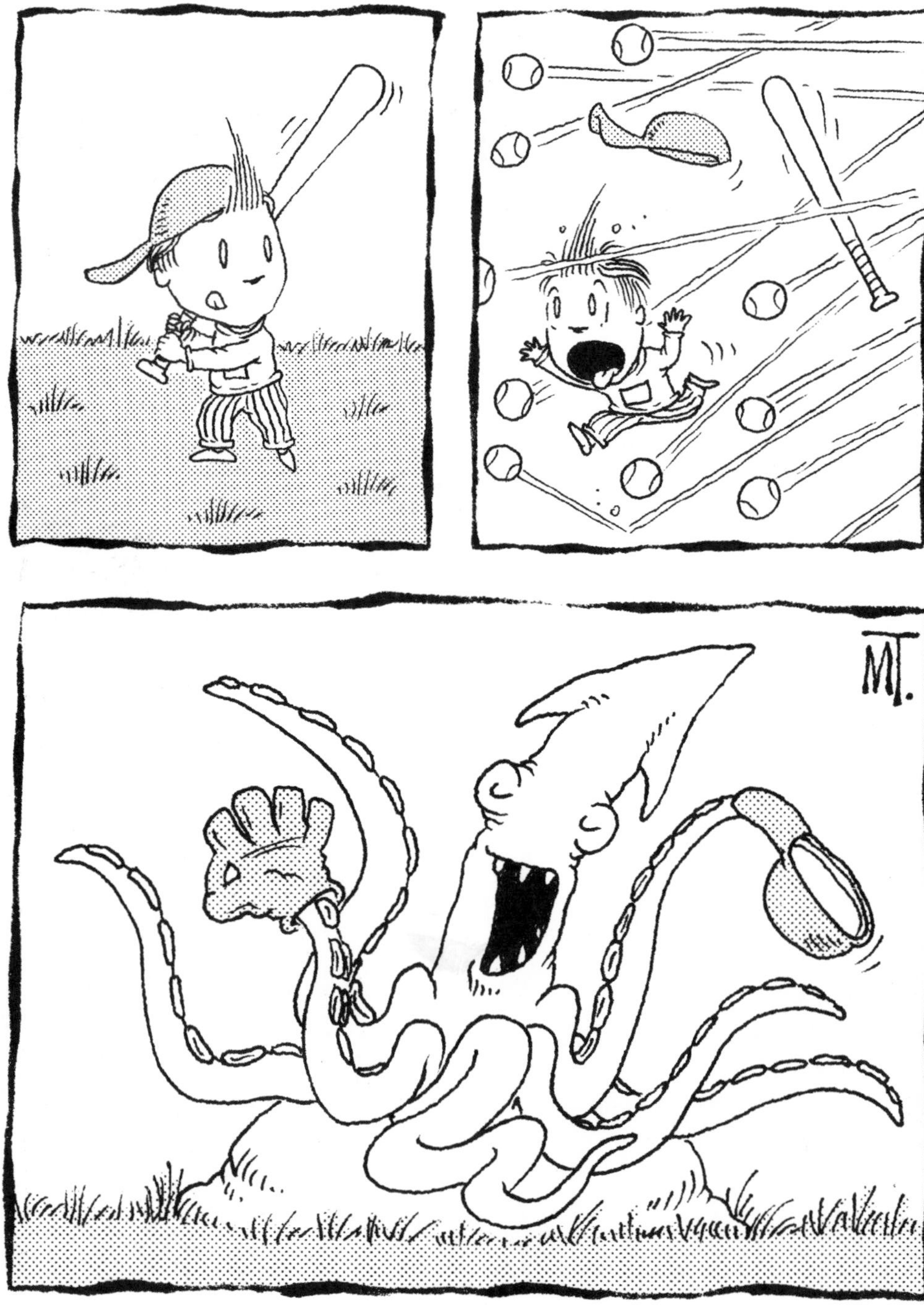
MT.

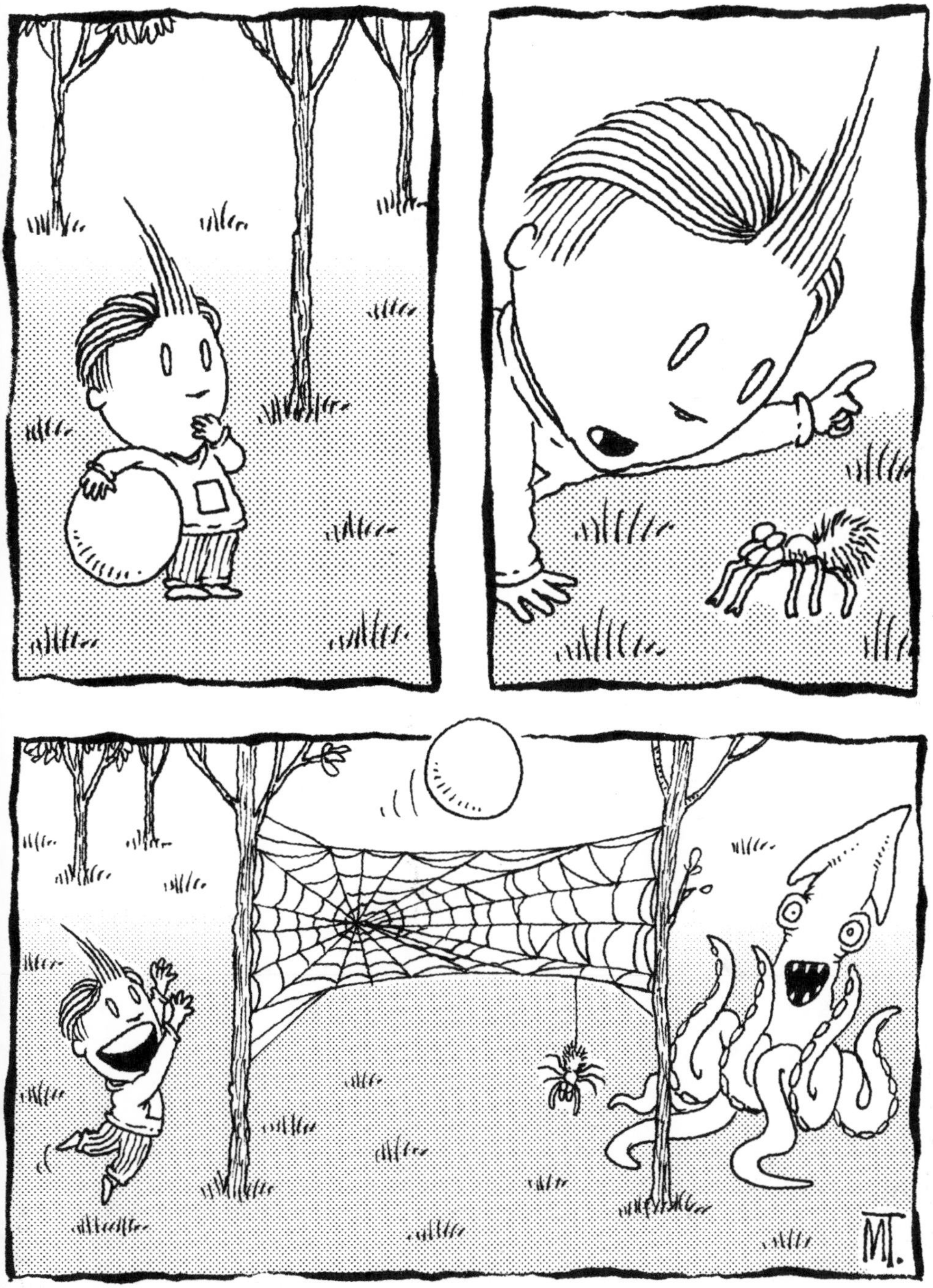
MT.

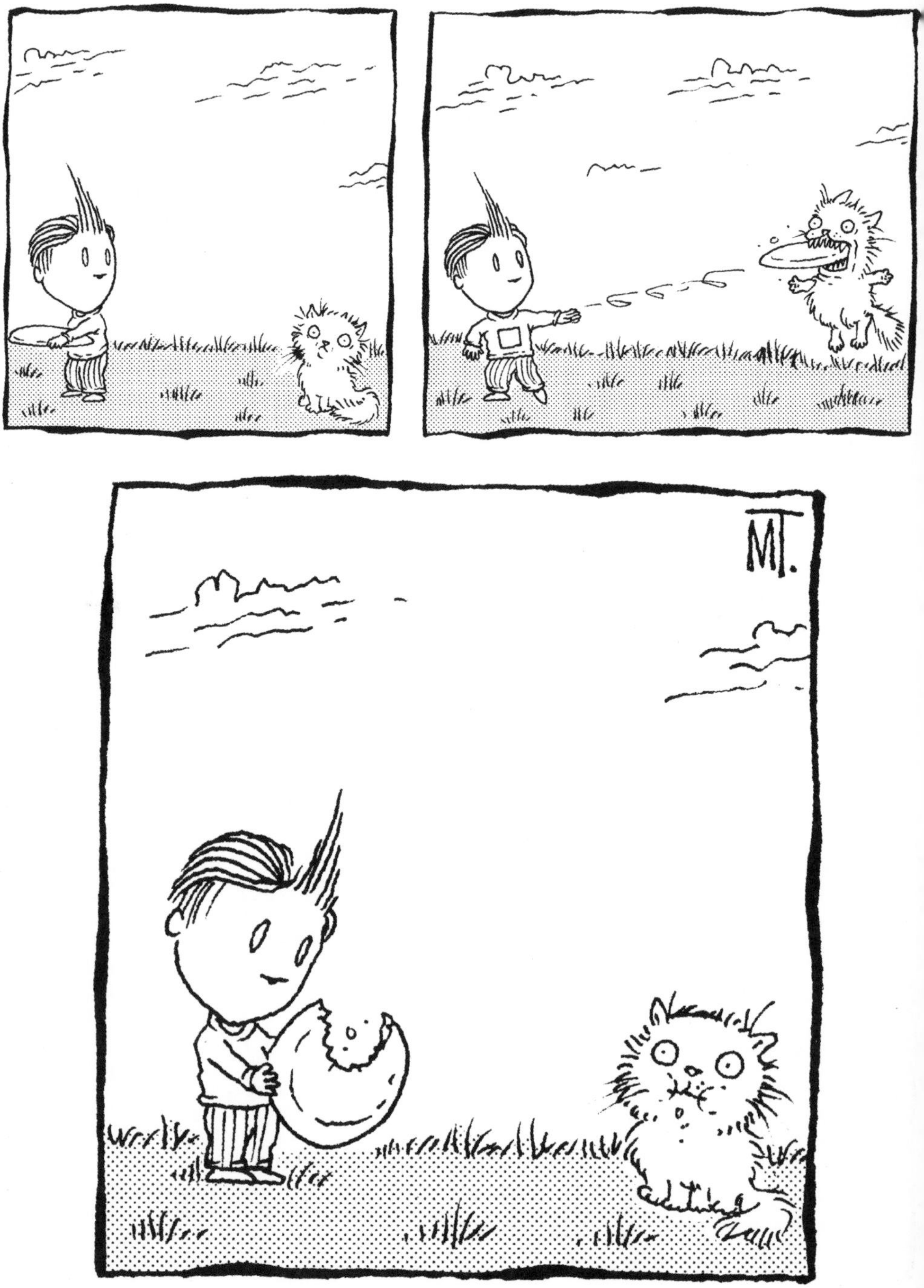
MT.

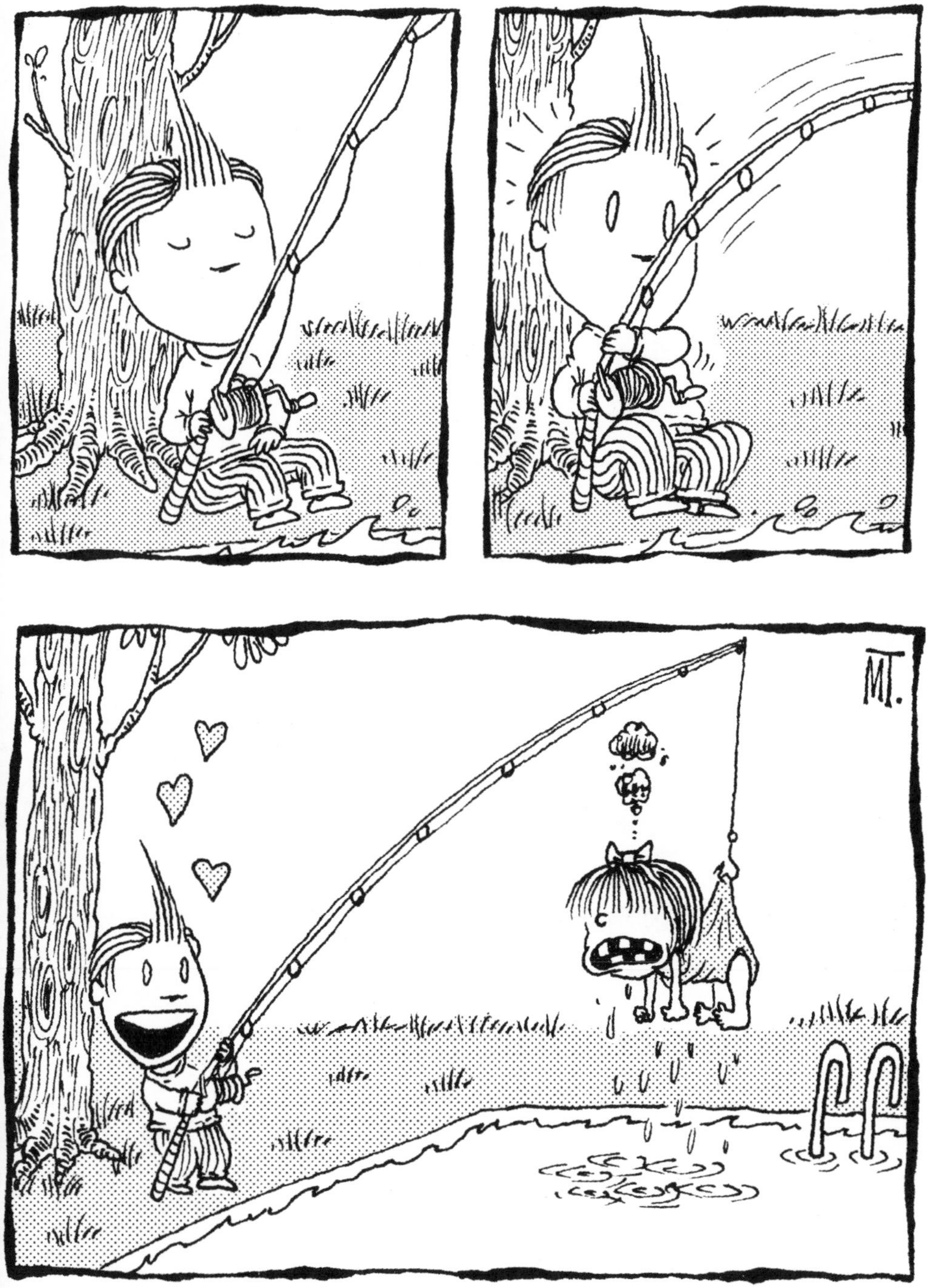
MT.

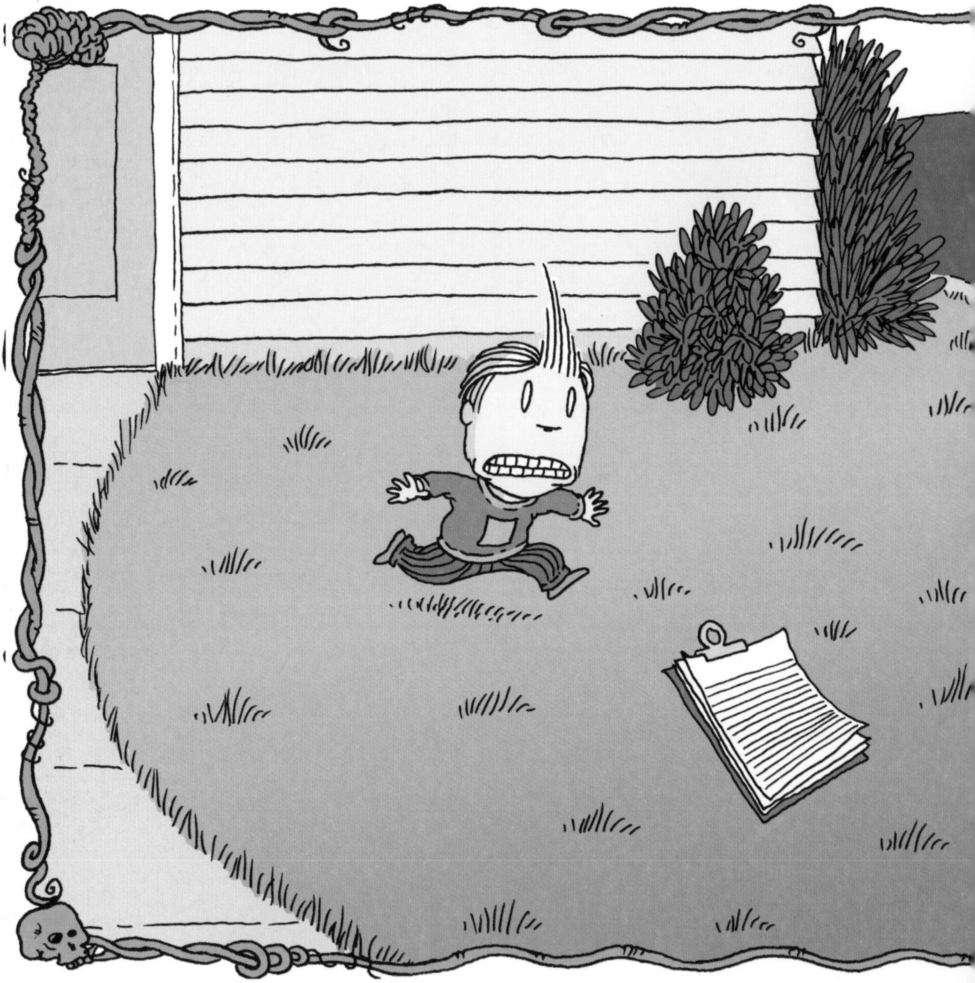

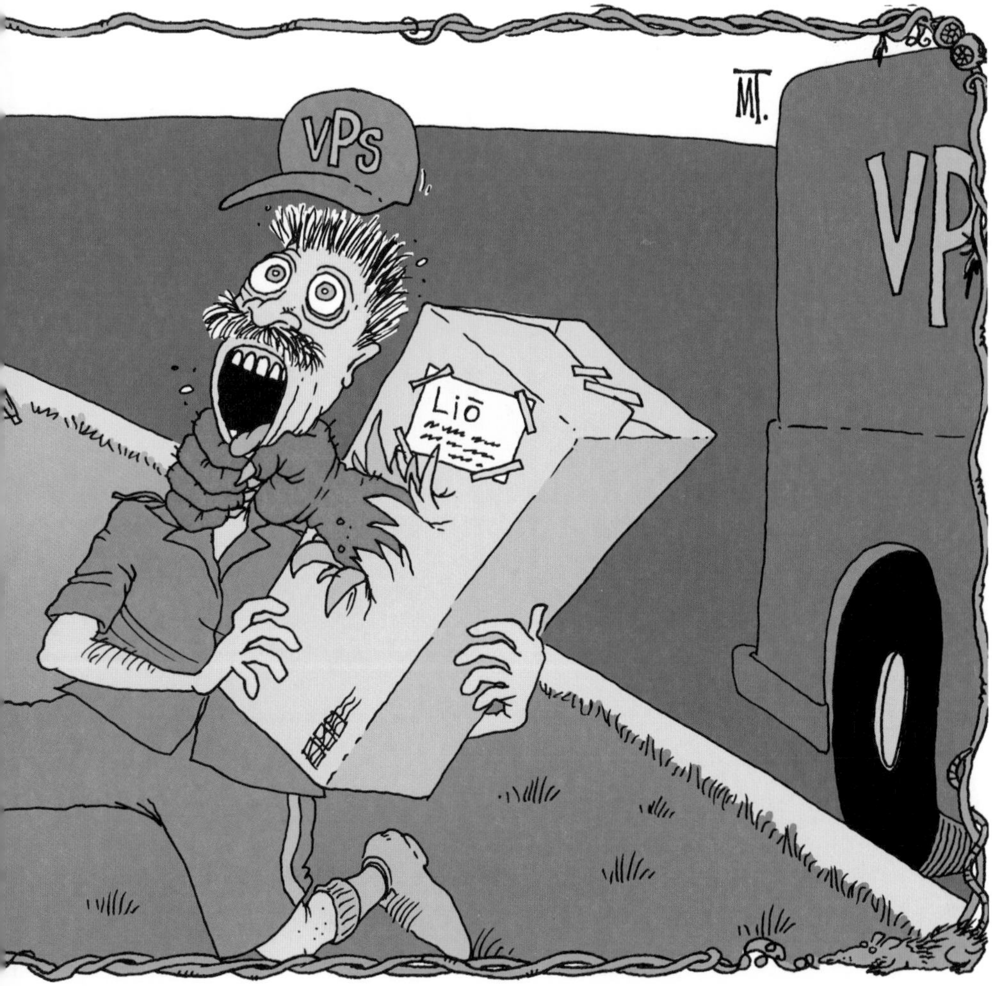
MT.
VPs
Liō
VP

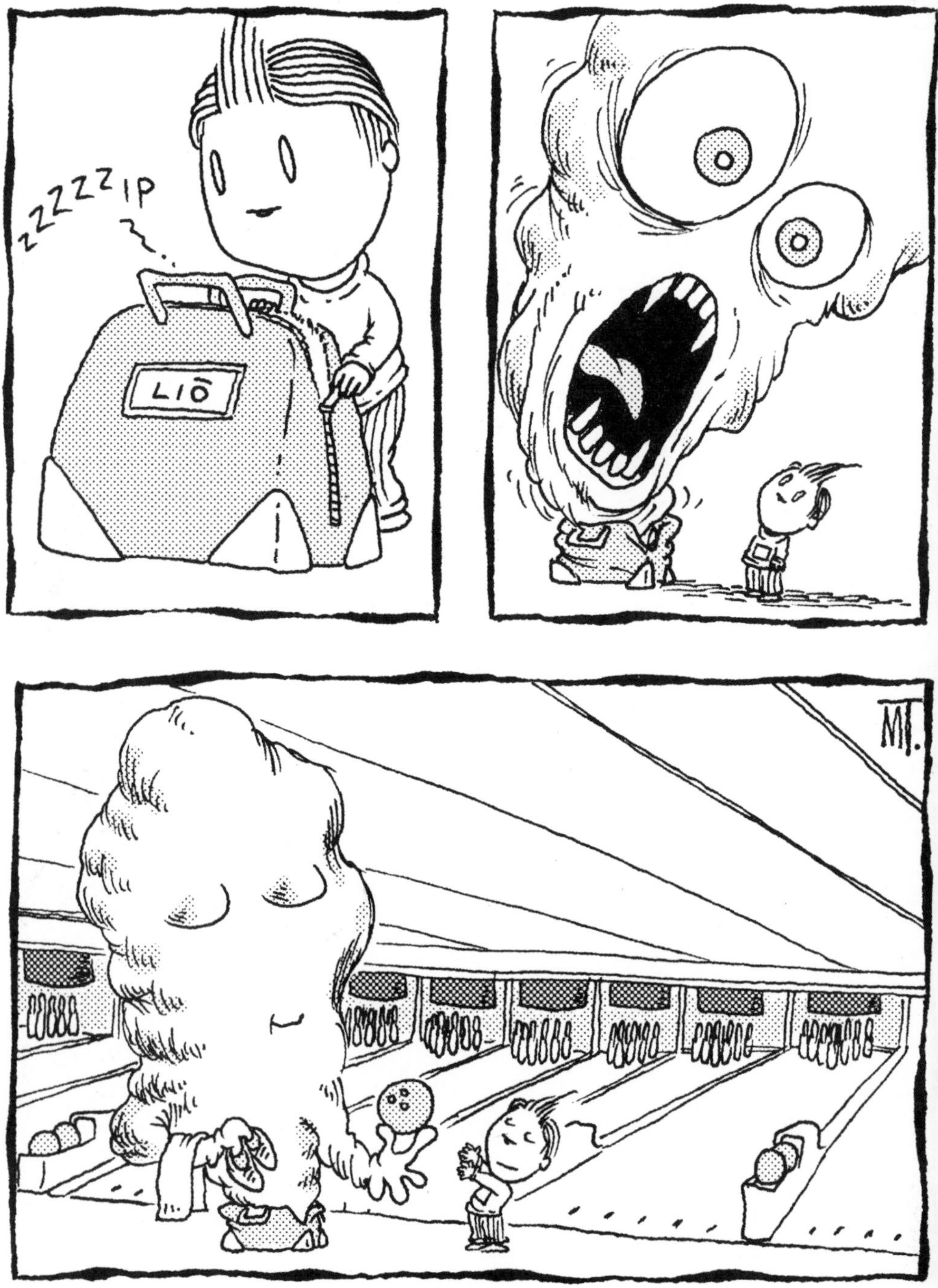

zZZZZIP
LIŌ
MT.

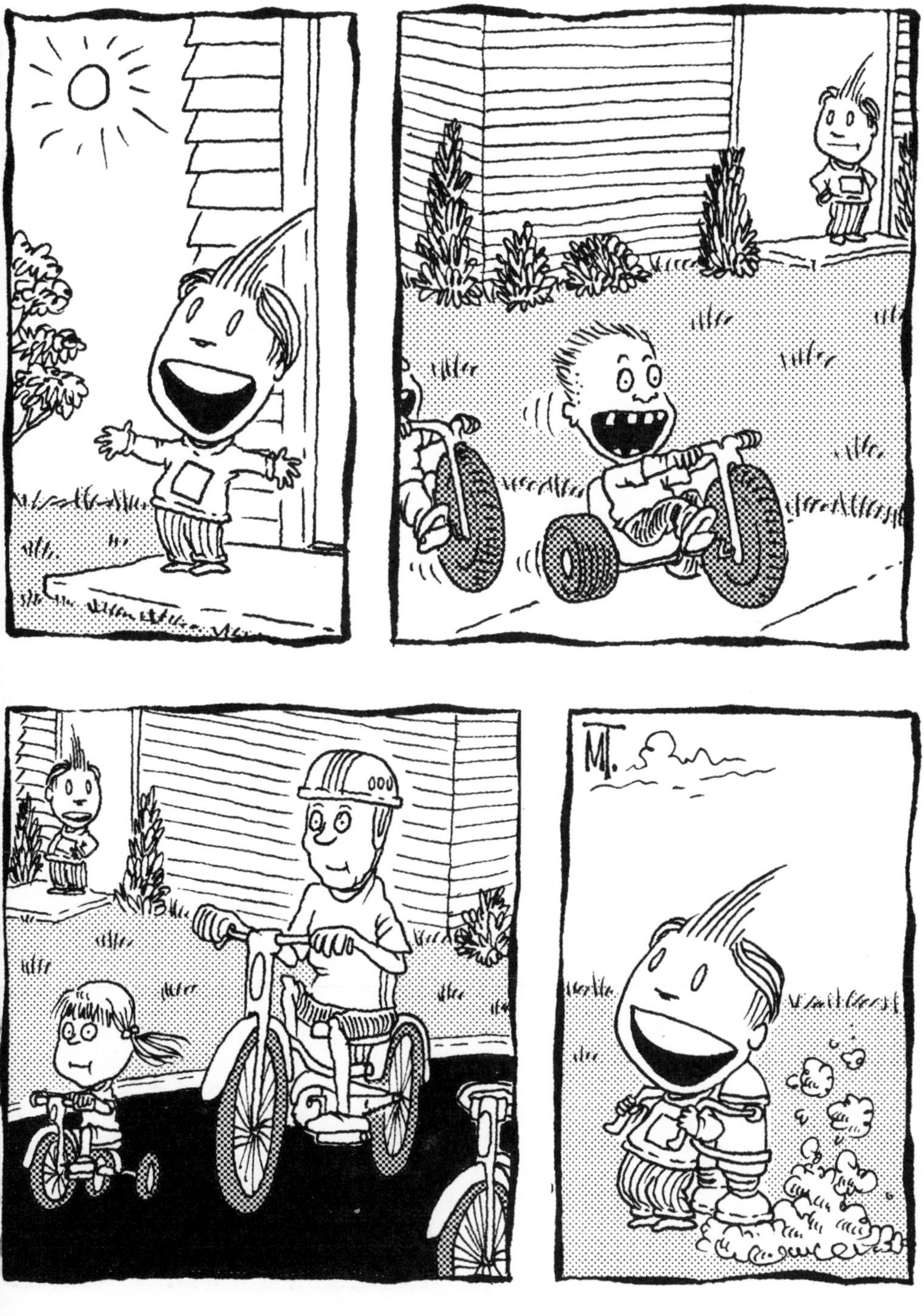
MT.

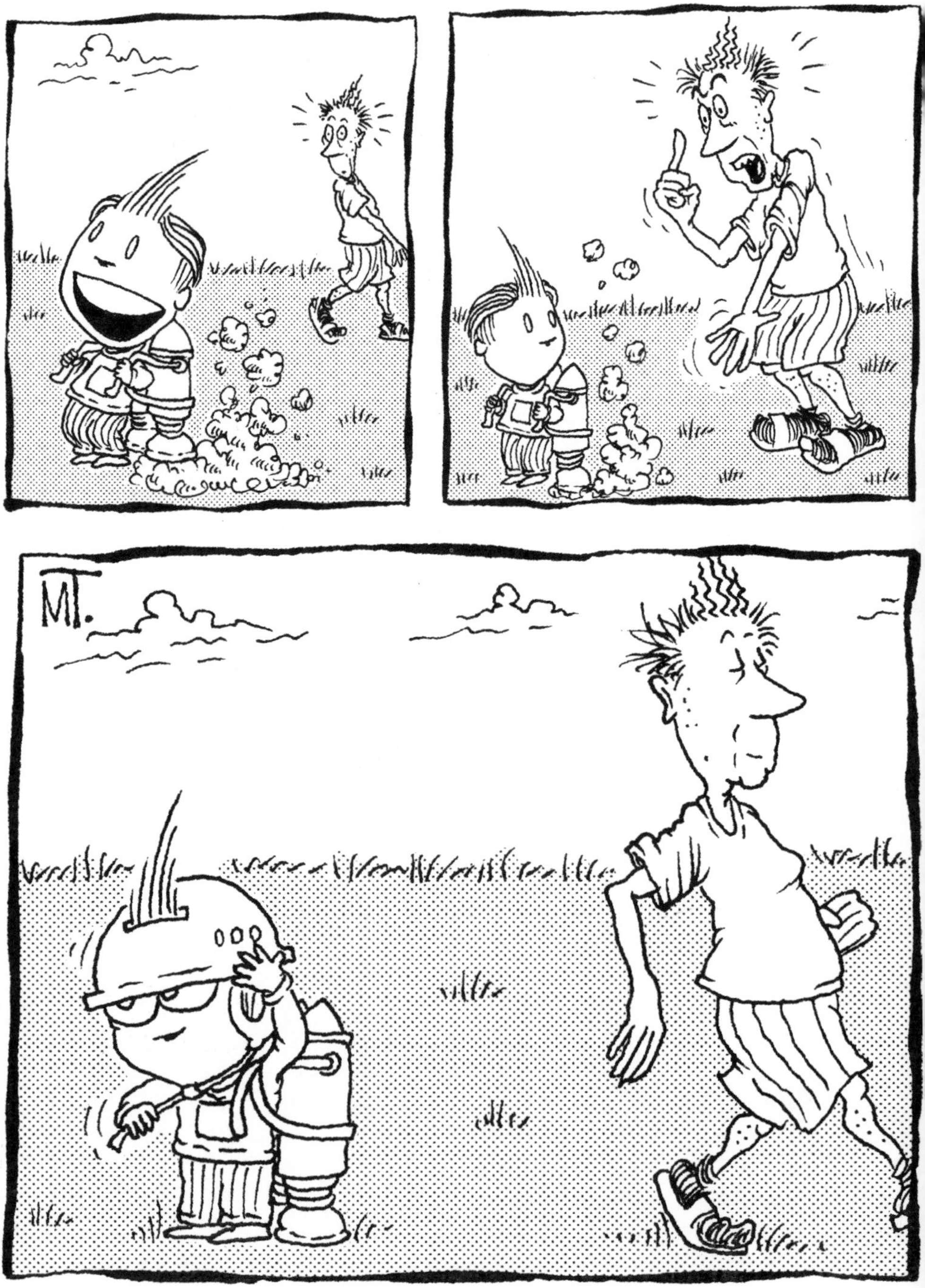

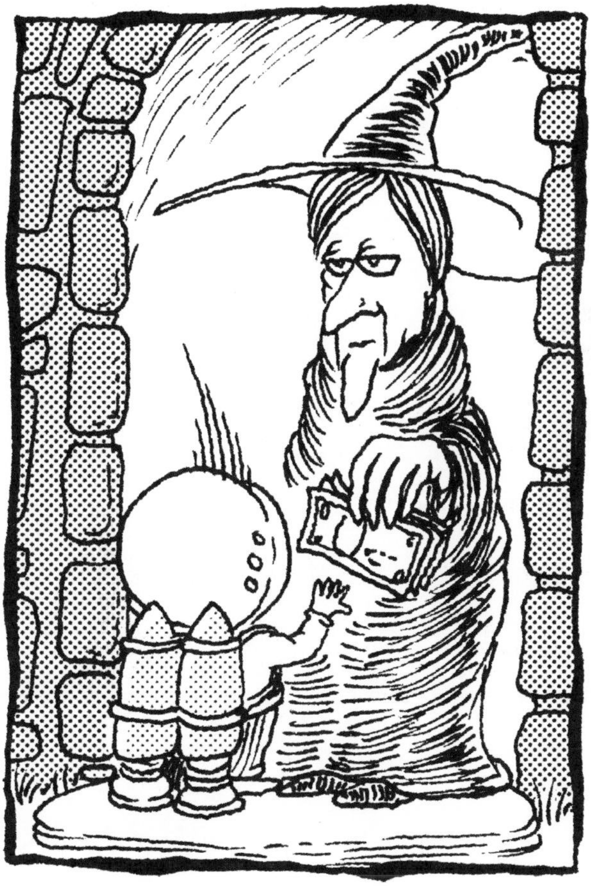

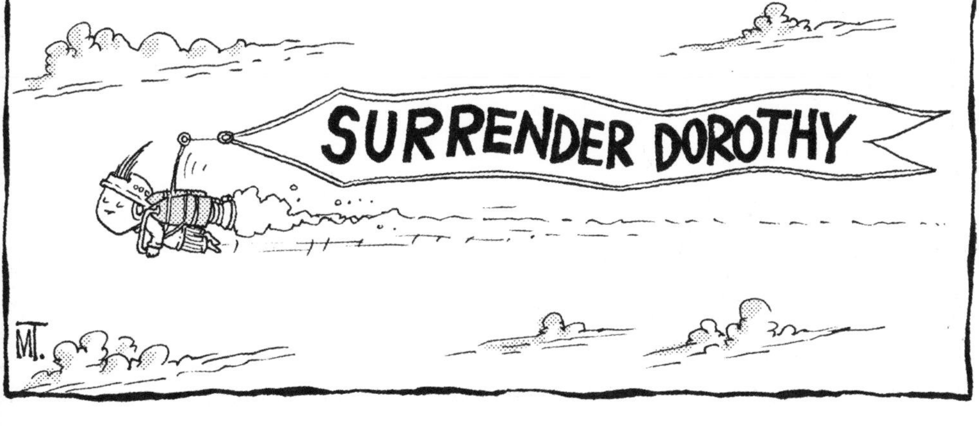

SURRENDER DOROTHY
MT.

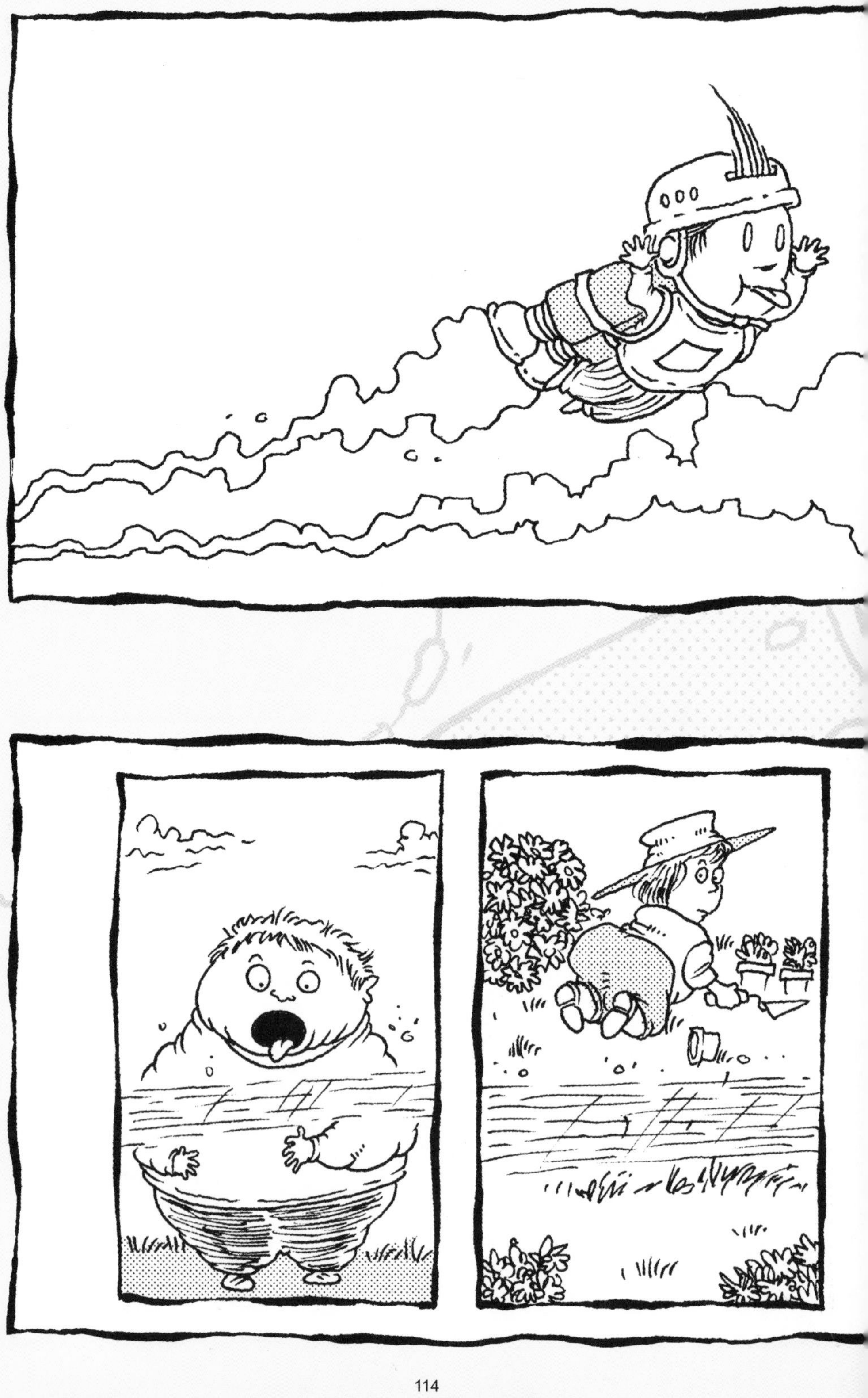

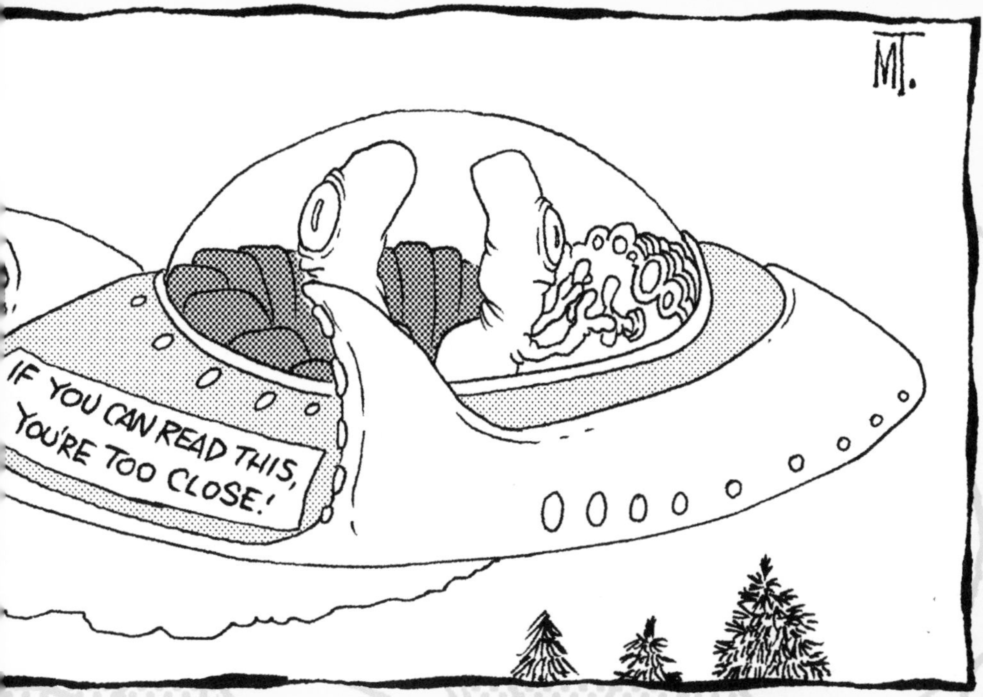
IF YOU CAN READ THIS, YOU'RE TOO CLOSE!

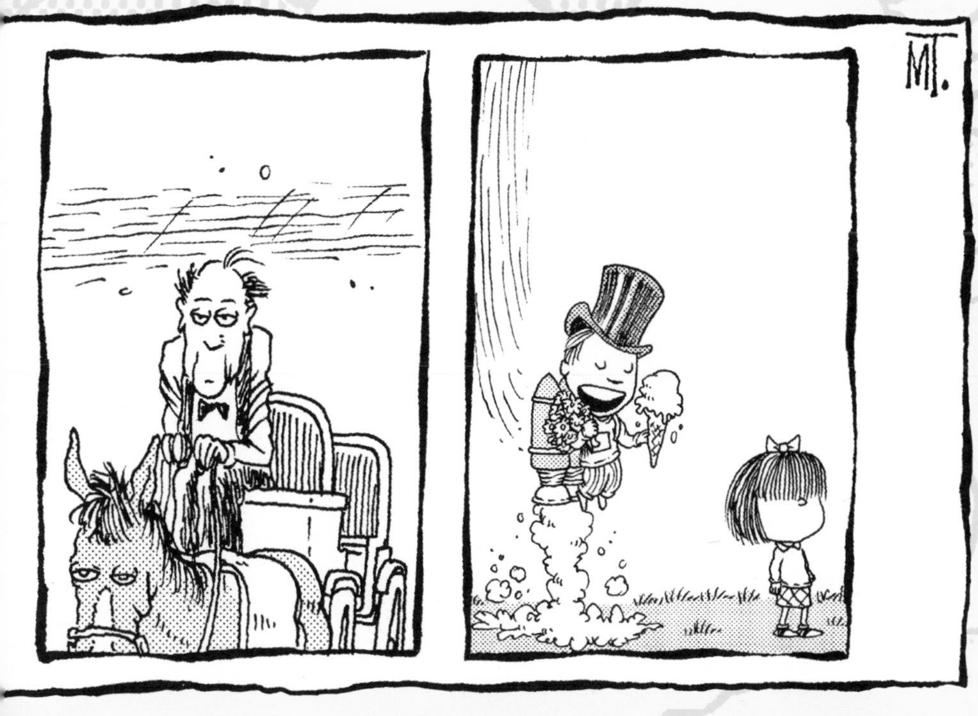

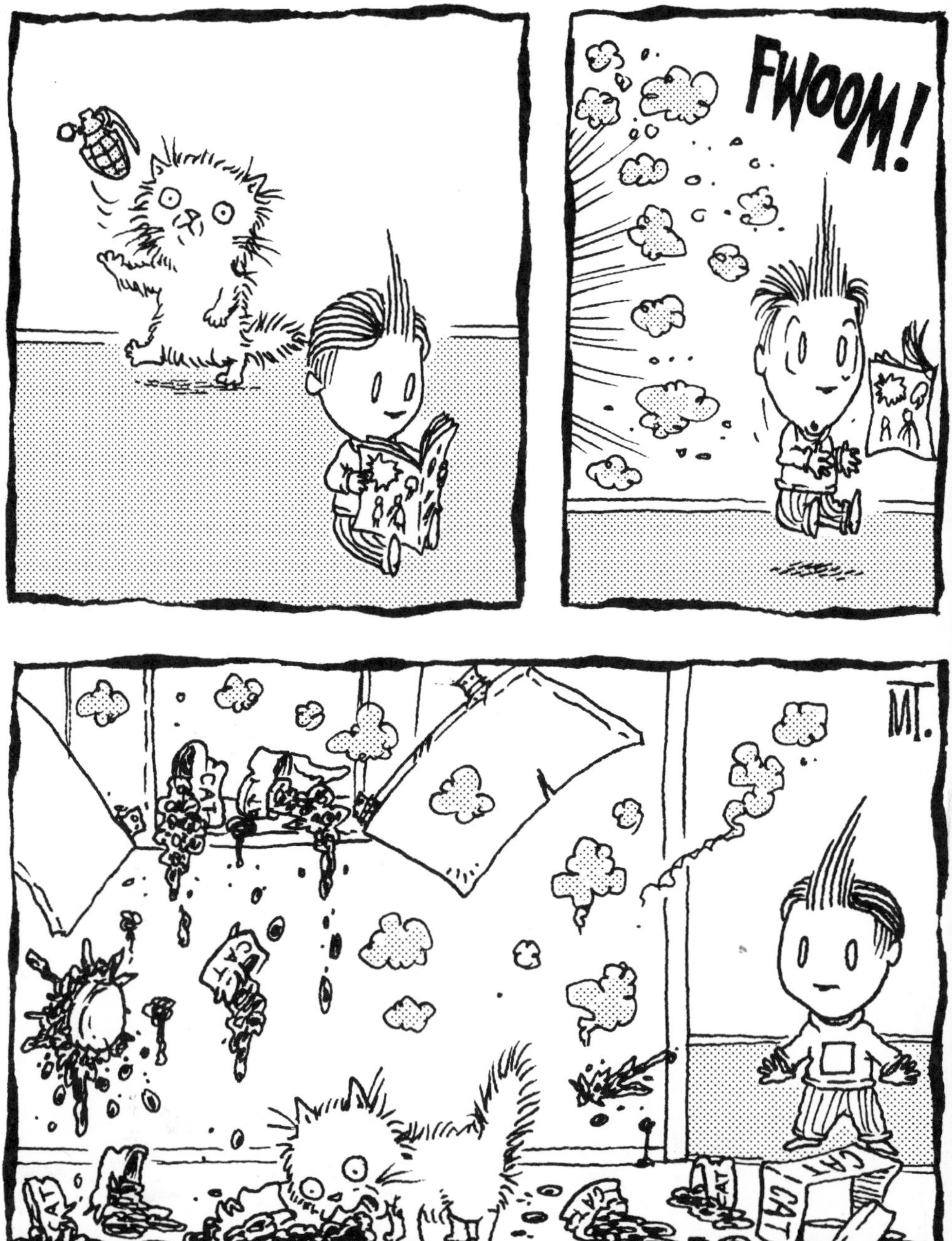
FWOOM!
CAT
CAT
CAT
CAT
CAT
MT.

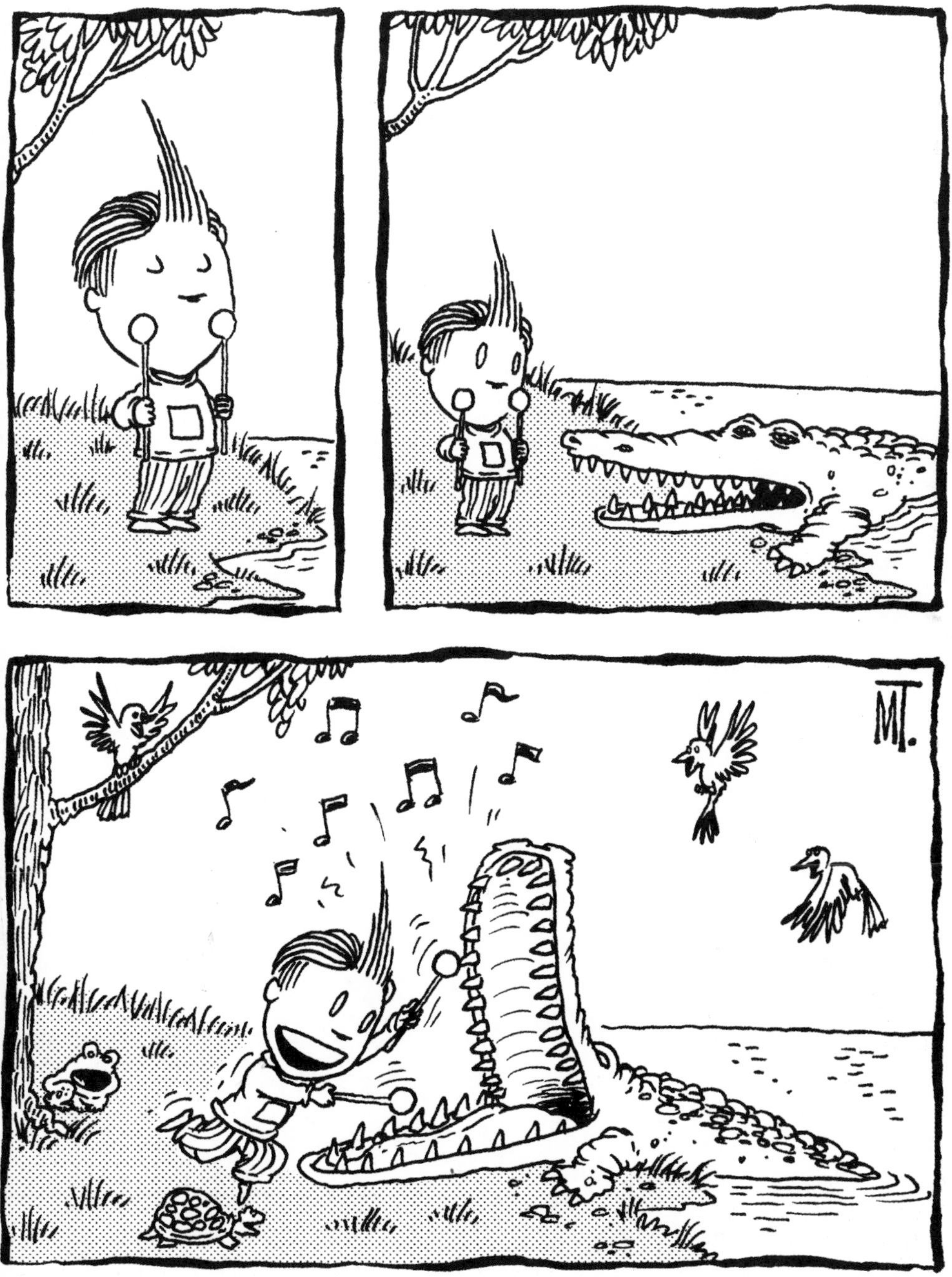
MT.

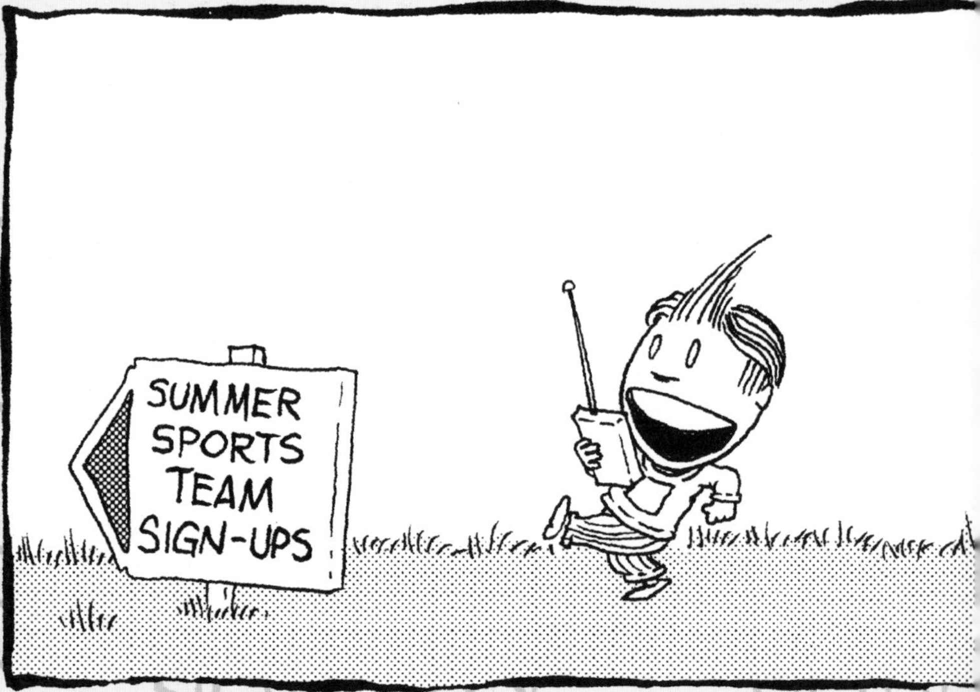
SUMMER
SPORTS
TEAM
SIGN-UPS

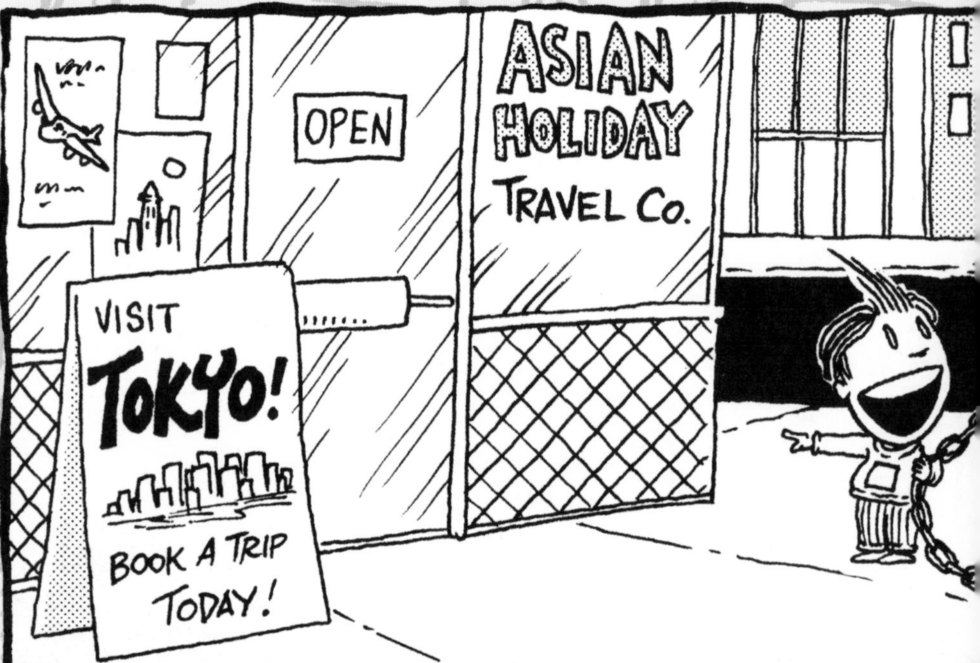
OPEN
ASIAN
HOLIDAY
TRAVEL Co.
VISIT
TOKYO!
BOOK A TRIP
TODAY!

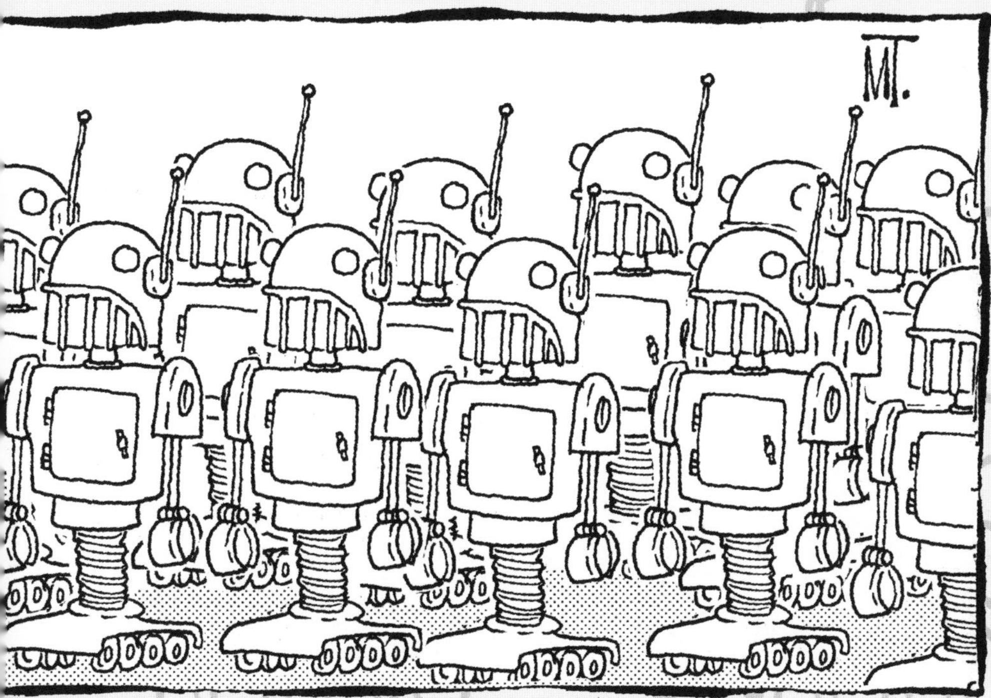
MT.

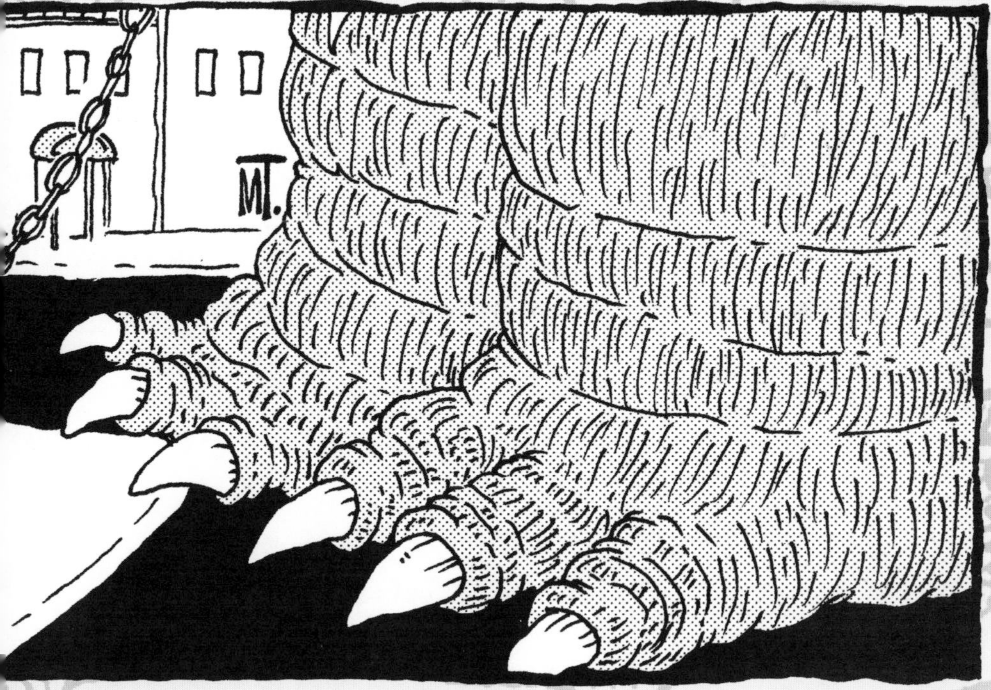
MT.

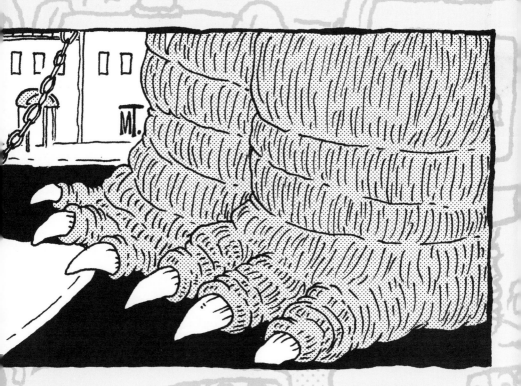

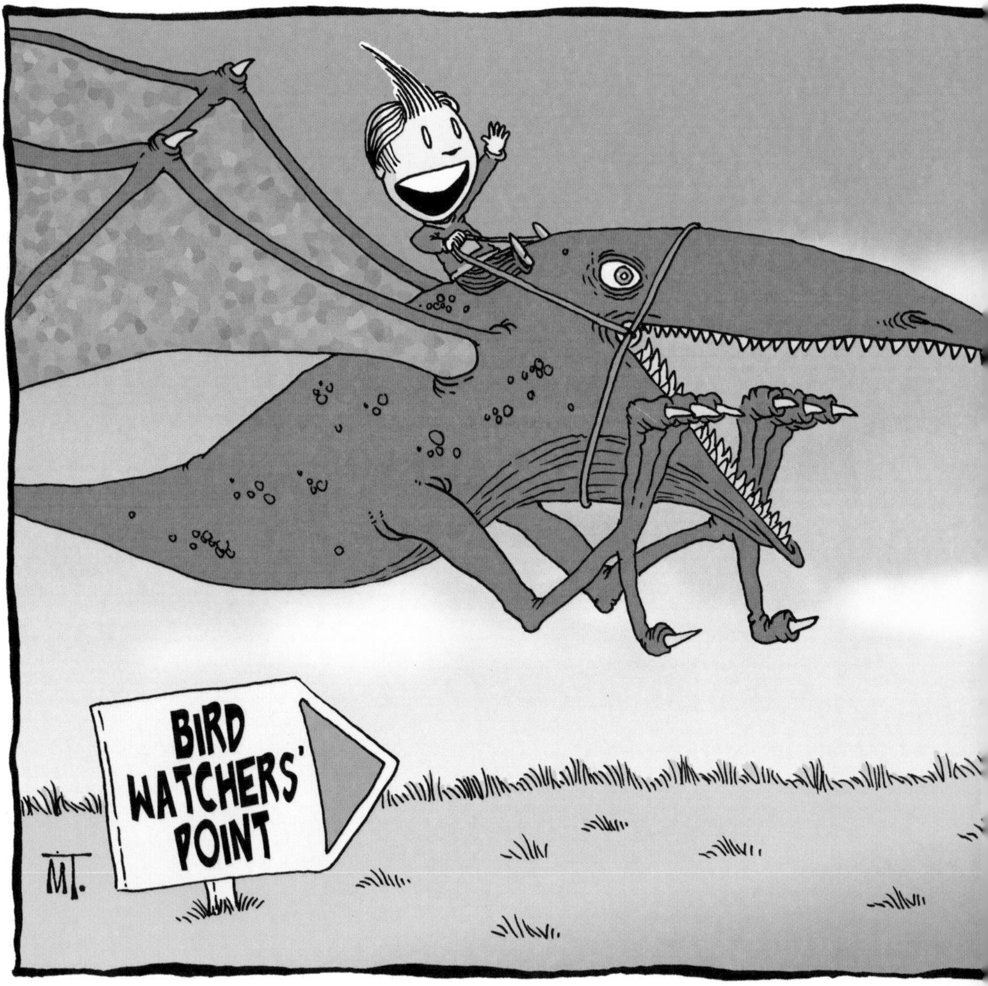
BIRD WATCHERS' POINT
MT.

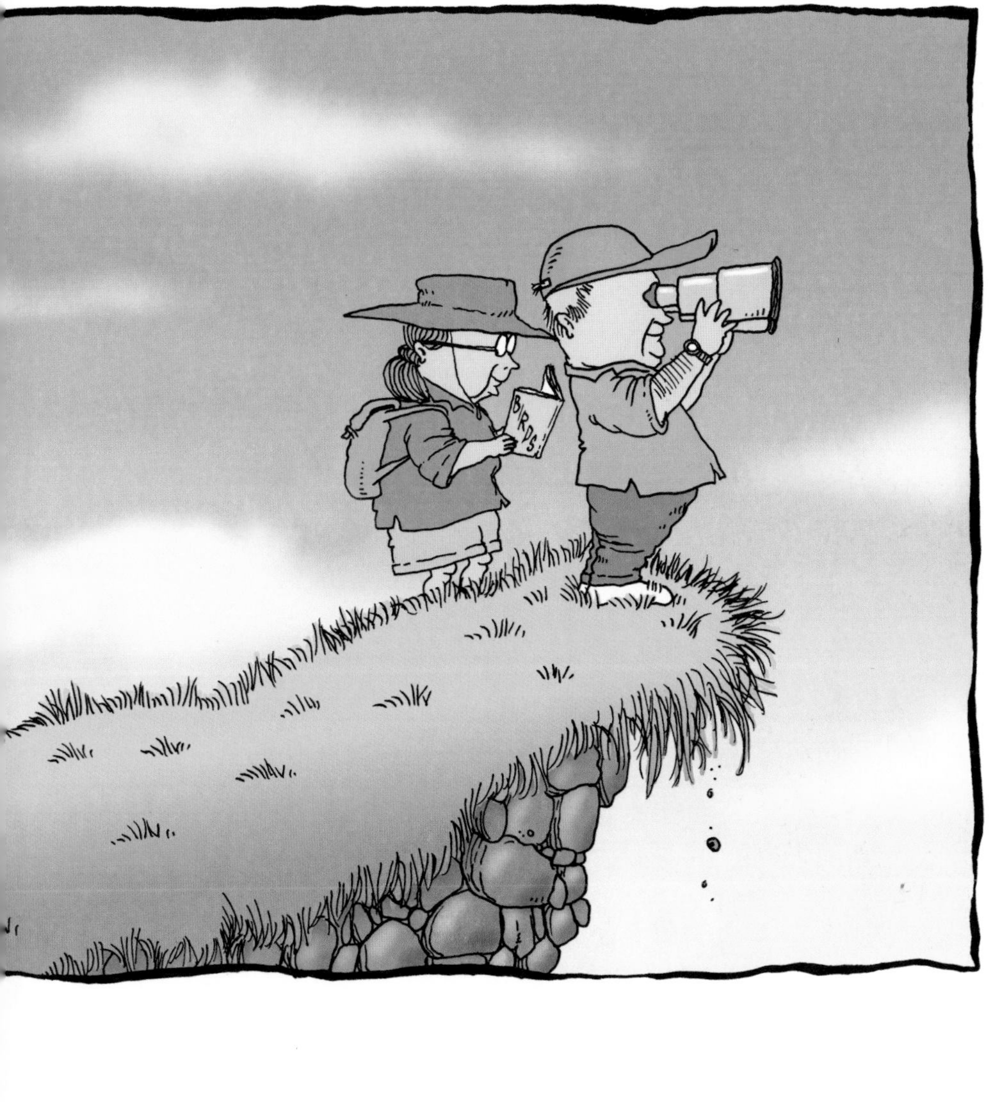
BIRDS

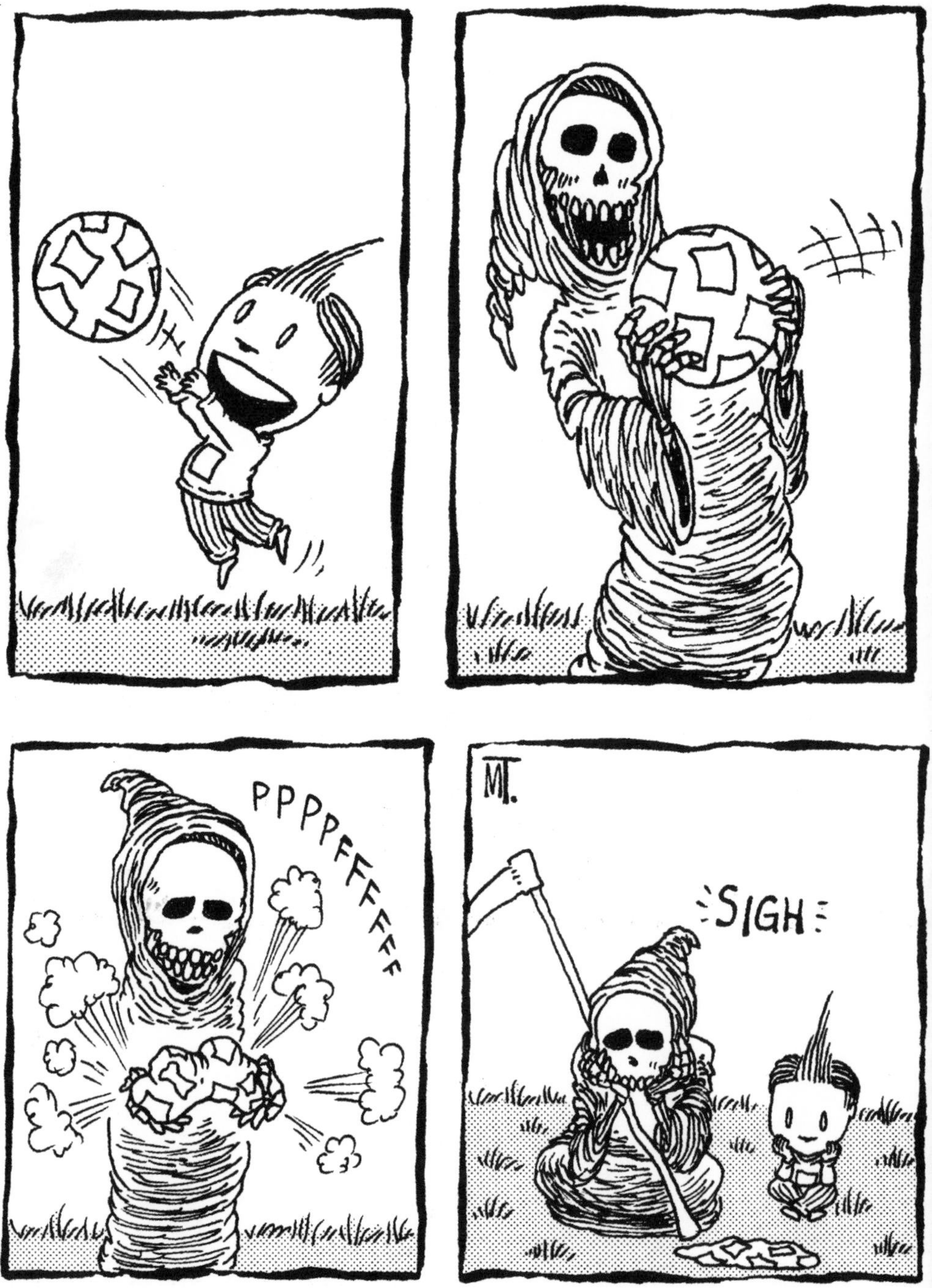
PPPPFFFFFFFF
MT.
SIGH

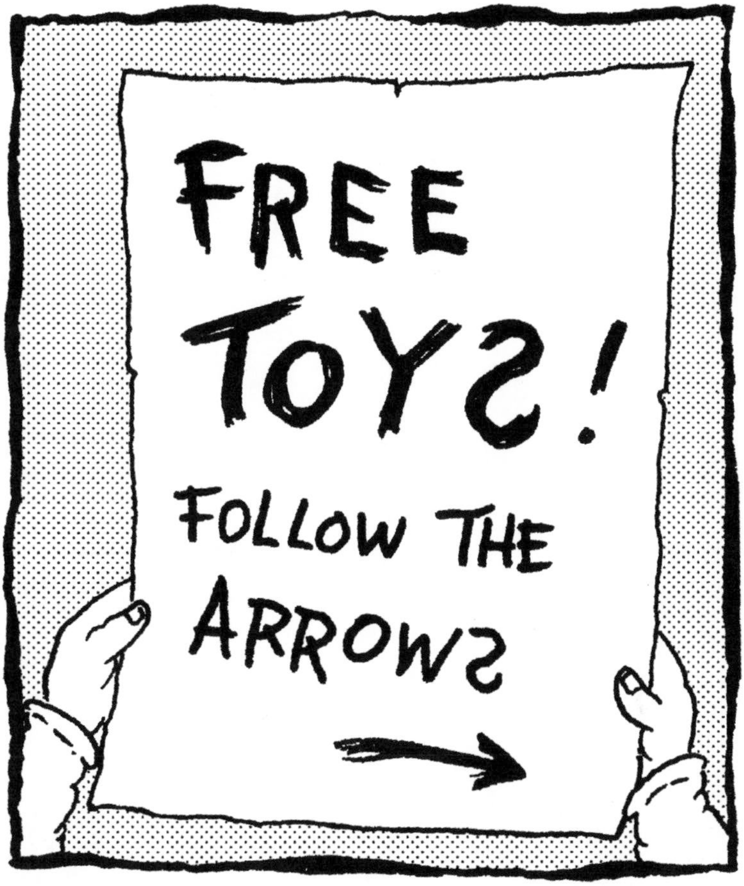
FREE
TOYS!
FOLLOW THE
ARROWS

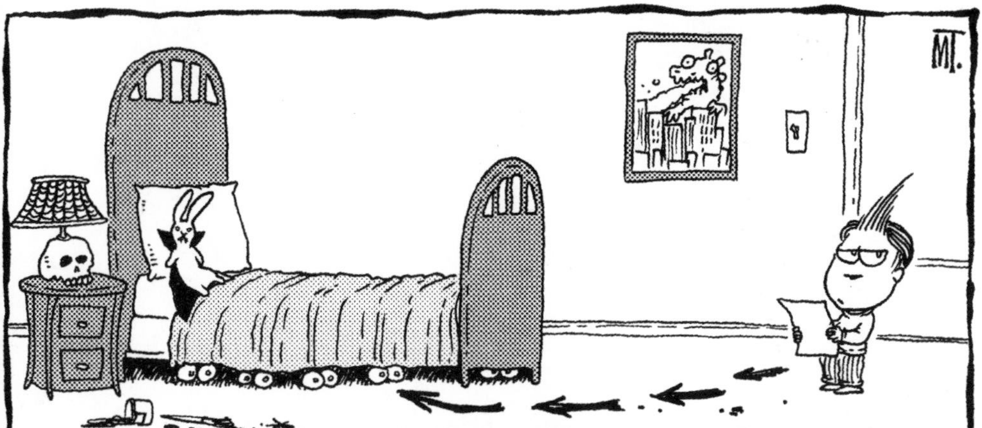
MT.

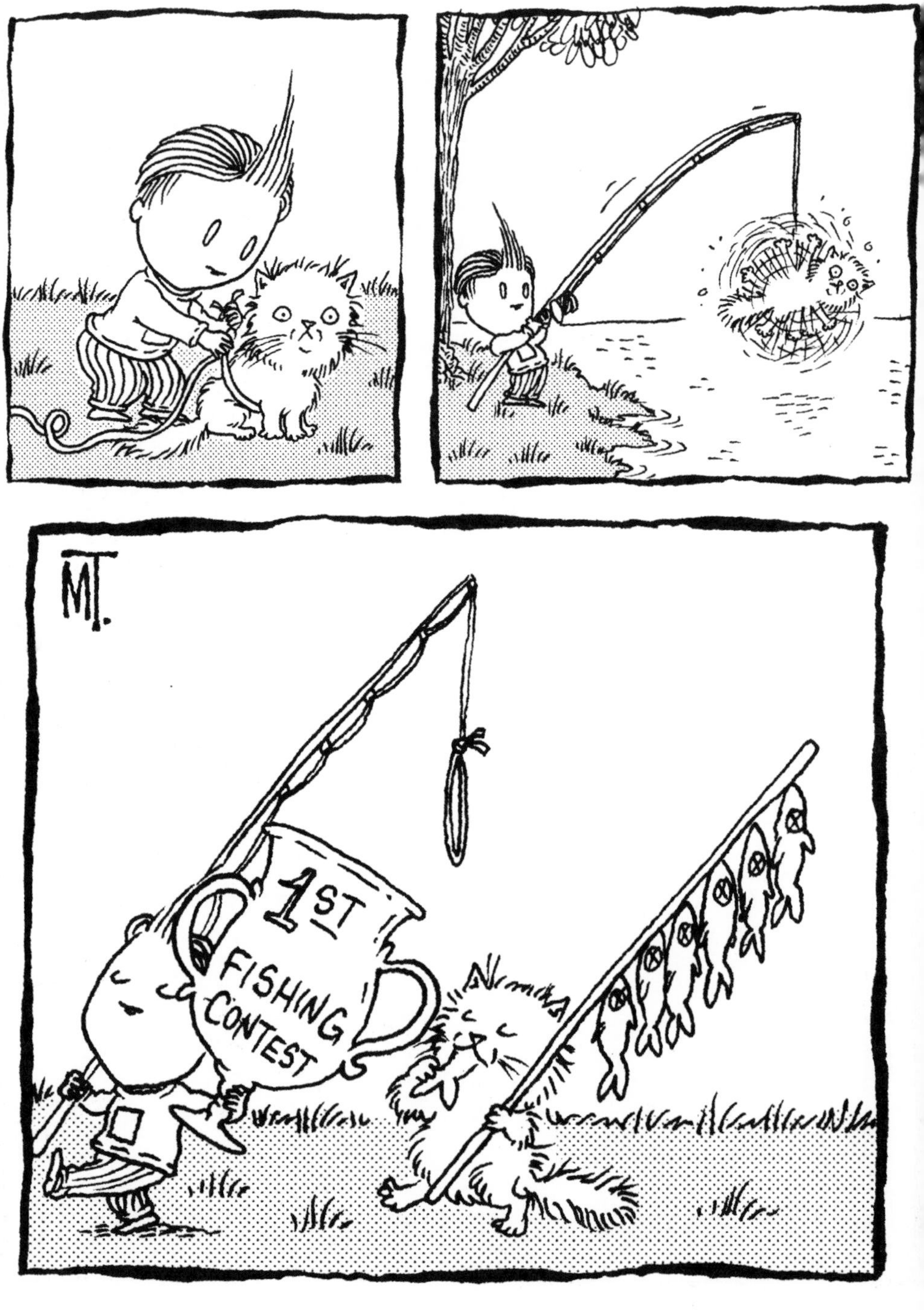
MT.
1ST
FISHING CONTEST

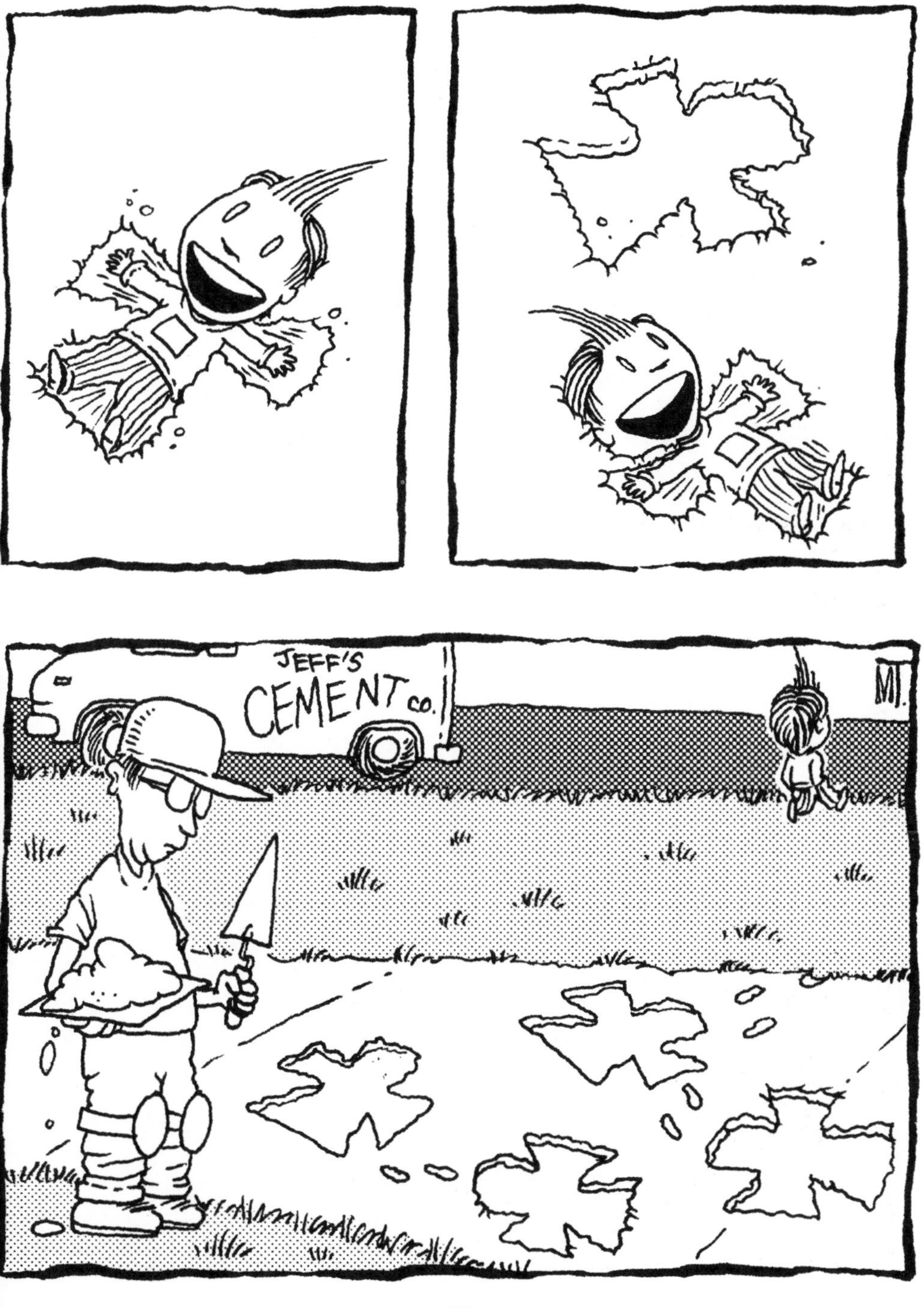

JEFF'S
CEMENT CO.
MT.

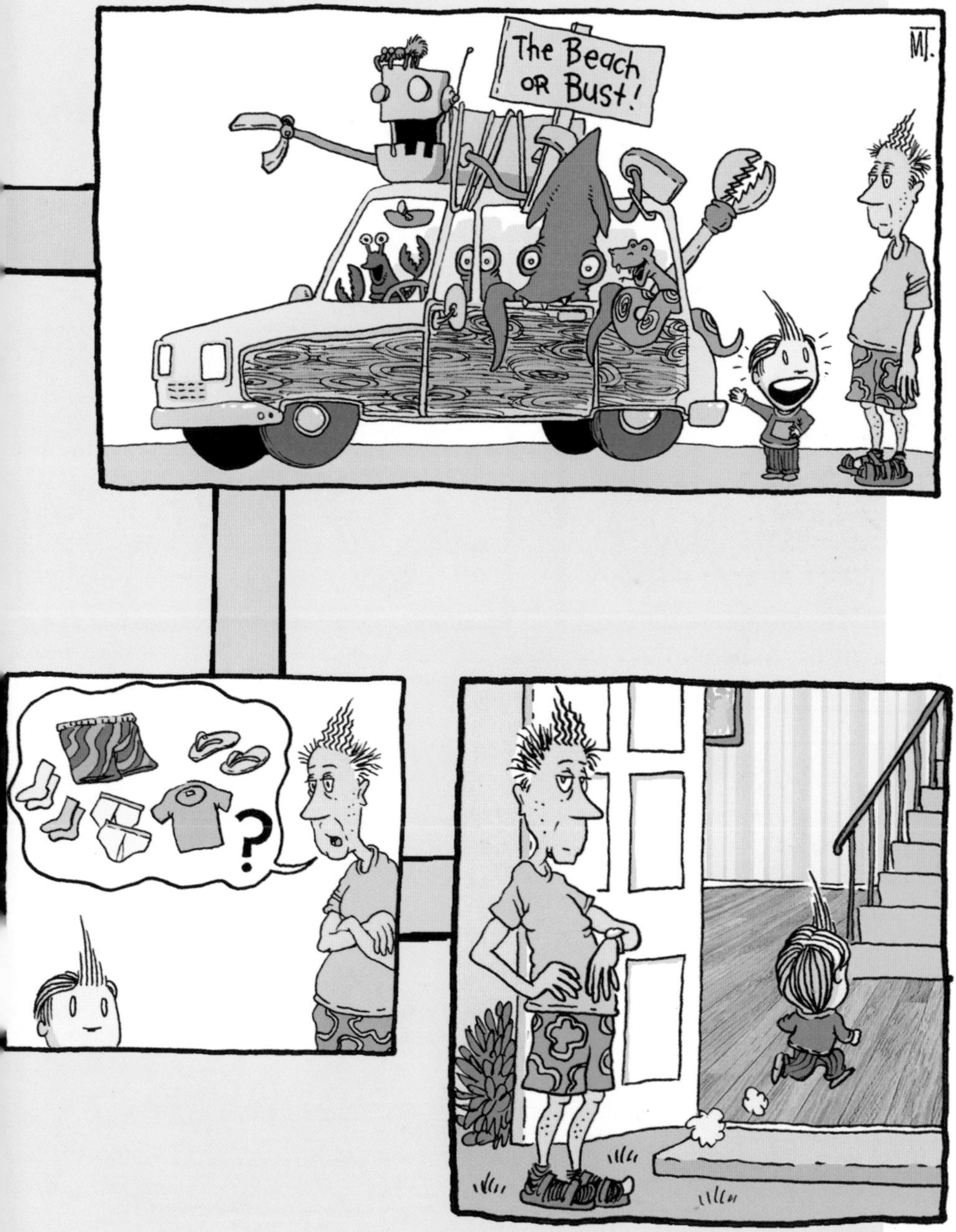
The Beach OR Bust!
MT.
?

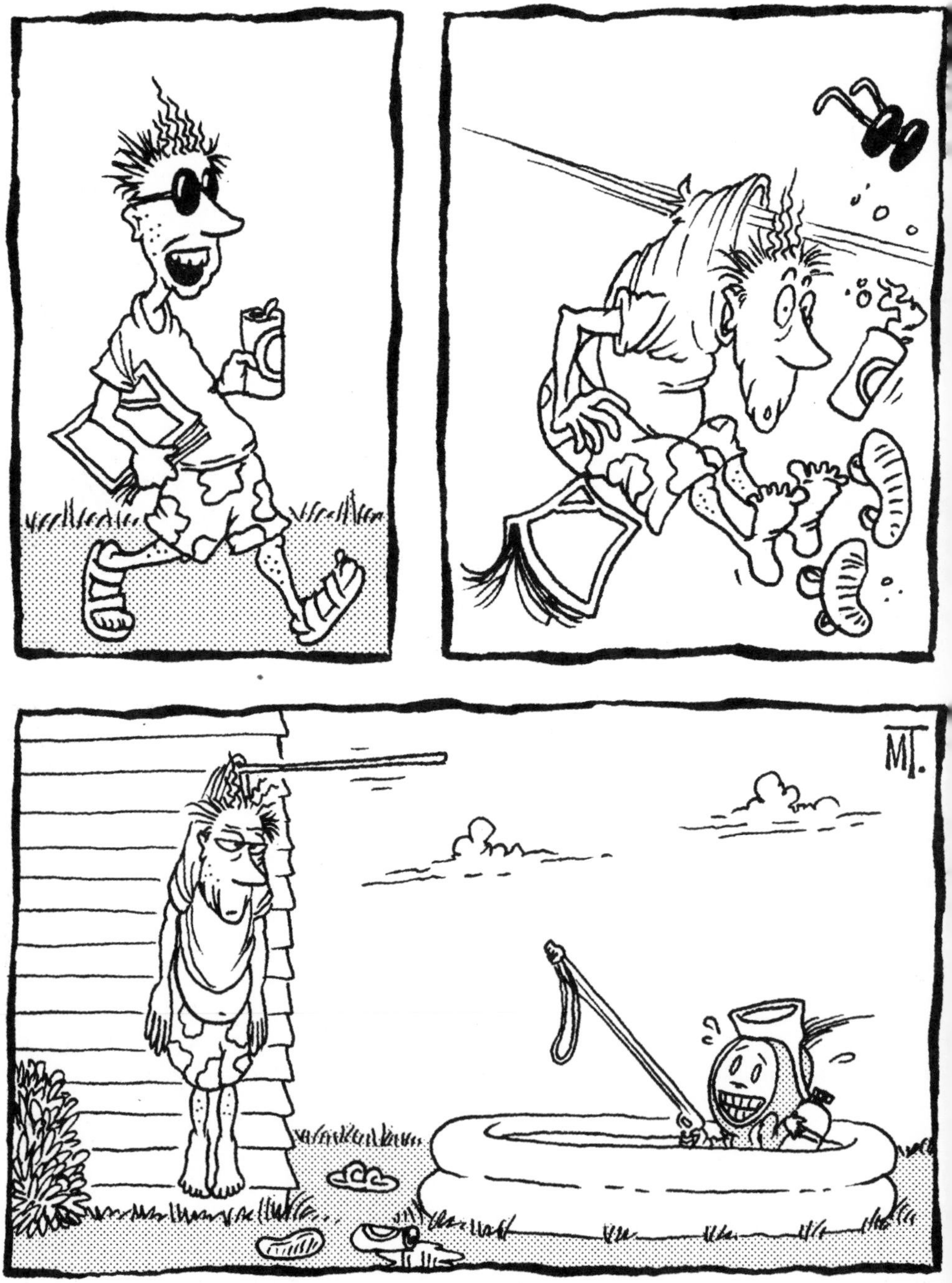
MT.

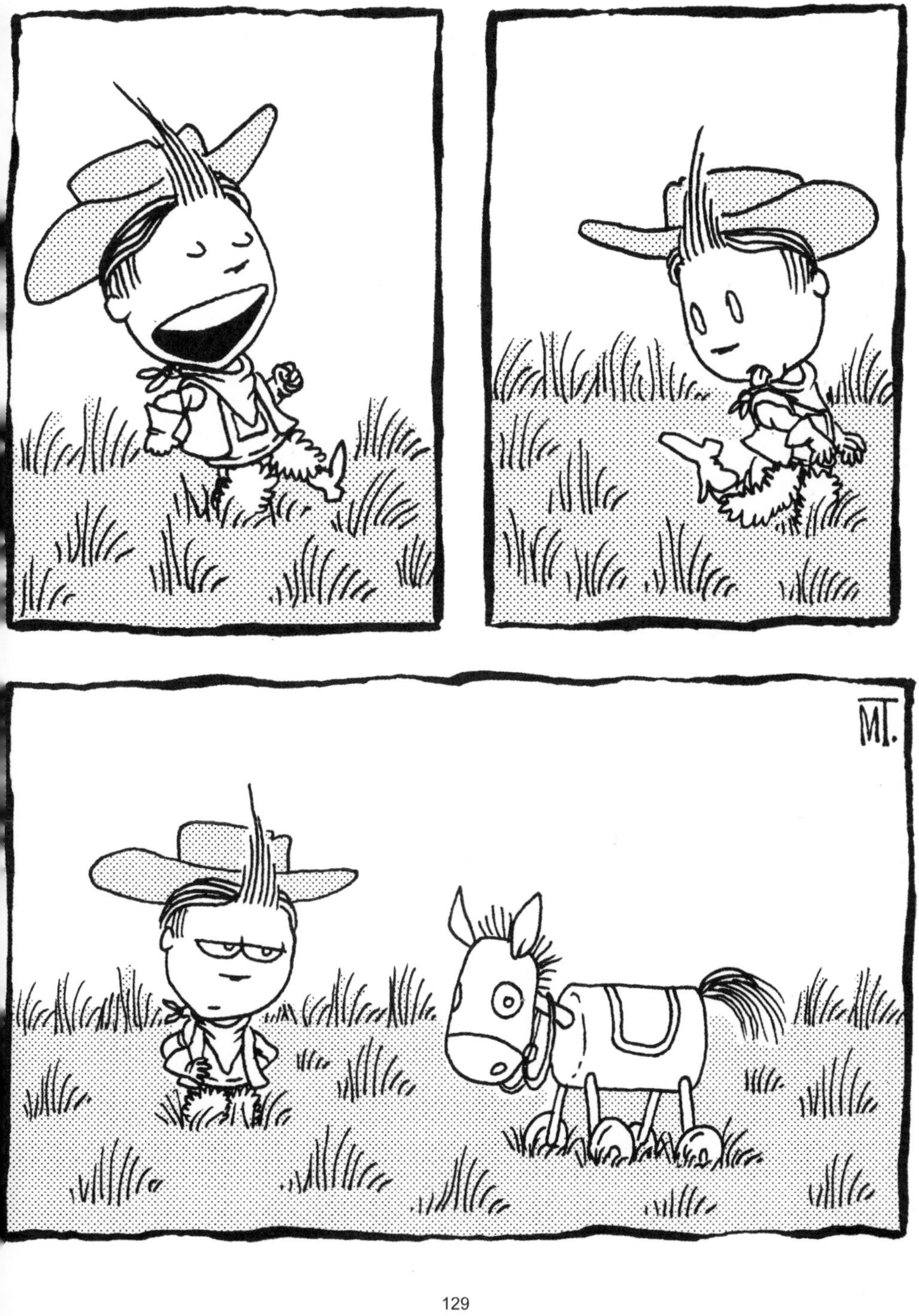
MT.

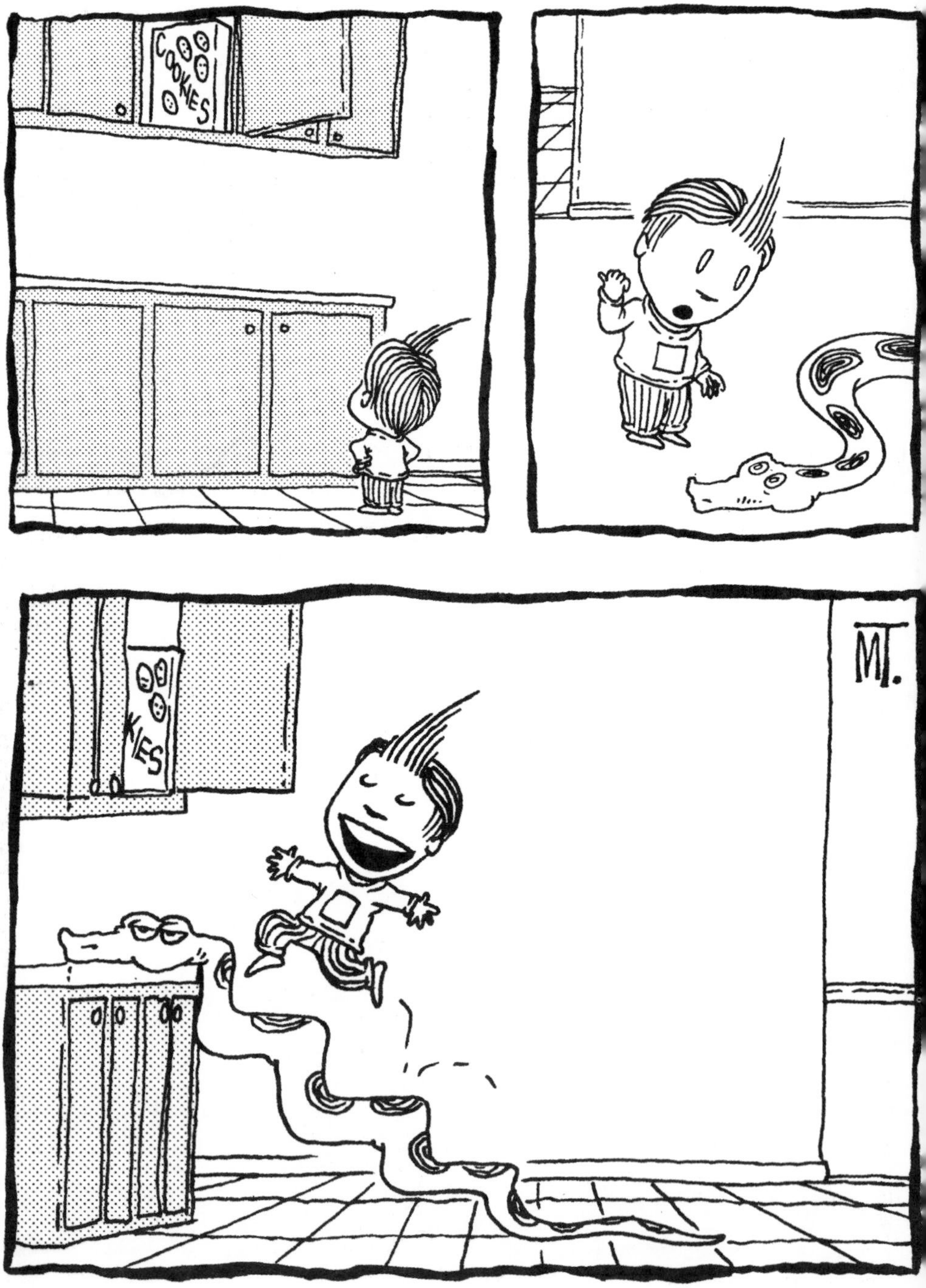
COOKIES
KIES
MT.

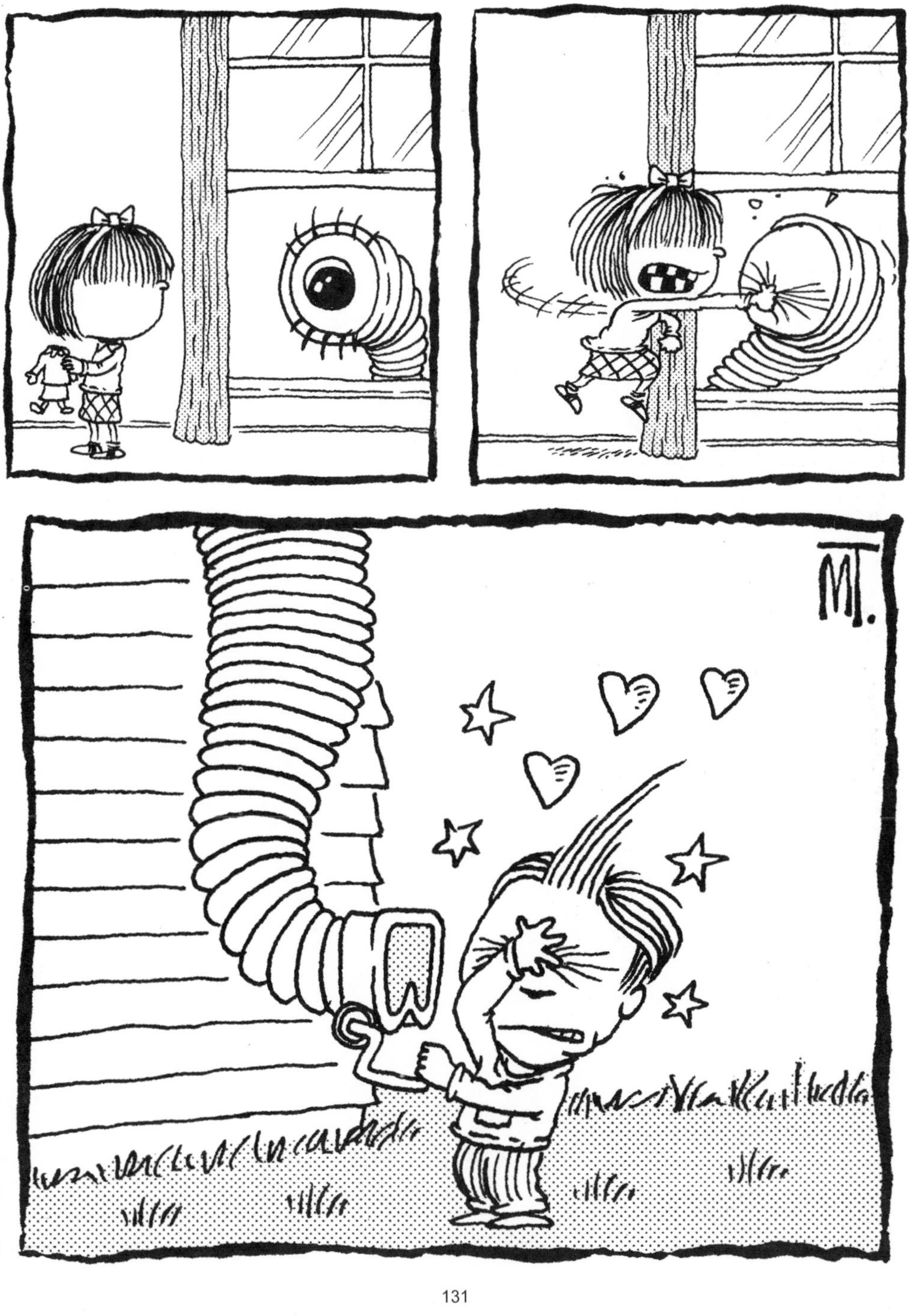

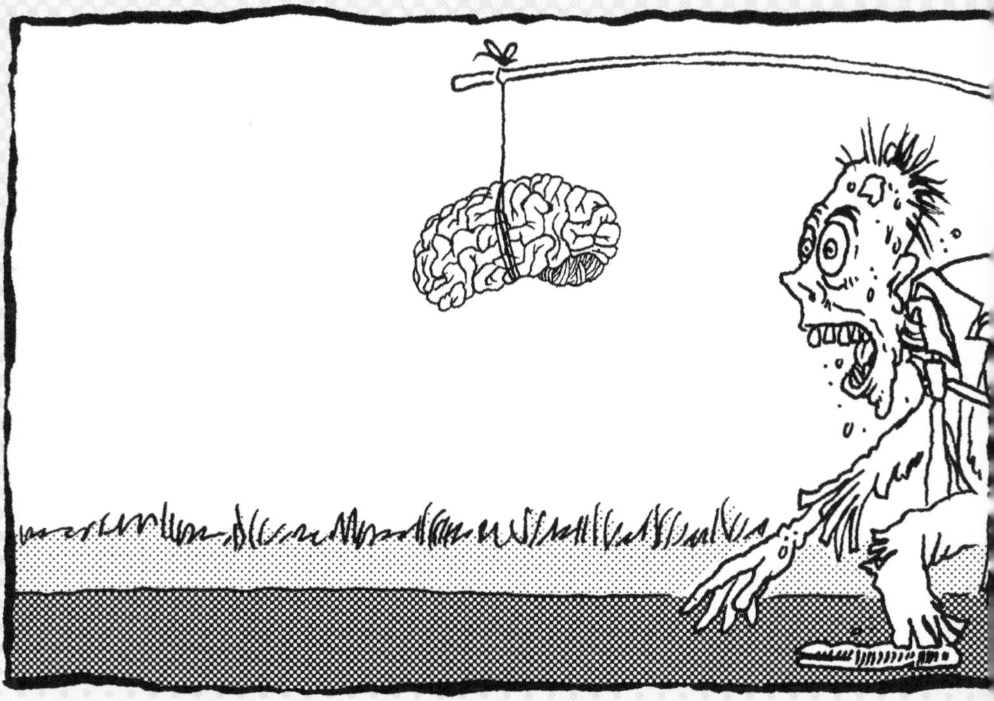

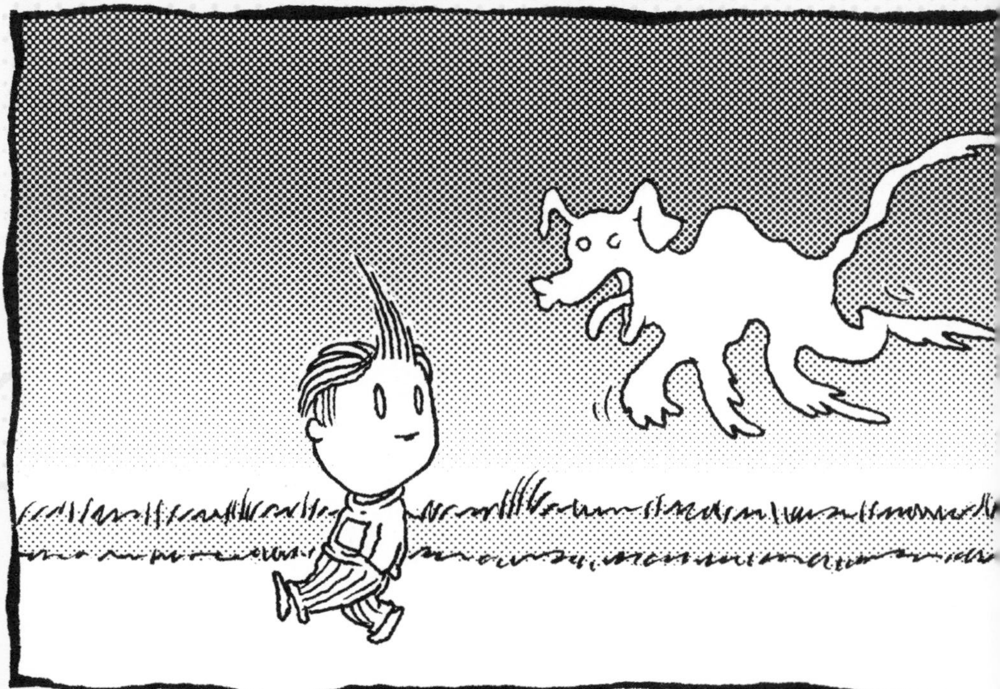

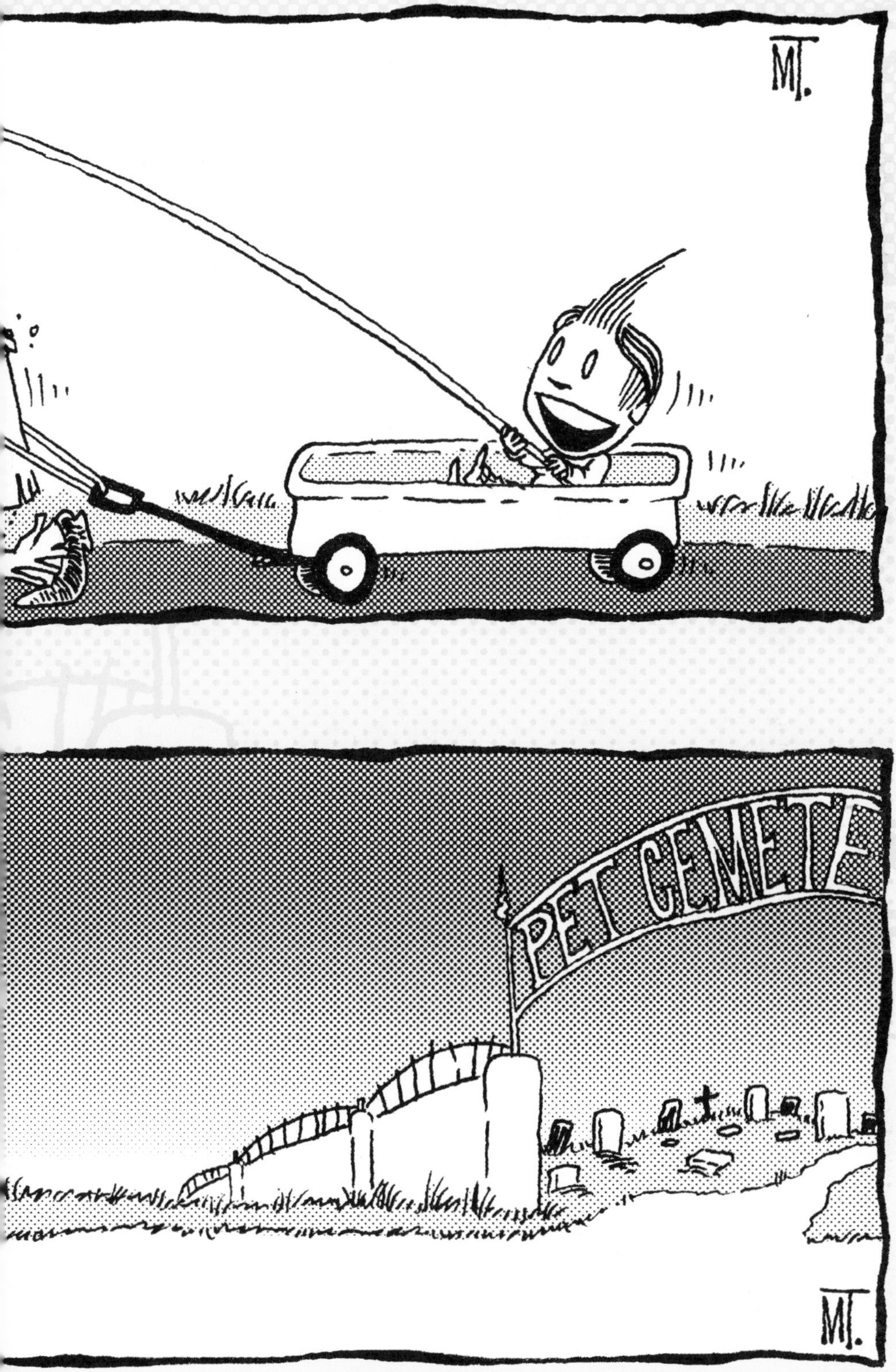
MT.
PET CEMETE
MT.

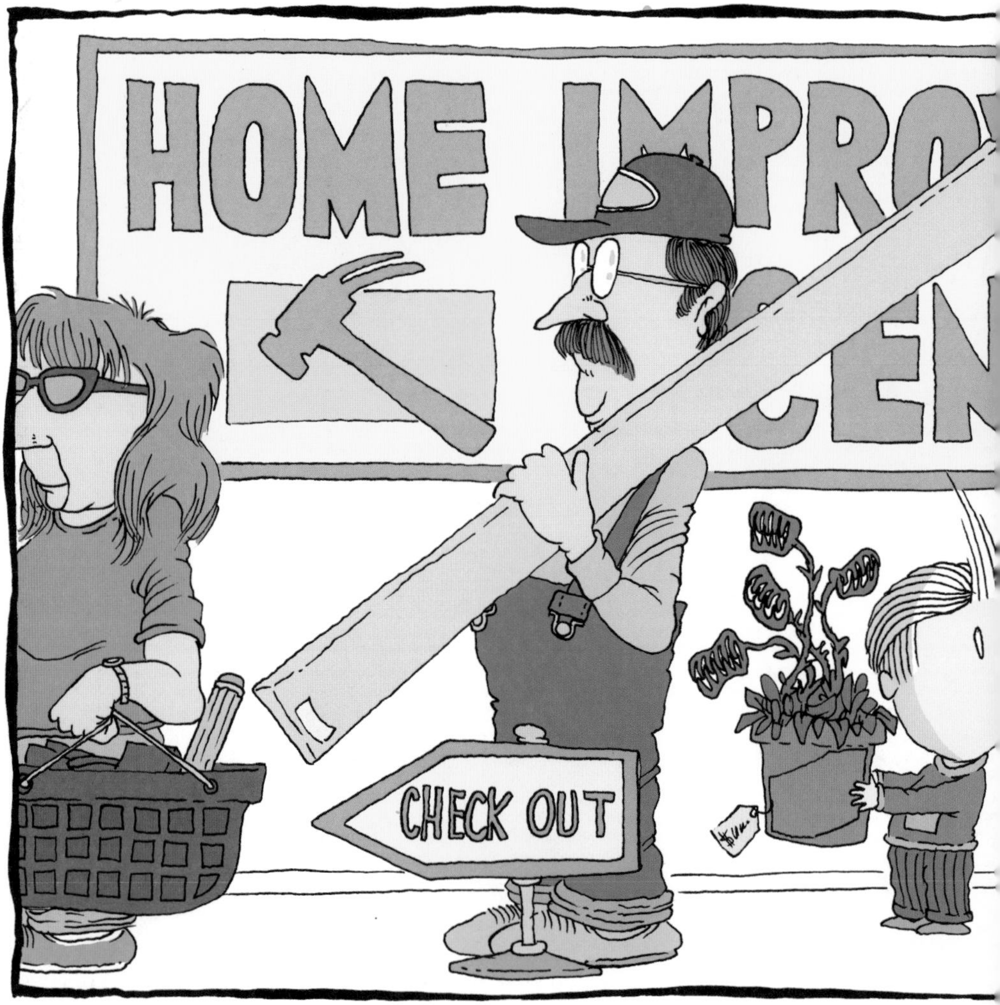
HOME
CHECK OUT

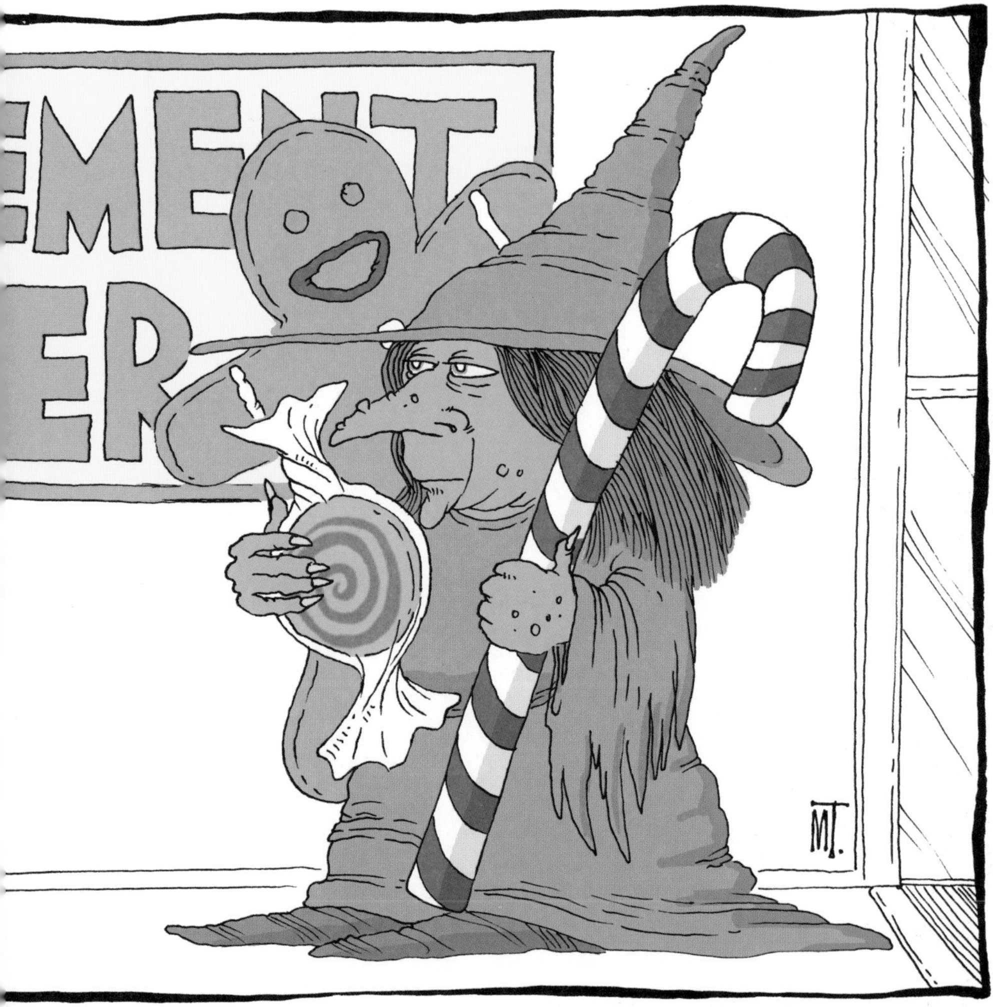
EMENT
ER

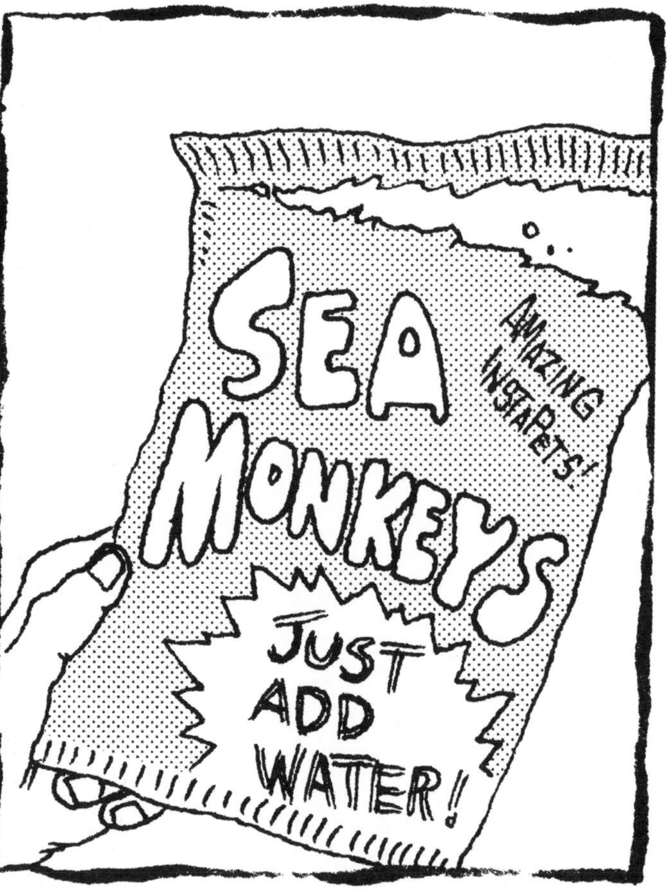
SEA MONKEYS
AMAZING INSTA-PETS!
JUST ADD WATER!

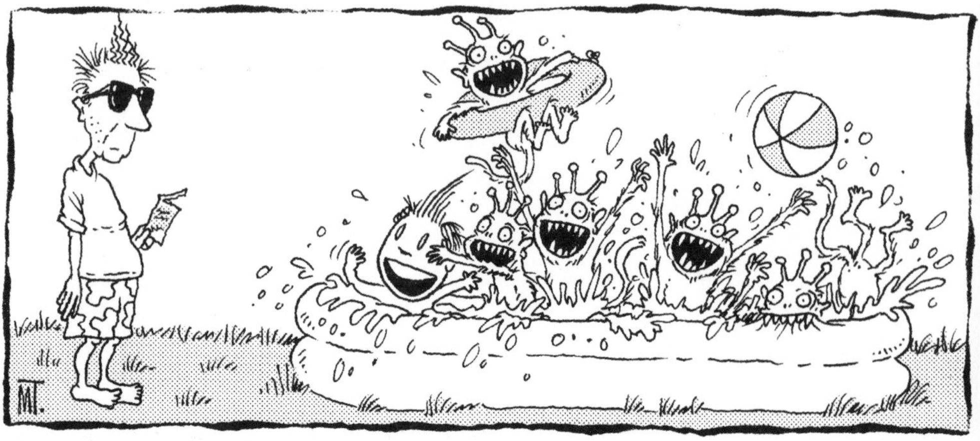

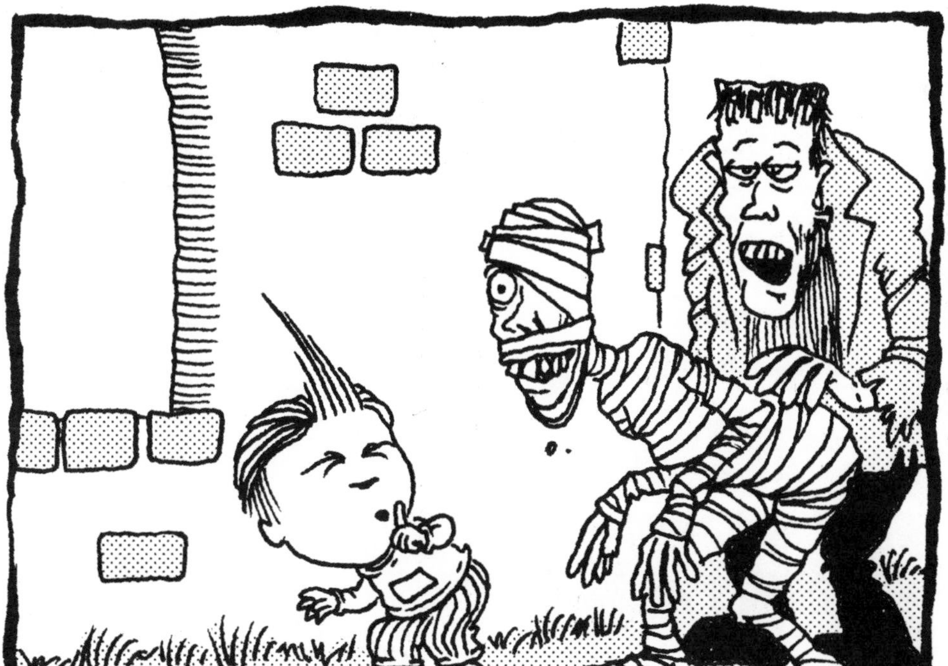

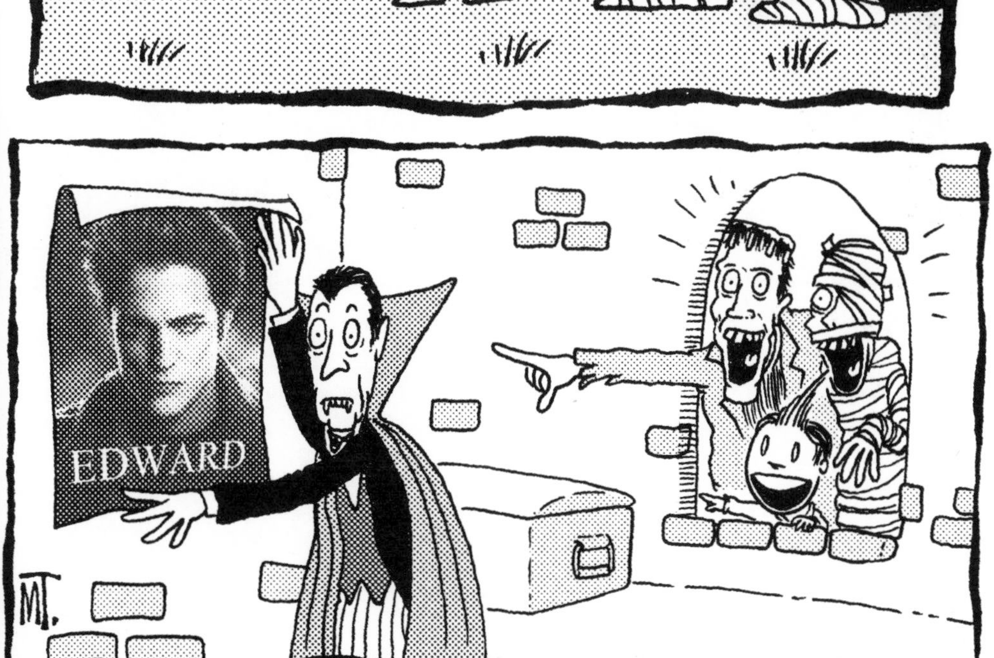
EDWARD
MT.

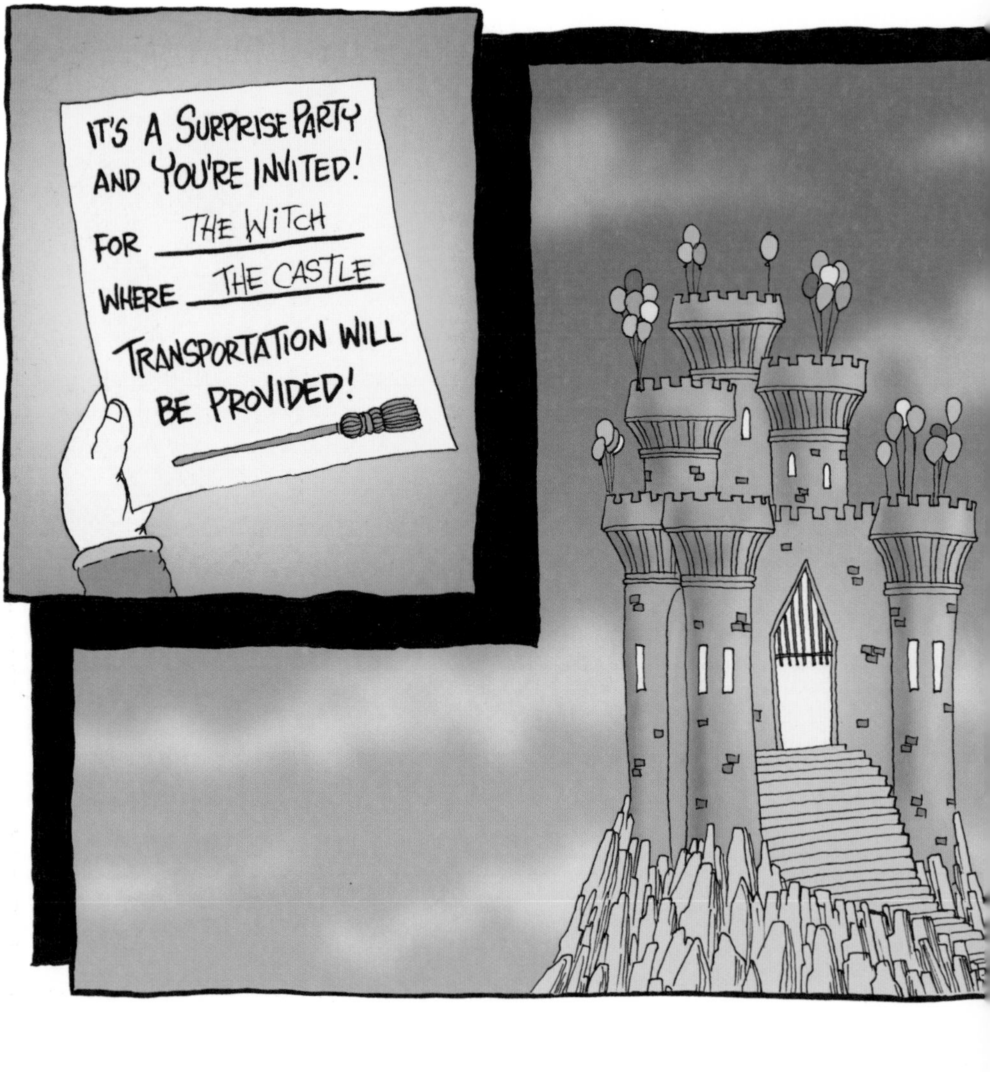
IT'S A SURPRISE PARTY
AND YOU'RE INVITED!
FOR THE WITCH
WHERE THE CASTLE
TRANSPORTATION WILL
BE PROVIDED!

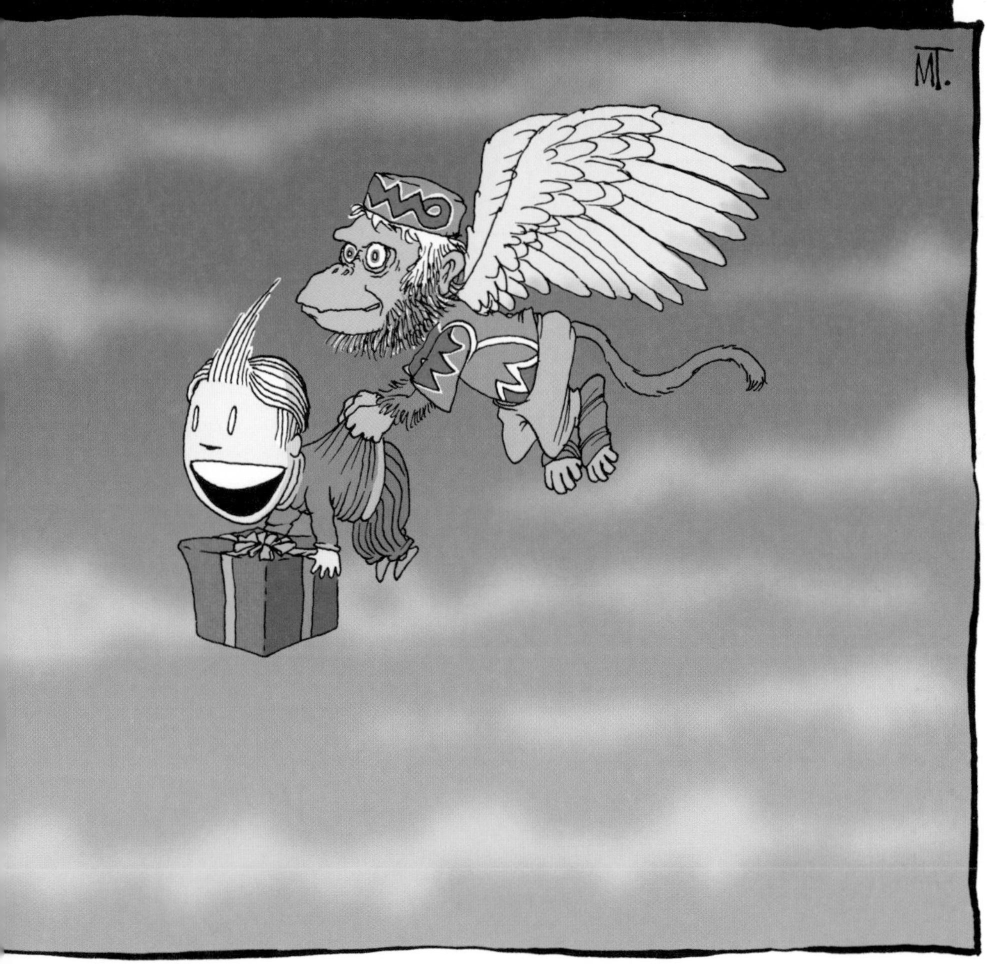

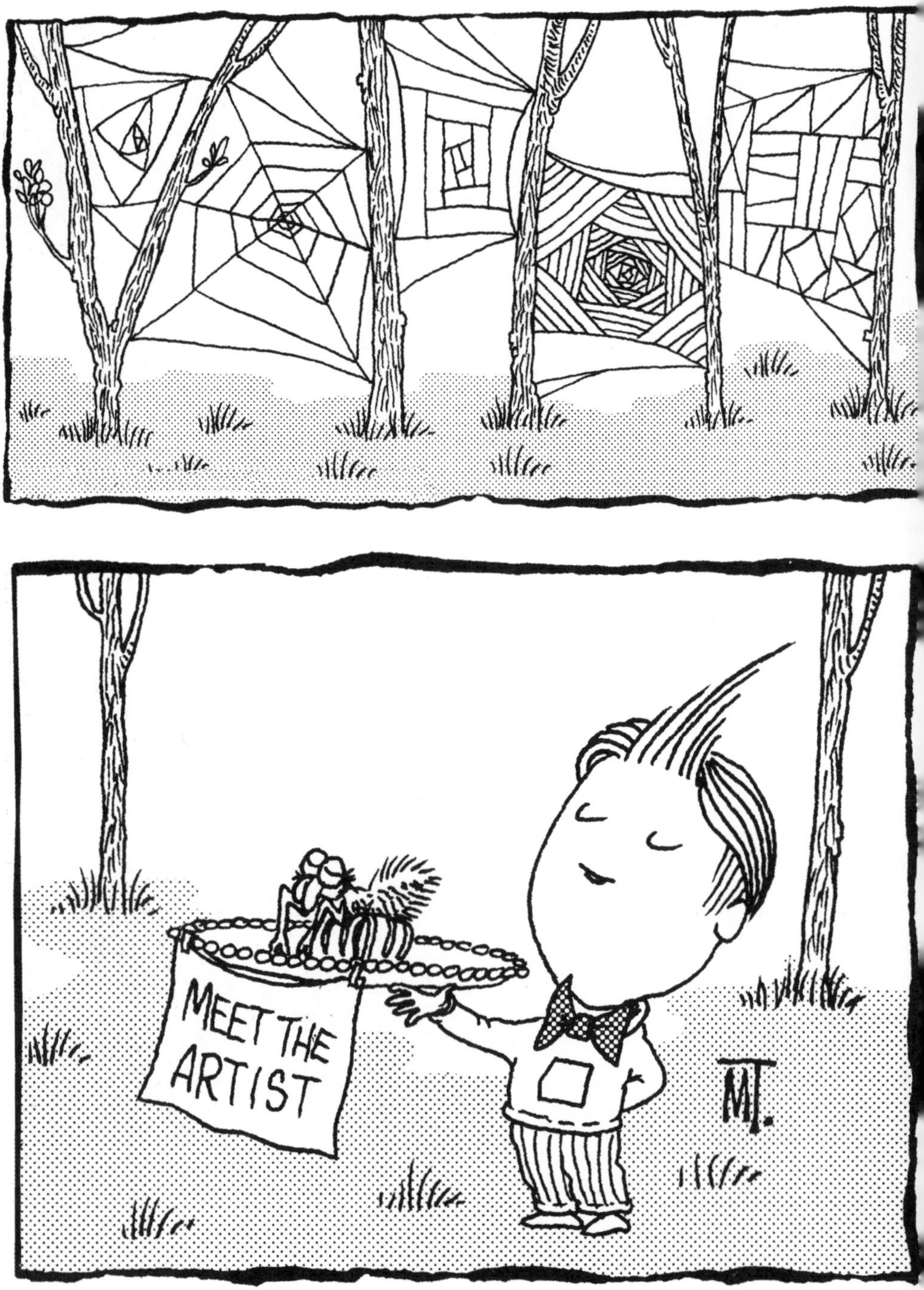
MEET THE ARTIST
MT.

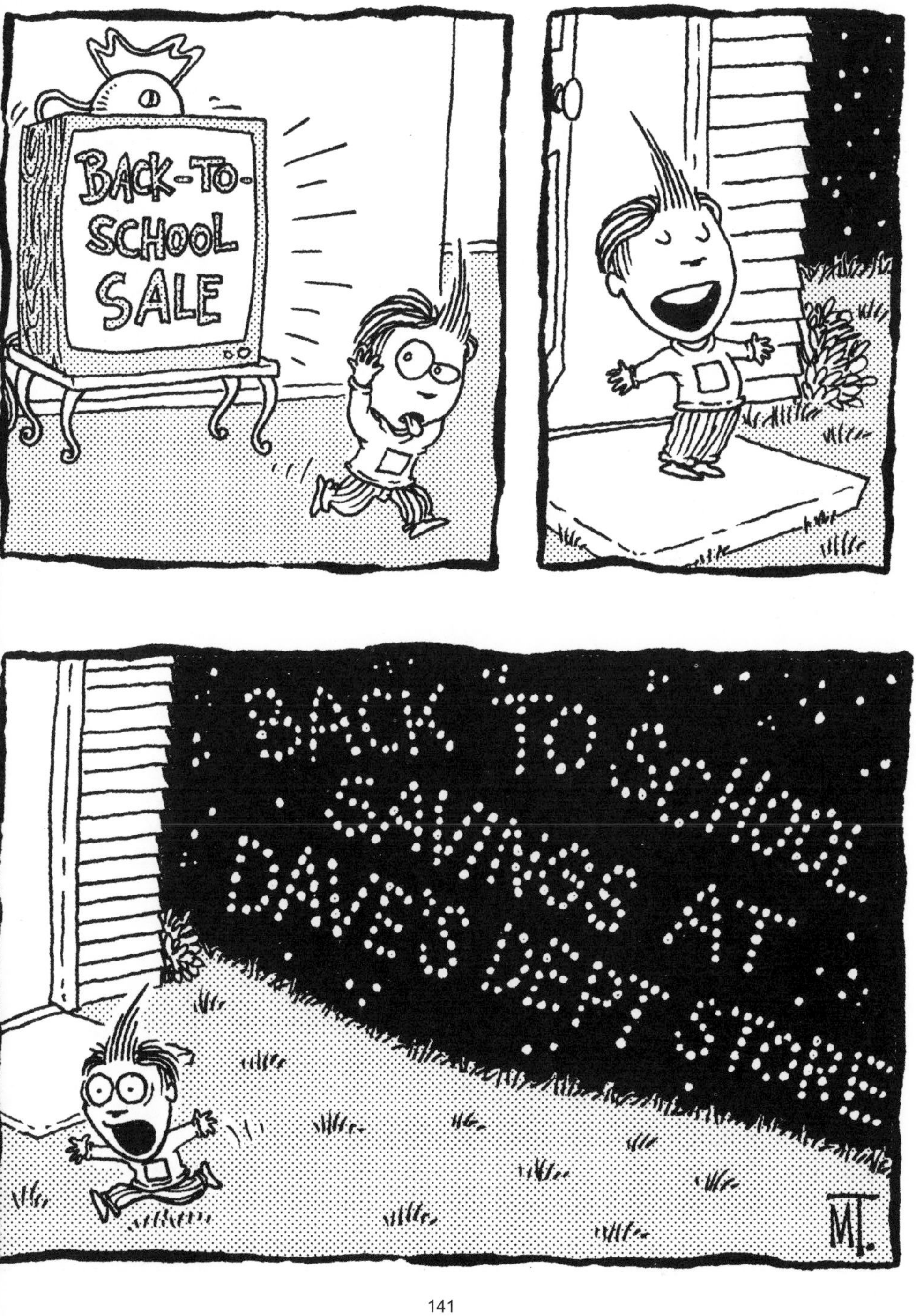
BACK-TO-SCHOOL SALE
BACK TO SCHOOL SAVINGS AT DAVE'S DEPT. STORE
MT

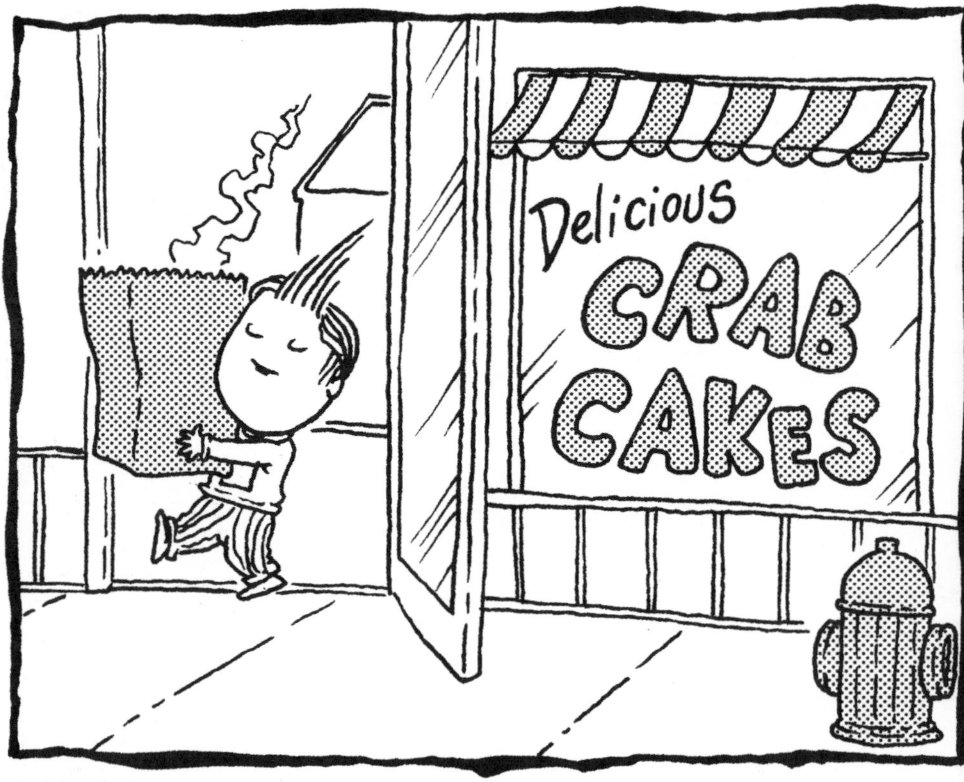
Delicious
CRAB
CAKES

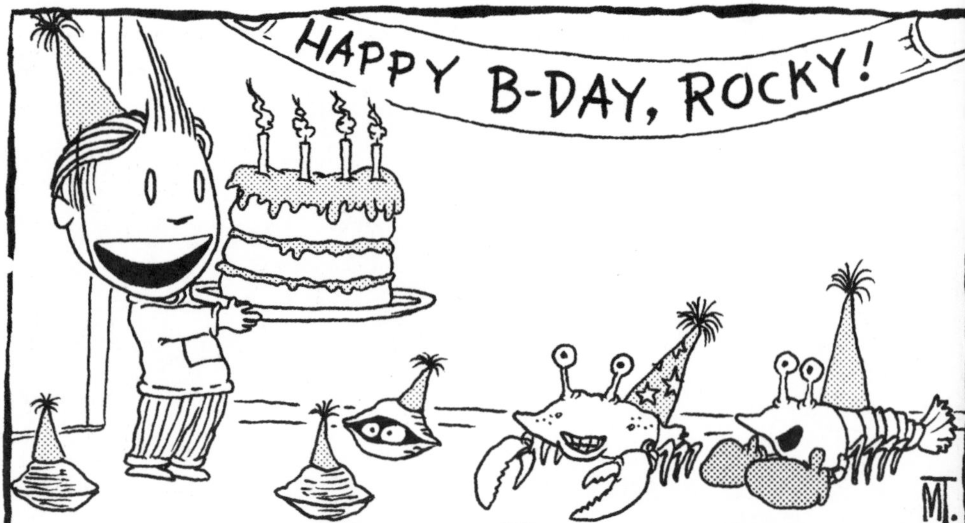
HAPPY B-DAY, ROCKY!
MT.

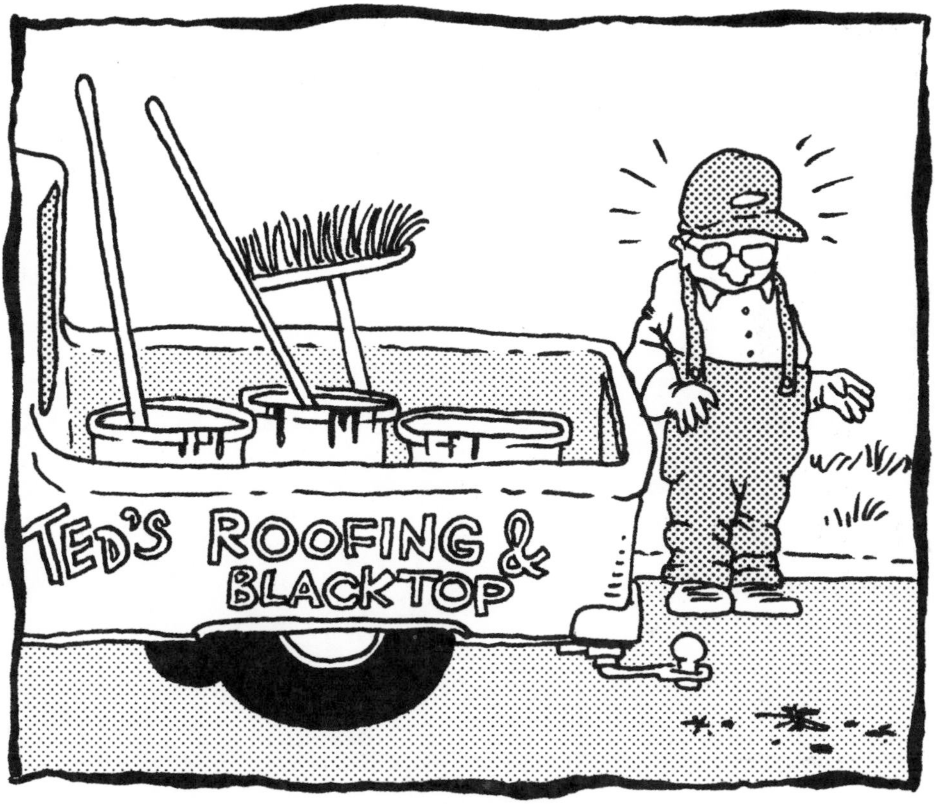
TED'S ROOFING & BLACKTOP

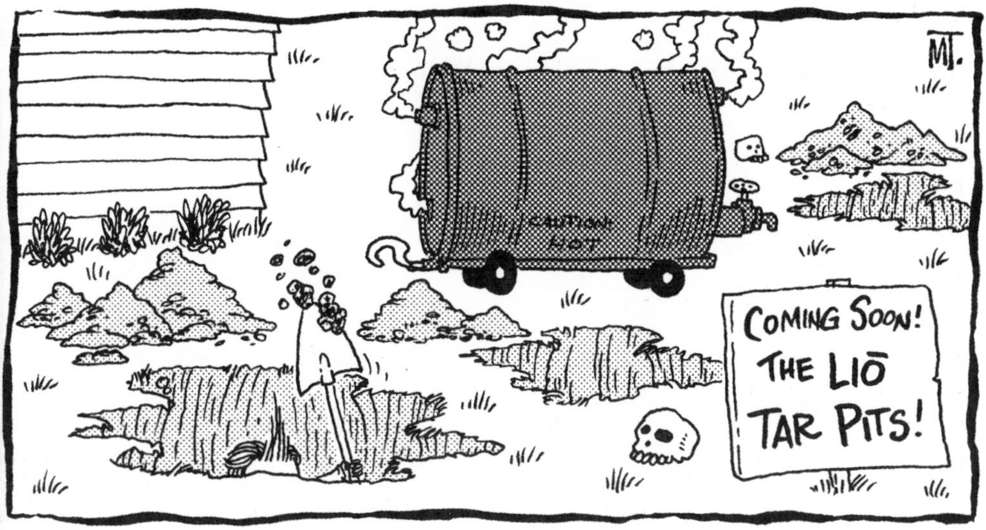
MT.
COMING SOON!
THE LIŌ
TAR PITS!

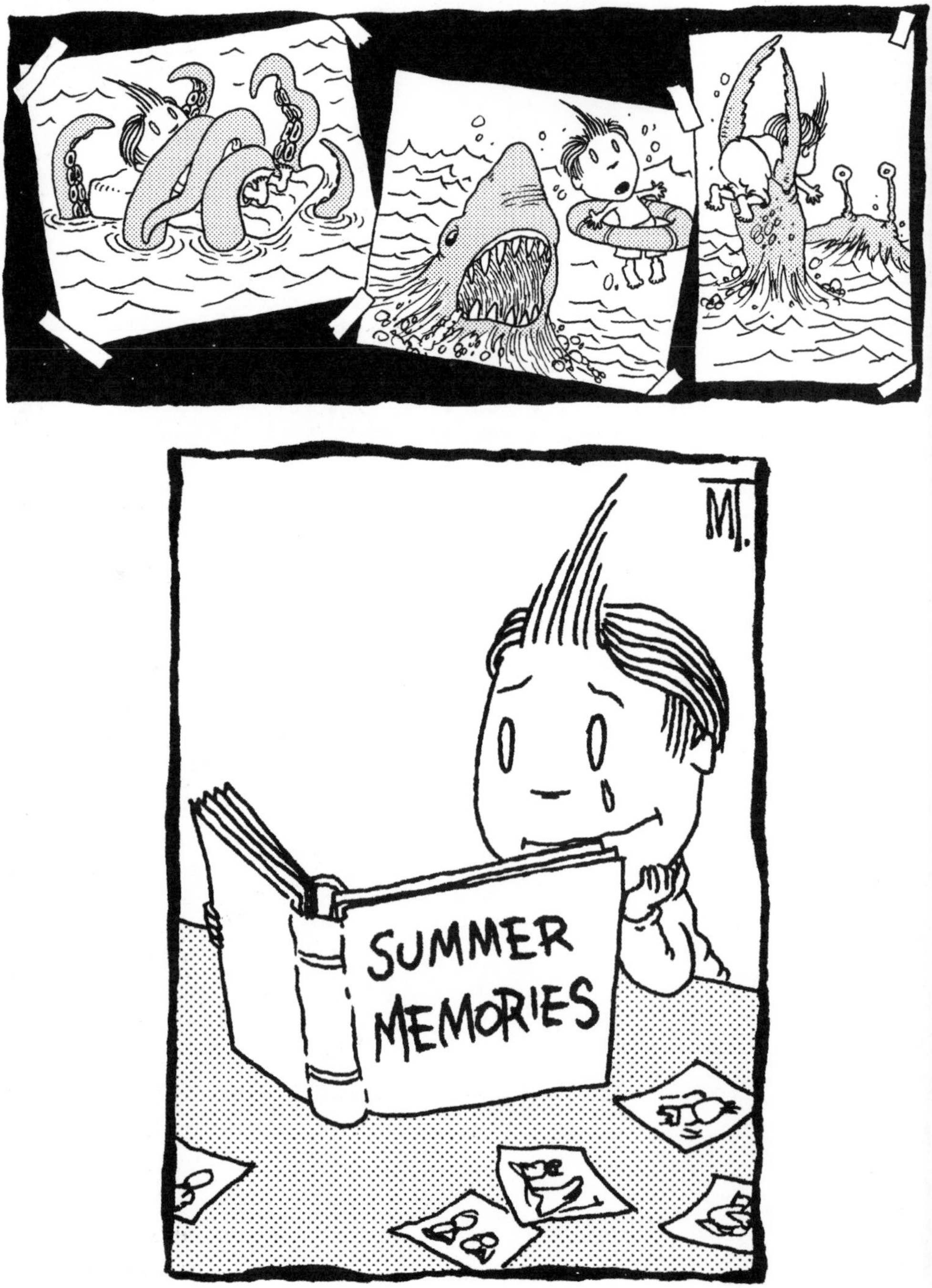
SUMMER
MEMORIES

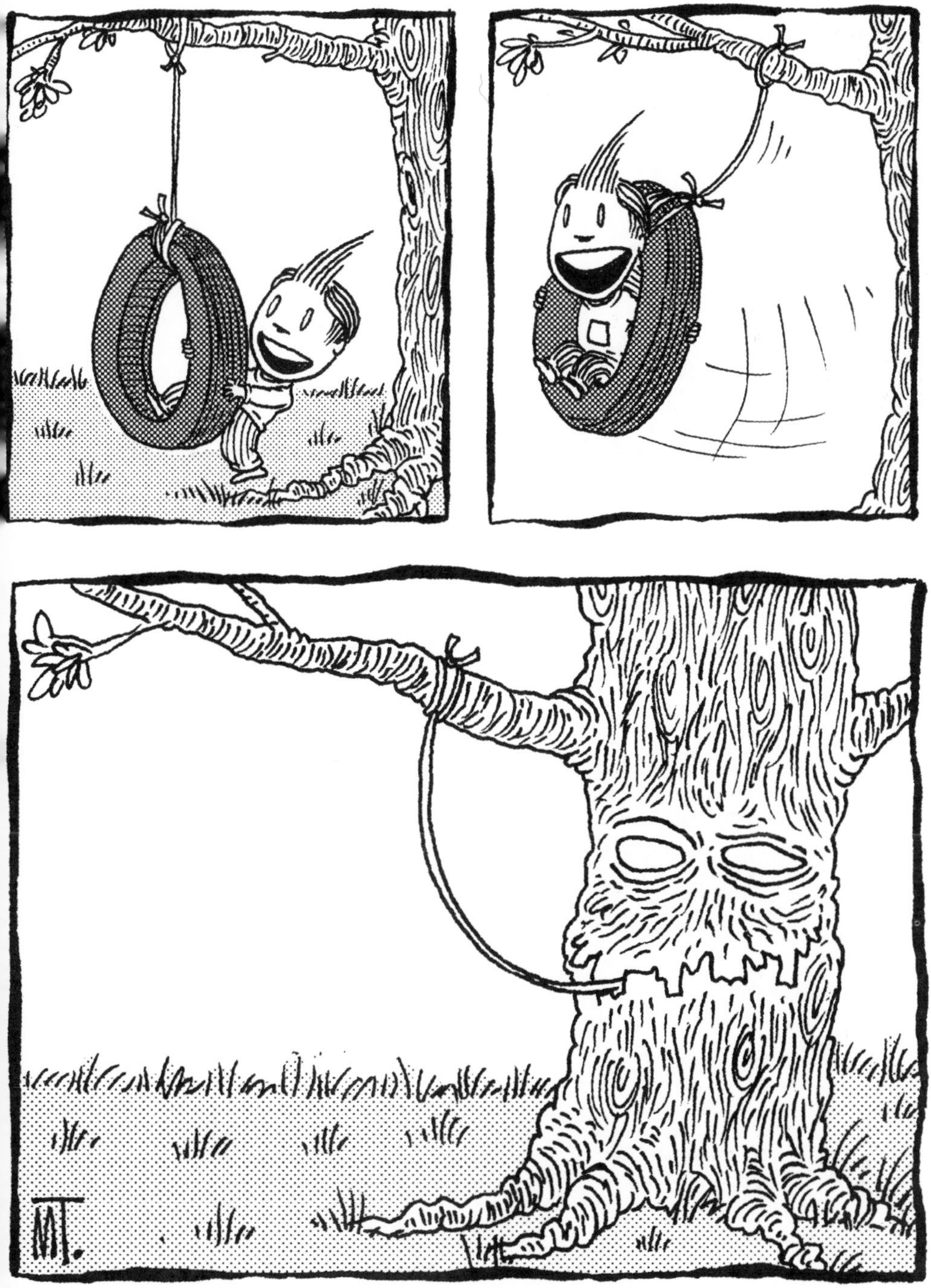
MT.

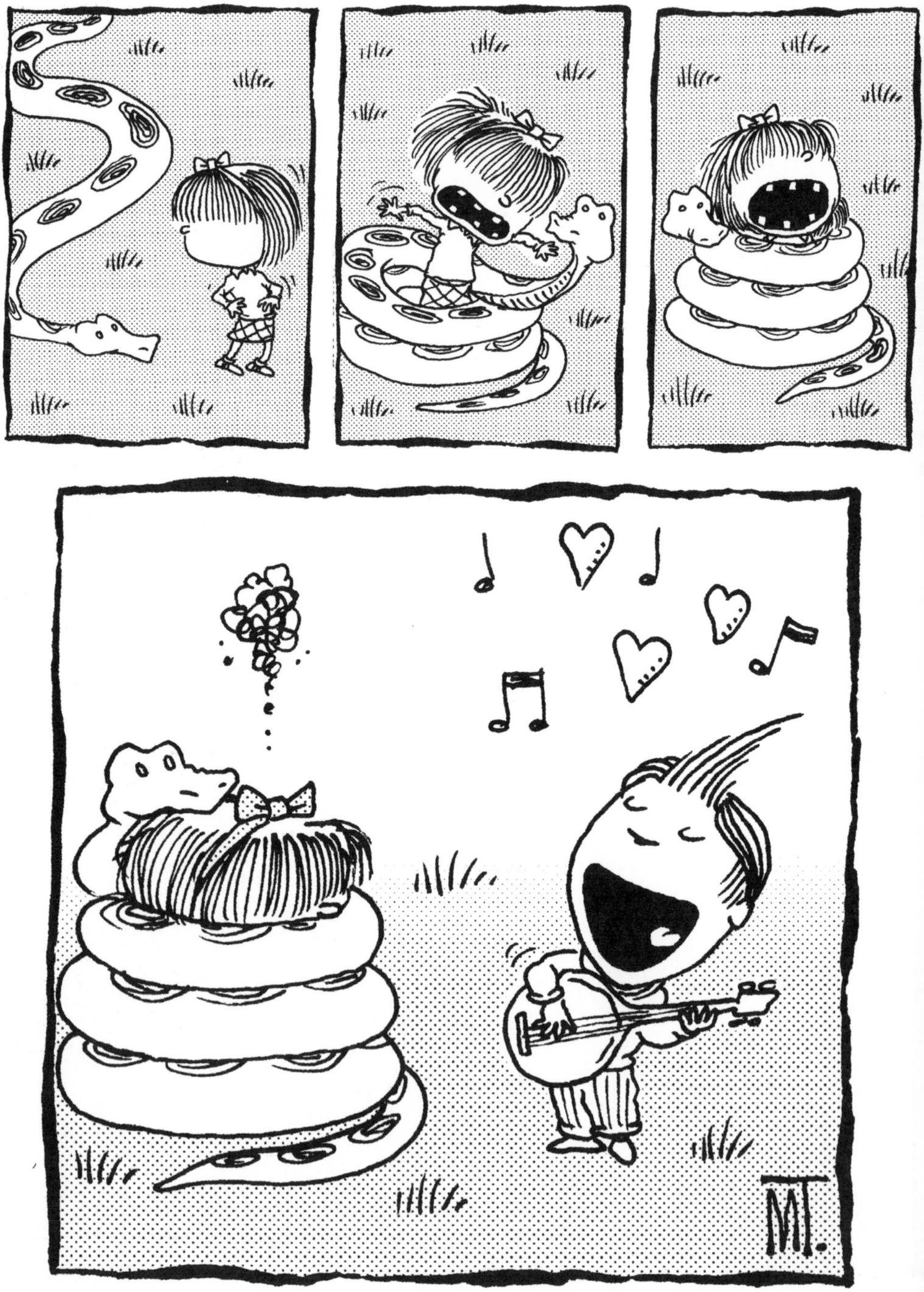
MT.

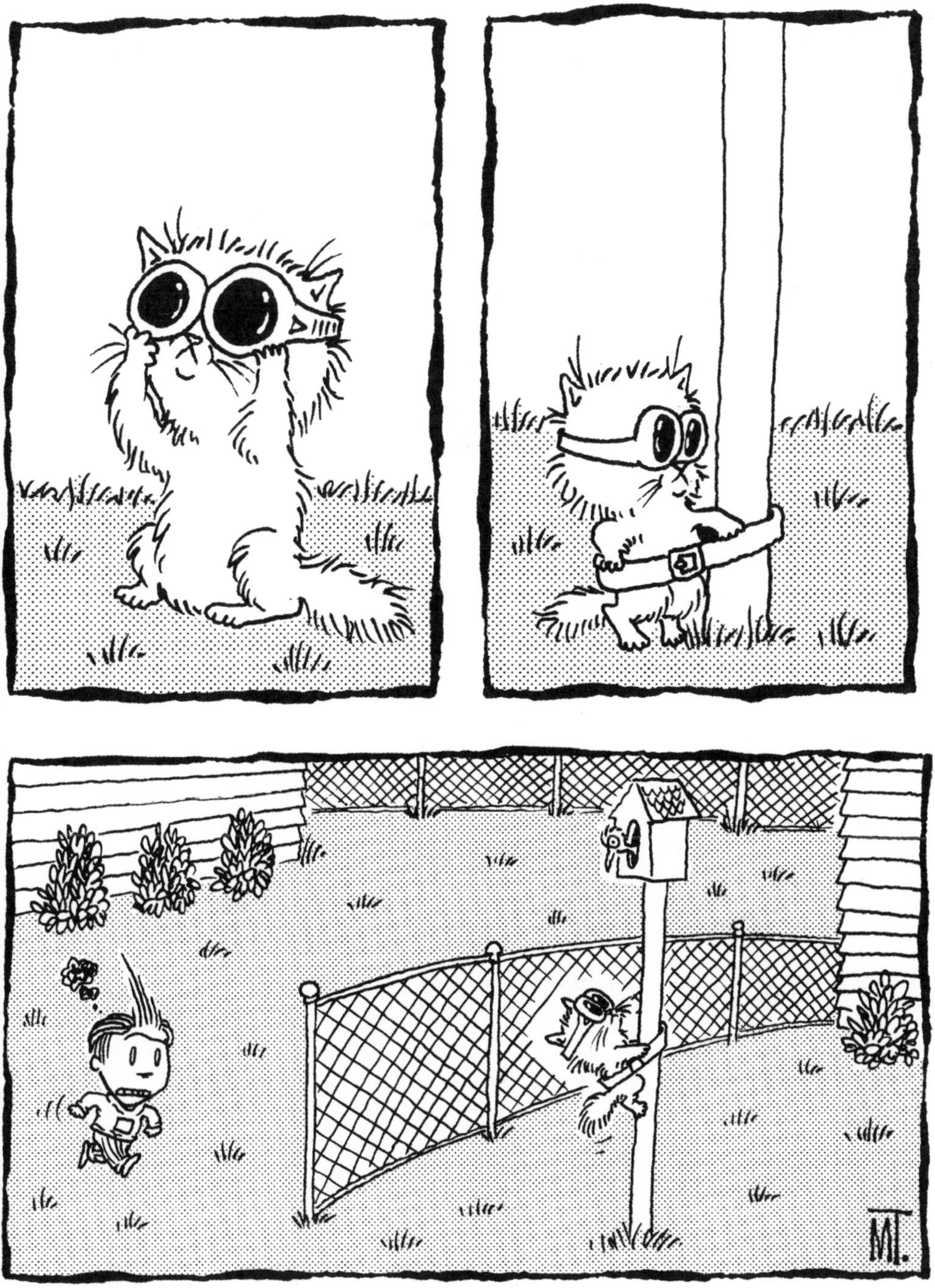
MT.

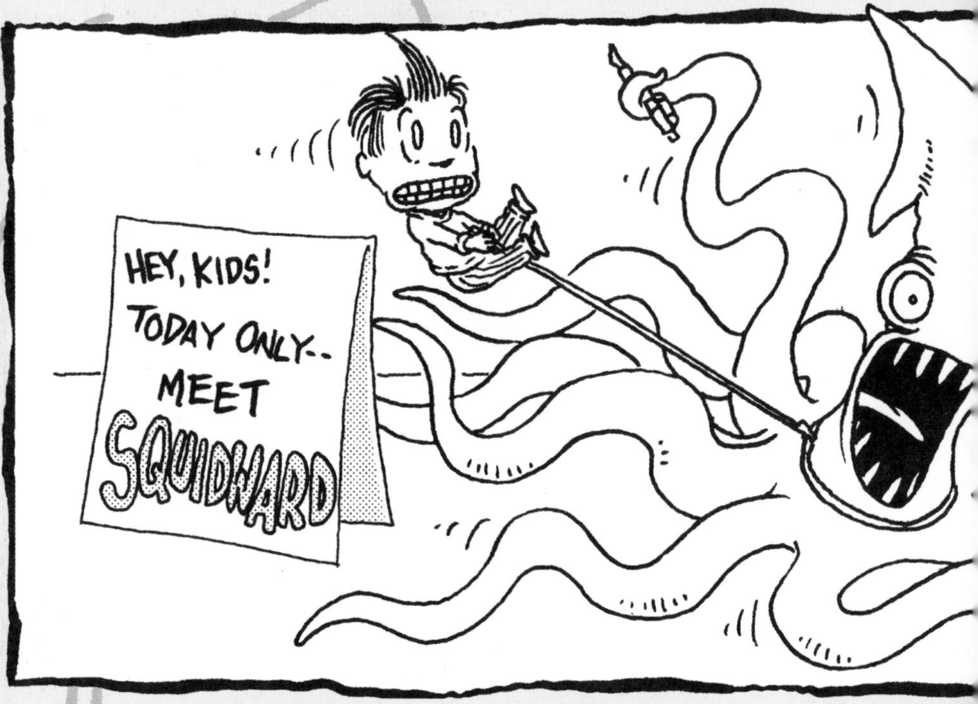
HEY, KIDS!
TODAY ONLY--
MEET
SQUIDWARD

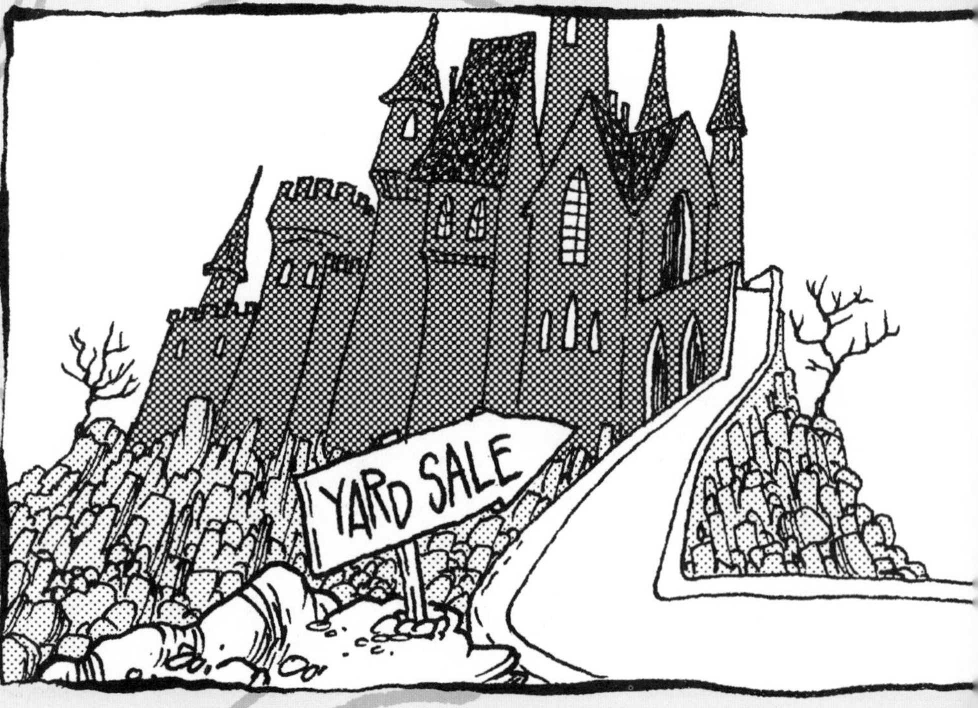
YARD SALE

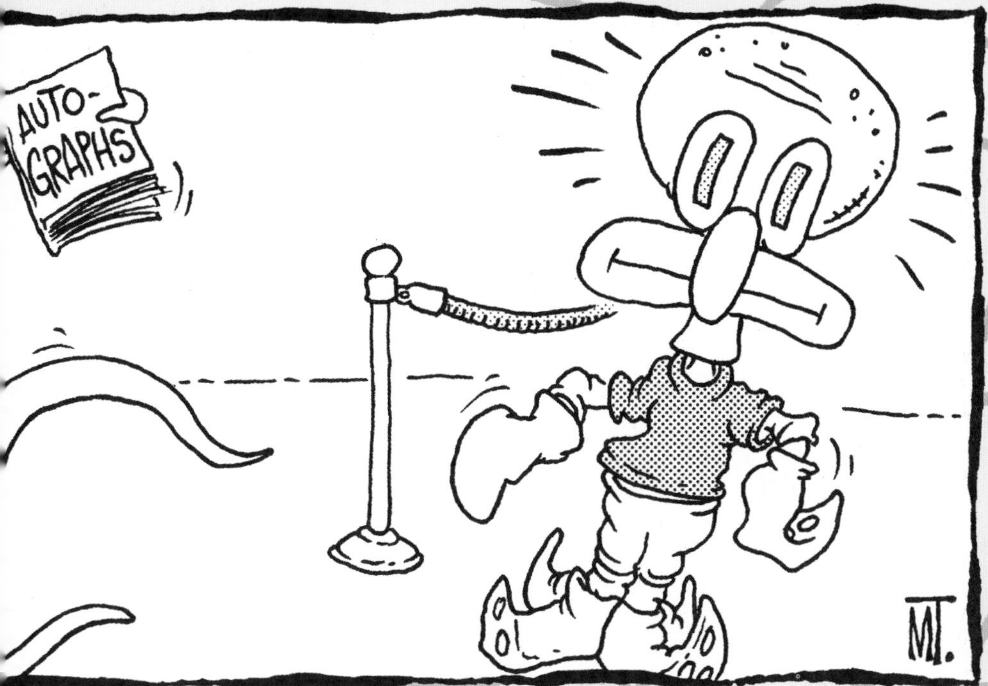
AUTO-
GRAPHS
MT.

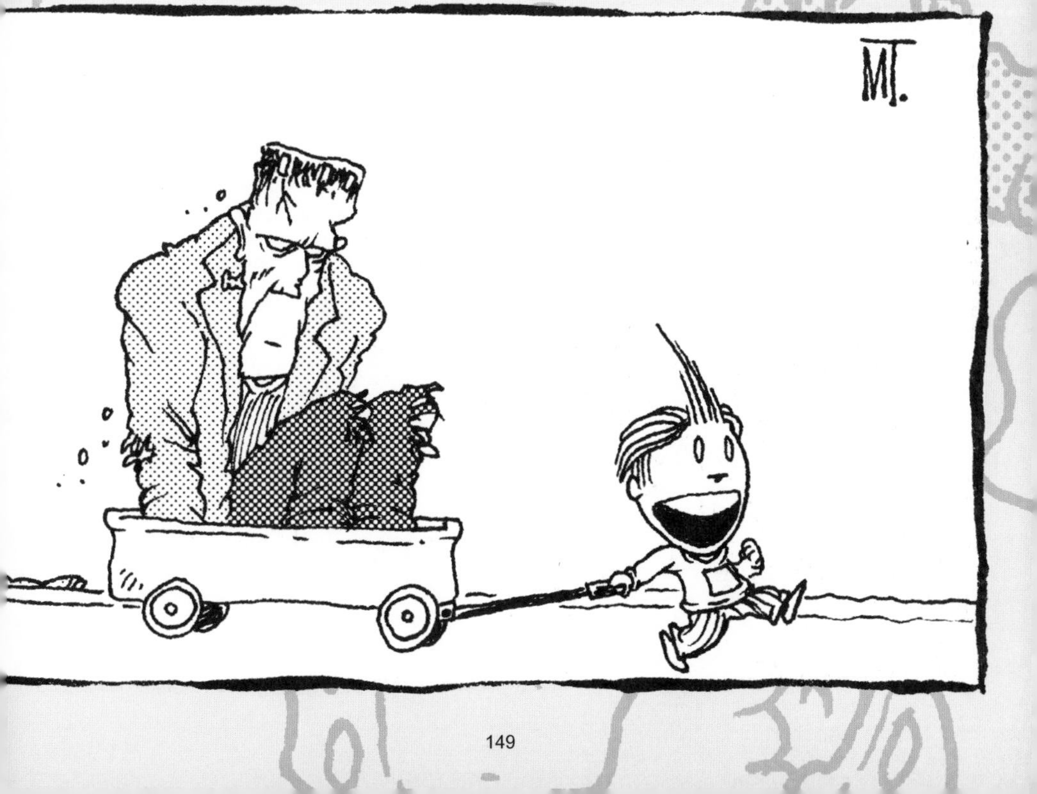
MT.

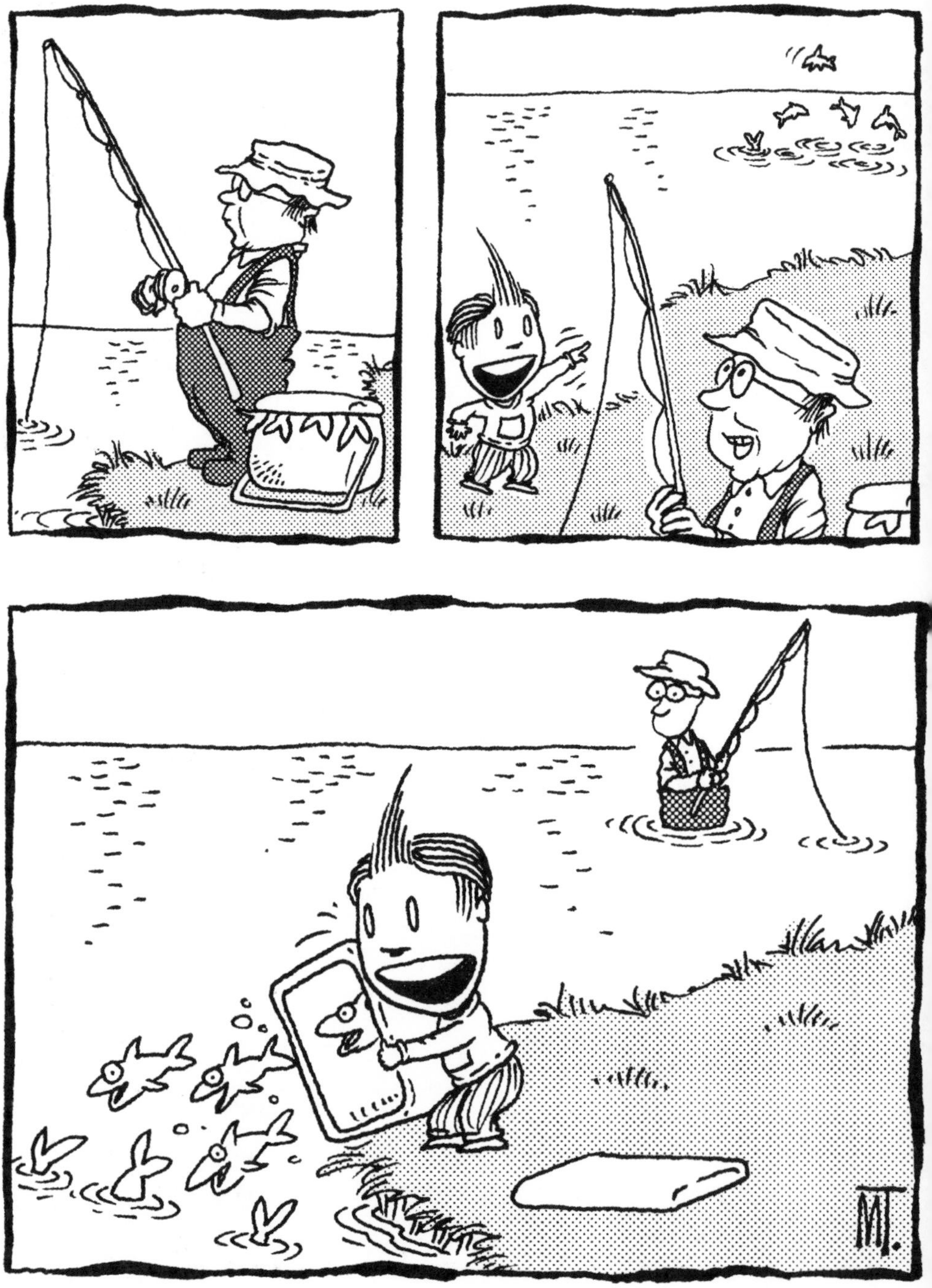

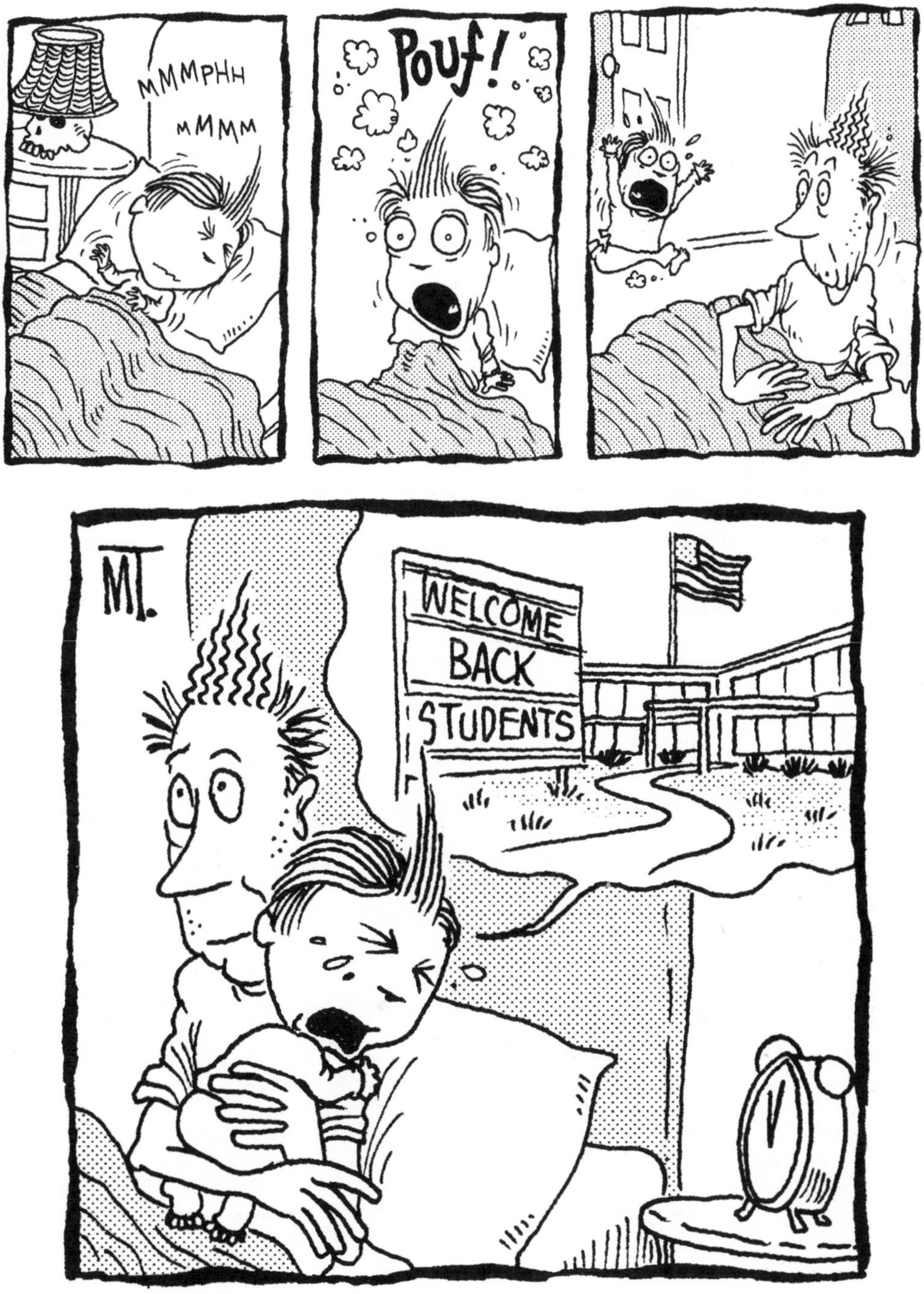
MMMPHH
MMMM
Pouf!
MT.
WELCOME
BACK
STUDENTS

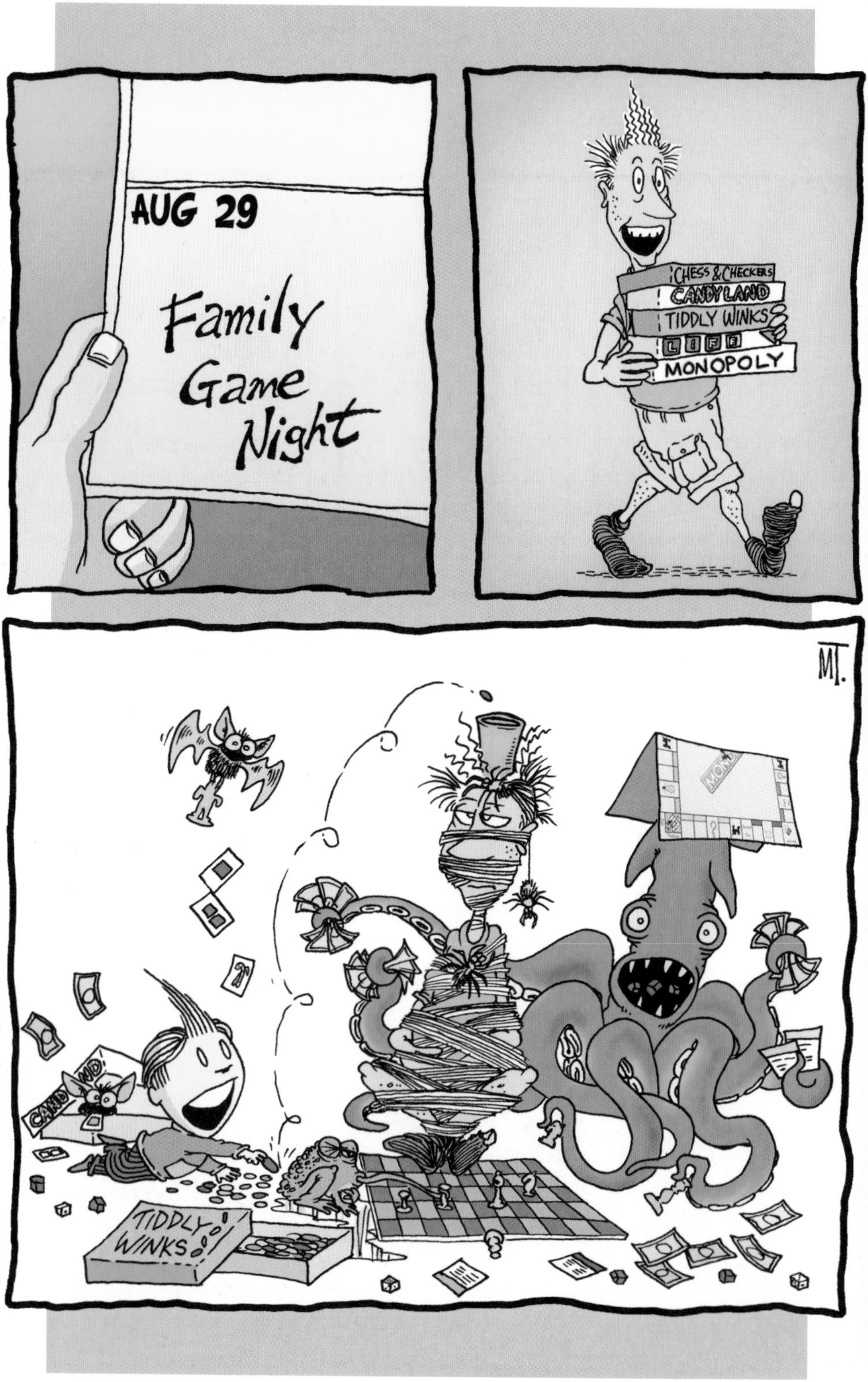
AUG 29
Family Game Night
CHESS & CHECKERS
CANDYLAND
TIDDLY WINKS
LIFE
MONOPOLY
MT.
TIDDLY WINKS

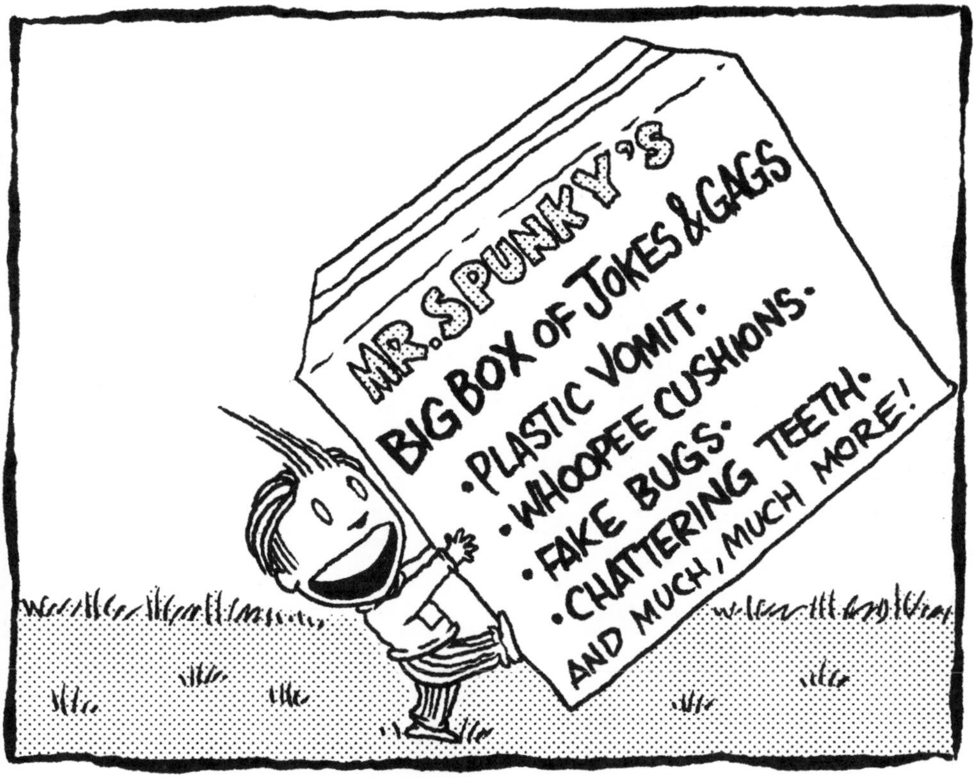
MR. SPUNKY'S
BIG BOX OF JOKES & GAGS
• PLASTIC VOMIT •
• WHOOPEE CUSHIONS •
• FAKE BUGS •
• CHATTERING TEETH •
AND MUCH, MUCH MORE!

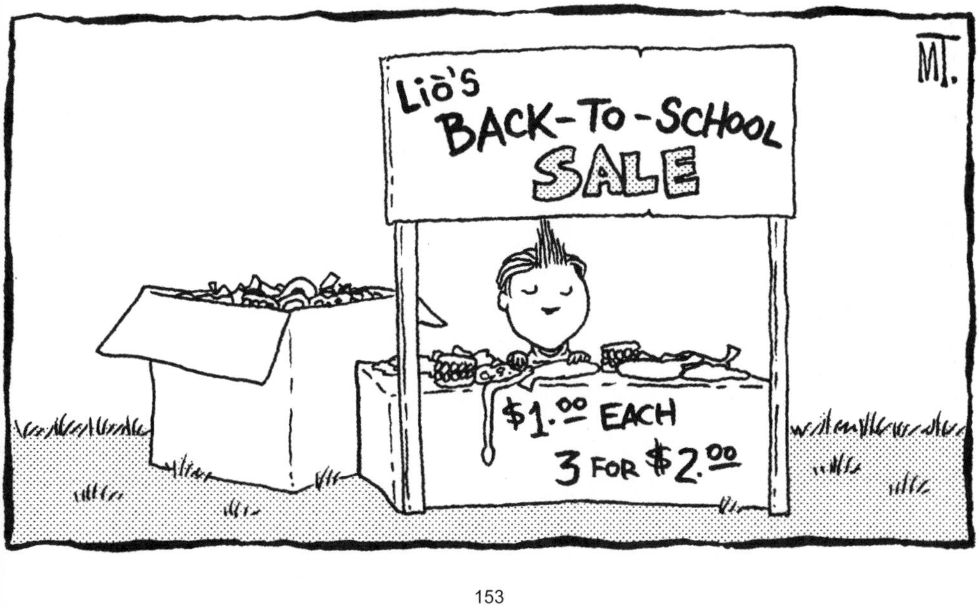
MT.
Liō's
BACK-TO-SCHOOL
SALE
$1.00 EACH
3 FOR $2.00

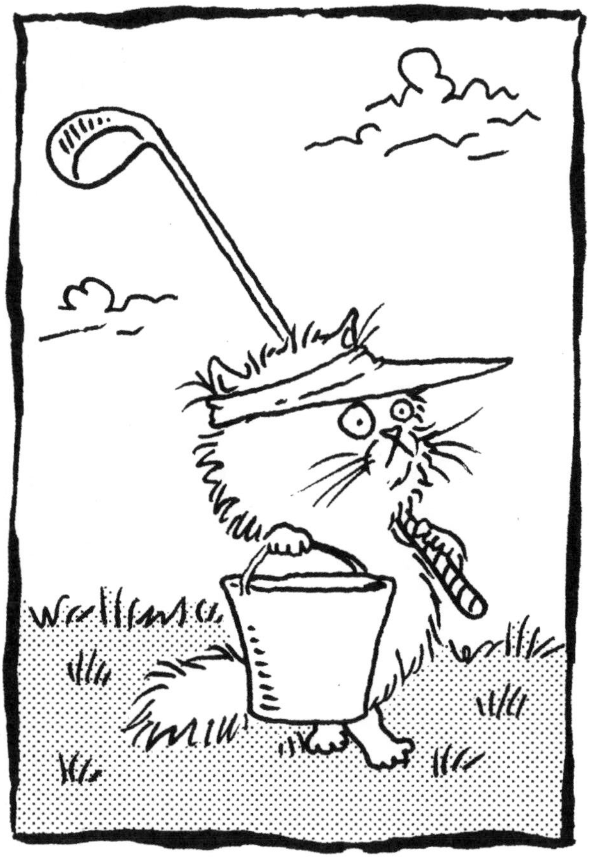

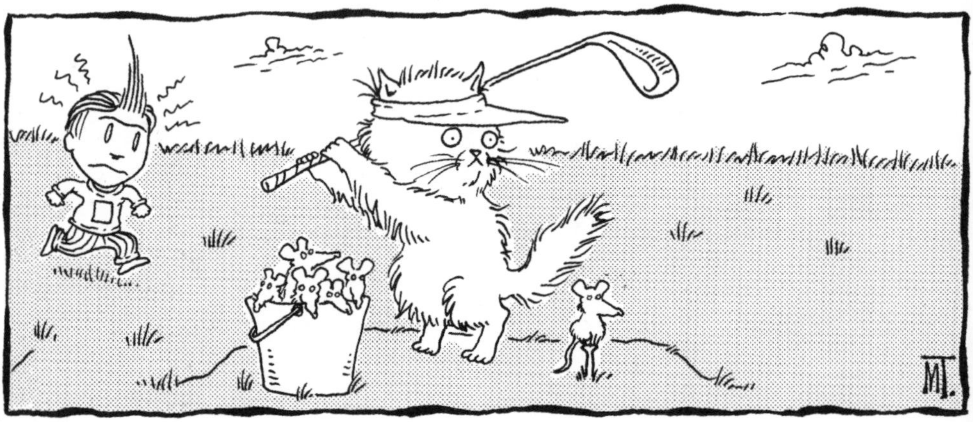

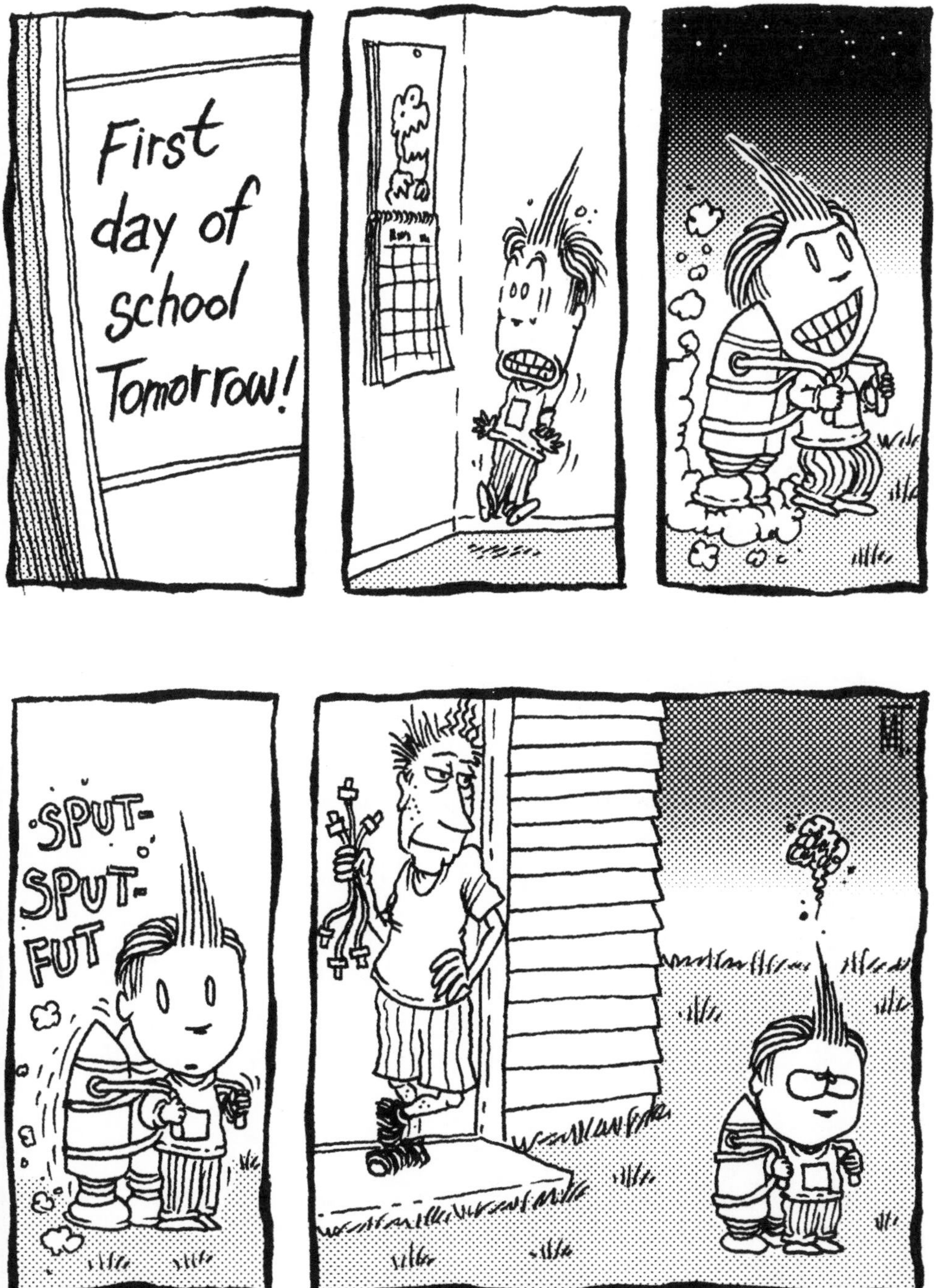
First day of school Tomorrow!
SPUT-
SPUT-
FUT

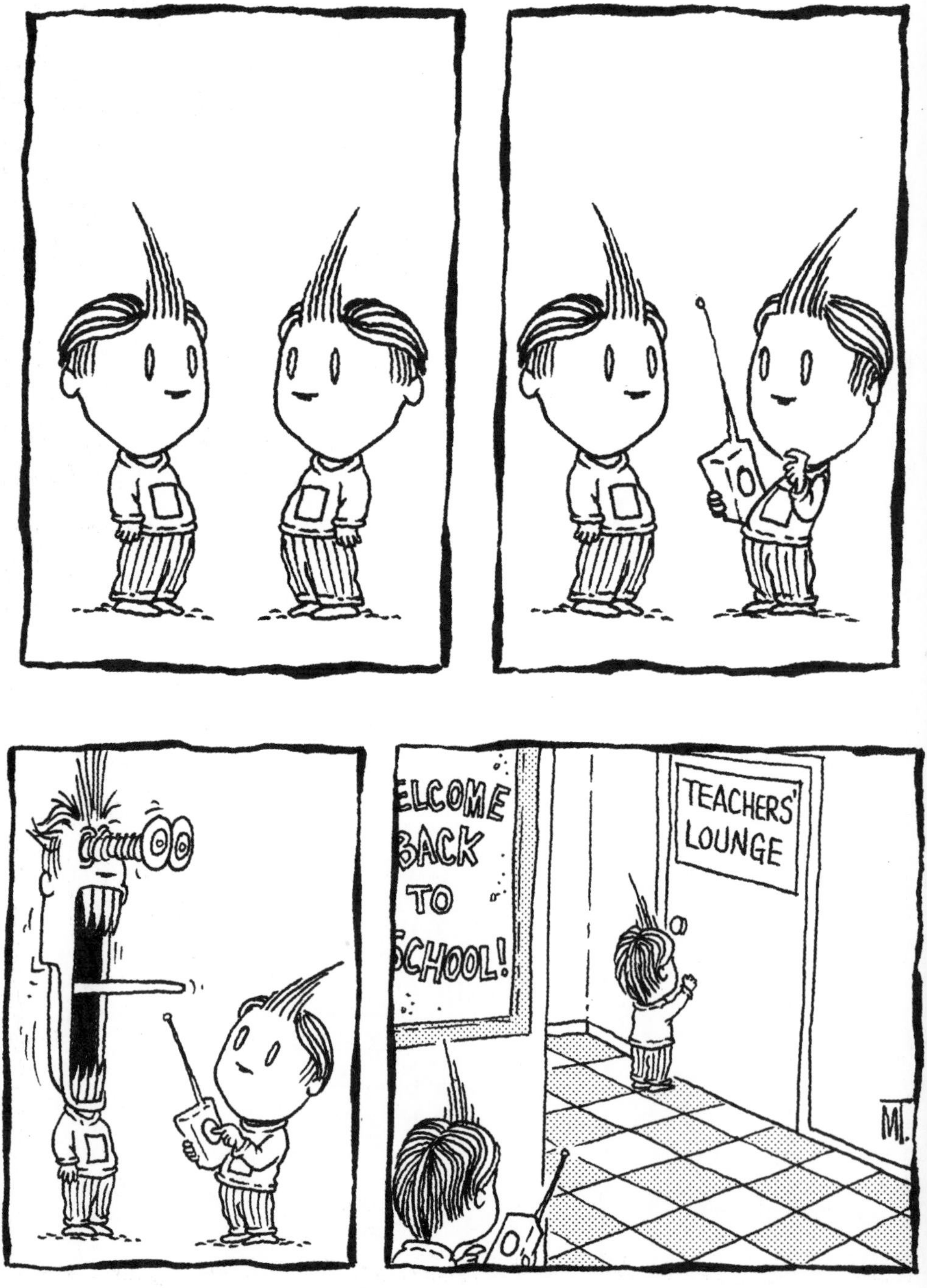
ELCOME
BACK
TO
SCHOOL!
TEACHERS'
LOUNGE
MT.

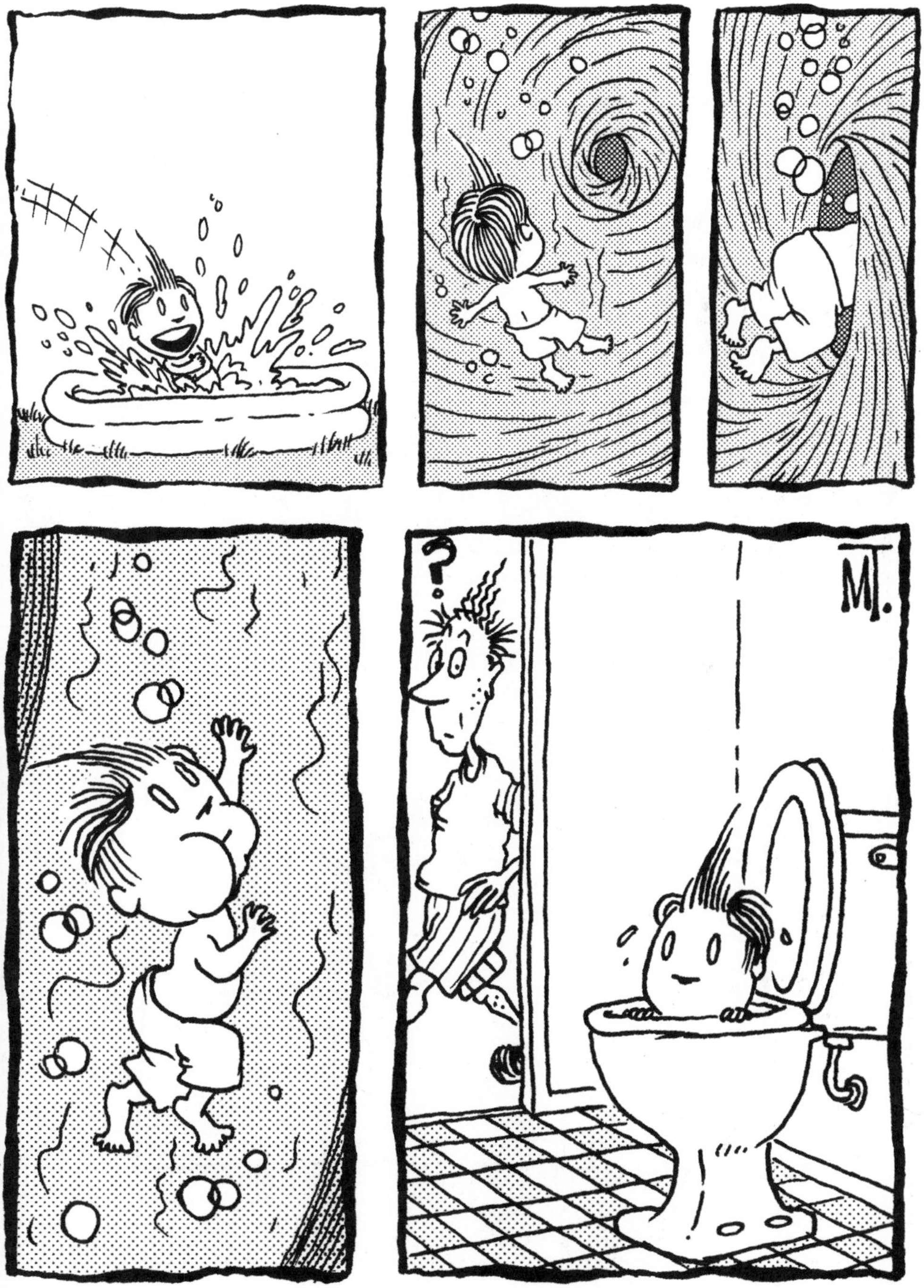
MT.

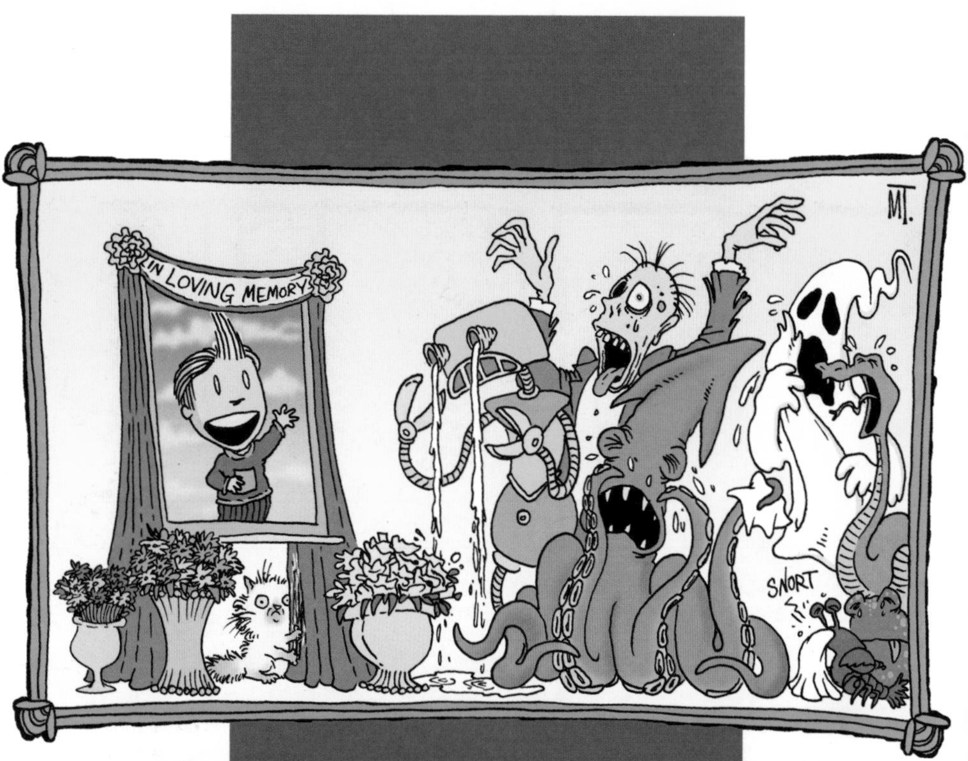
IN LOVING MEMORY
MT.
SNORT

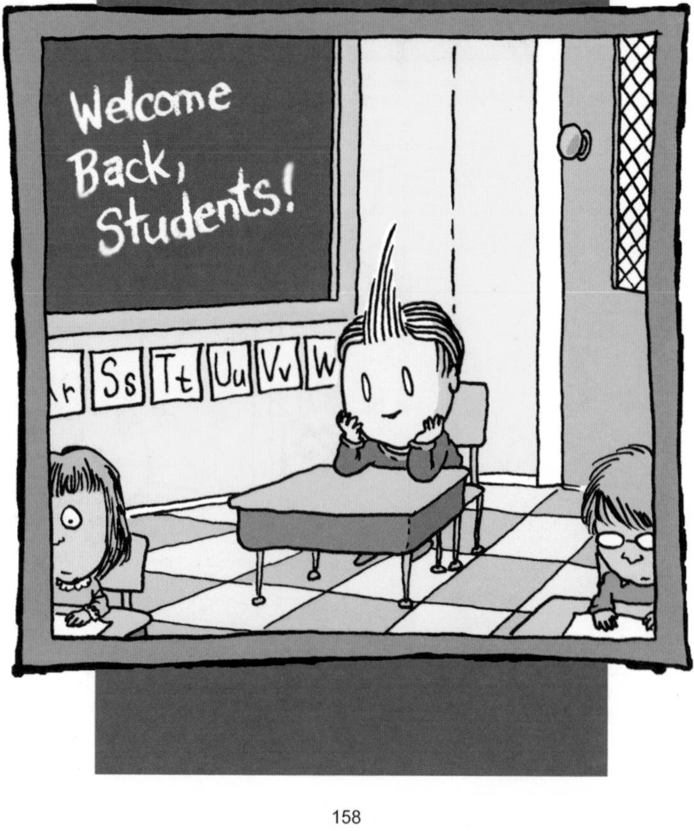
Welcome
Back,
Students!
Rr Ss Tt Uu Vv W

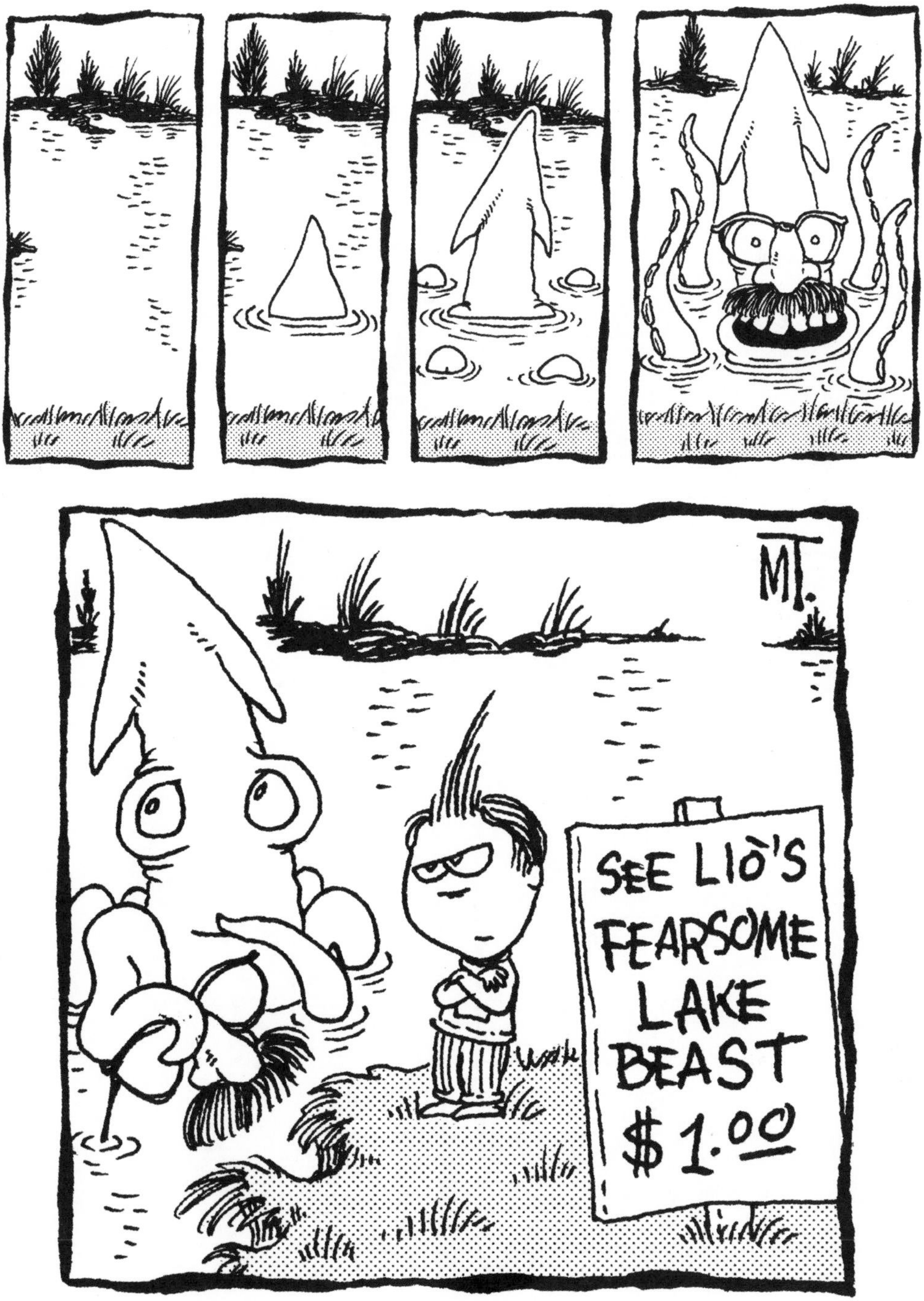
MT.
SEE LIO'S FEARSOME LAKE BEAST $1.00

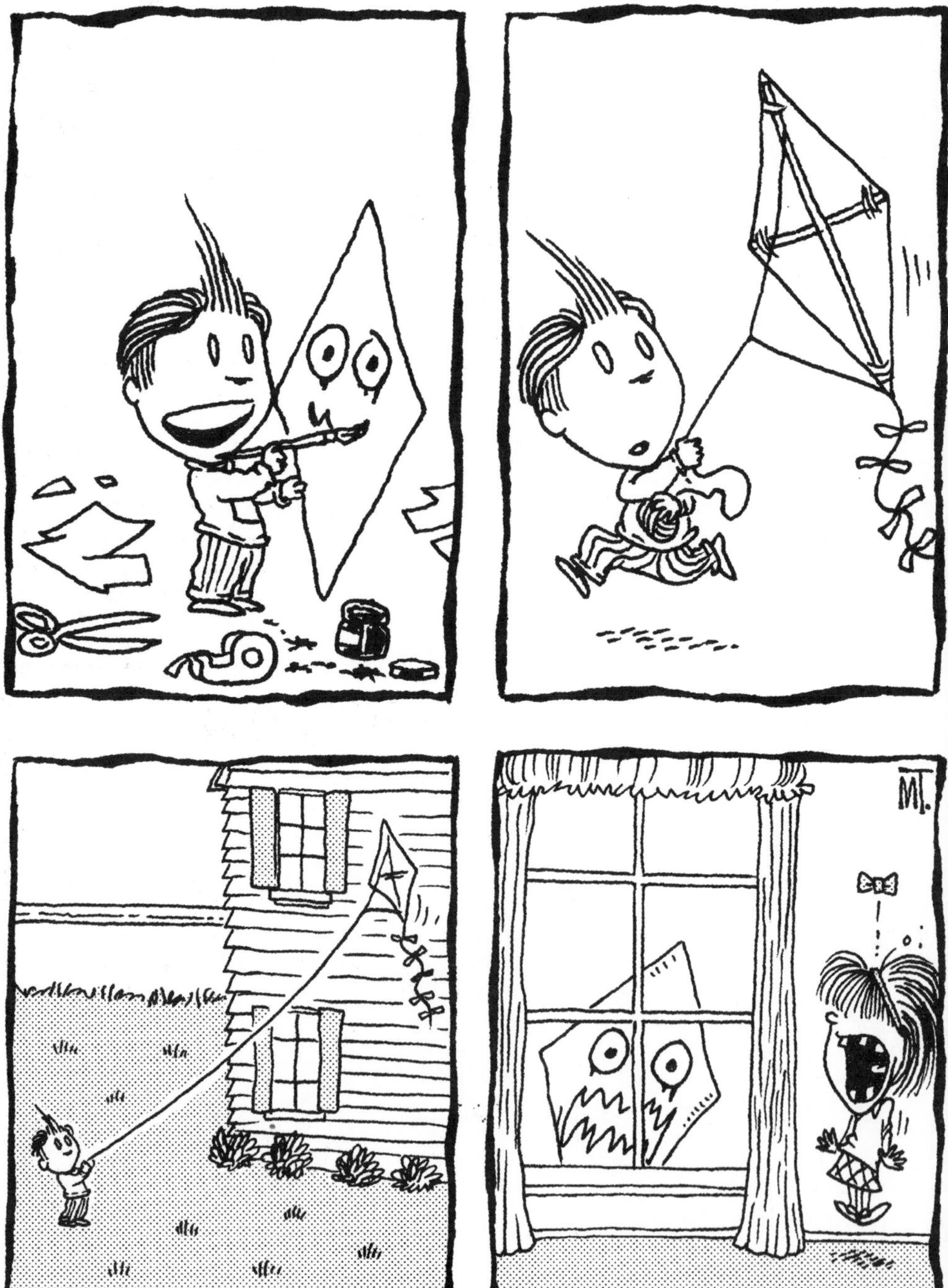

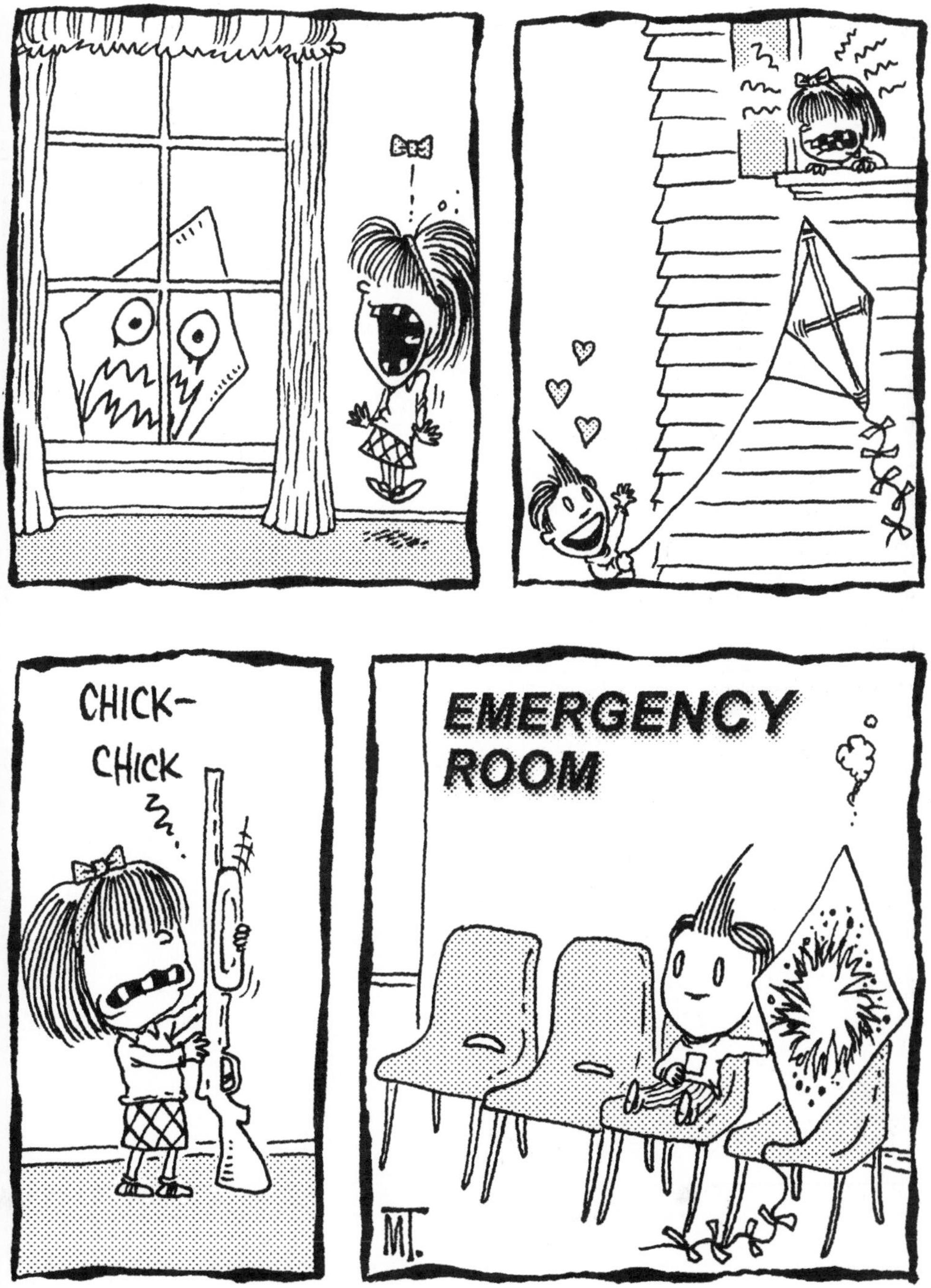
CHICK-
CHICK
EMERGENCY
ROOM
MT.

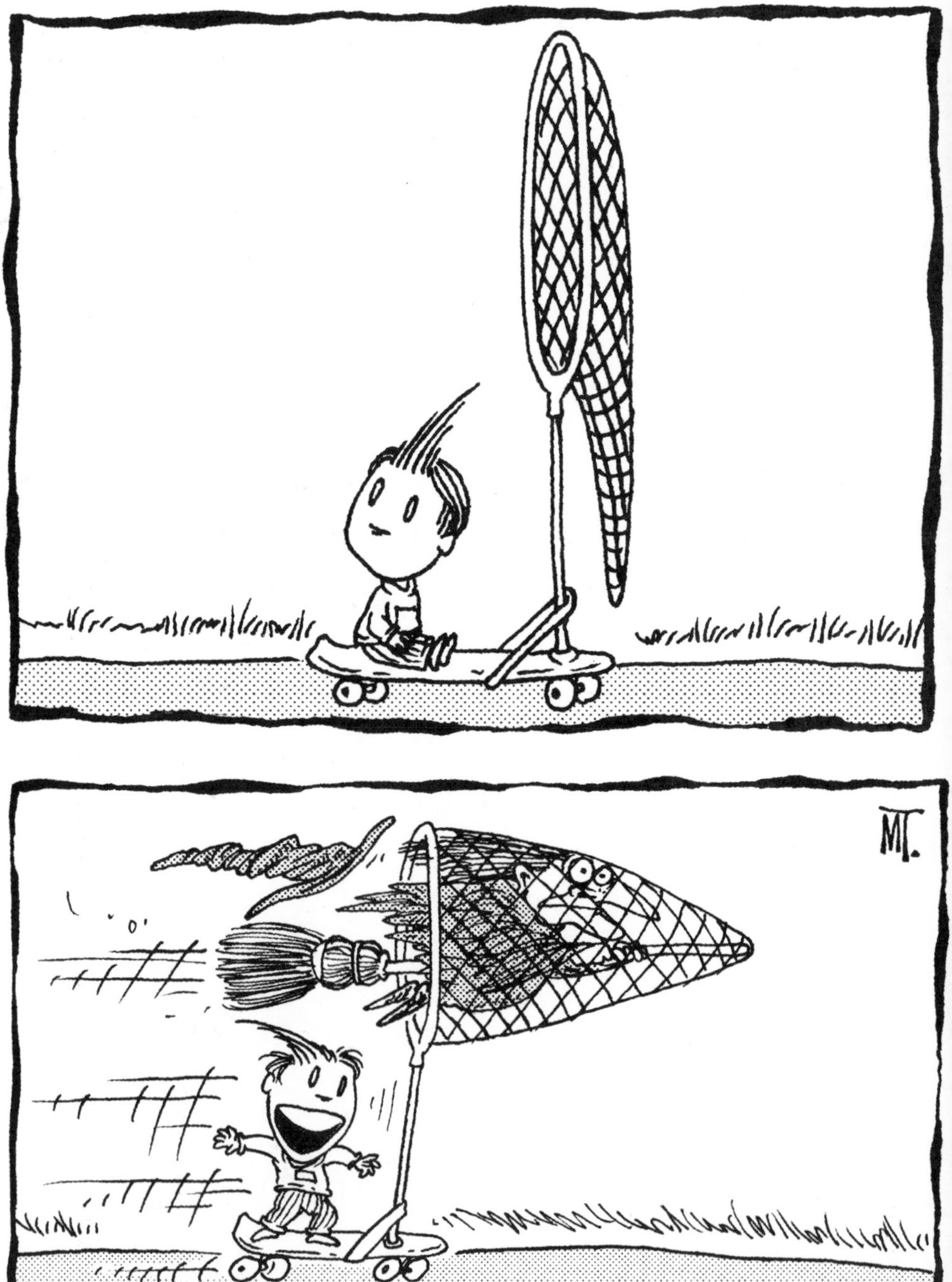

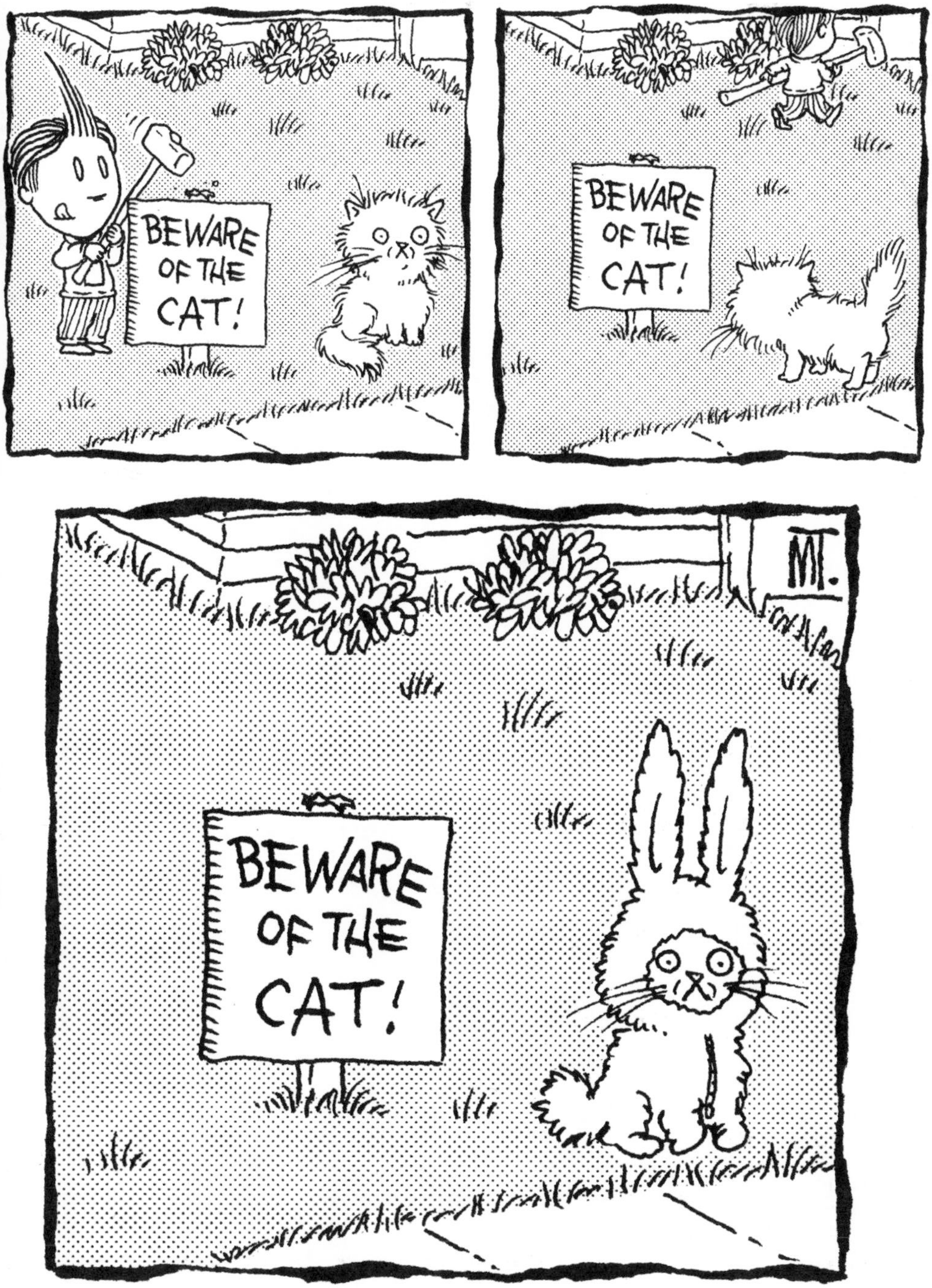
BEWARE OF THE CAT!
BEWARE OF THE CAT!
BEWARE OF THE CAT!
MT.

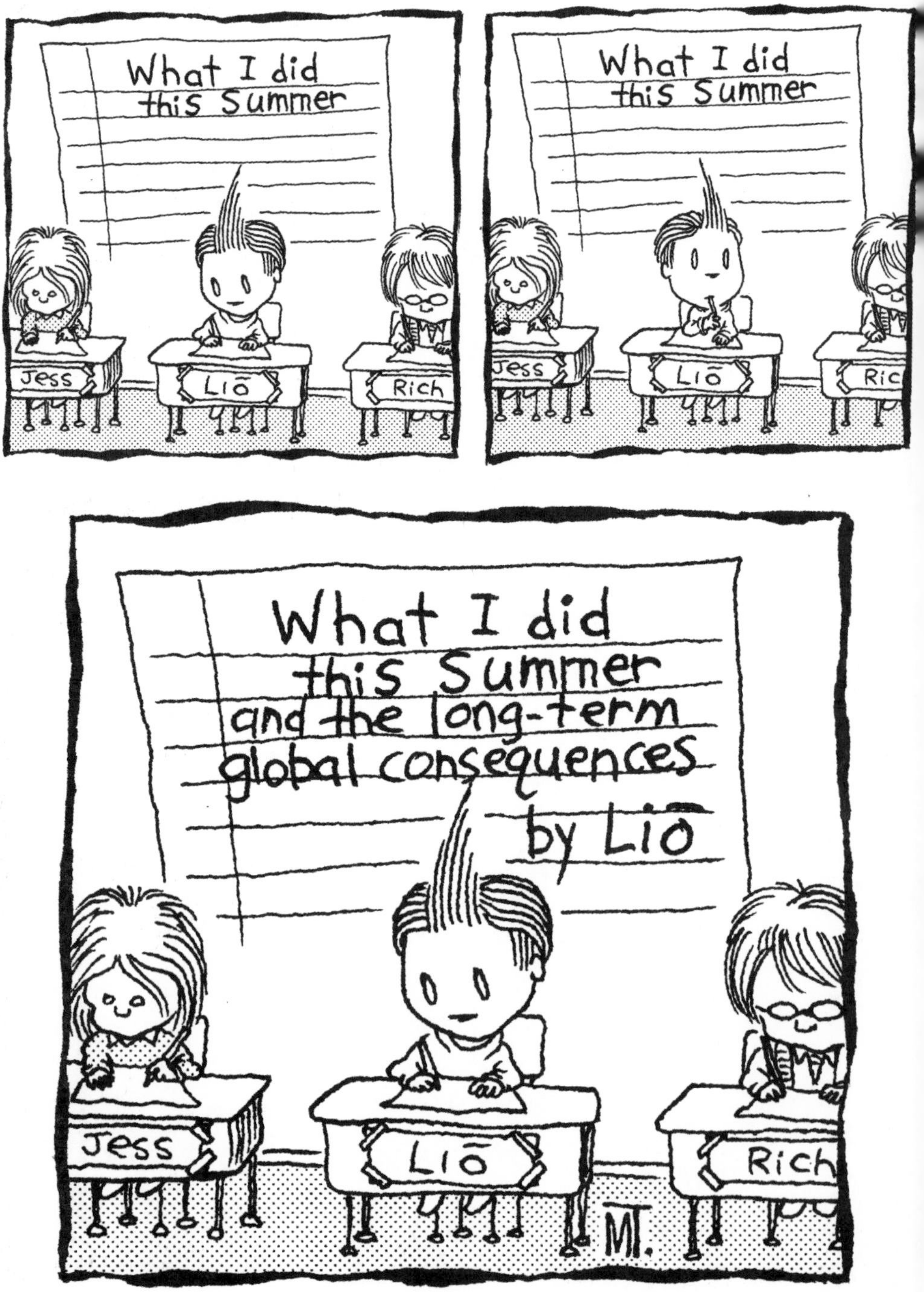
What I did this Summer
Jess
Liō
Rich
What I did this Summer
Jess
Liō
Ric
What I did this Summer and the long-term global consequences
by Liō
Jess
Liō
Rich
MT.

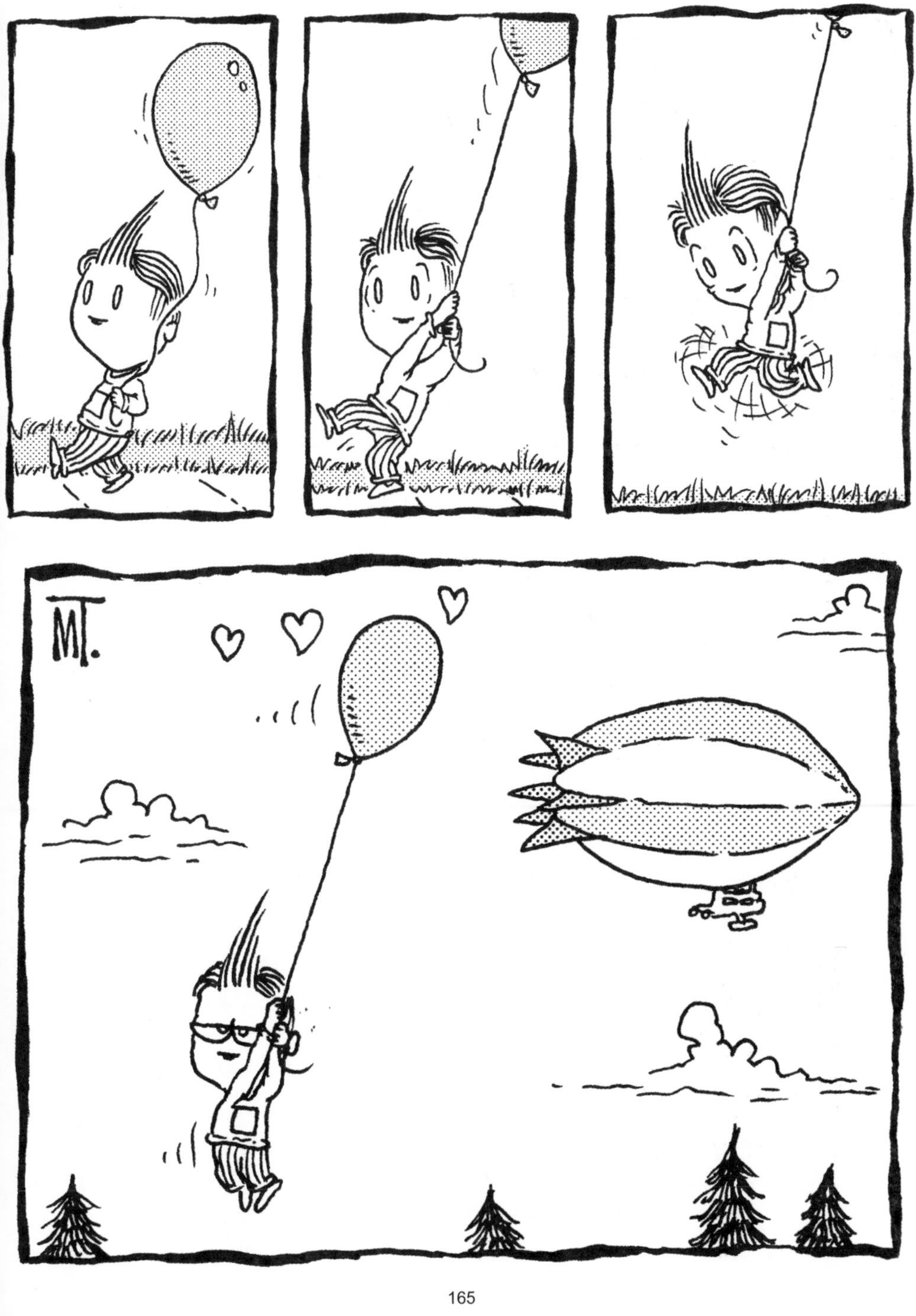
MT.

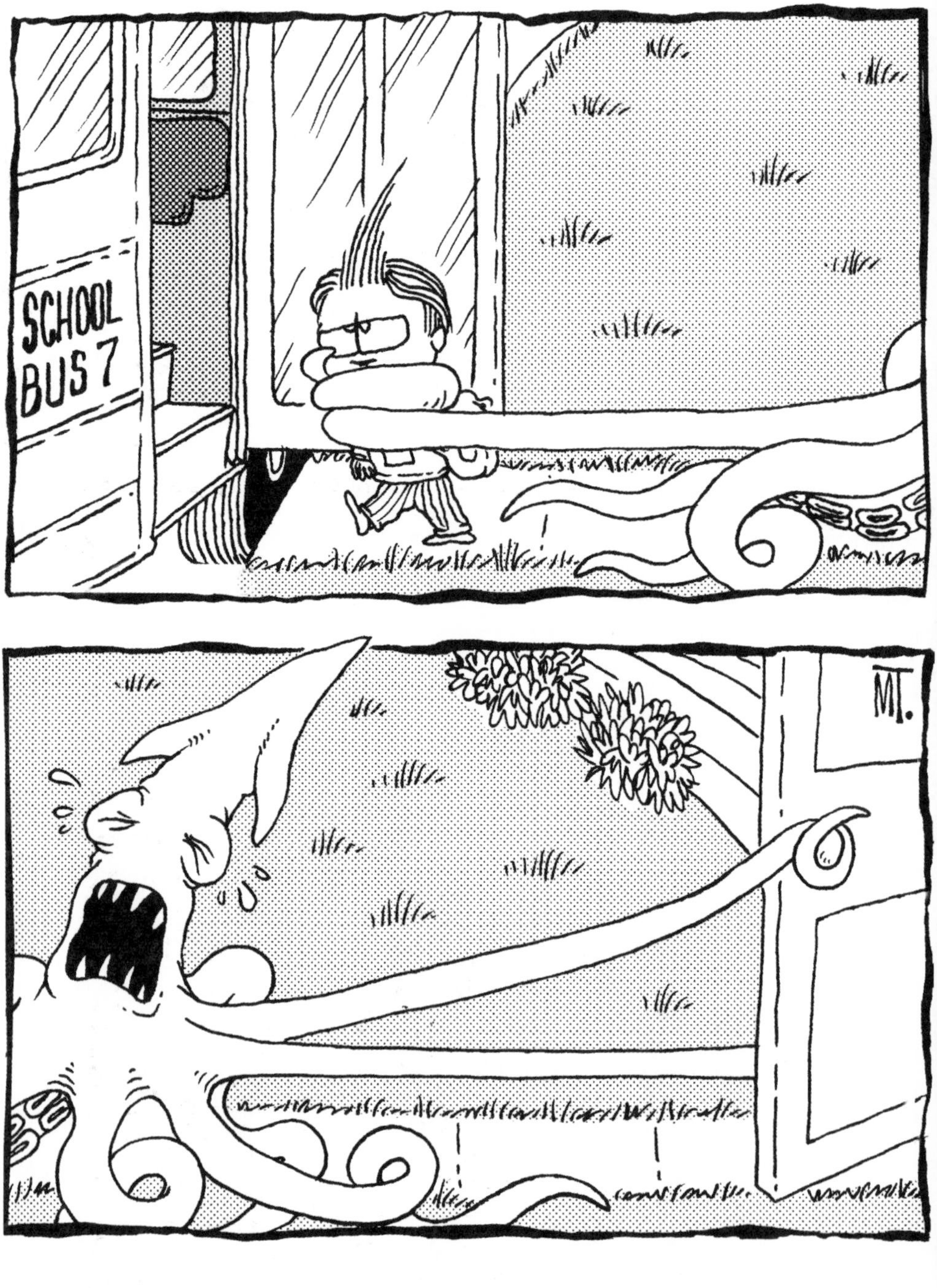
SCHOOL
BUS 7
MT.

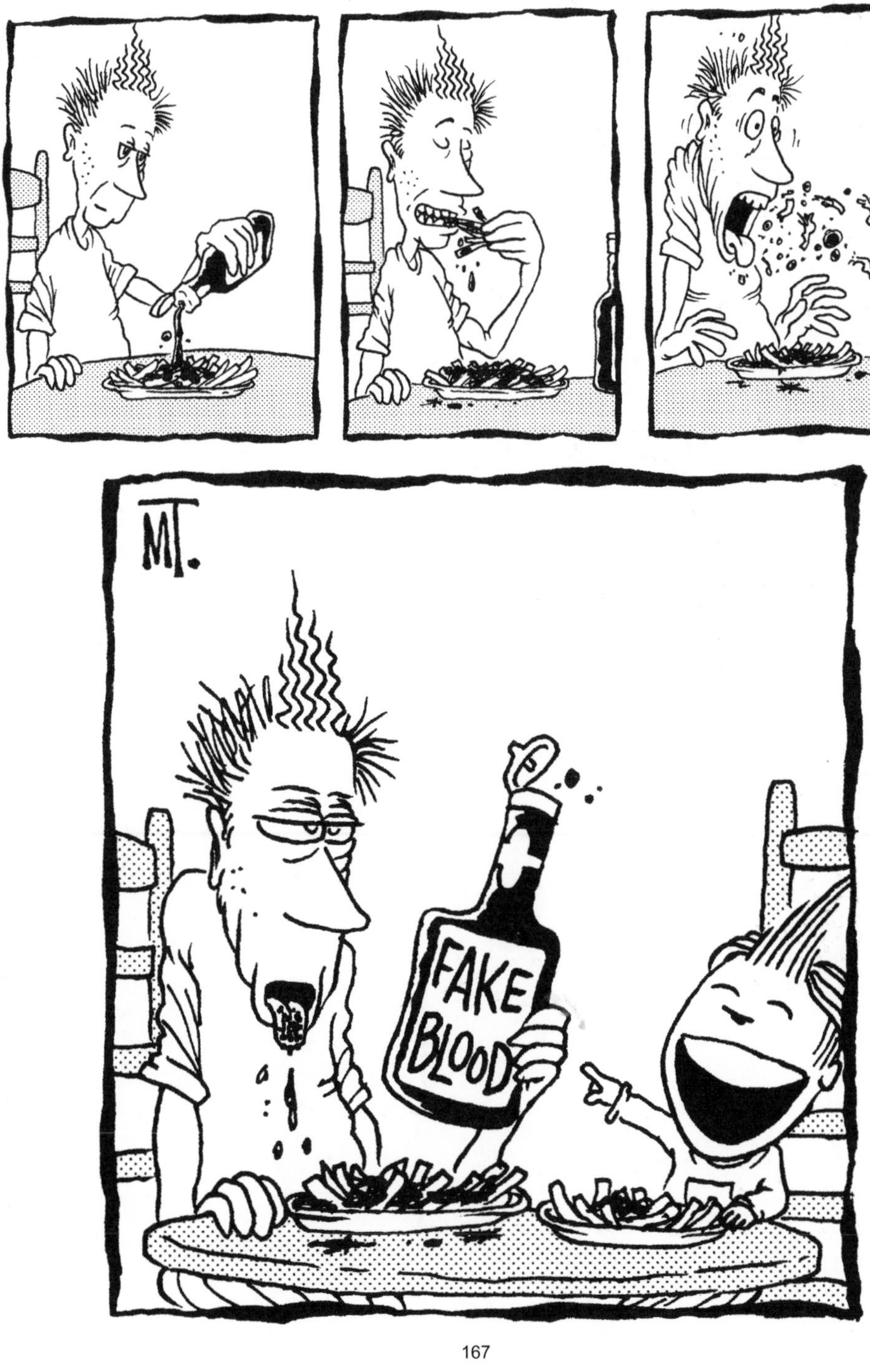
MT.
FAKE BLOOD

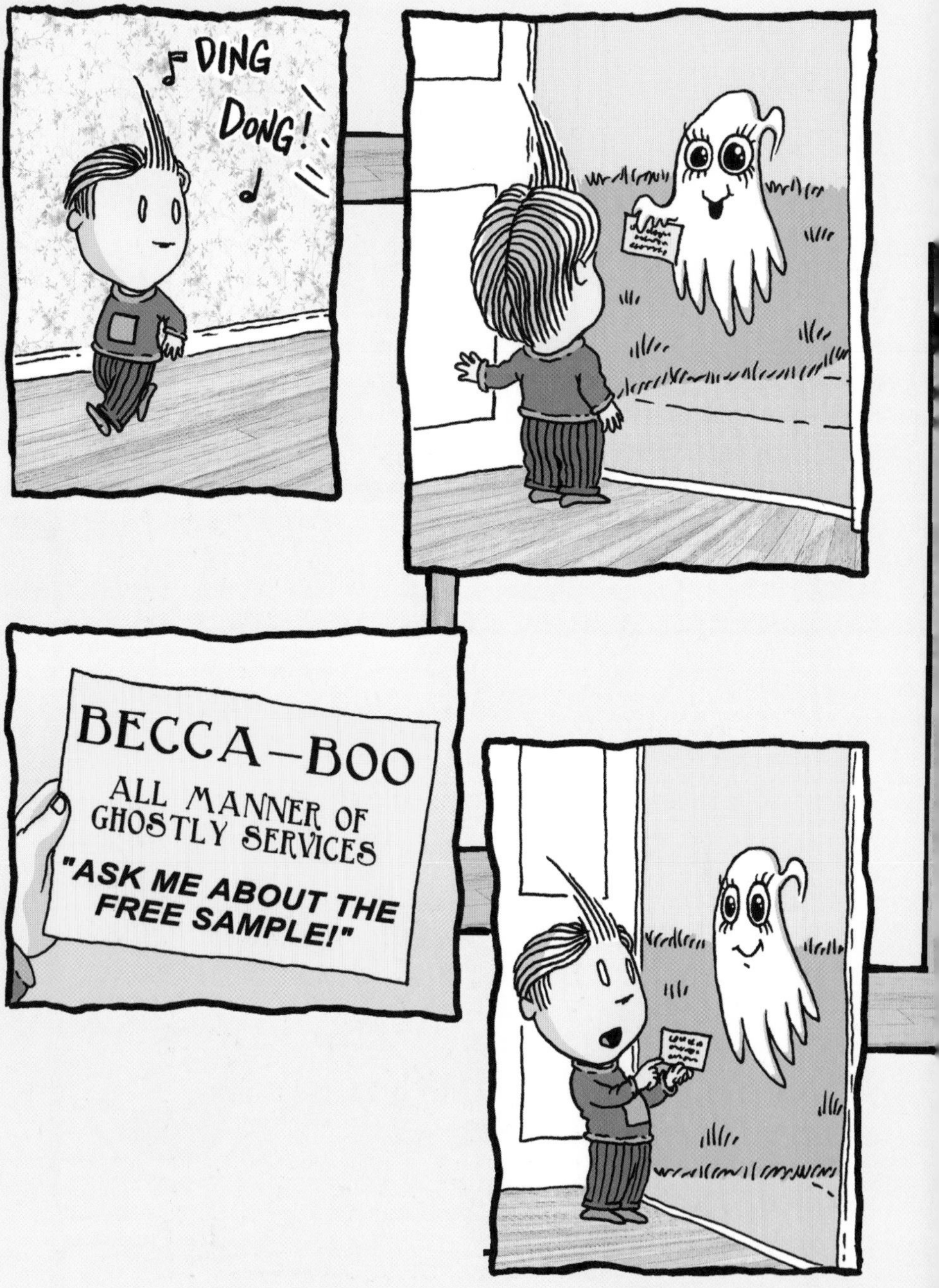
DING
DONG!
BECCA–BOO
ALL MANNER OF GHOSTLY SERVICES
"ASK ME ABOUT THE FREE SAMPLE!"

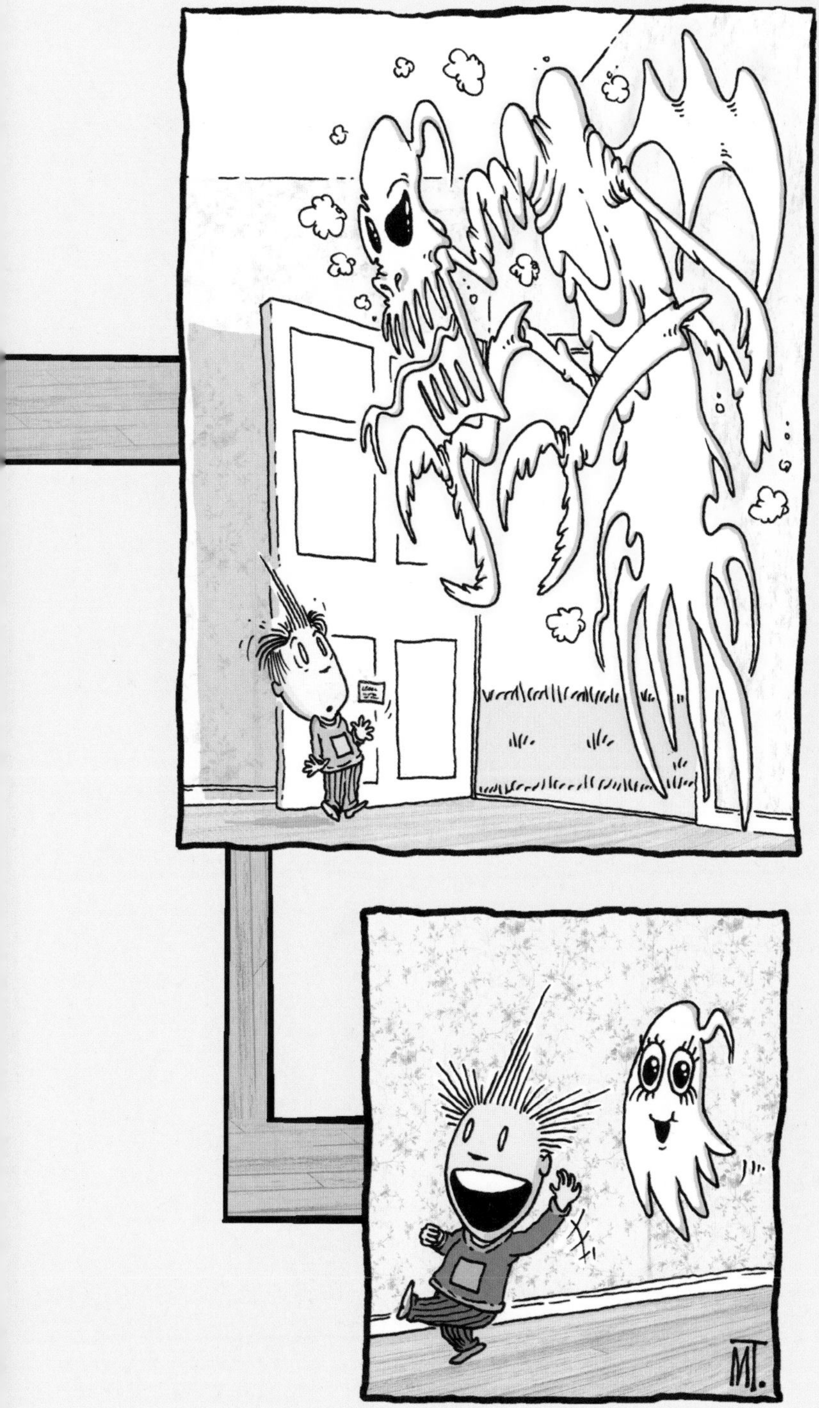

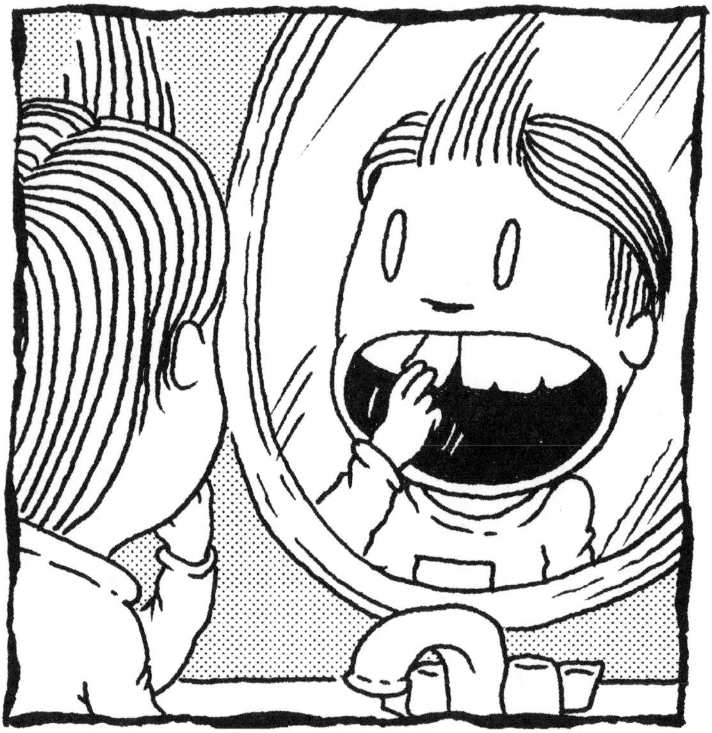

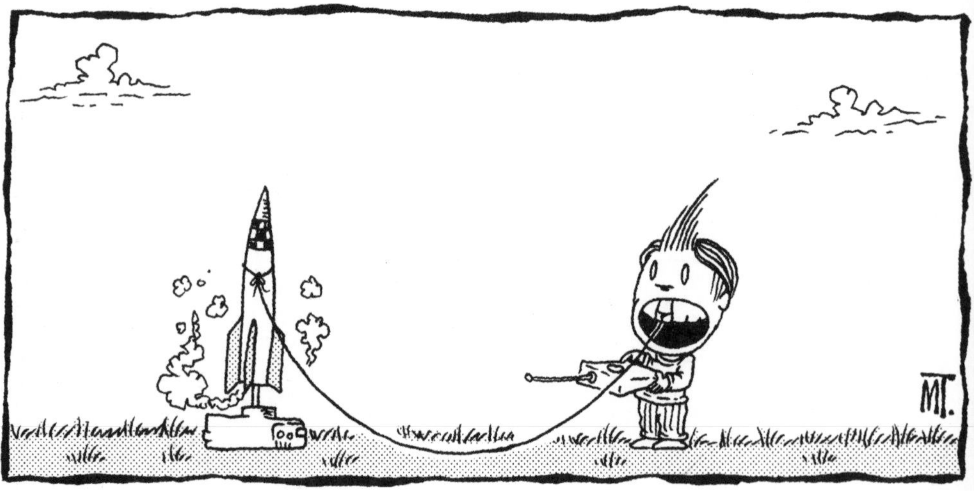
MT.

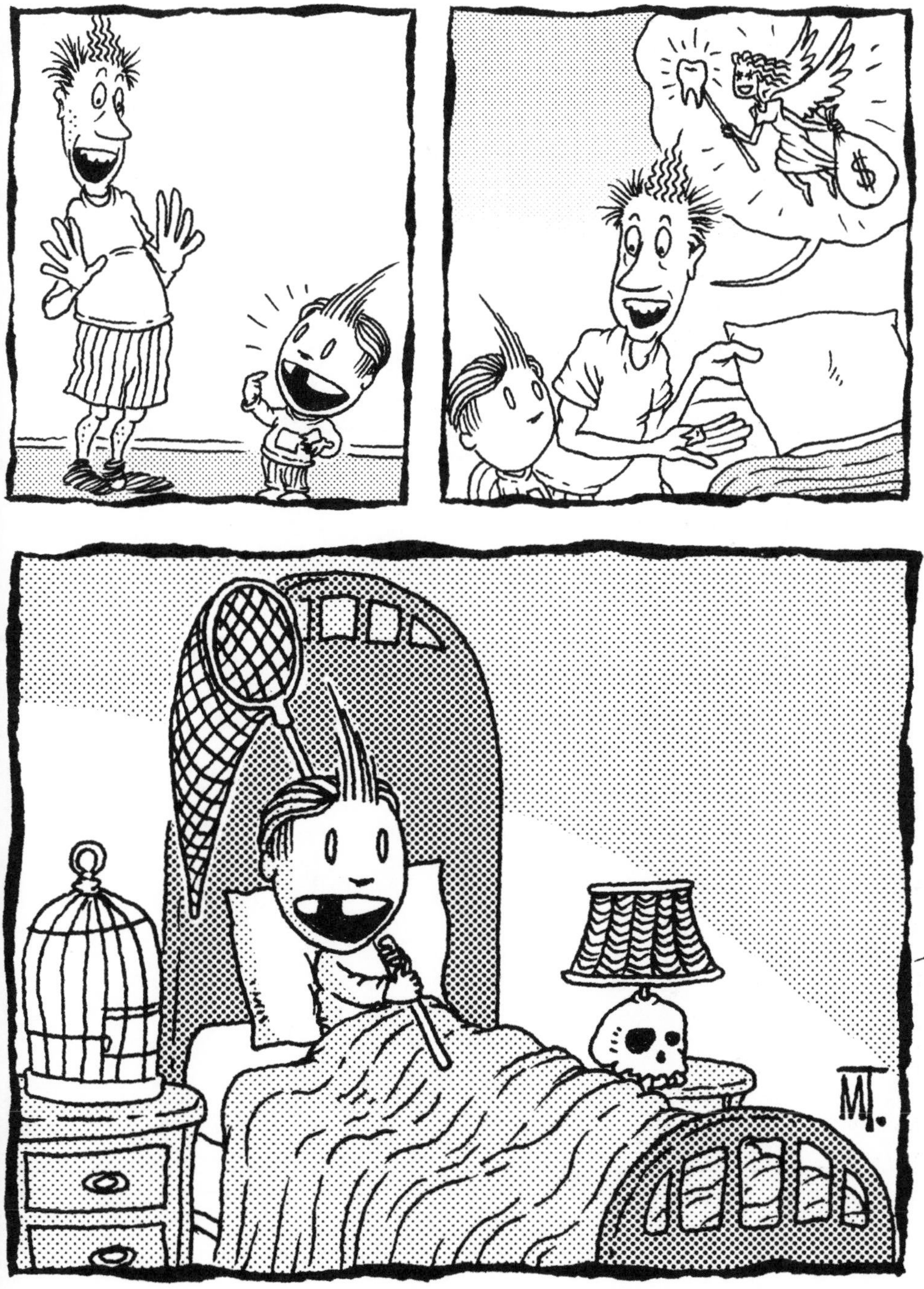

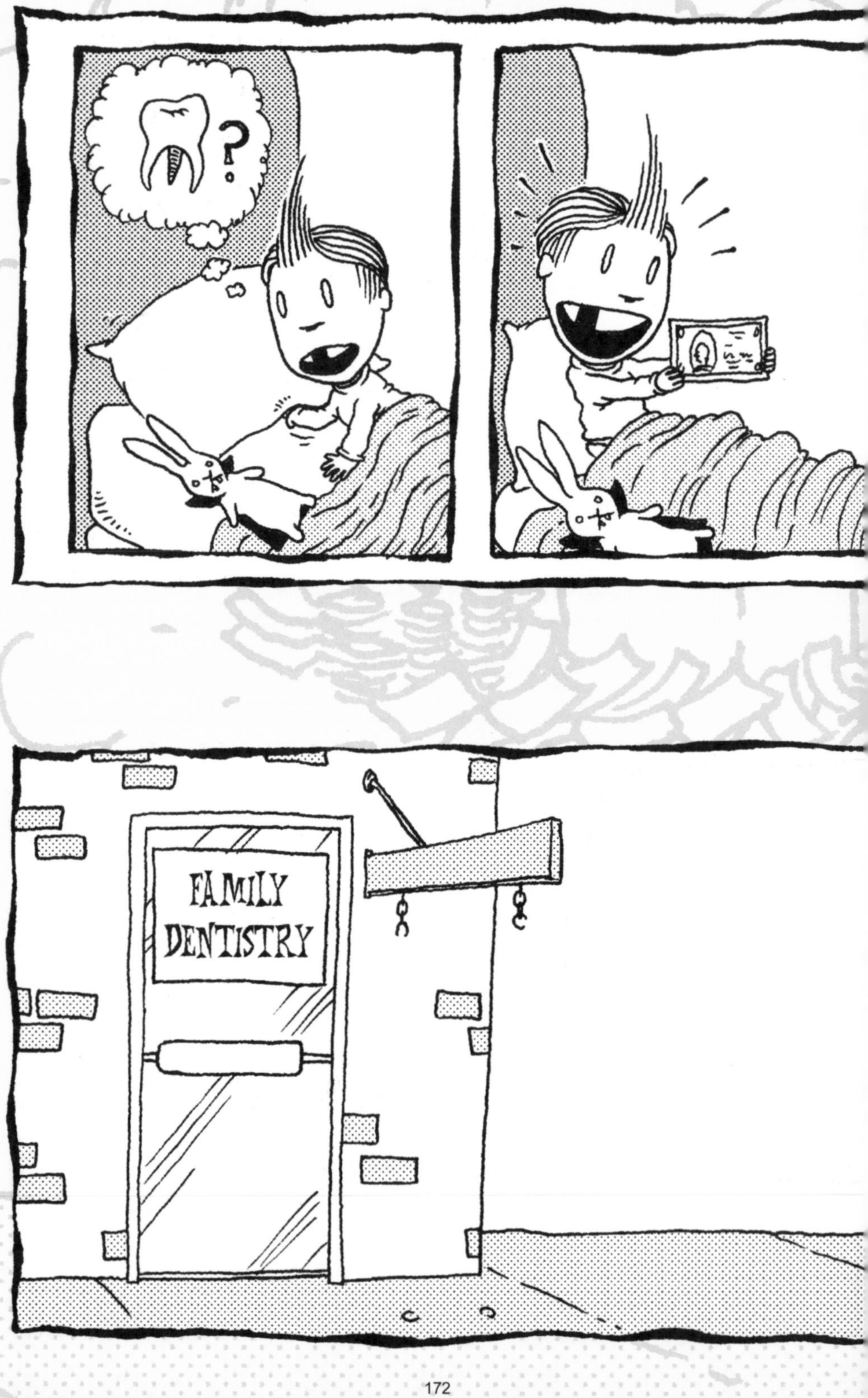

FAMILY
DENTISTRY

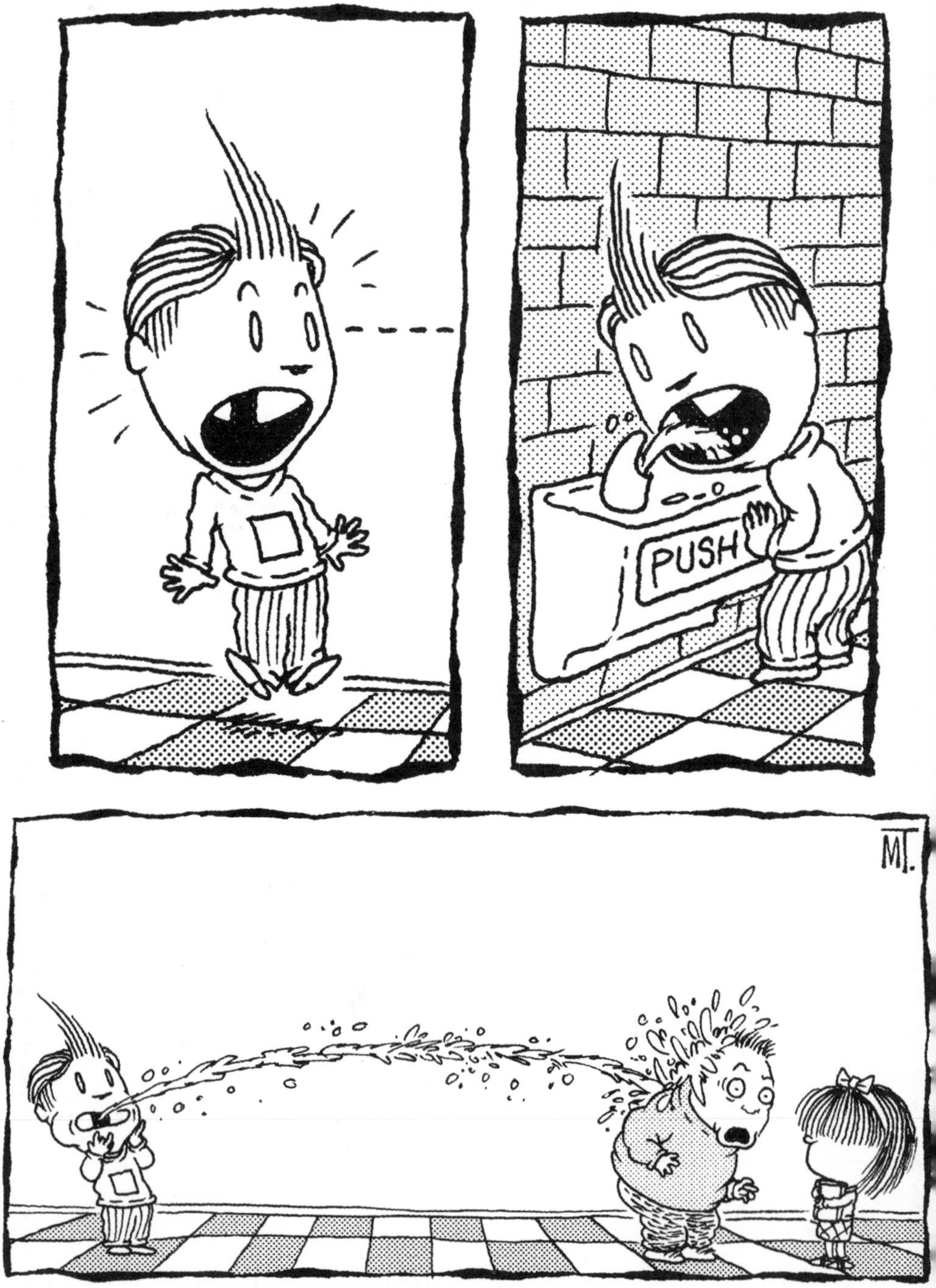
PUSH
MT.

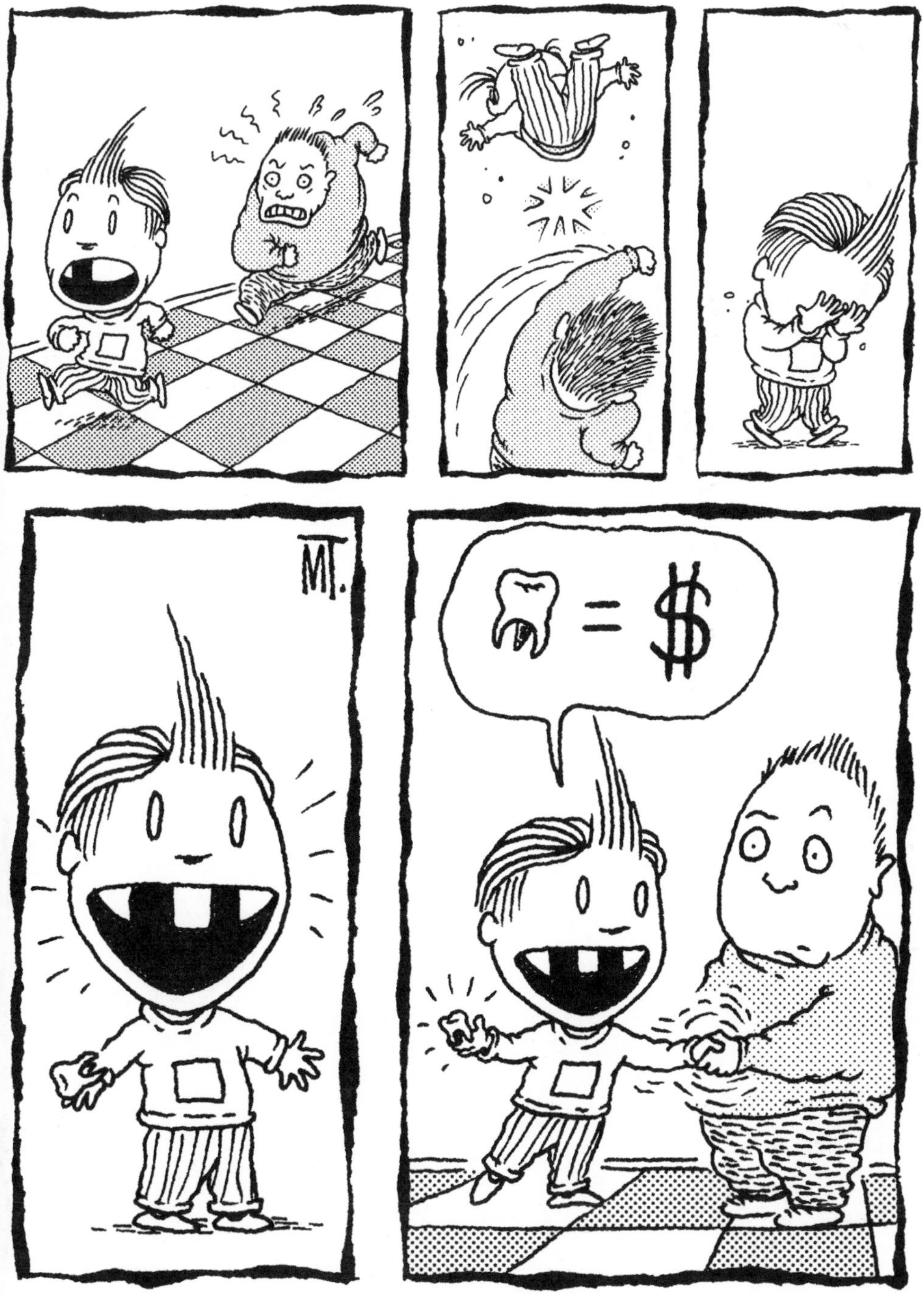
MT.
= $

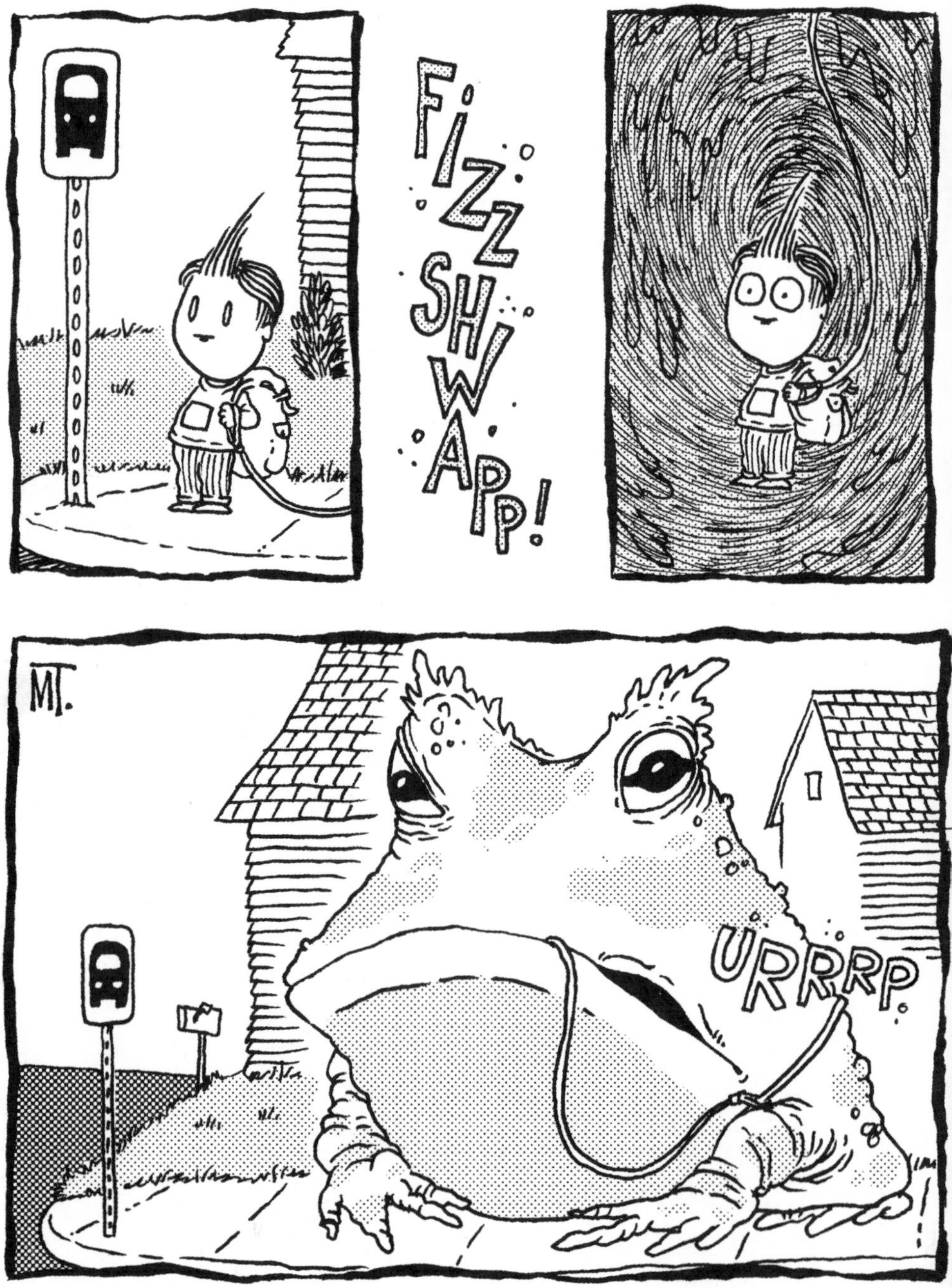
FIZZ
SHWAPP!
MT.
URRRP

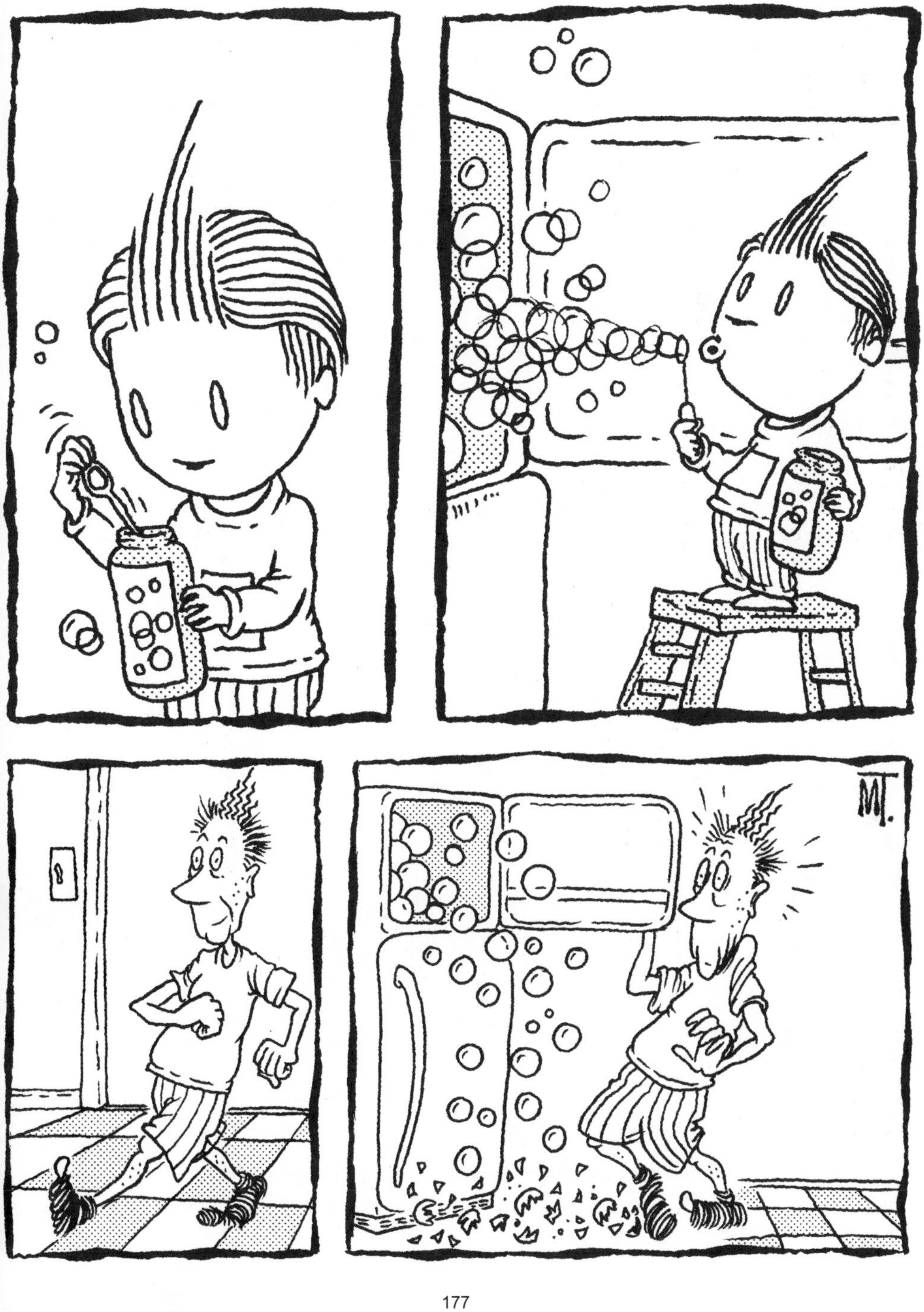
MT.

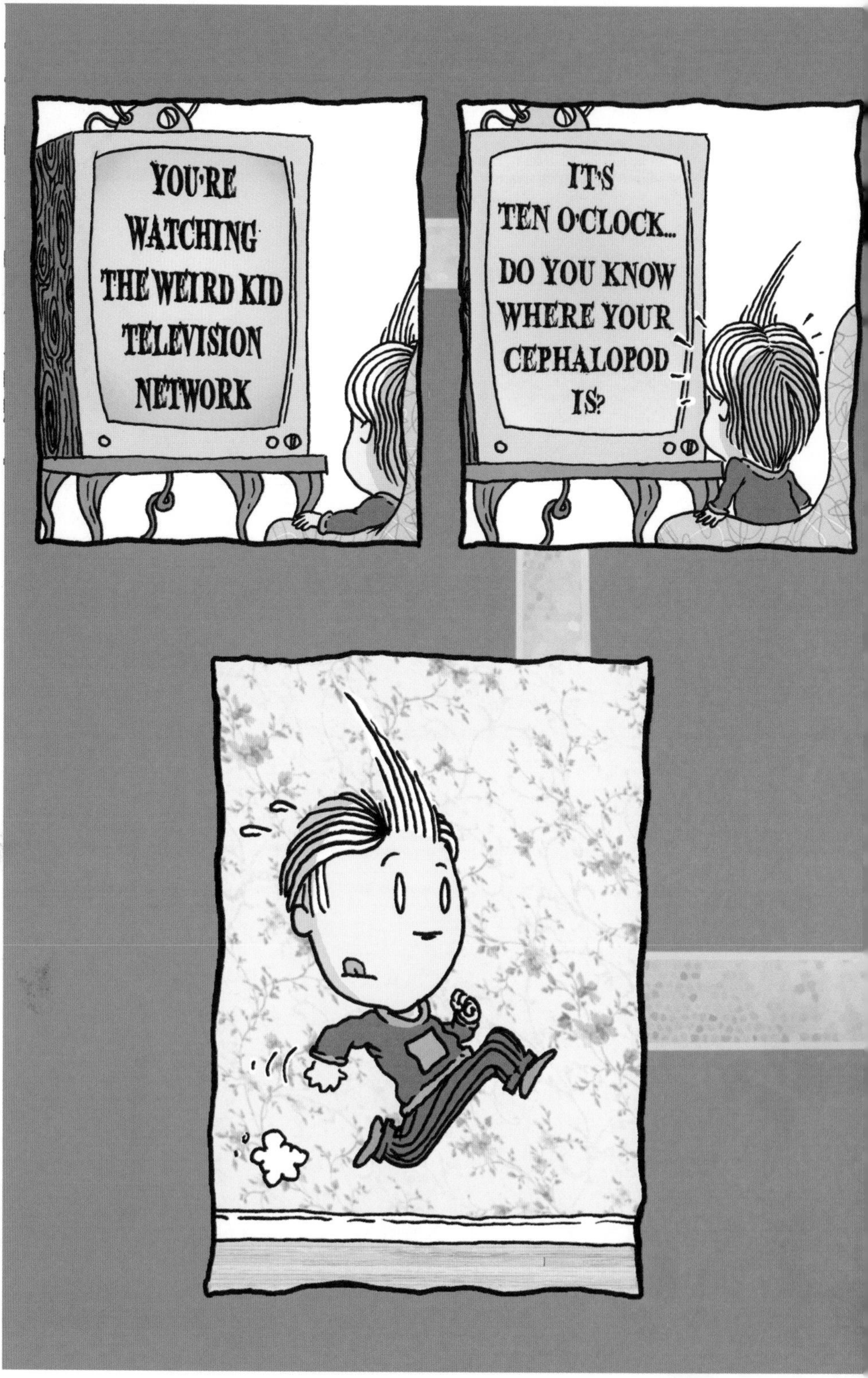
YOU'RE WATCHING THE WEIRD KID TELEVISION NETWORK
IT'S TEN O'CLOCK... DO YOU KNOW WHERE YOUR CEPHALOPOD IS?

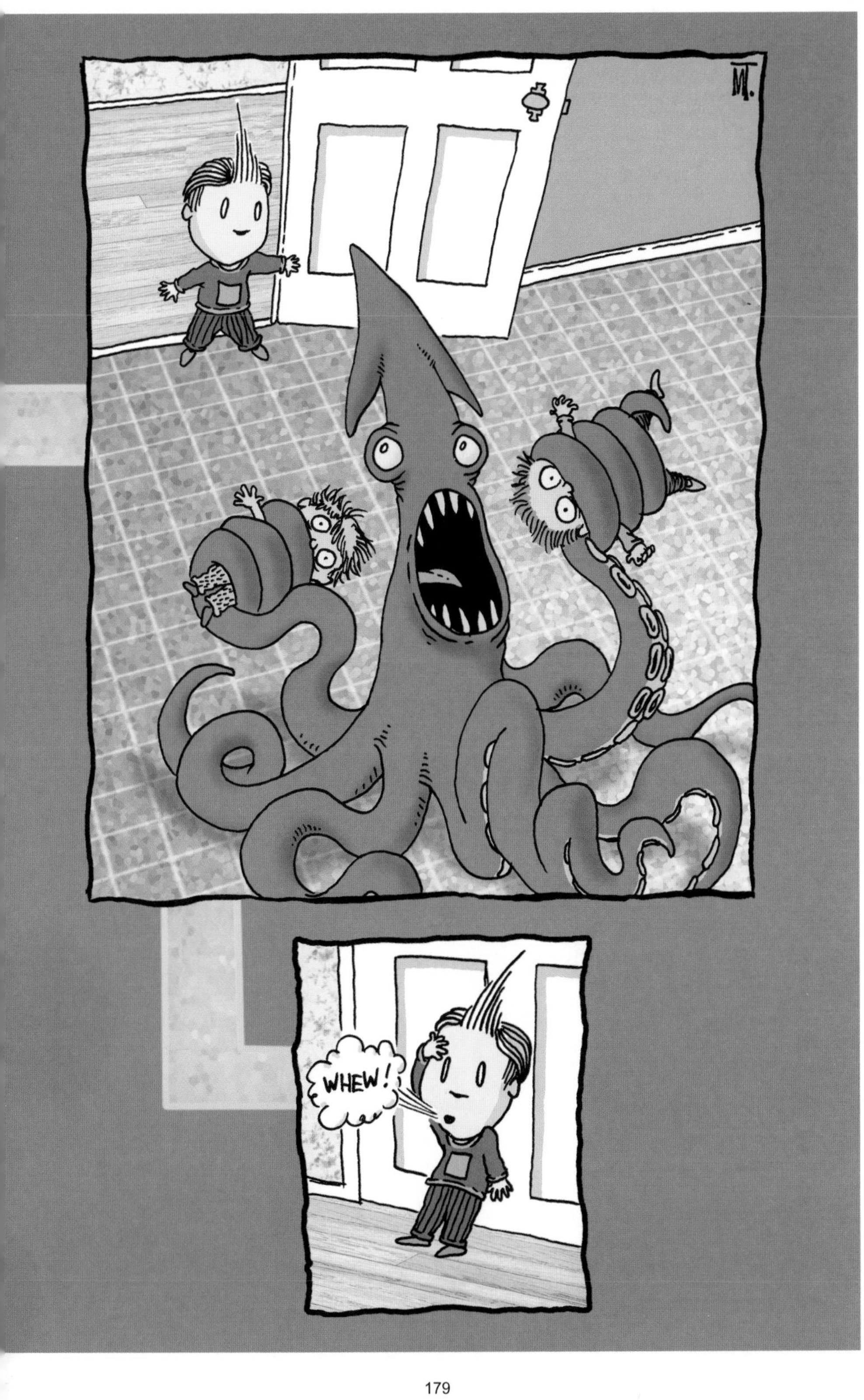
WHEW!

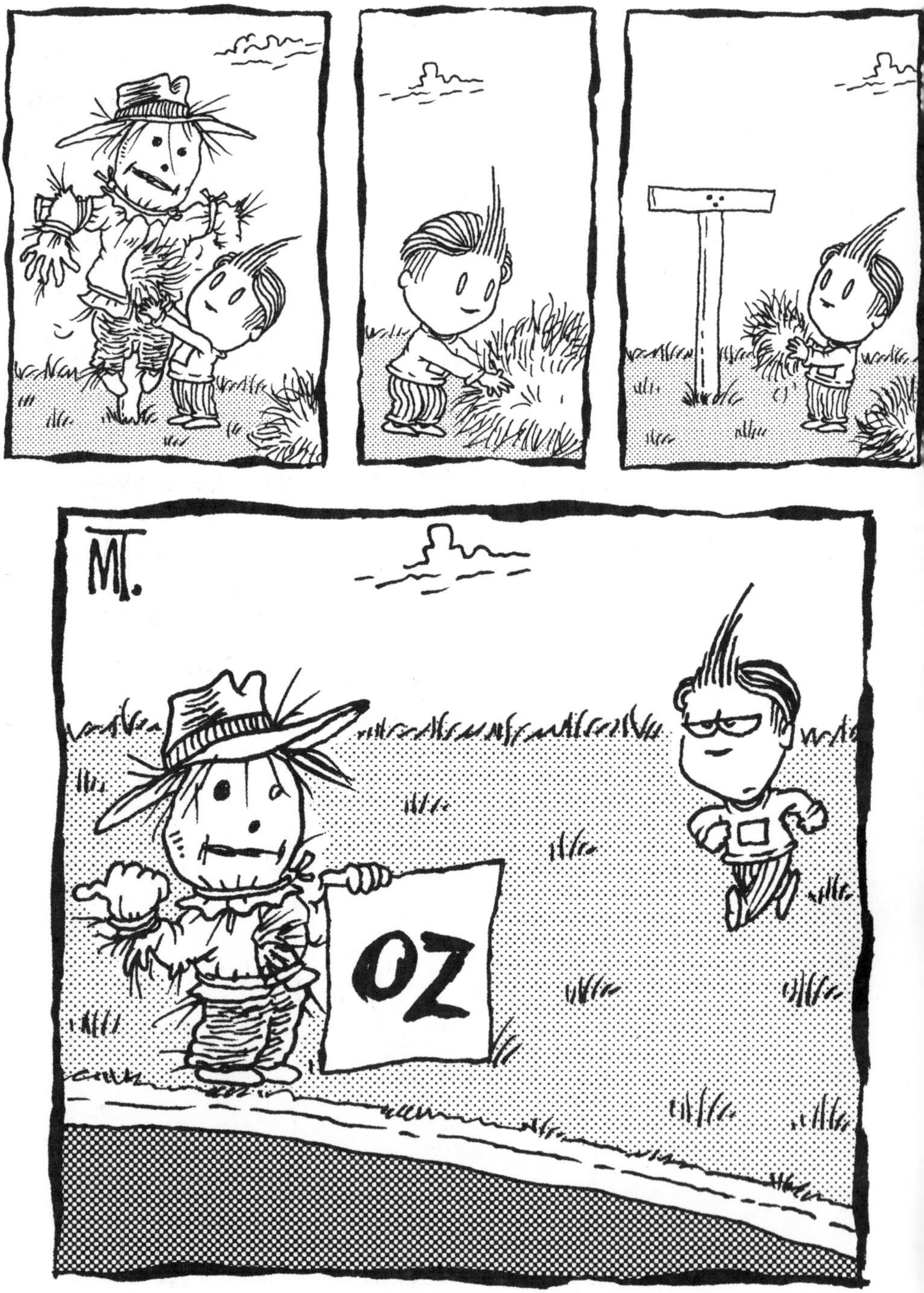
OZ

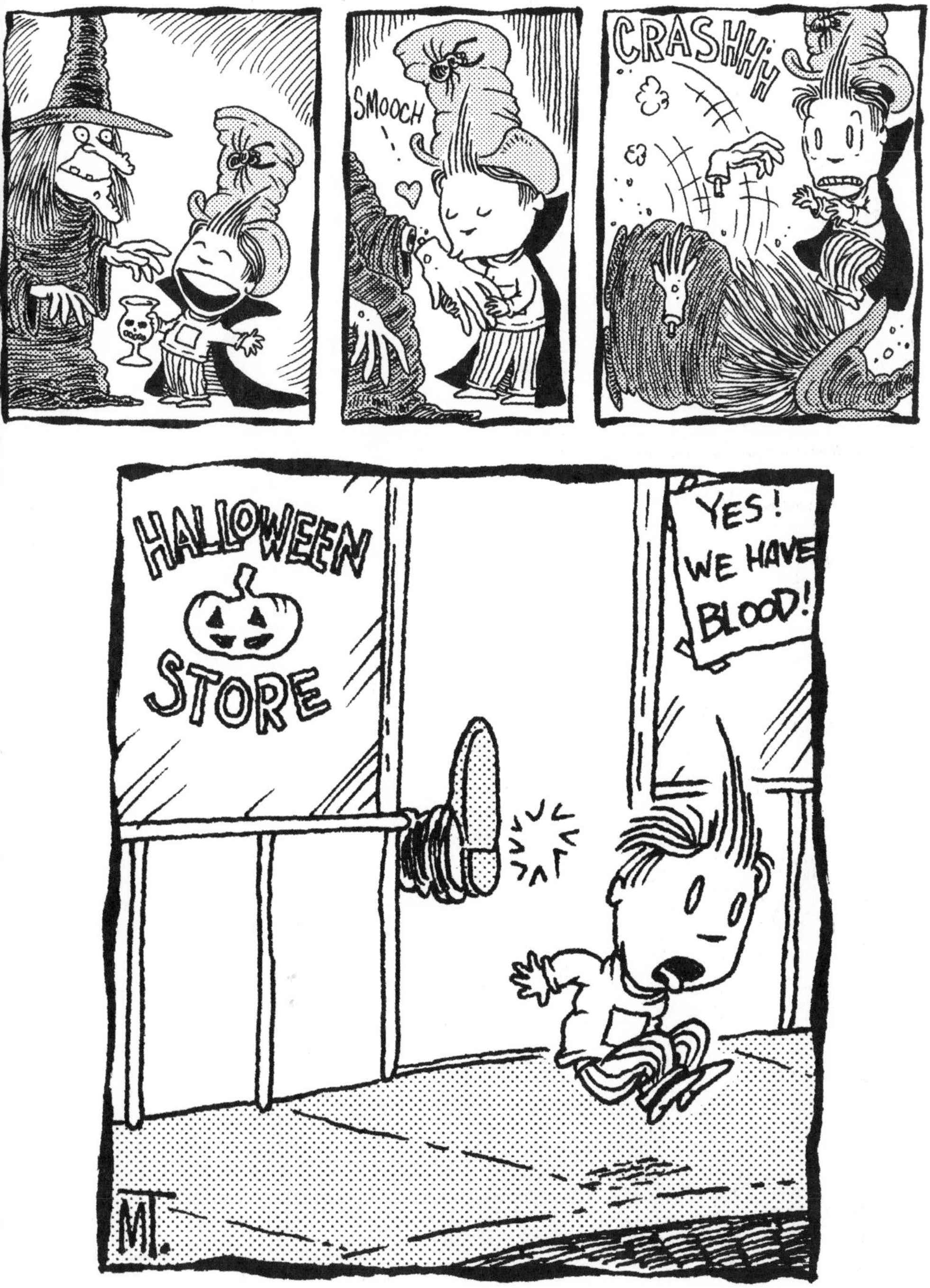
SMOOCH
CRASHHH
HALLOWEEN STORE
YES! WE HAVE BLOOD!
MT.

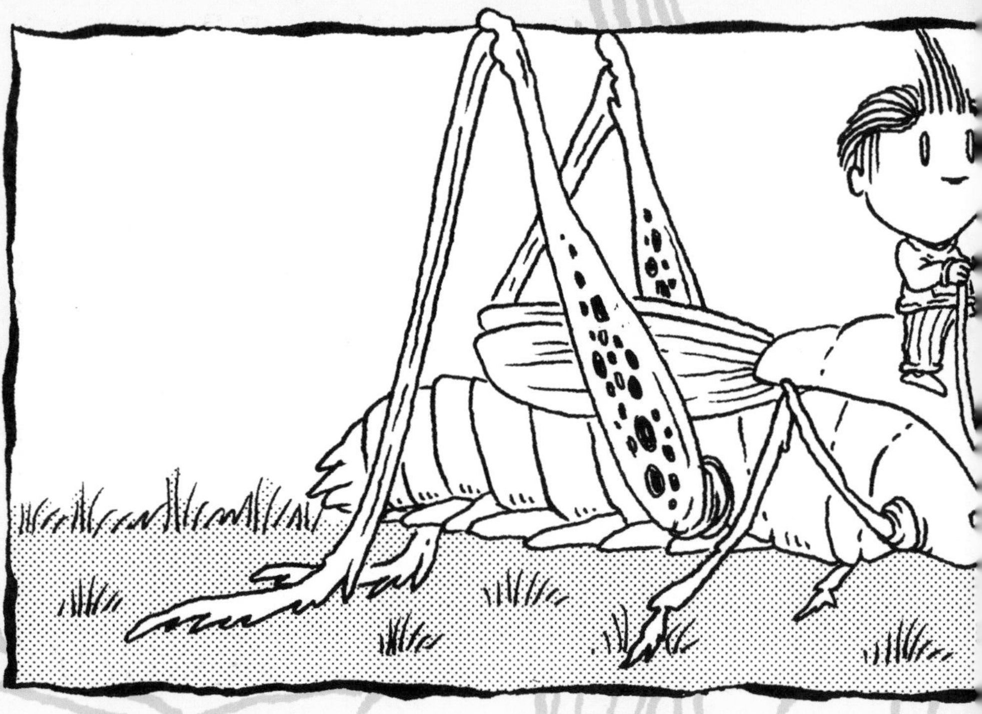

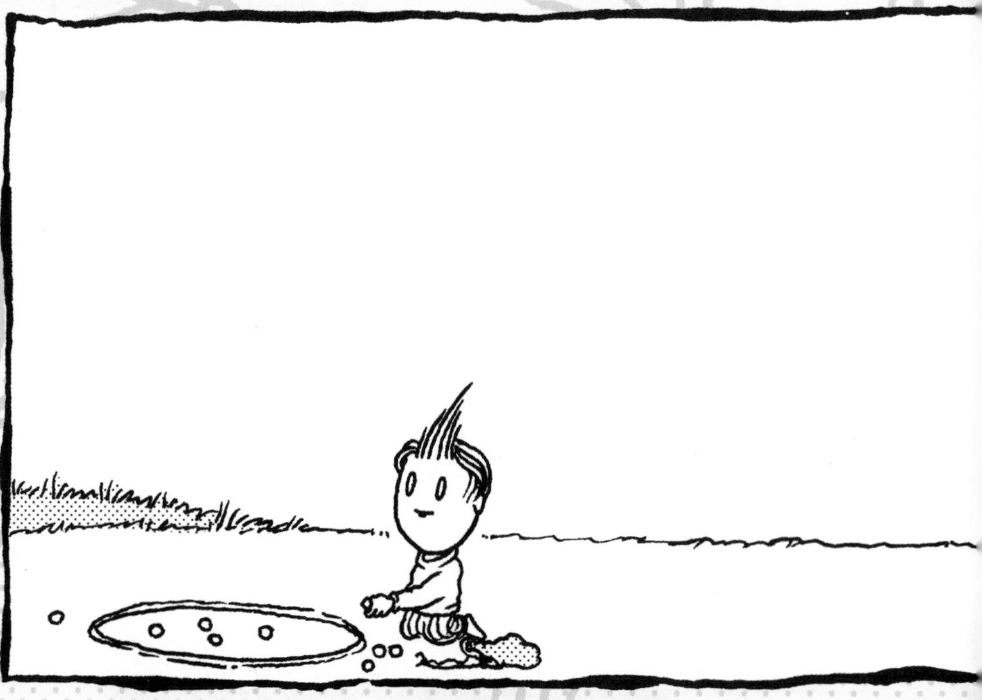

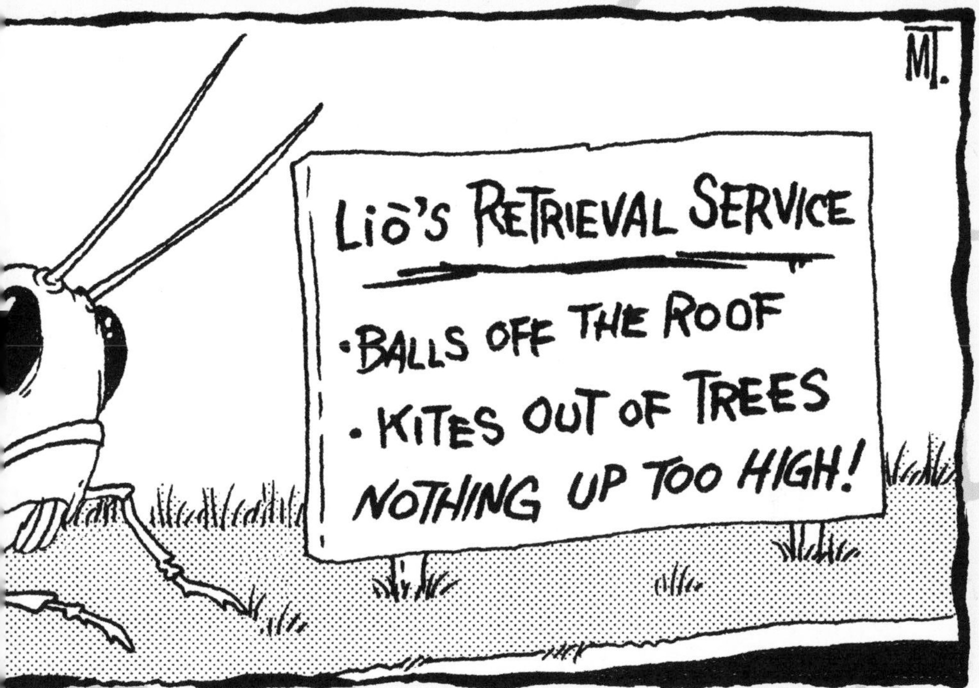
LIŌ'S RETRIEVAL SERVICE
•BALLS OFF THE ROOF
•KITES OUT OF TREES
NOTHING UP TOO HIGH!

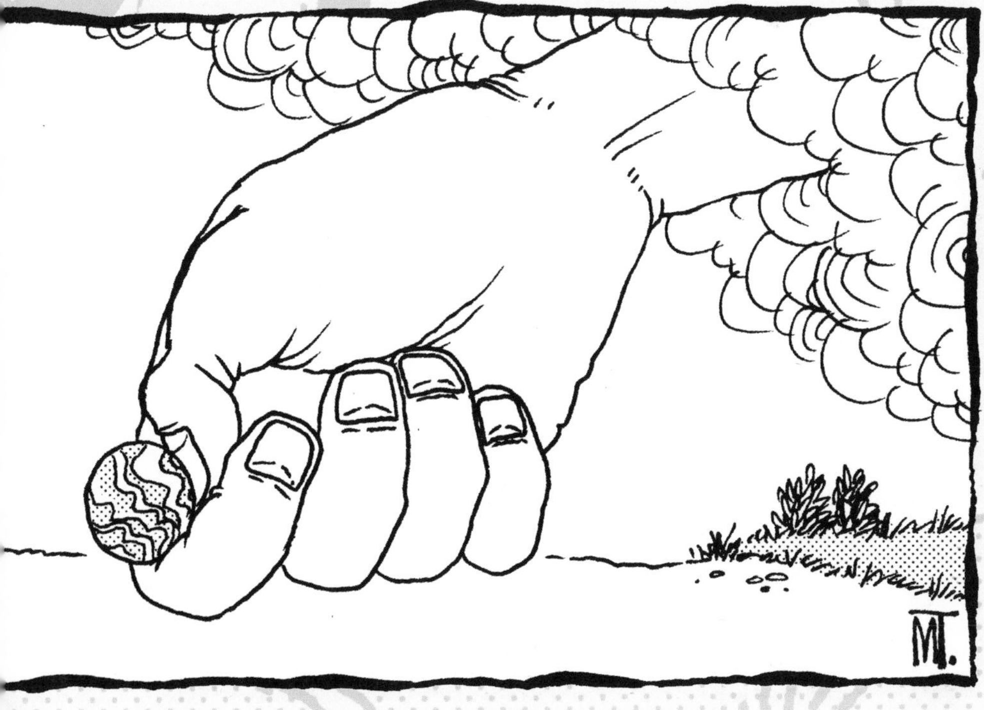

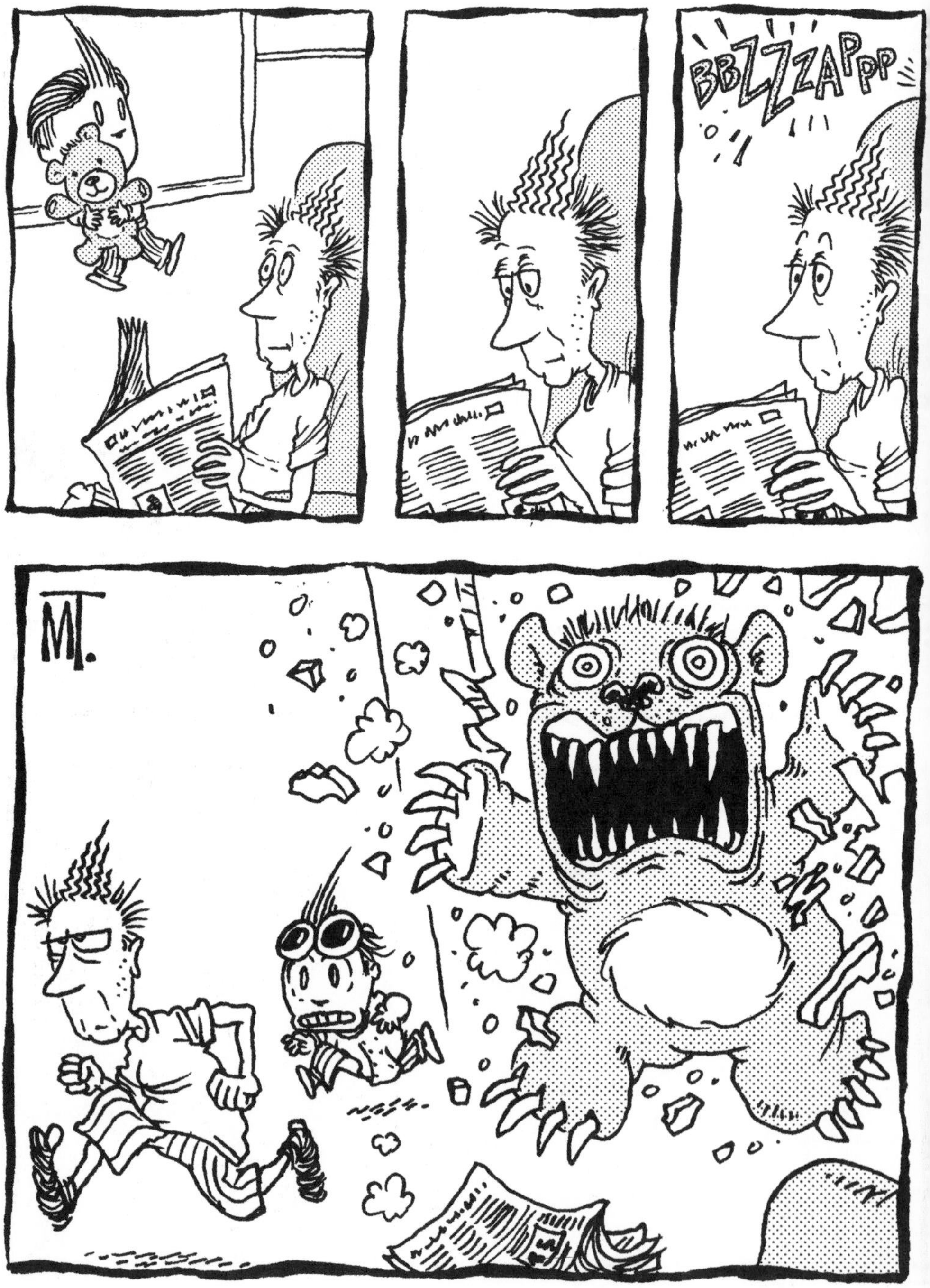
BBZZZAPPP

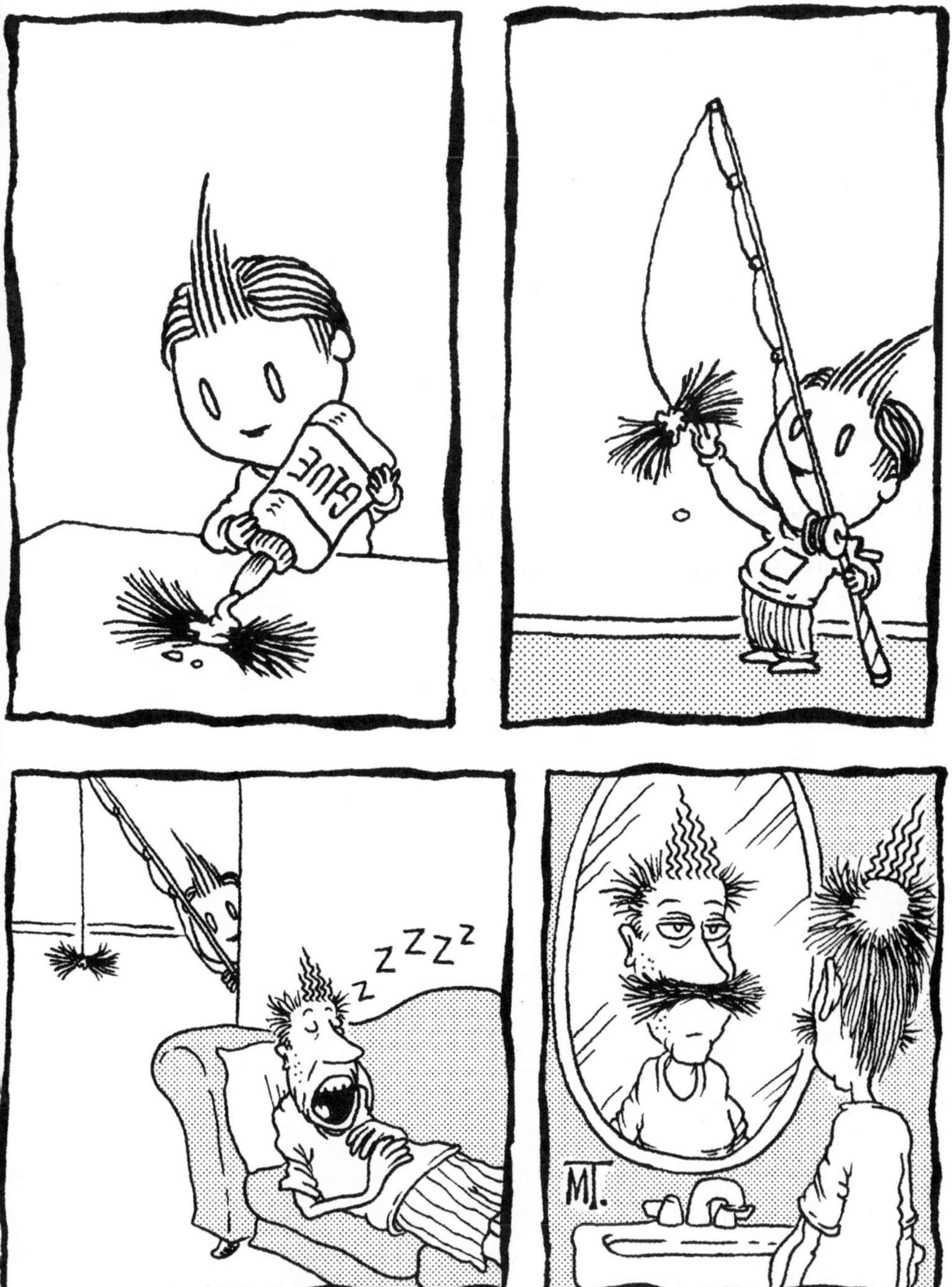
GLUE
z Z Z Z z
MT.

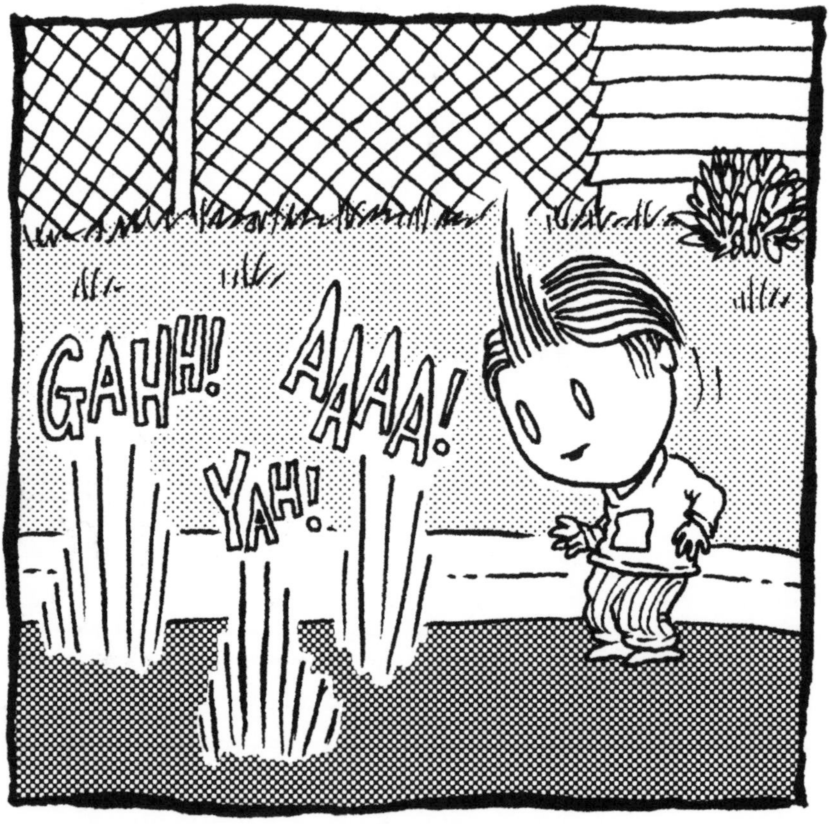
GAHH!
YAH!
AAAA!

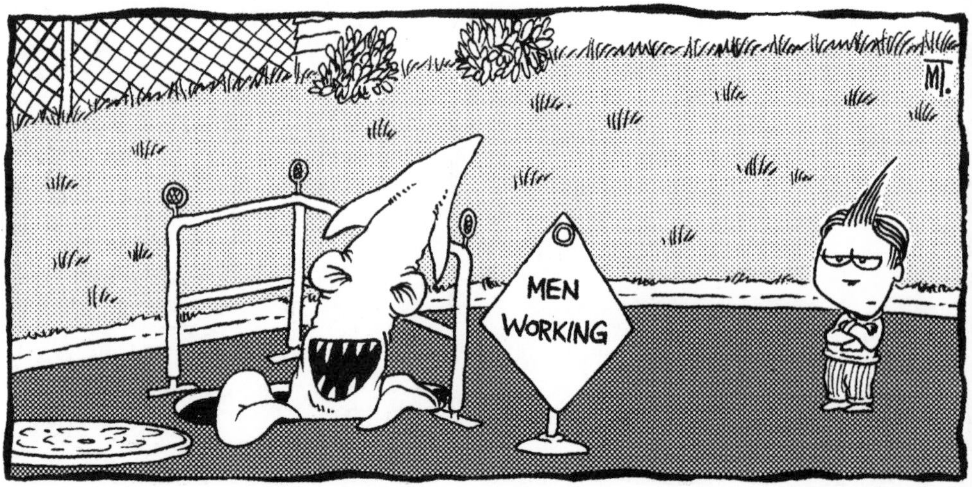
MT.
MEN
WORKING

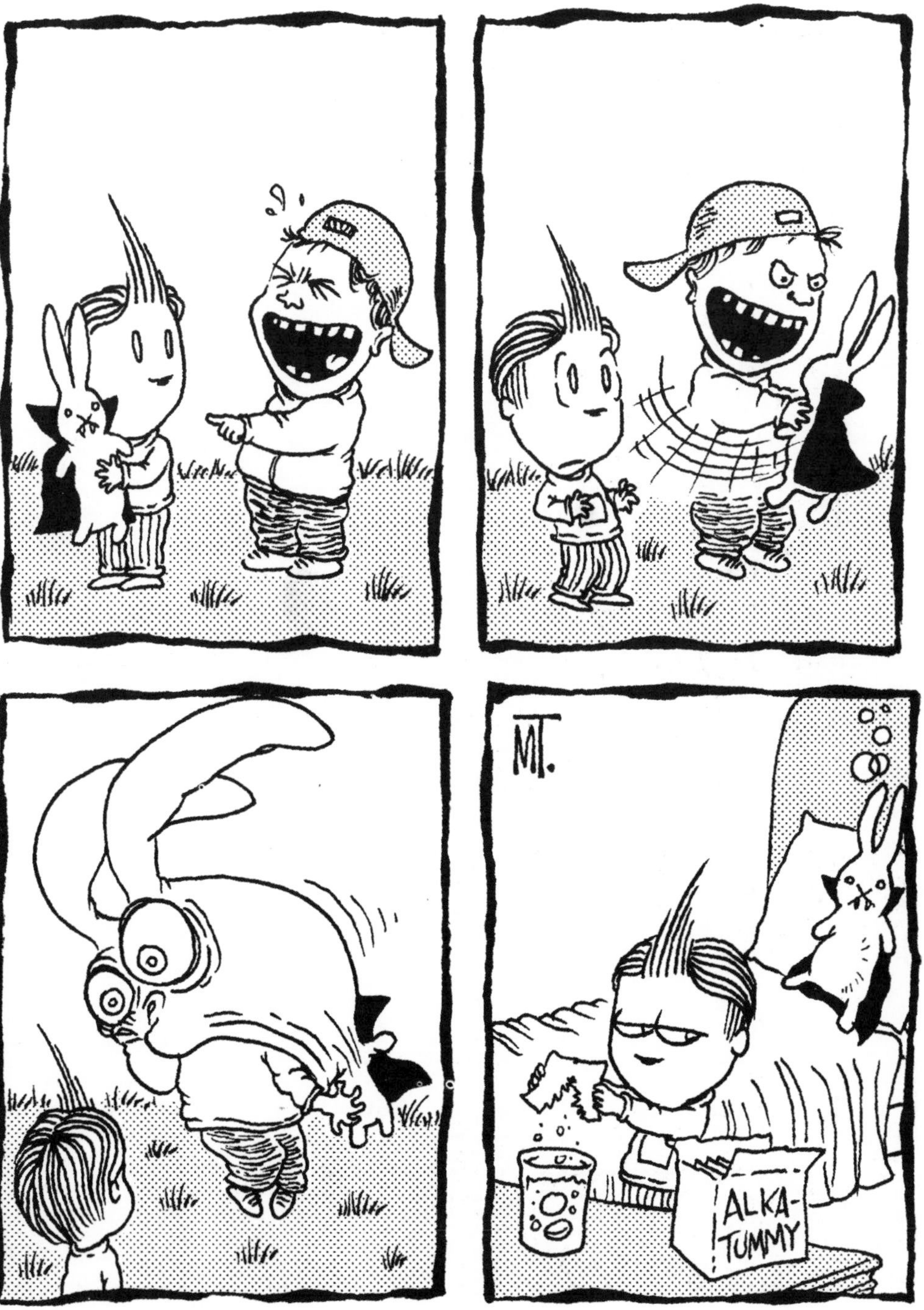

MT.
ALKA-
TUMMY

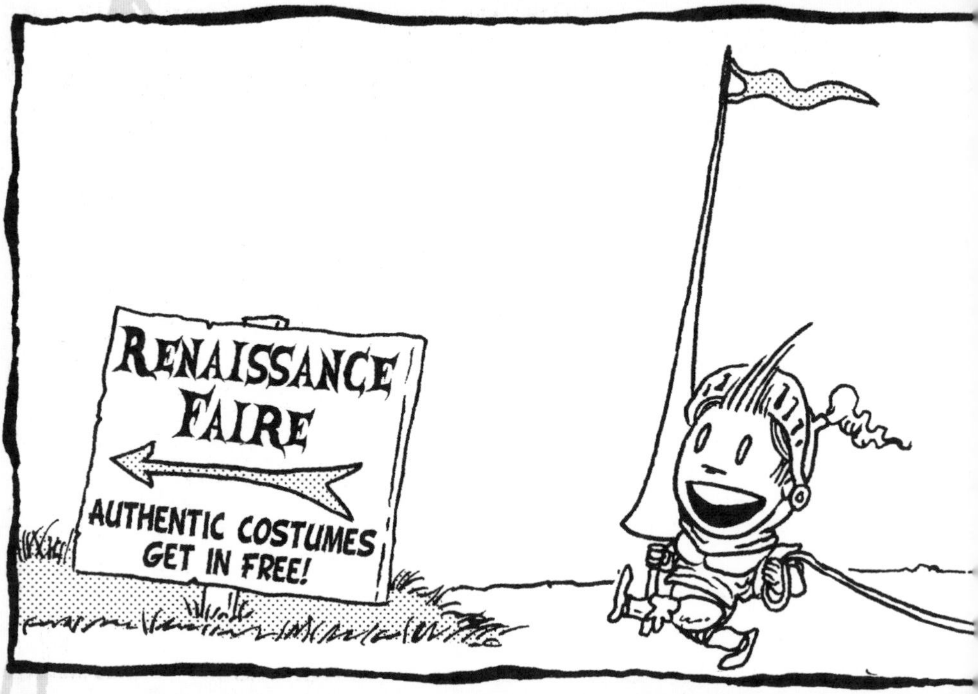
RENAISSANCE FAIRE
AUTHENTIC COSTUMES GET IN FREE!

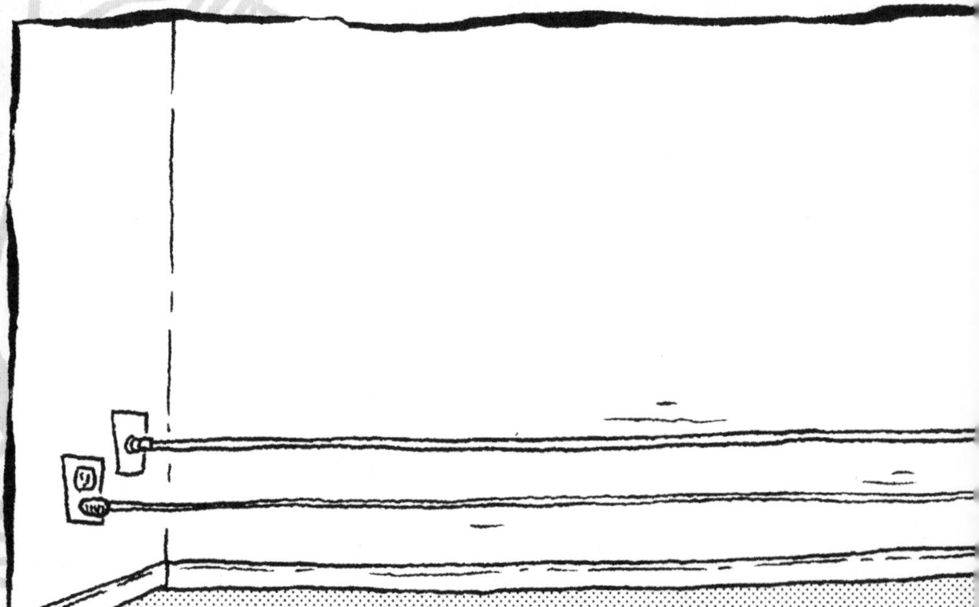

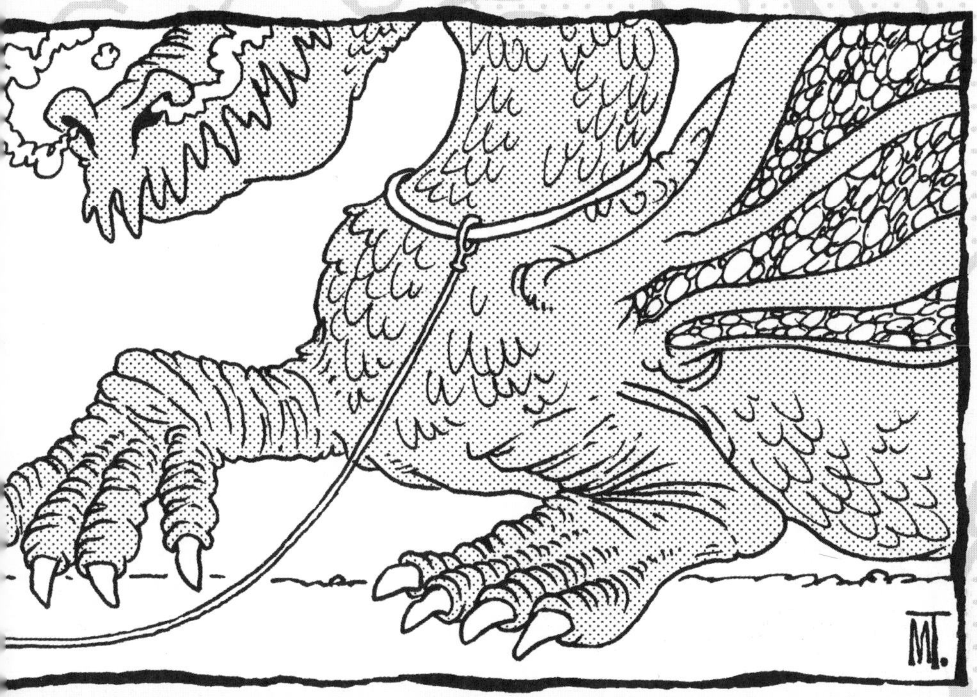

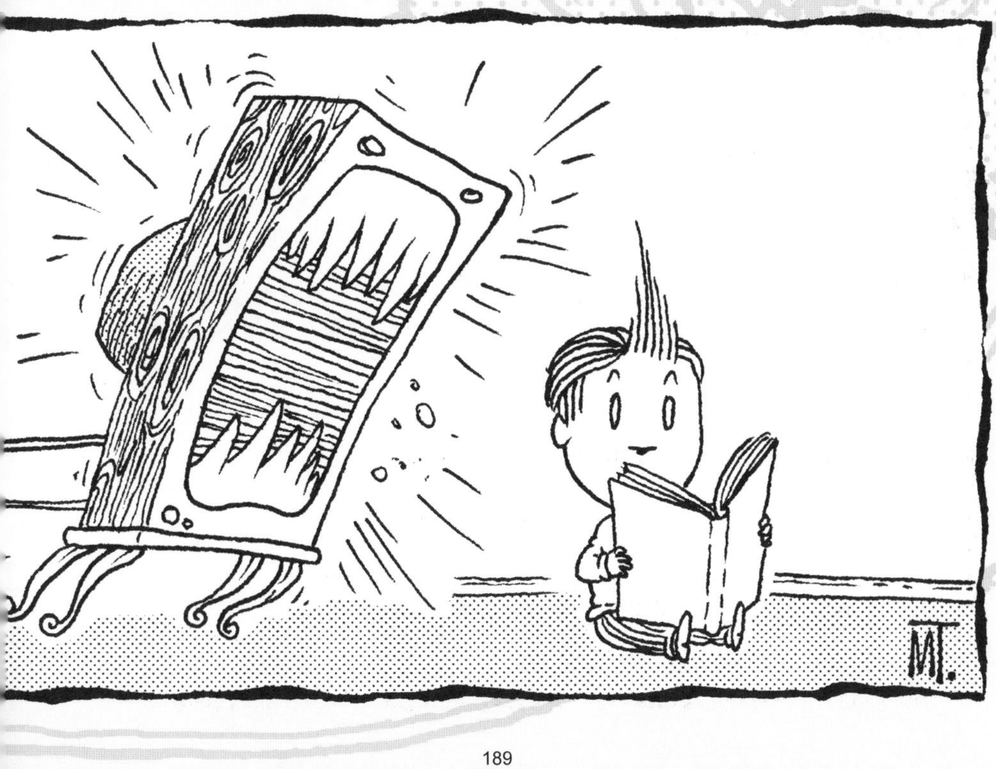

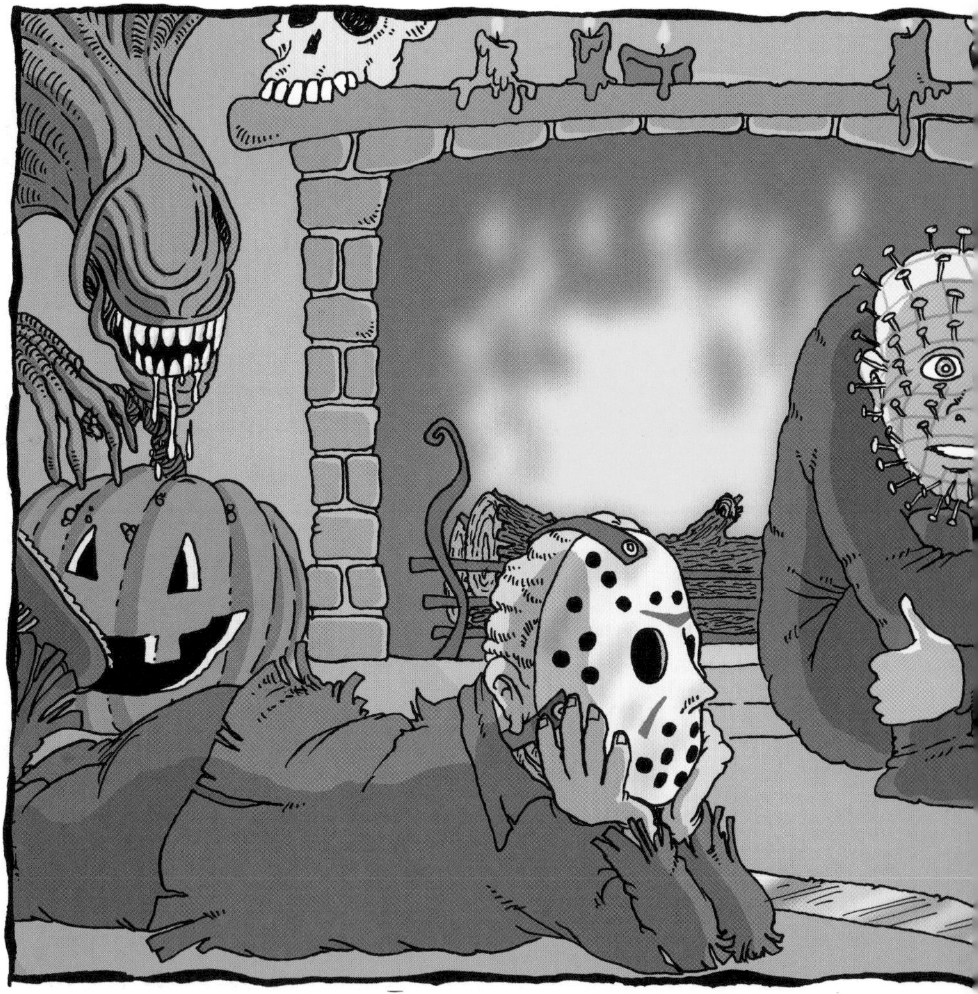

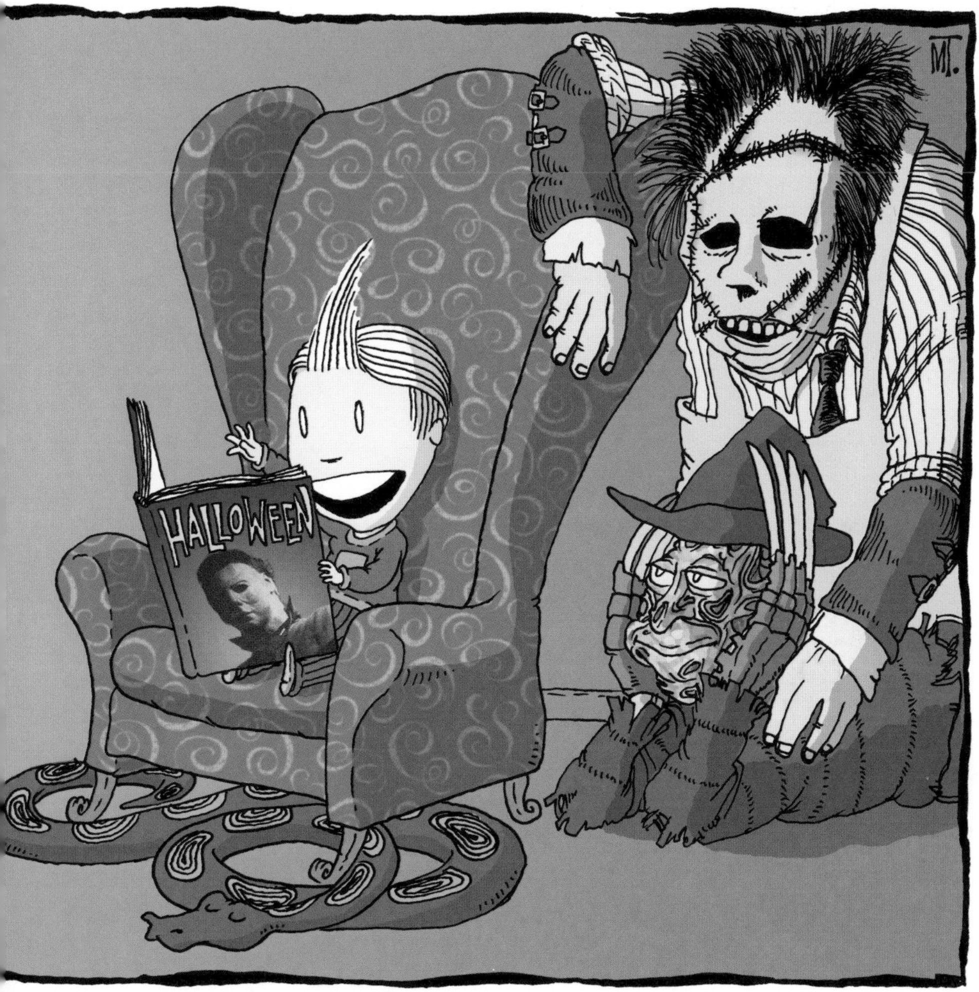
HALLOWEEN
MT.

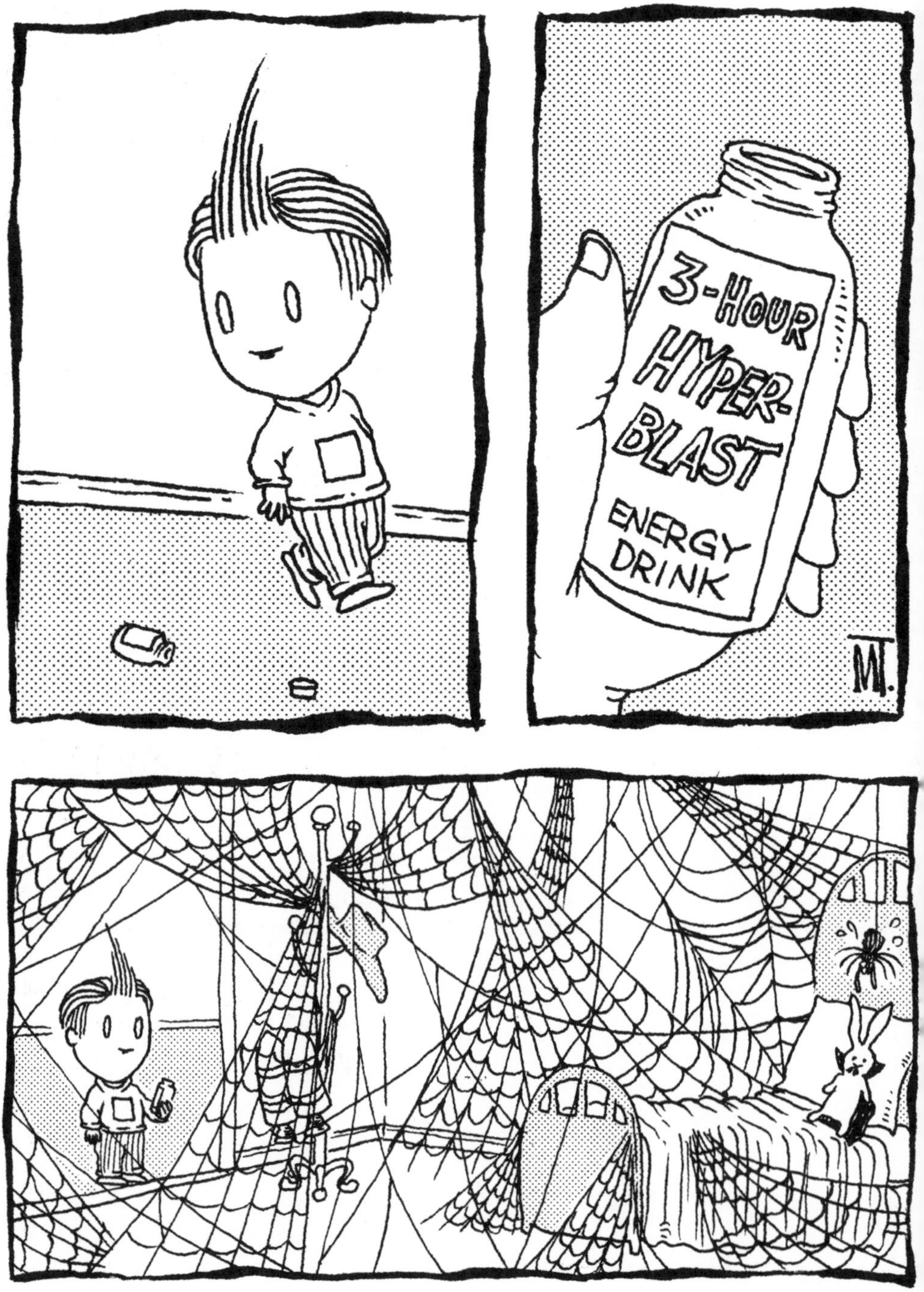
3-HOUR
HYPER-
BLAST
ENERGY
DRINK
MT.

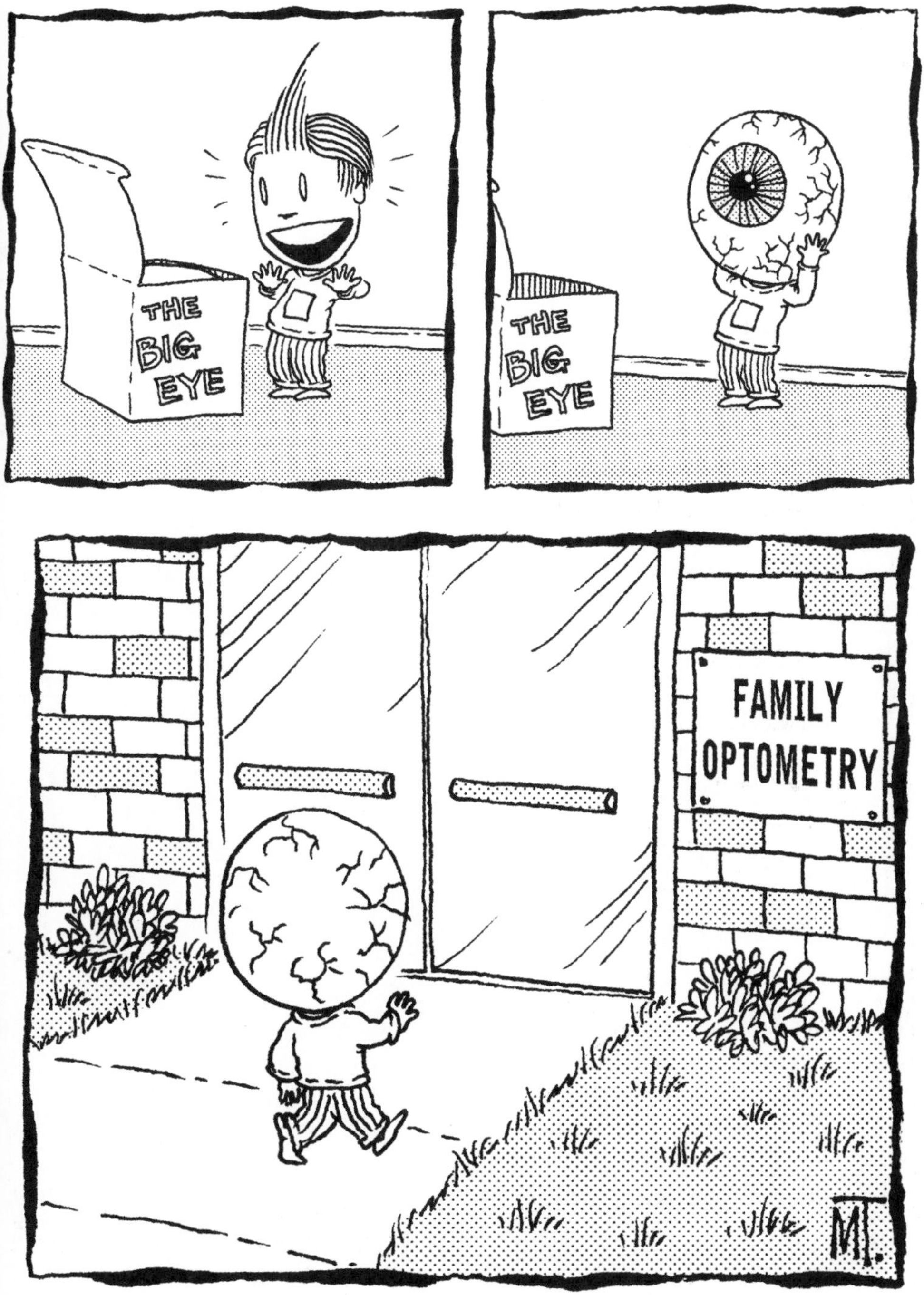
THE BIG EYE
THE BIG EYE
FAMILY OPTOMETRY

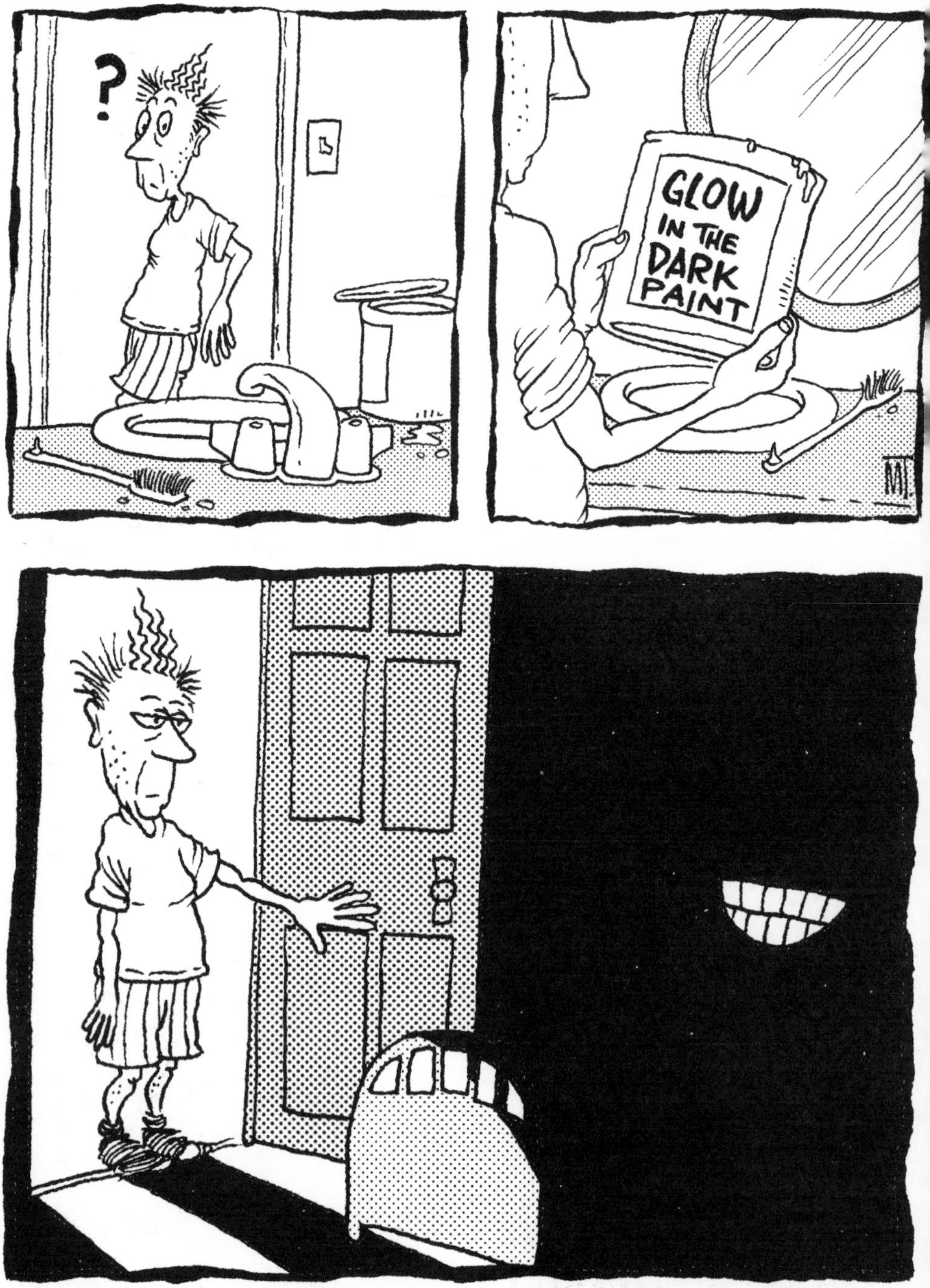
?
GLOW IN THE DARK PAINT

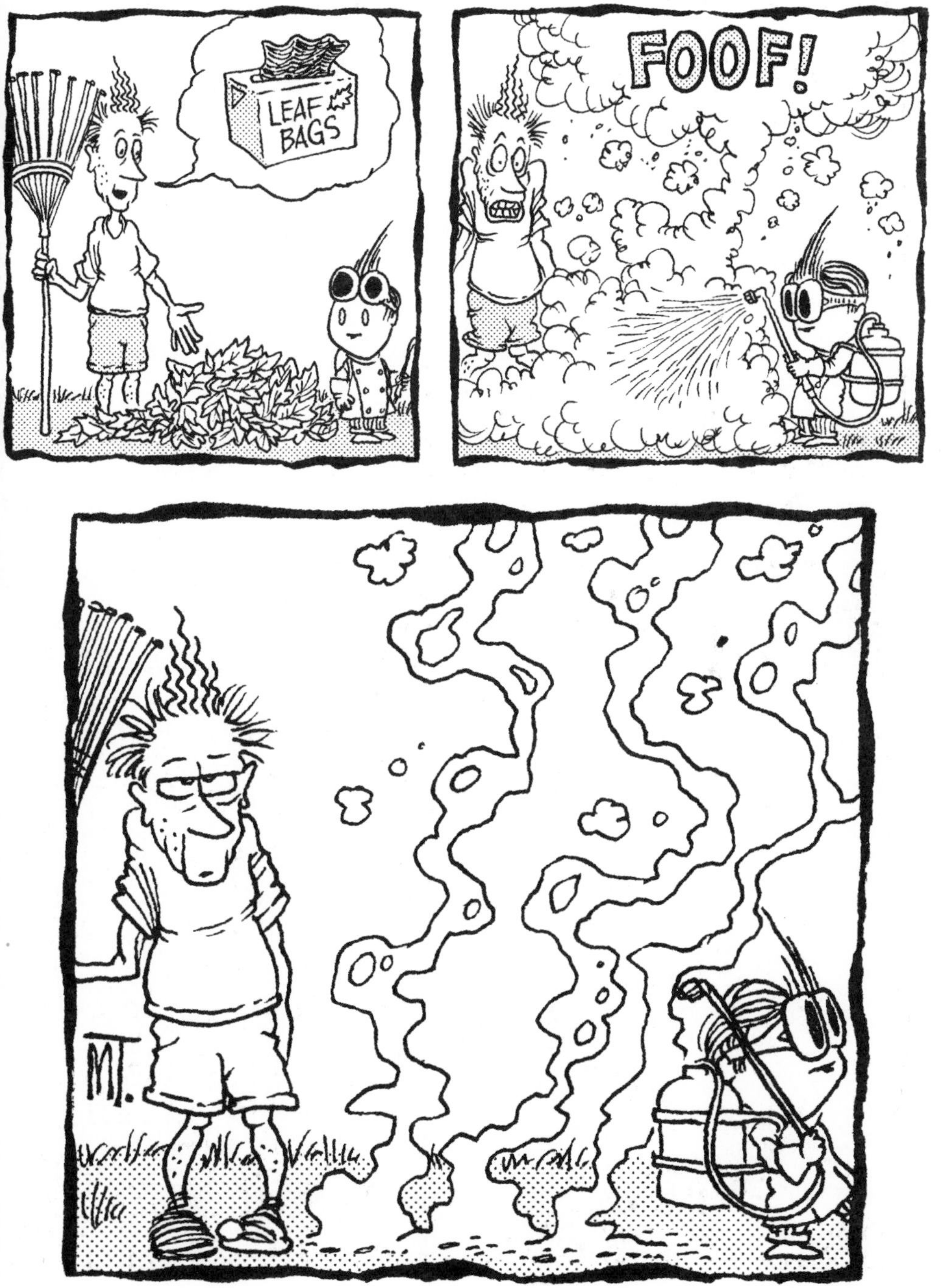
LEAF BAGS
FOOF!
MT.

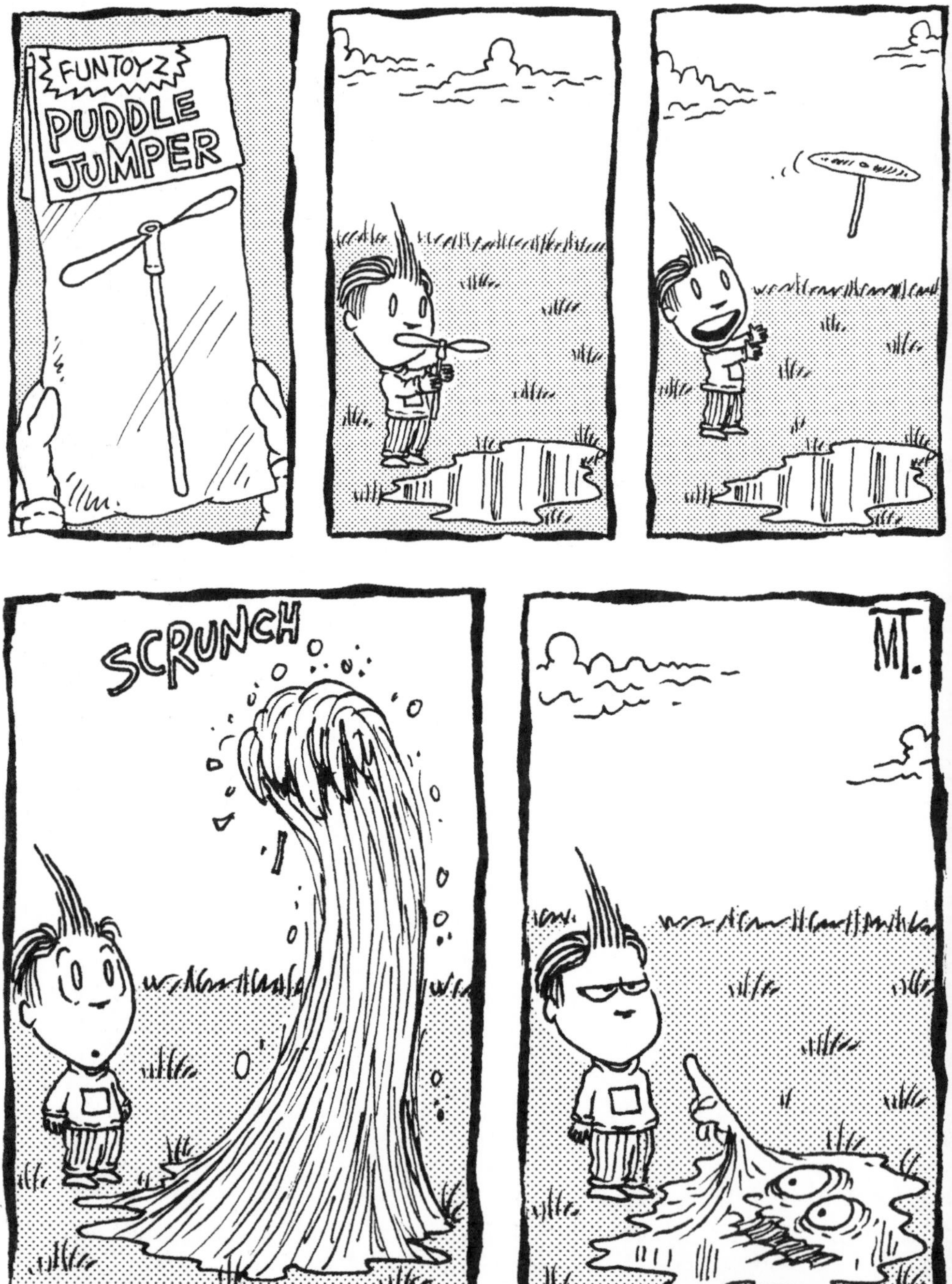
FUNTOYZ
PUDDLE JUMPER
SCRUNCH
MT.

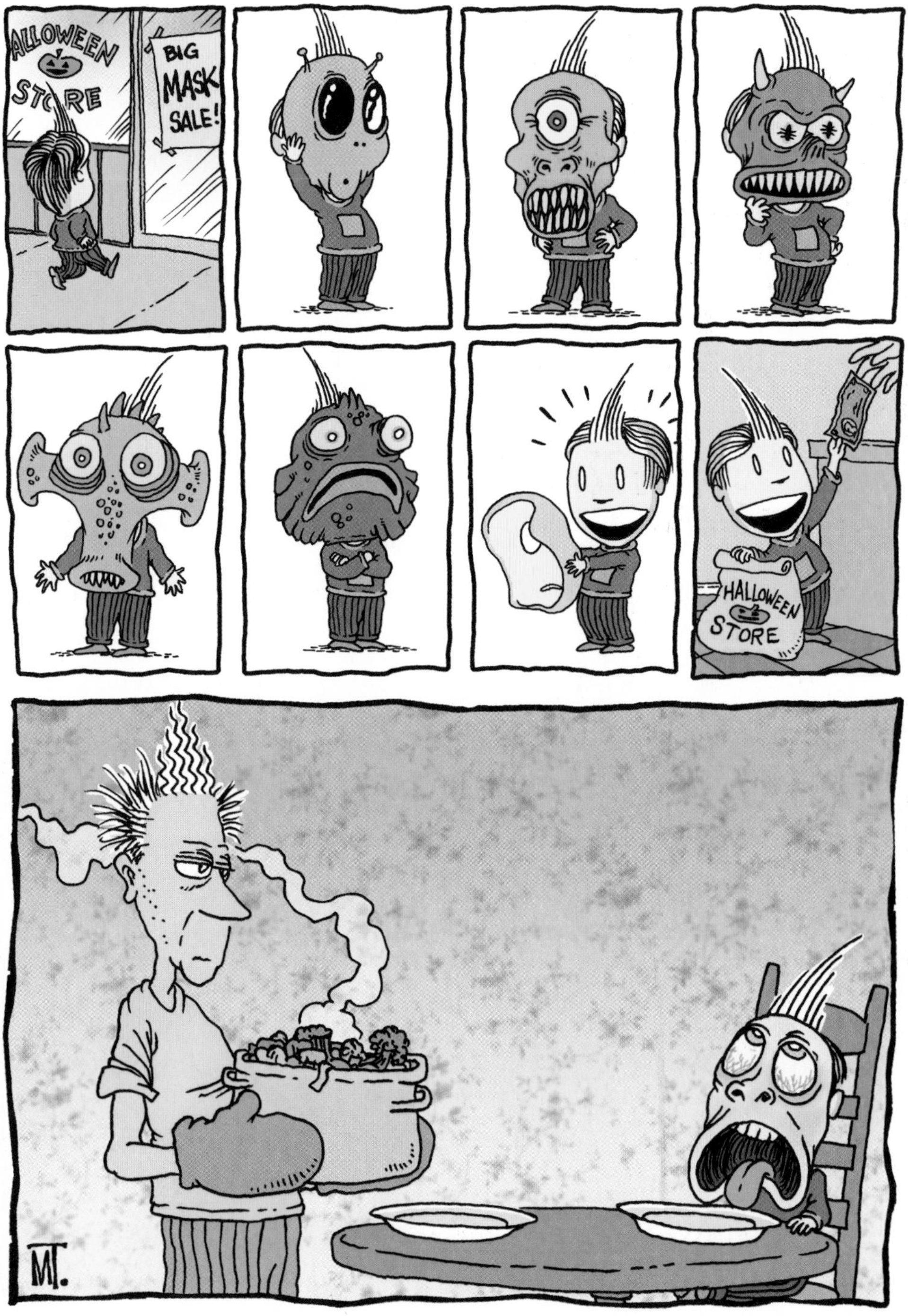
HALLOWEEN
STORE
BIG
MASK
SALE!
HALLOWEEN
STORE
MT.

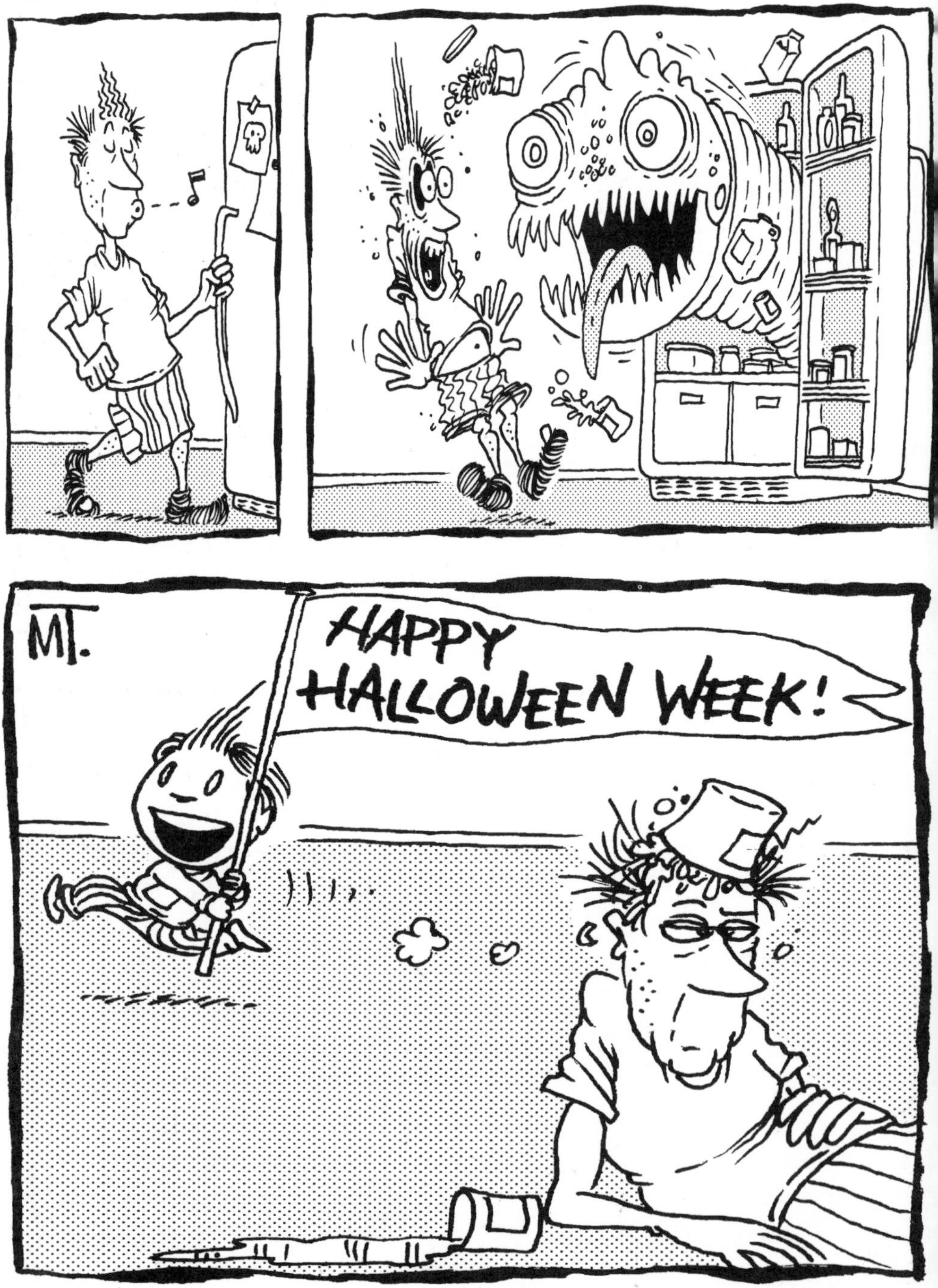
MT.
HAPPY HALLOWEEN WEEK!

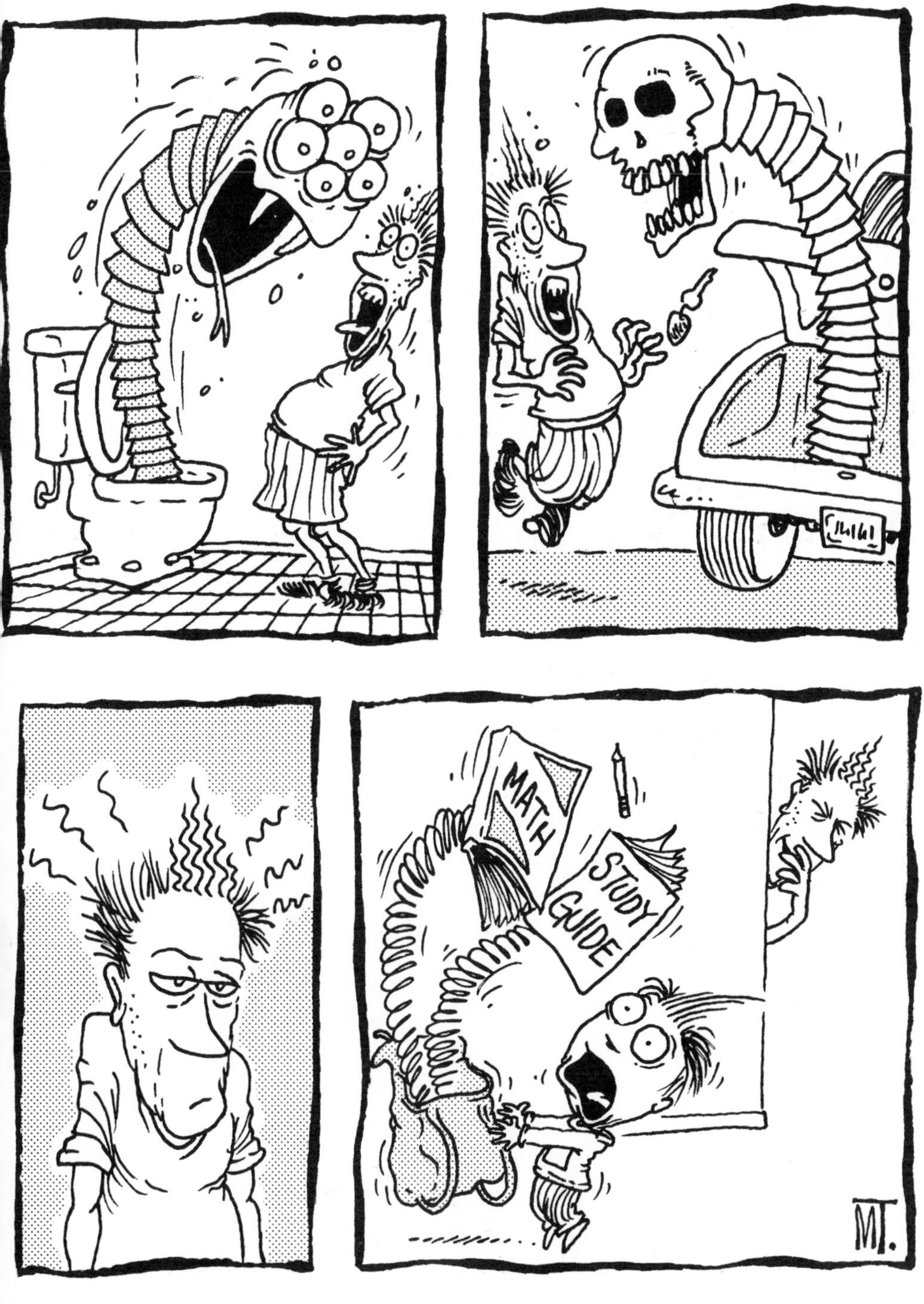
MATH
STUDY GUIDE
MT.

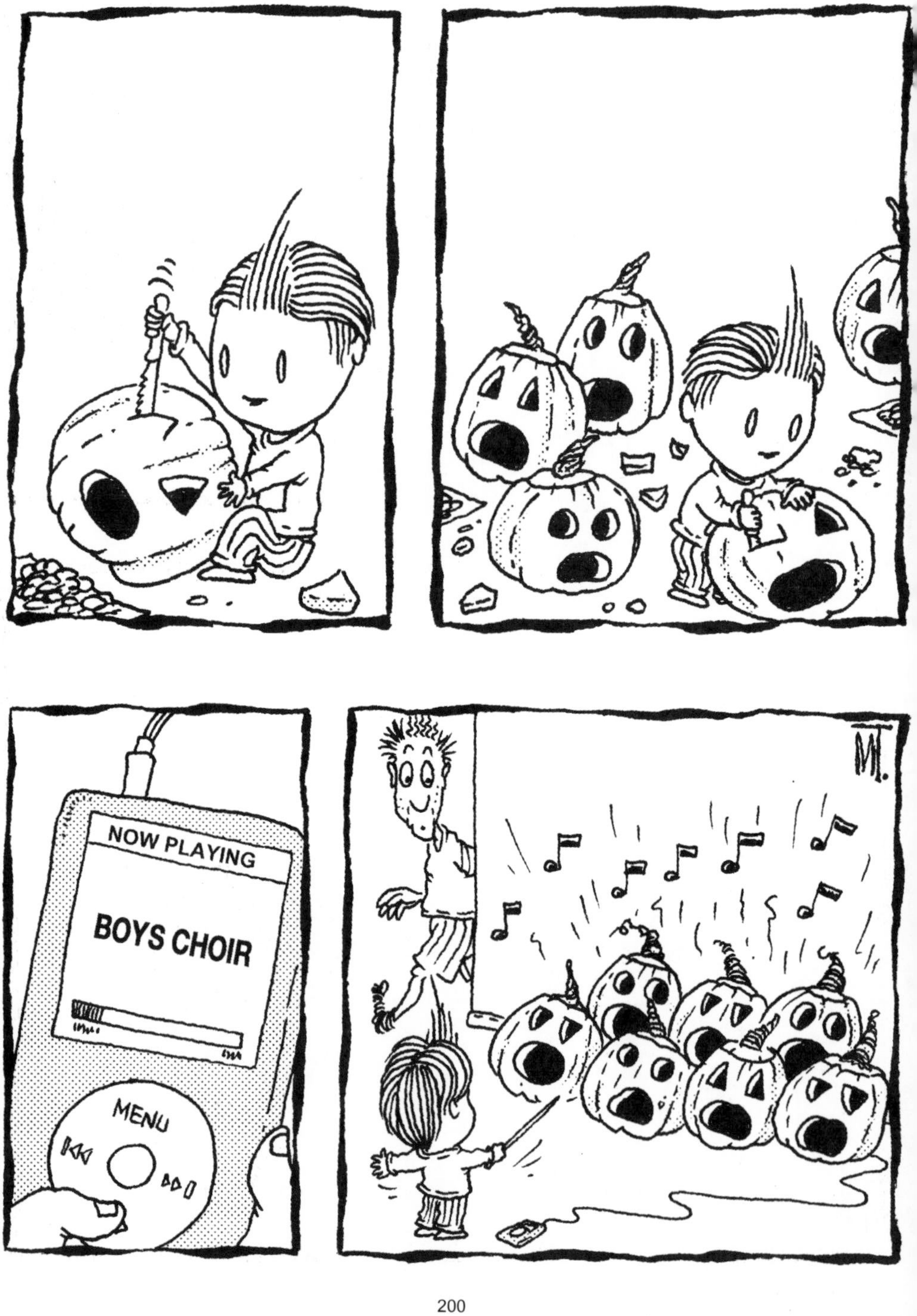
NOW PLAYING
BOYS CHOIR
MENU

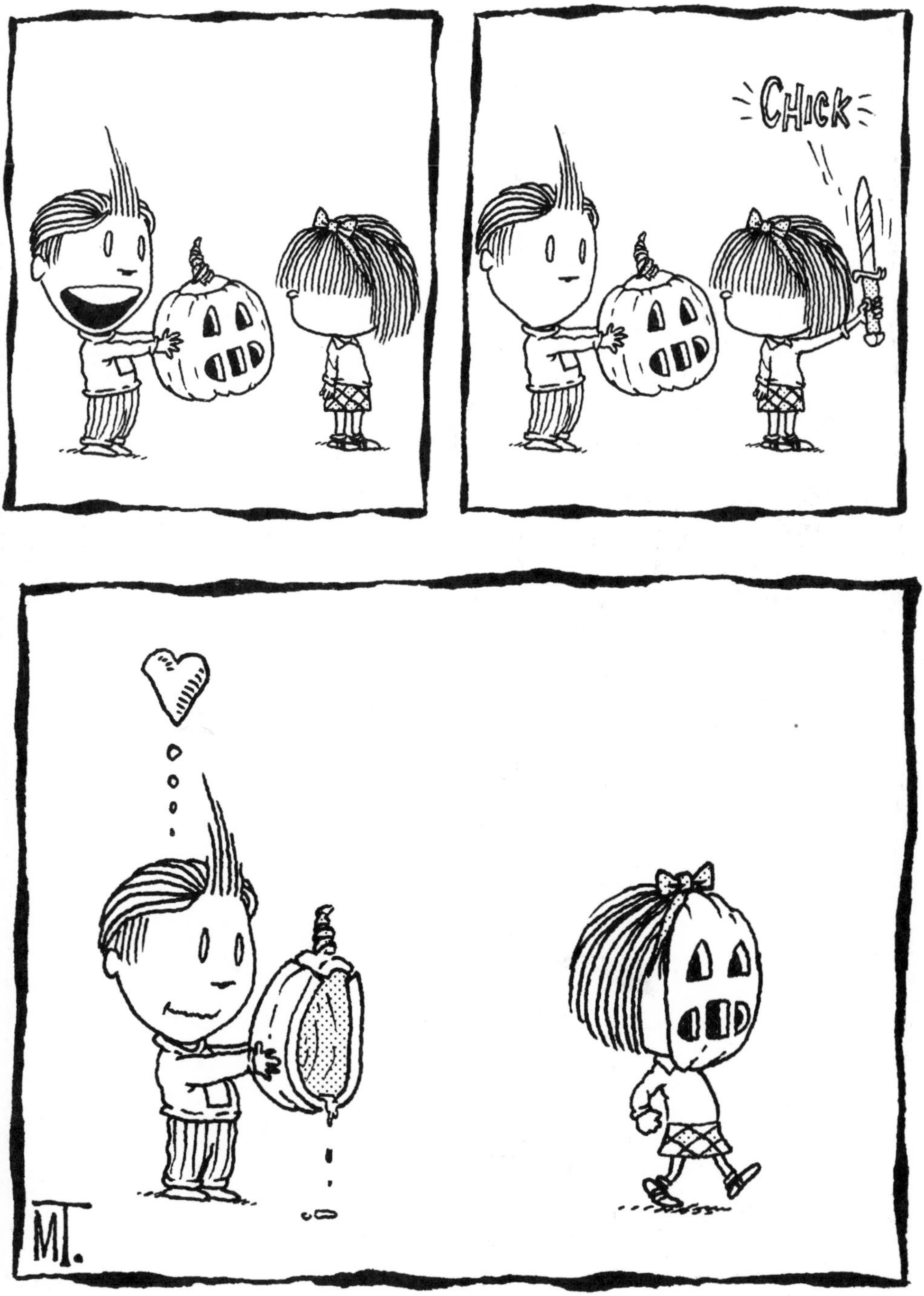
CHICK
MT.

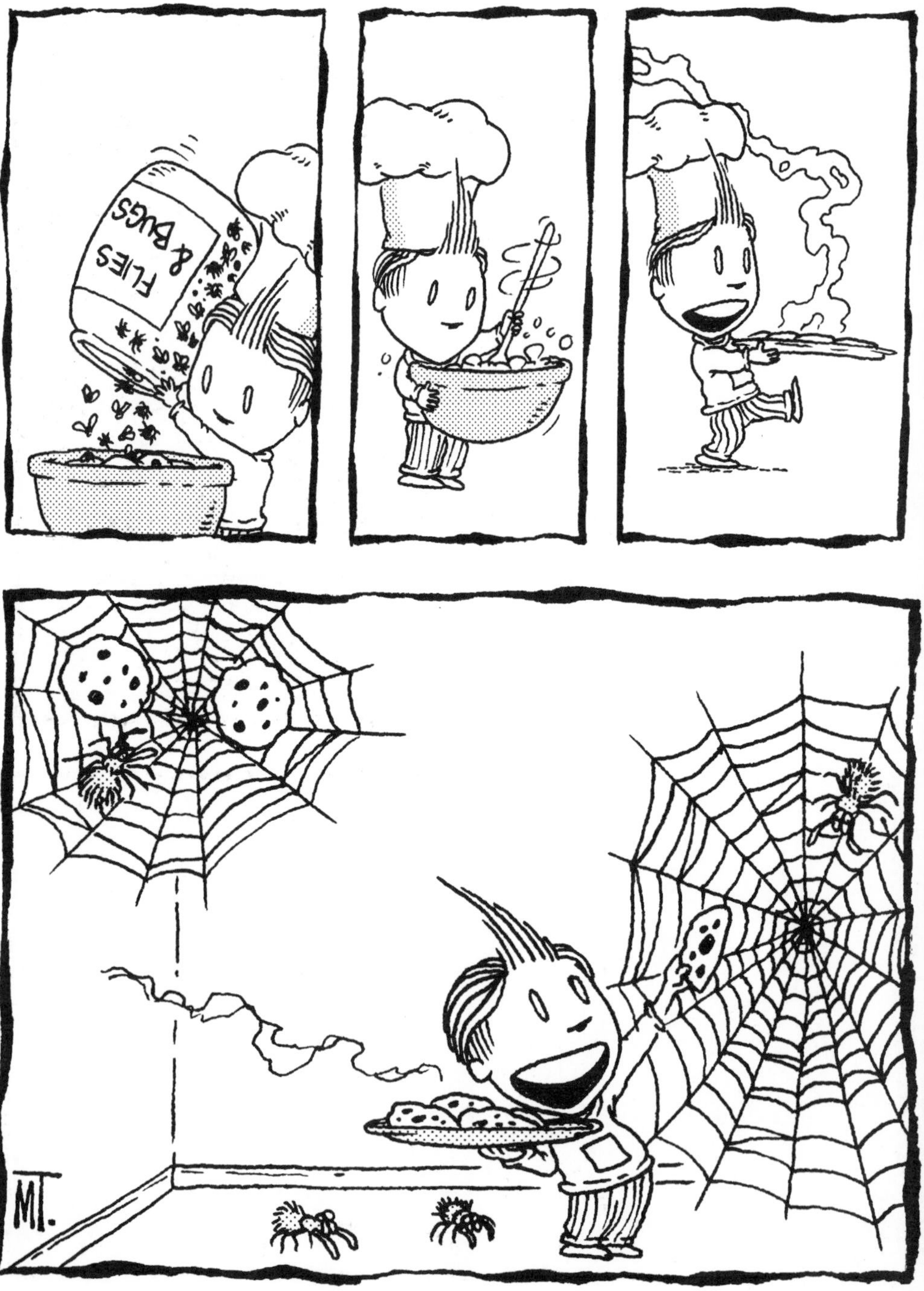
FLIES & BUGS
MT.

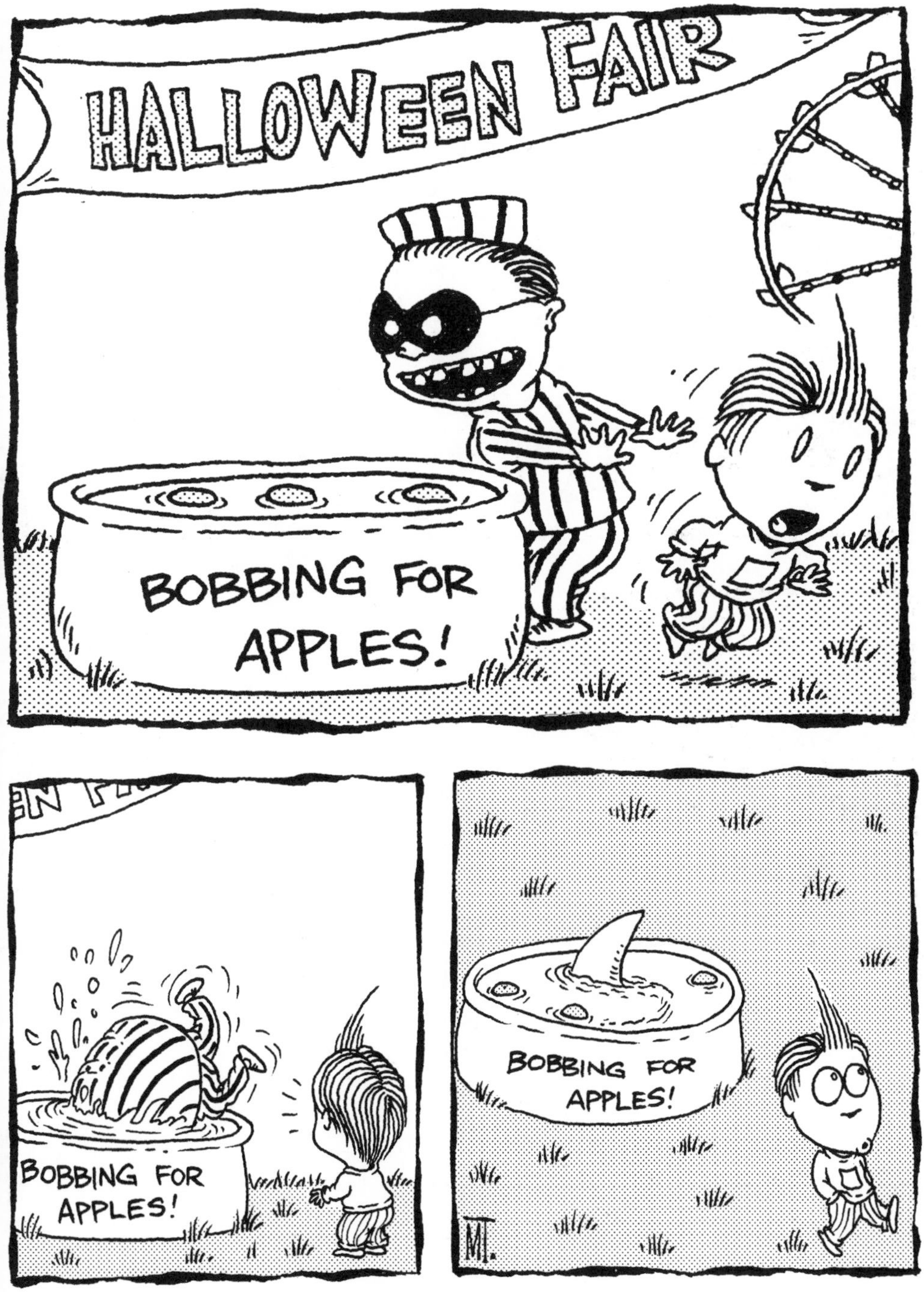
HALLOWEEN FAIR
BOBBING FOR APPLES!
BOBBING FOR APPLES!
BOBBING FOR APPLES!

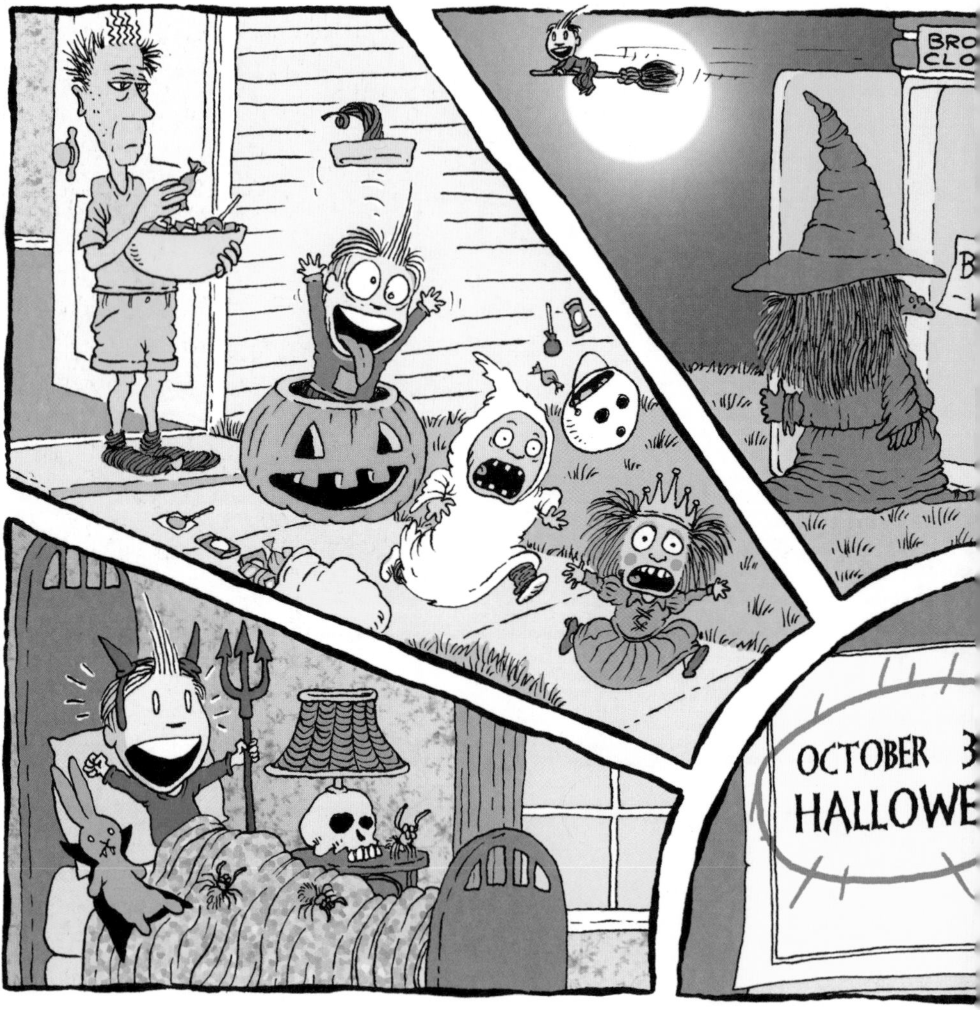
BRO
CLO
OCTOBER 3
HALLOWE

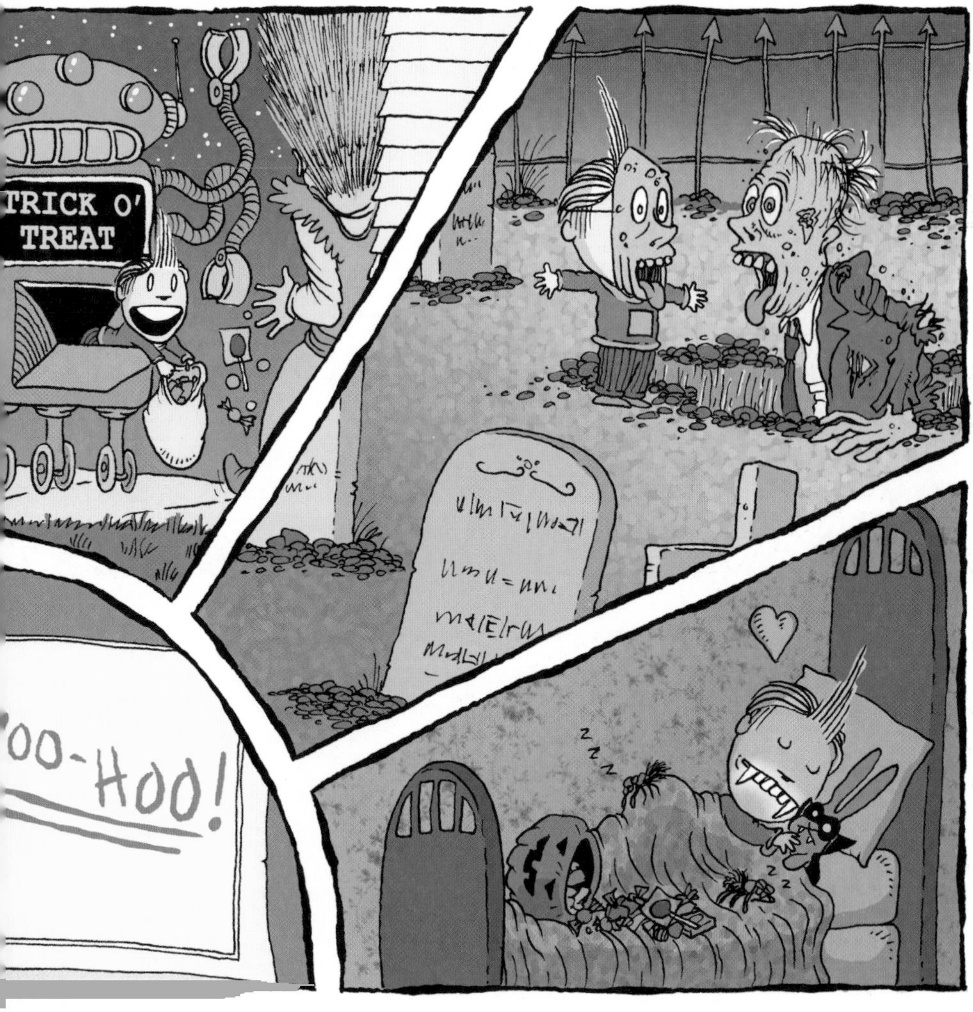
TRICK O' TREAT
OO-HOO!

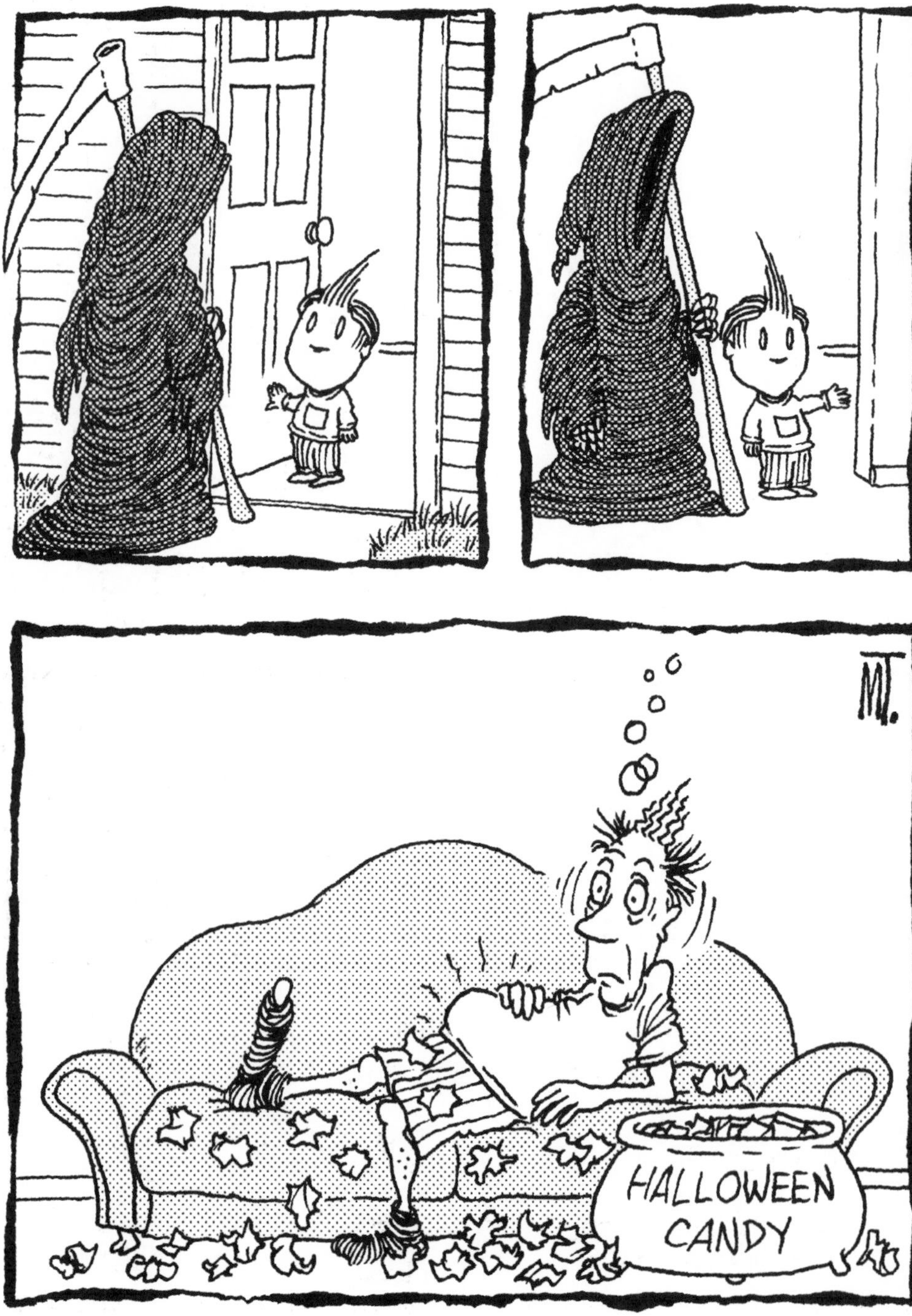
HALLOWEEN
CANDY

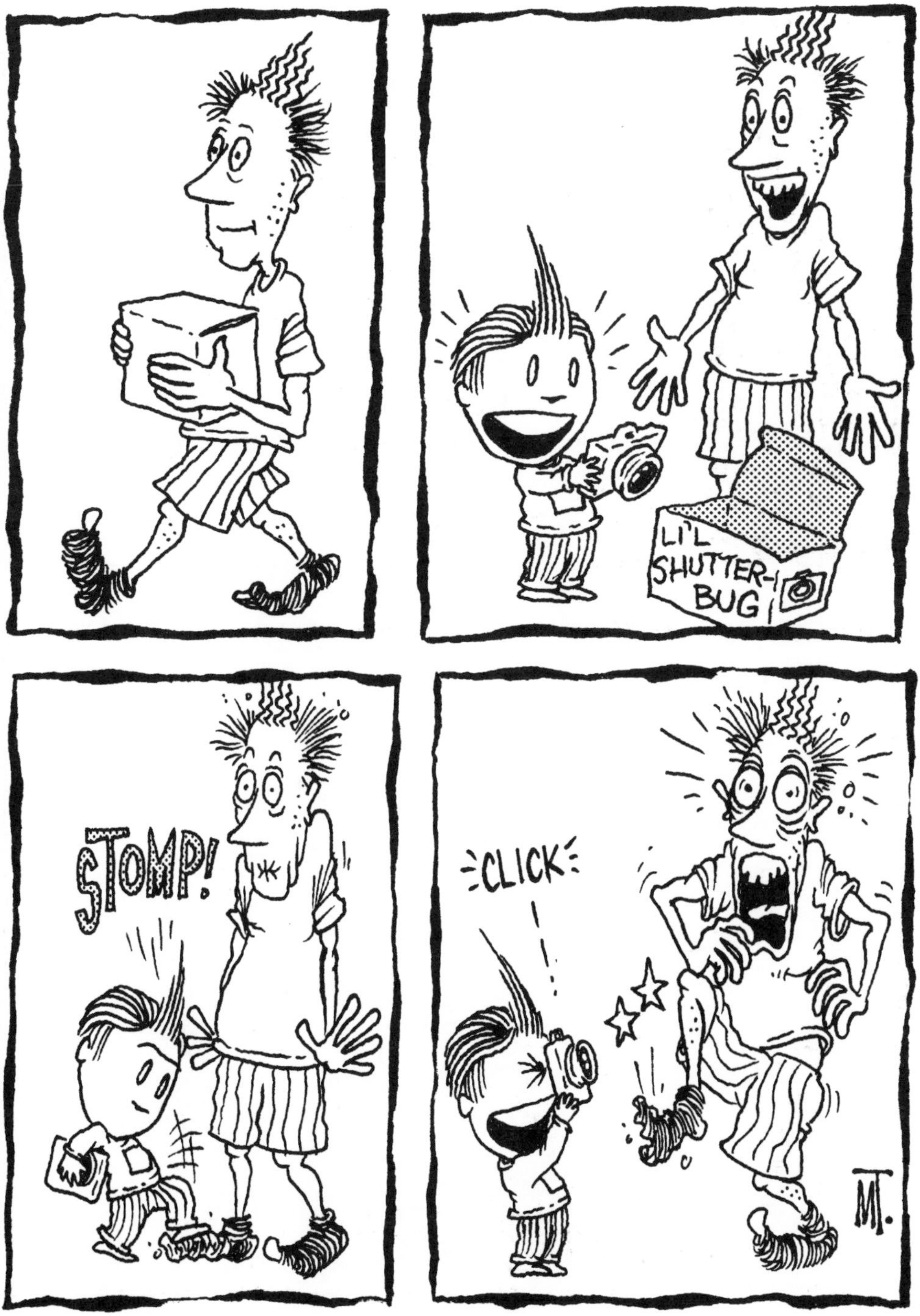
LI'L
SHUTTER-
BUG
STOMP!
CLICK
MT.

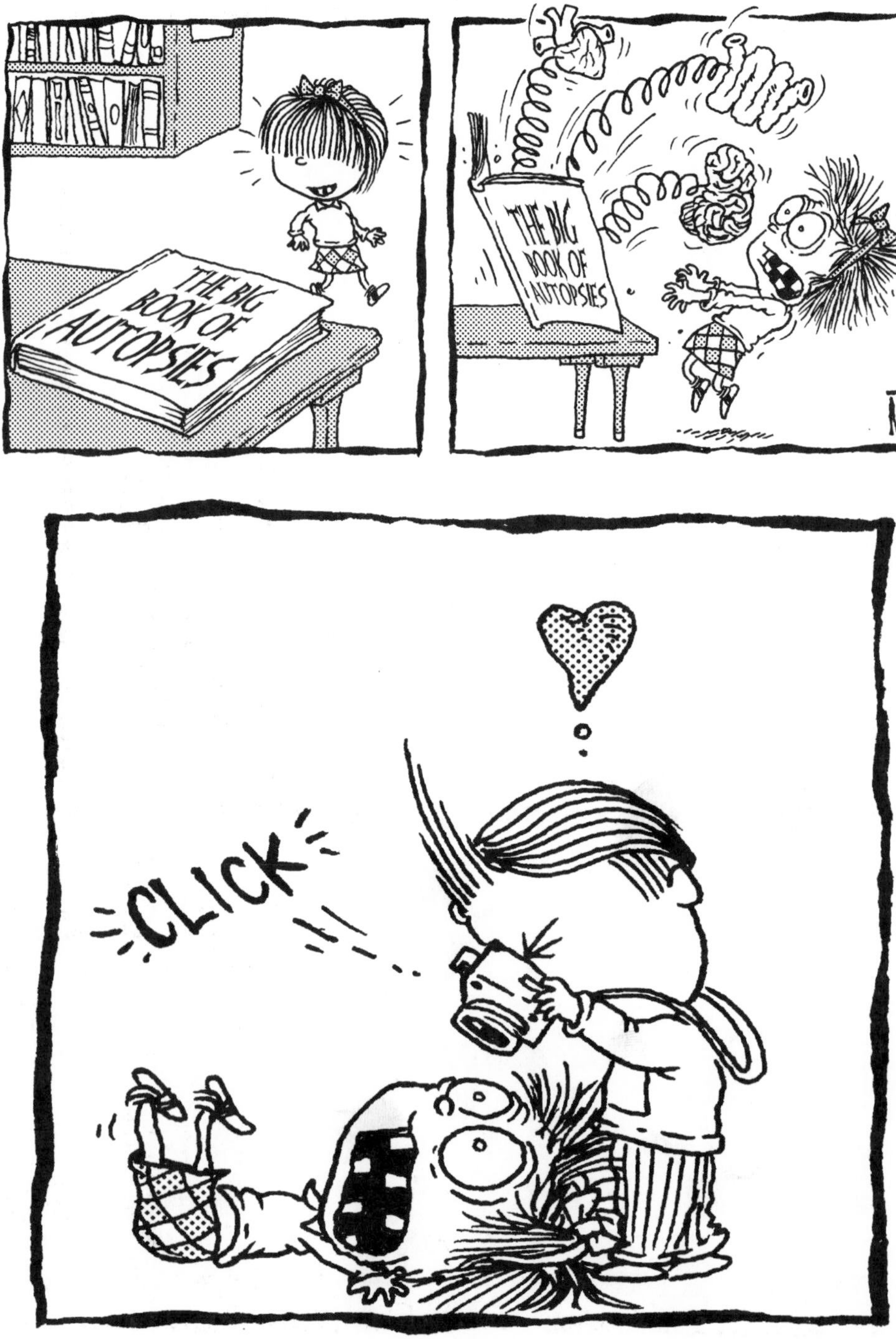
THE BIG BOOK OF AUTOPSIES
THE BIG BOOK OF AUTOPSIES
MT.
CLICK

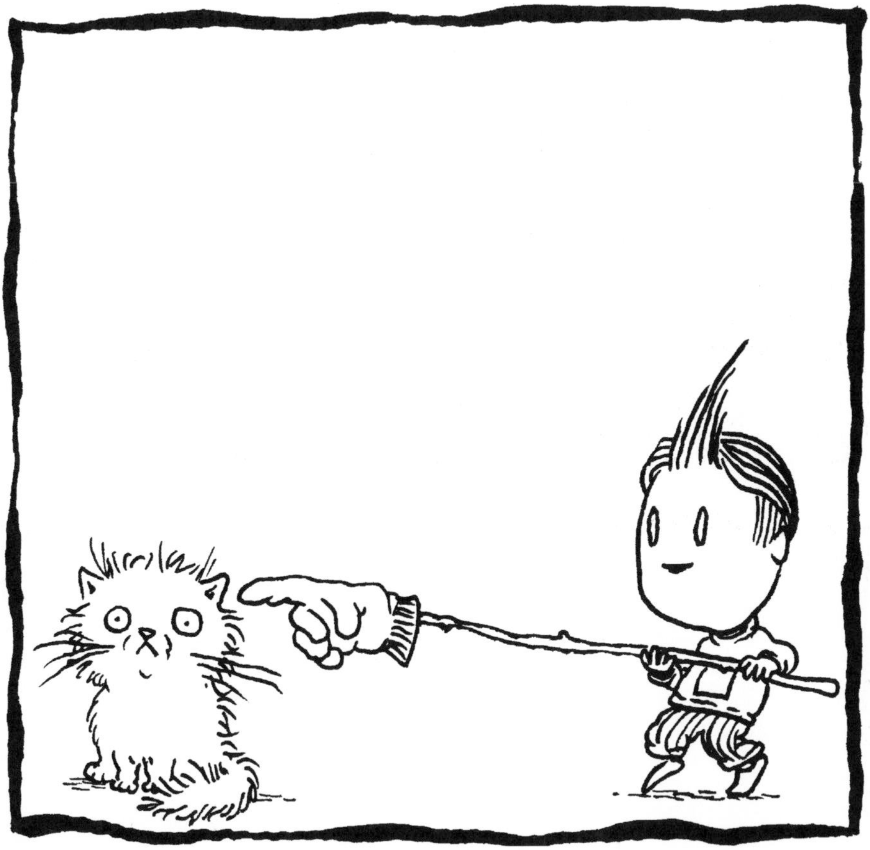
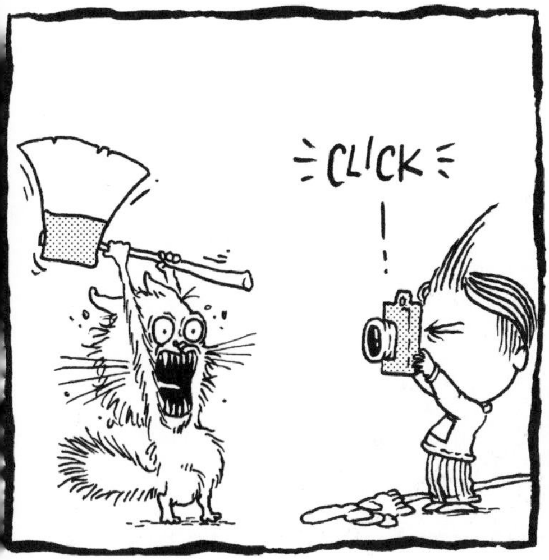
CLICK
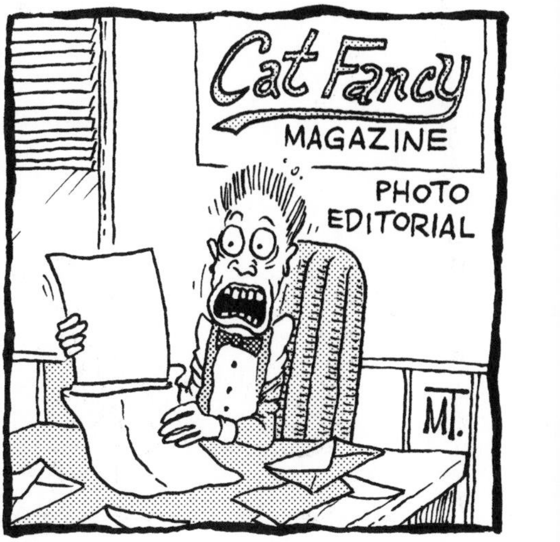
Cat Fancy
MAGAZINE
PHOTO
EDITORIAL
MI.

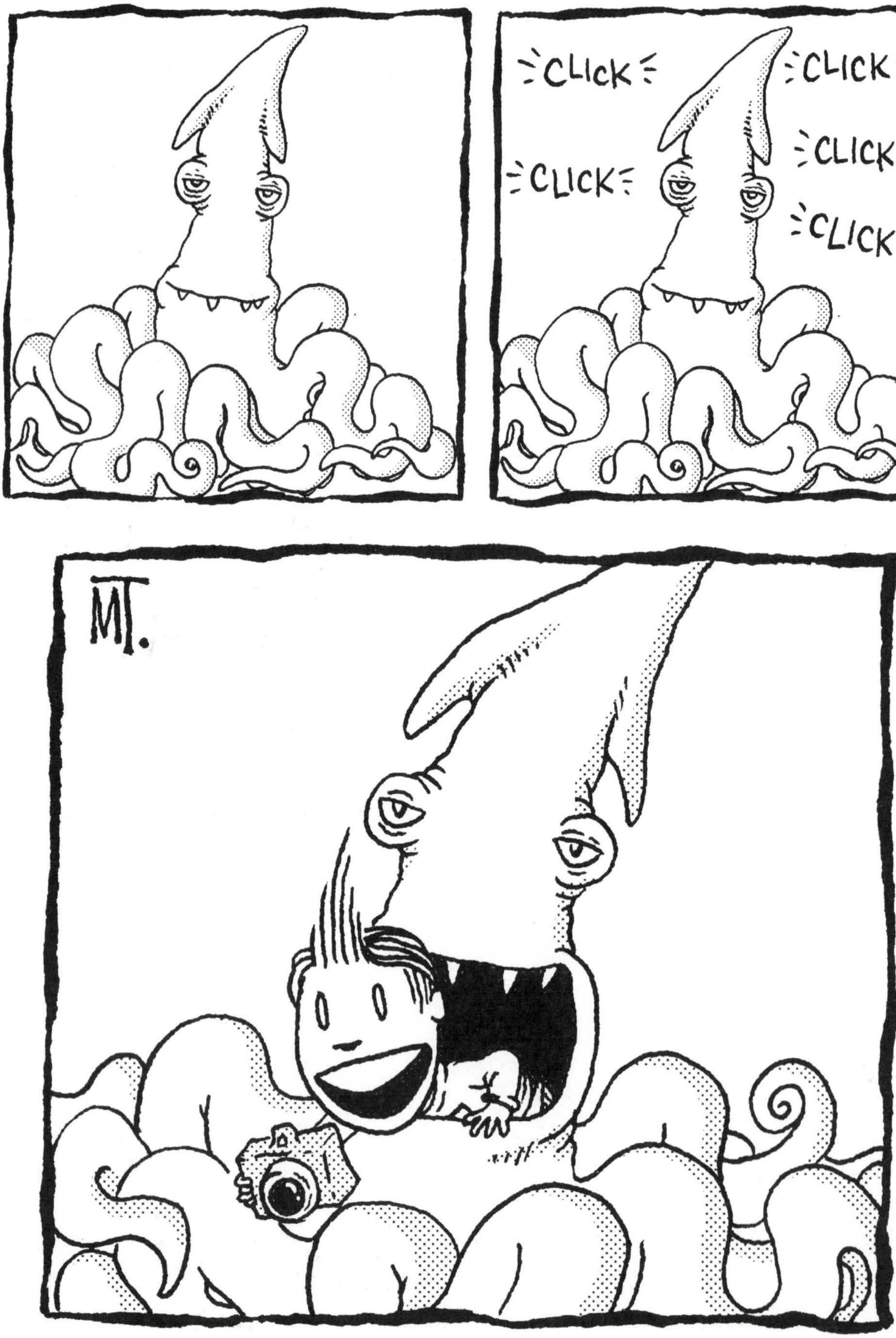
CLICK
CLICK
CLICK
CLICK
CLICK
MT.

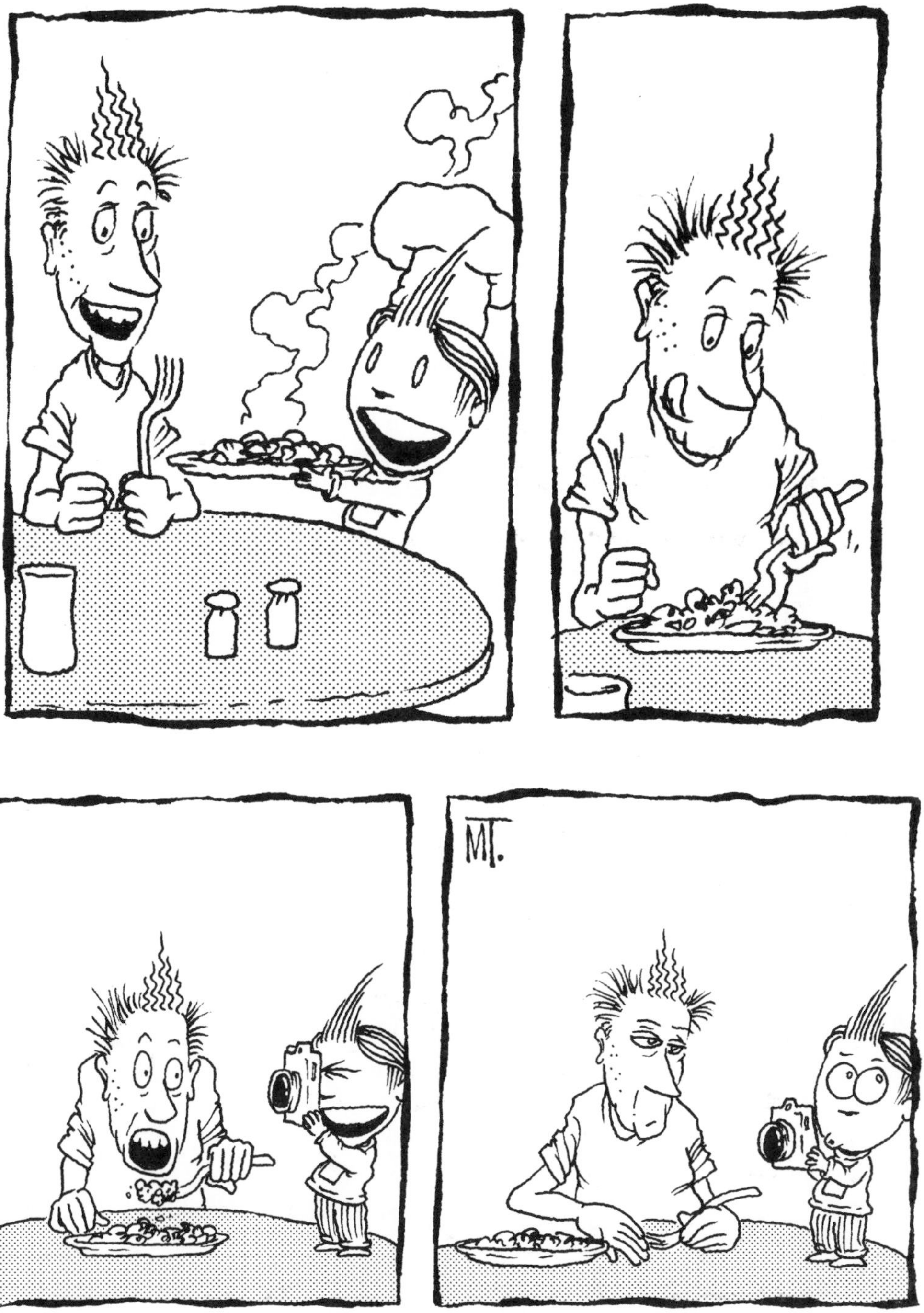
MT.

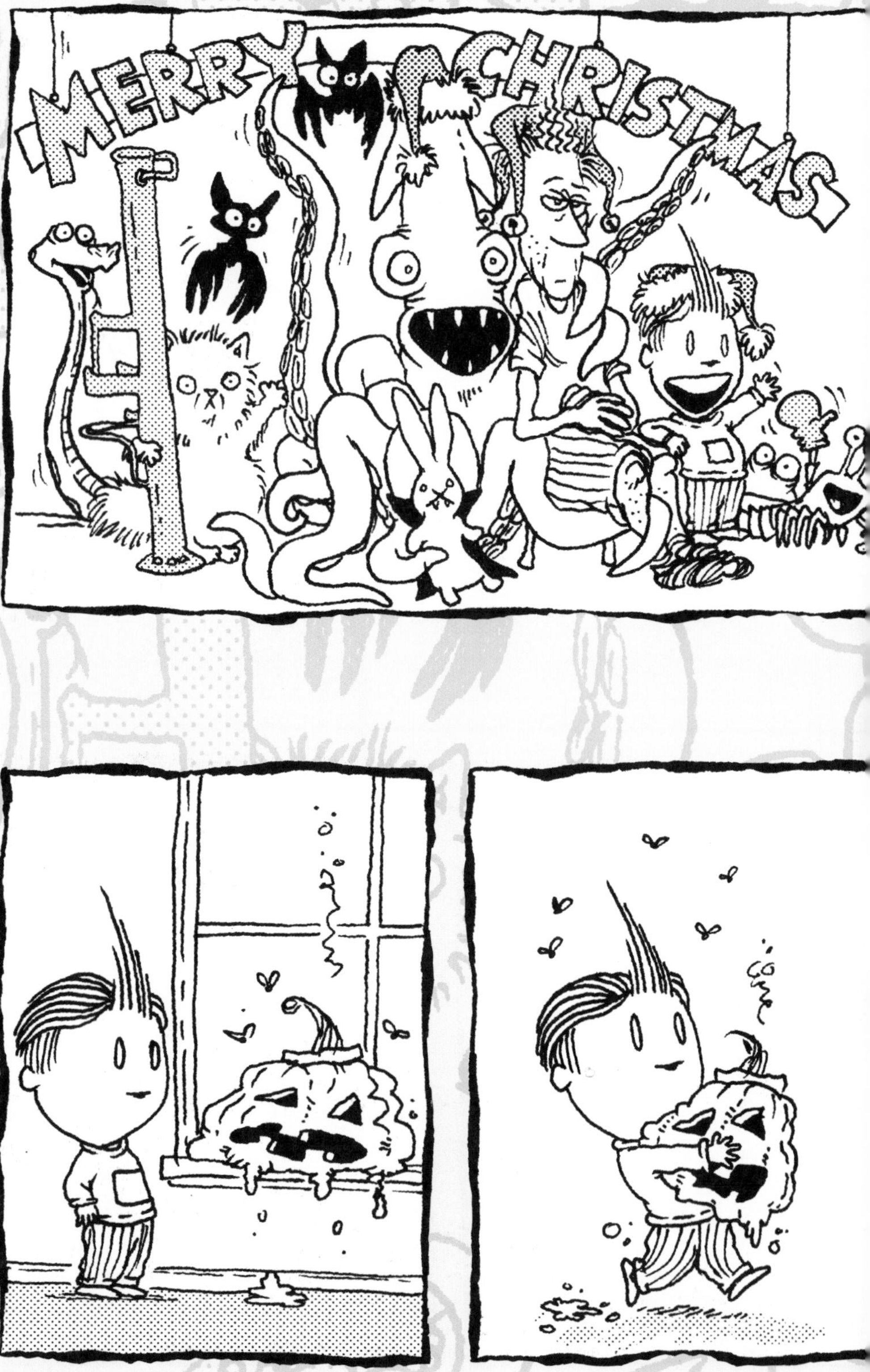
MERRY CHRISTMAS

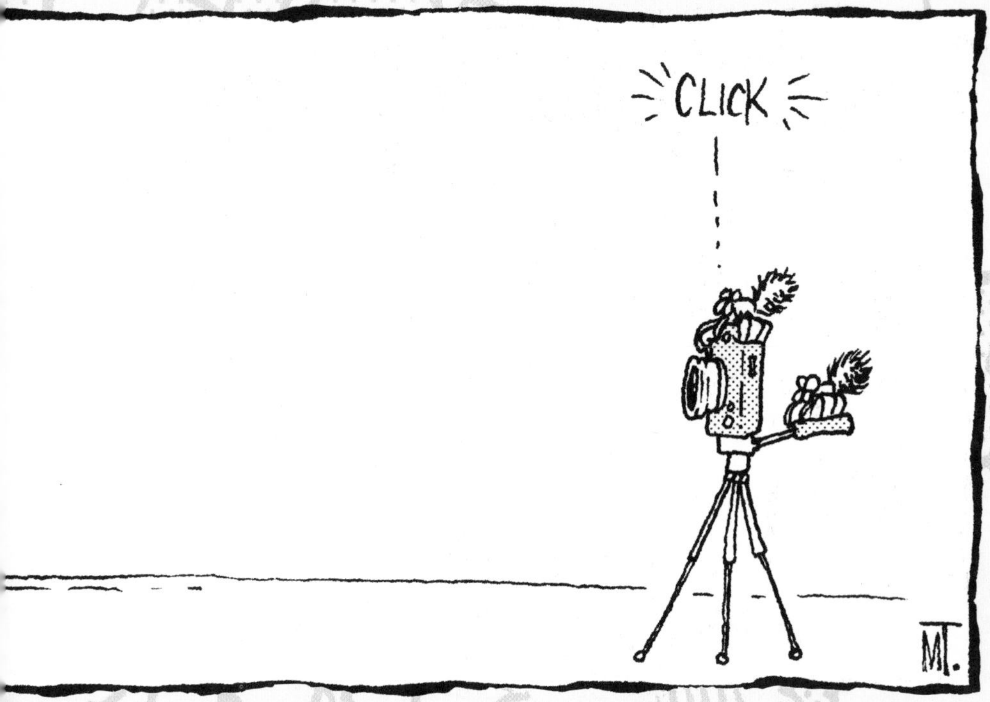
CLICK
MT.

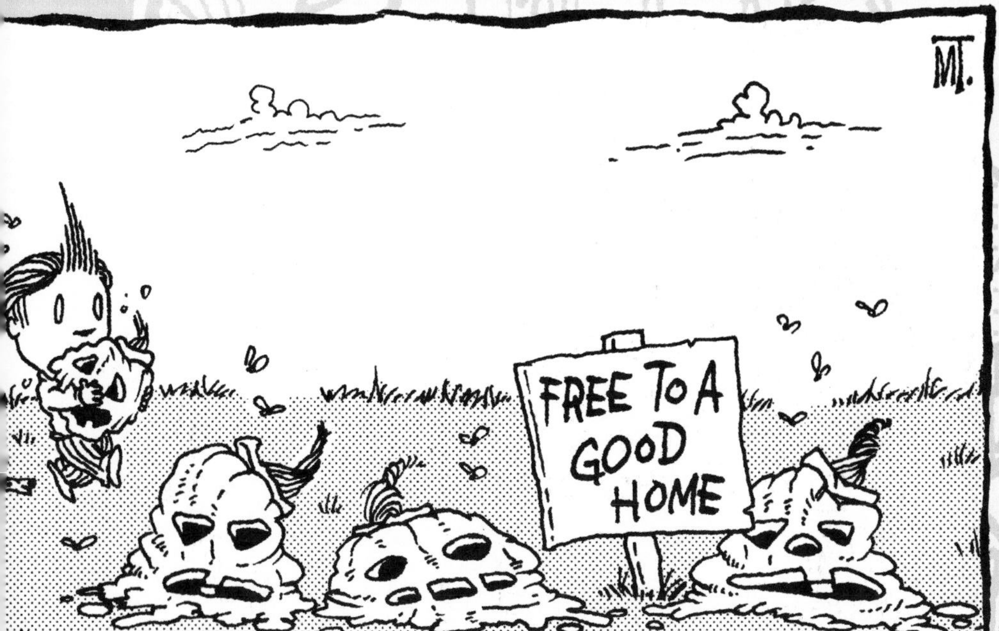
MT.
FREE TO A GOOD HOME

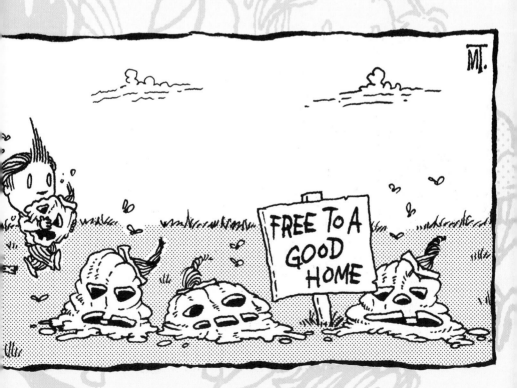

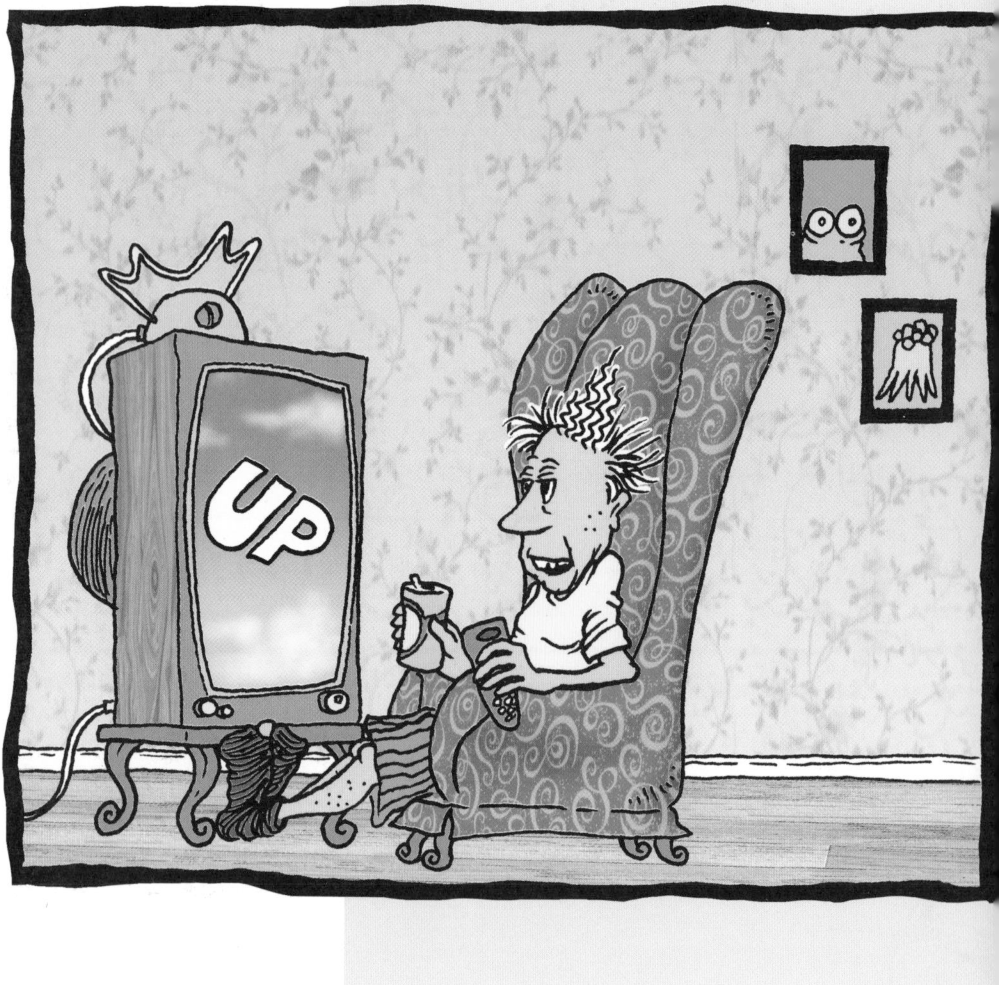
UP

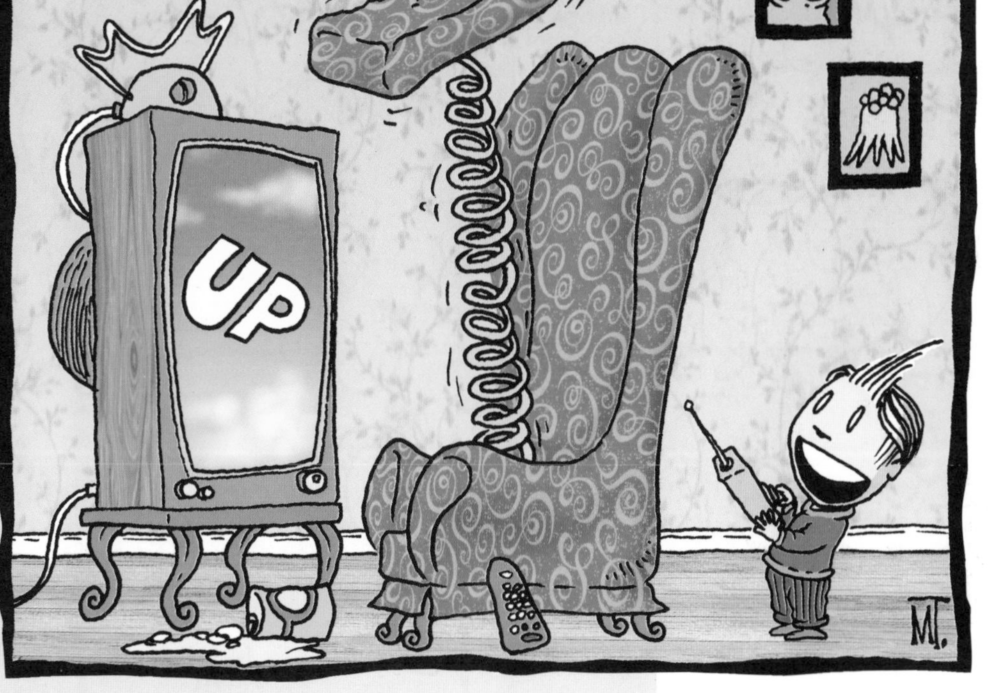
UP

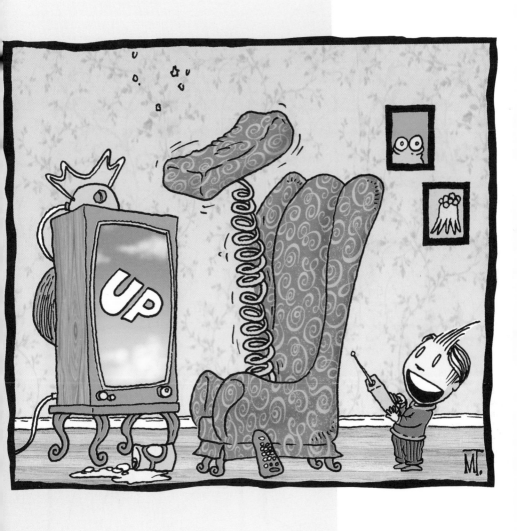

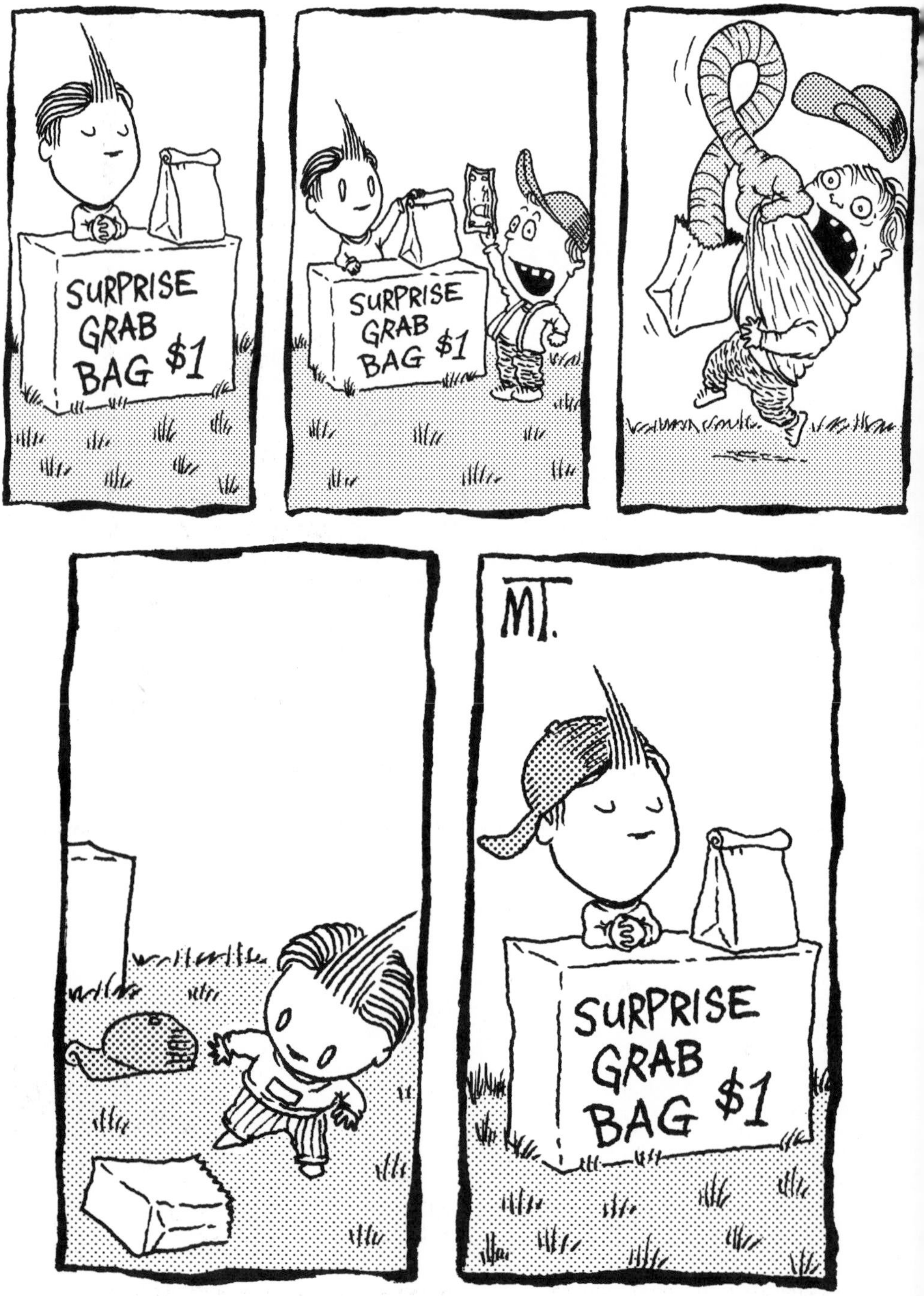

SURPRISE GRAB BAG $1
SURPRISE GRAB BAG $1
SURPRISE GRAB BAG $1

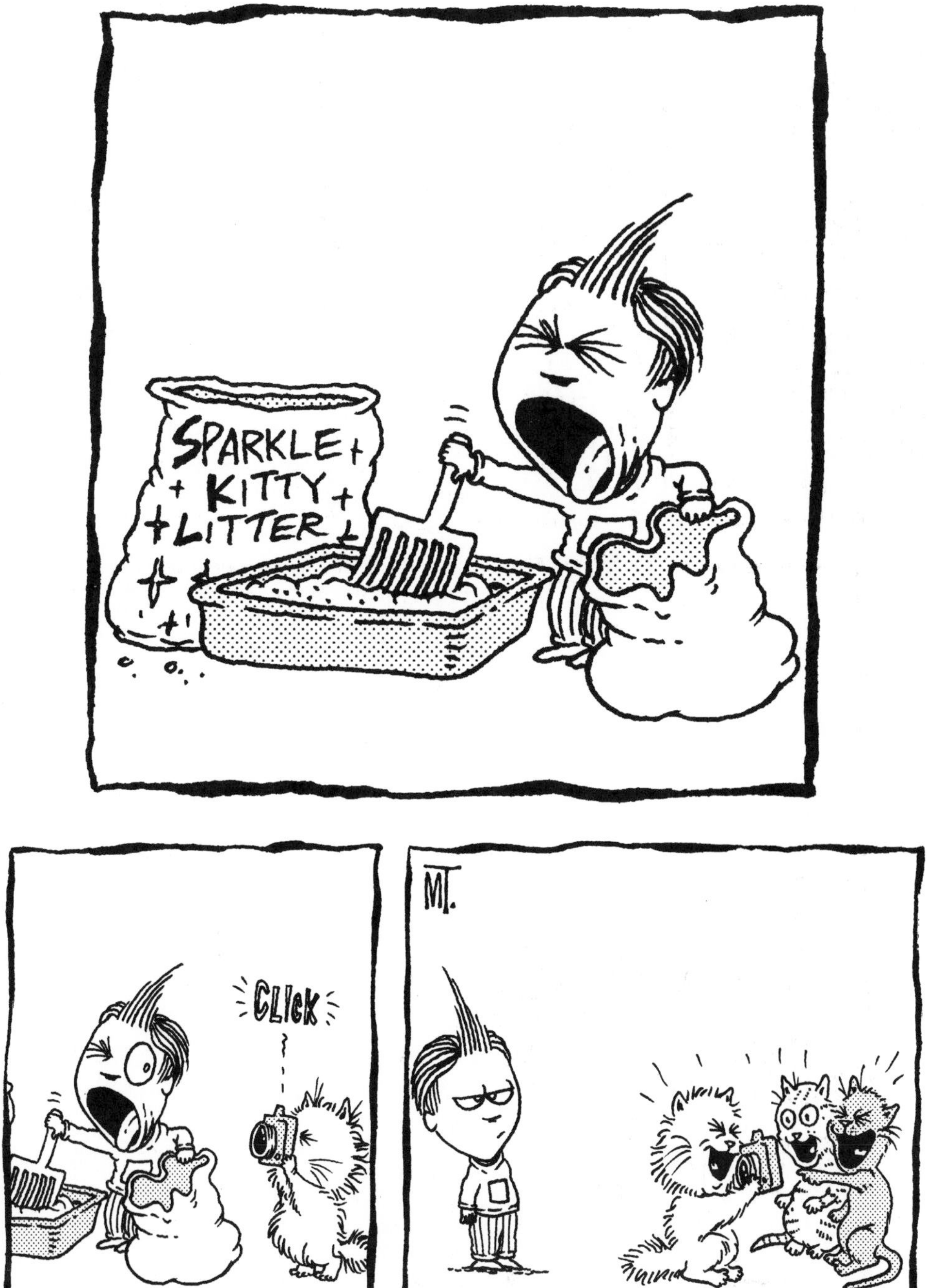
SPARKLE
KITTY
LITTER
CLICK
MT.

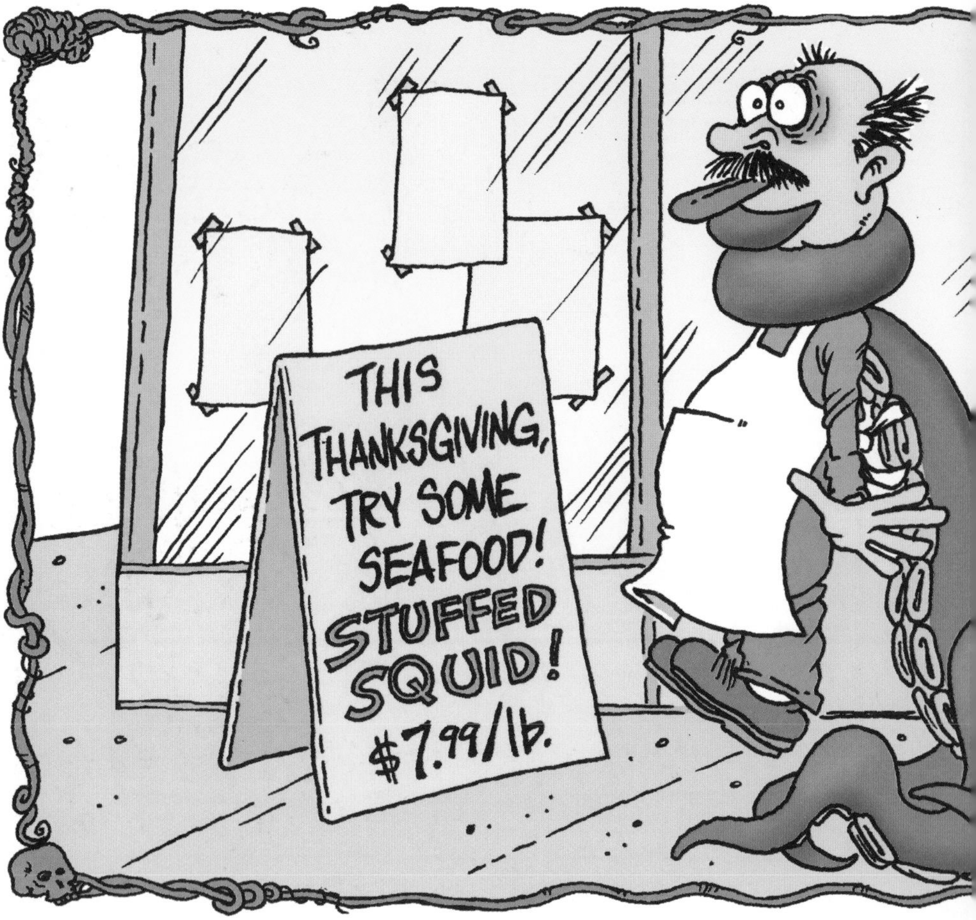
THIS THANKSGIVING, TRY SOME SEAFOOD!
STUFFED SQUID!
$7.99/lb.

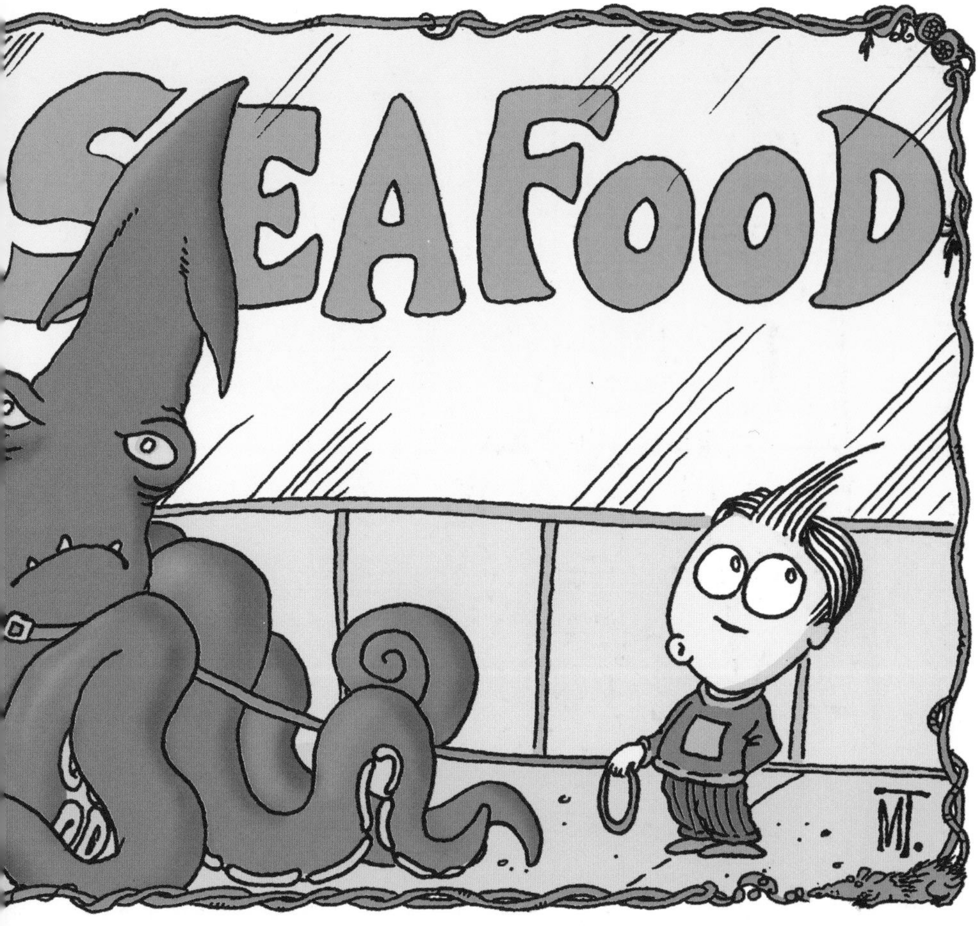
SEAFOOD
MT.

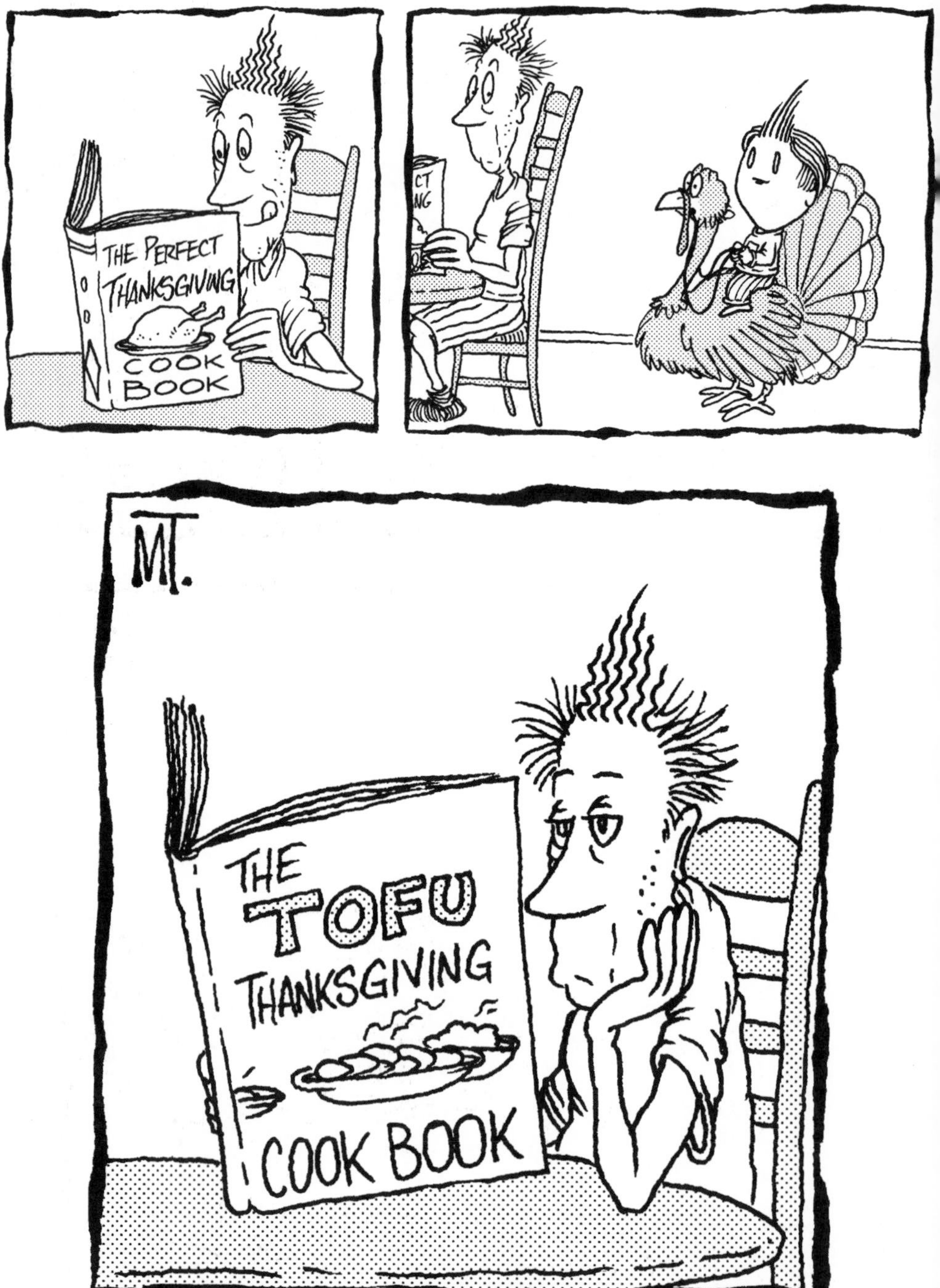
THE PERFECT
THANKSGIVING
COOK
BOOK
MT.
THE
TOFU
THANKSGIVING
COOK BOOK

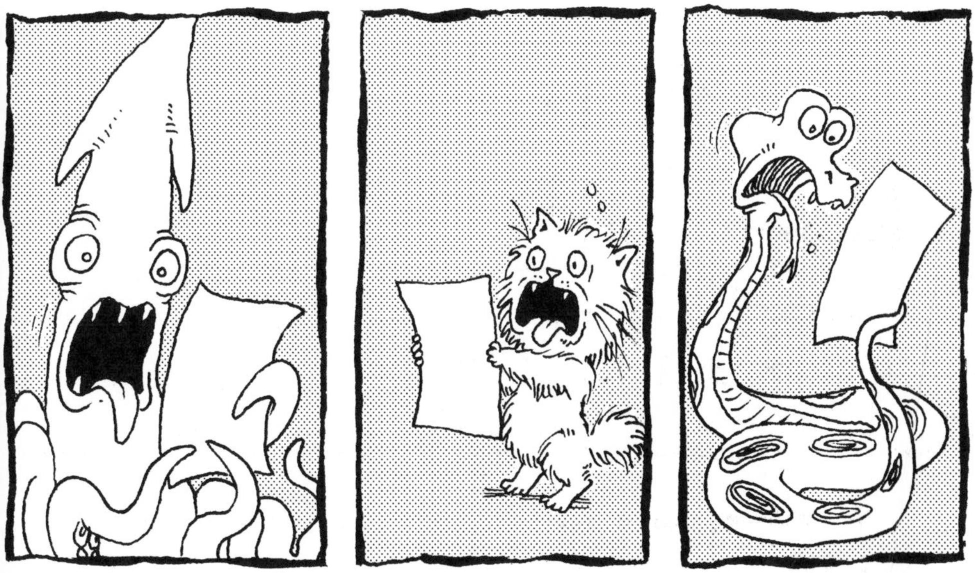

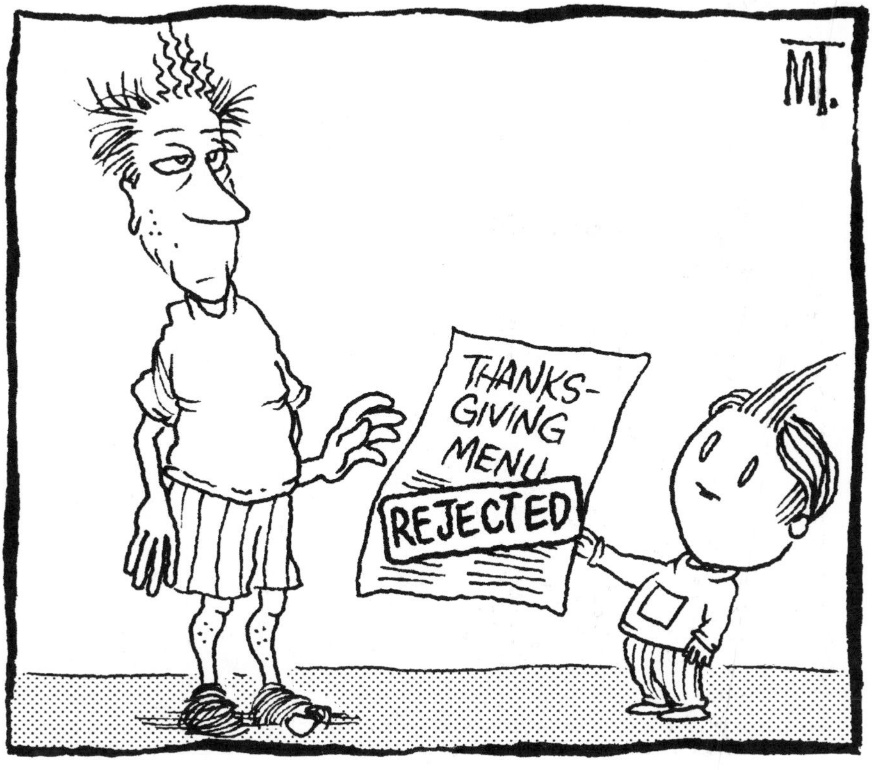
MT.
THANKS-
GIVING
MENU
REJECTED

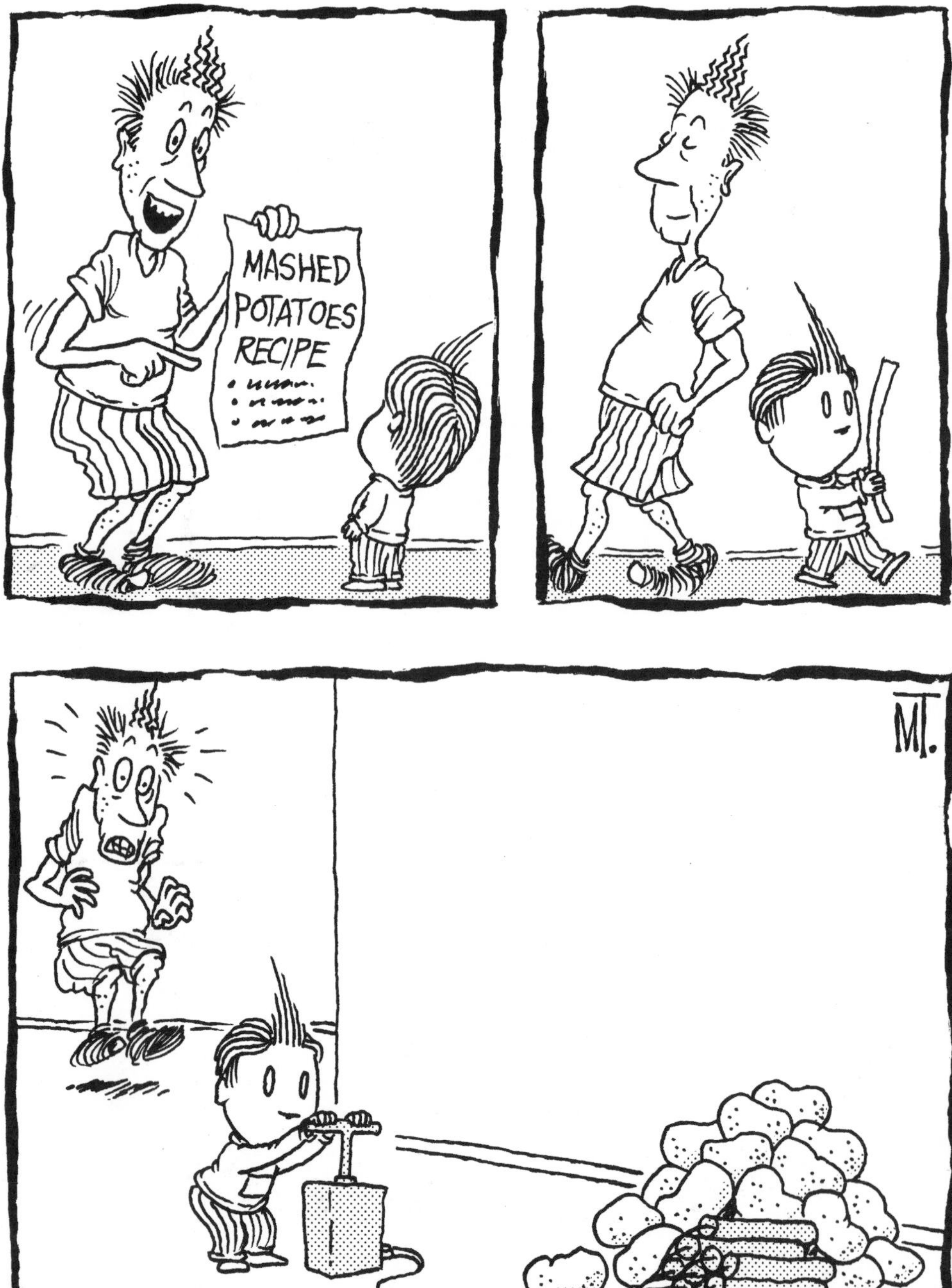
MASHED
POTATOES
RECIPE
MT.

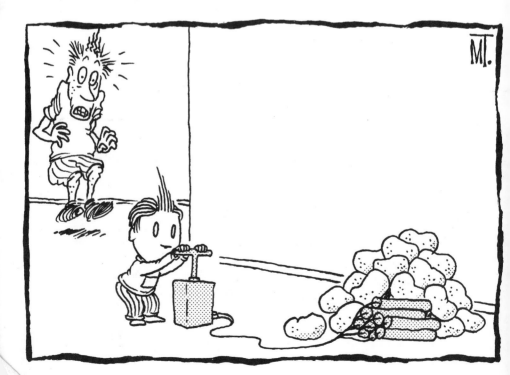

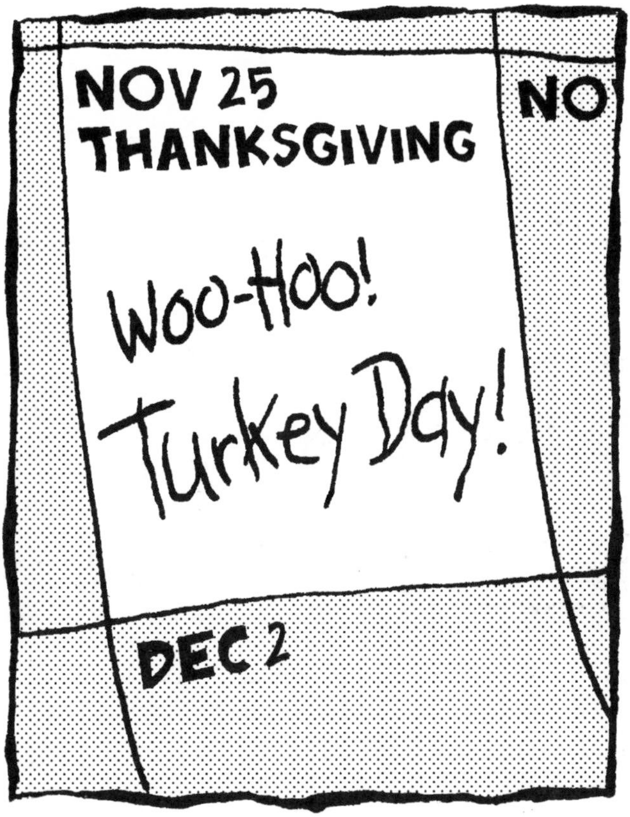
NOV 25
THANKSGIVING
NO
Woo-Hoo!
Turkey Day!
DEC 2

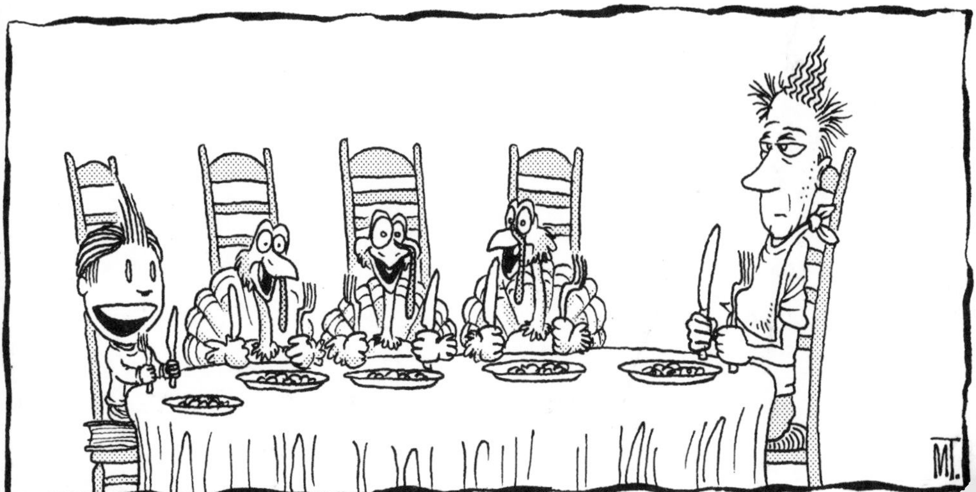
MI.

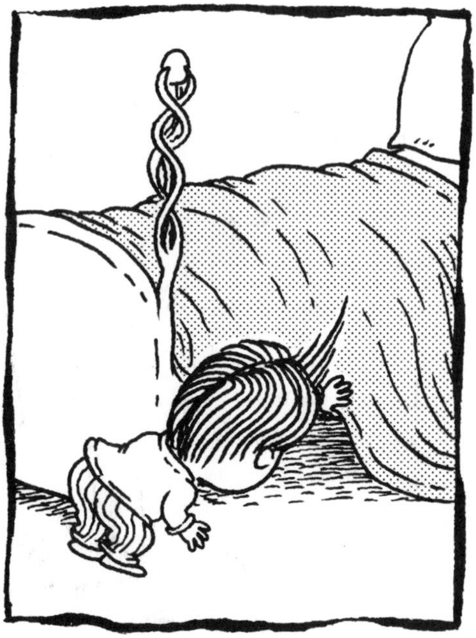

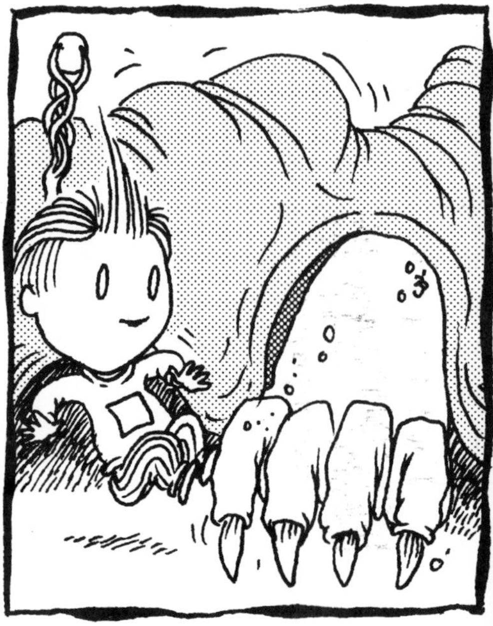

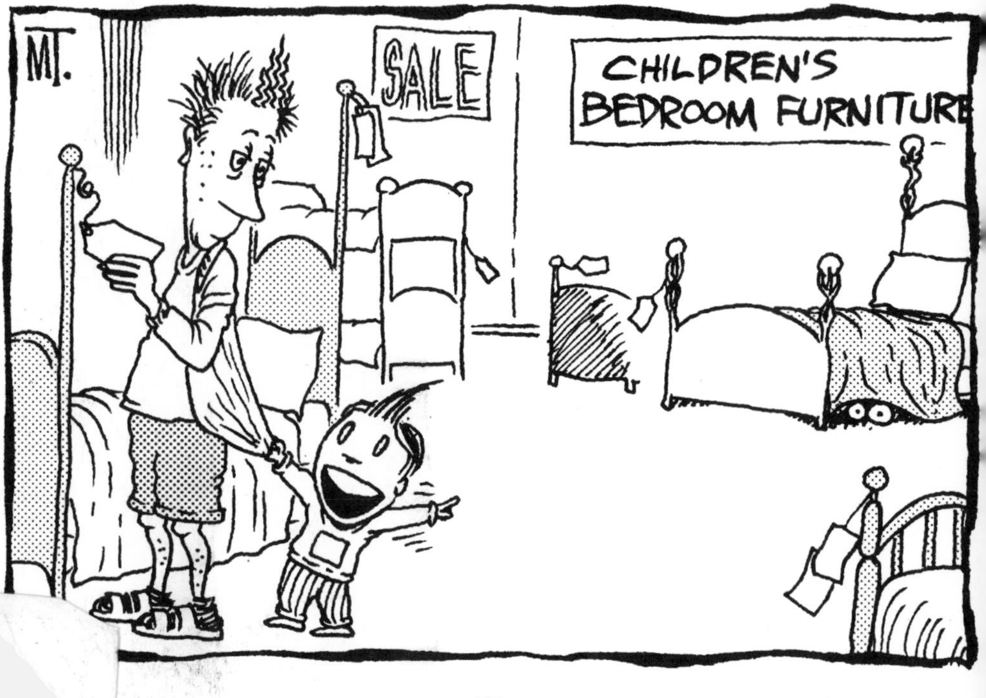

MT.
SALE
CHILDREN'S
BEDROOM FURNITURE